El PEÓN

Michael Crump

El PEÓN

Michael Crump

PENMAN HOUSE
PUBLISHING

Disclaimer

El Peon and Other Stories From the Campo is a work of fiction. With exceptions noted below, names, characters, and incidents derive solely from the imagination of the author or are used fictitiously. Any resemblance to actual persons, living or dead, is purely coincidental. The novel, *El Peon*, is set in an unnamed Central American country. The short stories, *The River*, is set in Turrubares de San Jose, Costa Rica, *The Good Policeman* is set in various locations of Costa Rica. Don Pepe (Figueres) is a historical figure who led the 1948 revolution and served as the first president thereafter. *La Novena* is set in Guanacaste, Costa Rica and the story is fictional. *The Last Indio* is partly modeled on an actual village school (not named Yamiya) but the story and the characters are entirely fictional. The initial description of Rigo is based on actual learnings taught to me by a real employee, but the rest of Rigo's life is entirely fictional. Although I have made a conscious attempt to create a realistic setting through the use of place and some historical events, they too are used in a fictional manner to support entirely fictitious stories.

Acknowledgements

Curiosity sated, it takes fortitude to re-read, and re-read, a manuscript. I am especially indebted to Lenny Karpman and Joan Hall for their unflagging support of this and all my work. I am grateful for the attention and contributions of these friends, each an expert in some aspect of writing or of life in Central America: Nuria Alfaro, Greg Bascom, Vidya Bolz, Chris Clarke, Ken Cline, Carole Evans, Alberto Guindon, Angelina Guindon, Paul Hastings, Dev Joslin, Harriet Joslin, Jim Just, Irina Just, Robin Kazmir, Ingo Krommer, Frans Lamers, Steve Macik, Margaret Macik, Hobbit Merritt, Elias Newswanger, Jonathan Ogle, Luisa Rodriguez, Kevin Ryan, Greg Seymour, Marilyn Stevens, Josephine Stuart, Bob Stickney, Lyn Stickney, Mary Stuckey, Jannelle Wilkins, Stacie Wolfe and Kirby Wolfe. I am most grateful to Greg, Lenny and Robin for hanging in for the endless early revisions. To friends who read for sound, wording and grammar: Sandra Hoehne, Jamie Aiken and Fred Holmes. To my Buddhist book and meditation group whose contributions are the most subtle of all. And finally to Janet who proofed, proofed and re-proofed. Only a wife could dredge up that kind of commitment, and this story is dedicated to her.

With special gratitude to Jim Harrison for permission to quote his poems. As some of the short stories attest, Jim's poetry is the well I return to when my own imagination fails. To Barry Johnson, Ph.D., a long time friend and mentor who contributed the intellectual structure and process for managing polarities to the world. And to Gabriel Garcia Marquez who showed the world that truth is not necessarily material and that magic is in the mind of the beholder.

For Janet
And
The Expats Who've Chosen Central America
And
Friends: The Real Guito and his Family

El PEÓN[1]

By
Mike Crump

---

[1] Pay-OWN

"Consider the deer. There are tens of thousands of them and they are rarely seen because they don't wish to be seen. Learn the traits of peasants and deer was my advice. They do their best not to be shot." – Jim Harrison, In Search of Small Gods.

Table of Contents

Prologue

I have a story. It began shortly after I arrived in this country in the mid 1990's. I didn't know it was a story until about five years after I had settled in. I'd taken a small inheritance as an excuse to throw over the boredom of underwriting insurance and a failed marriage to retire early. Live simply, read a lot and try writing was my plan. What I did not foresee was the extent to which I would become involved with the Ariza family. It almost certainly would not have happened at all except that I hired Rigo as a dayworker, a *peón* on my farm. He was the first to tell me an Ariza family secret. It was his story to begin with, but his life was so intimately connected to theirs that the whole thing naturally came out over several years. Rigo worked with me for over five years and as time went on, he introduced me to the family with whom he had lived during his adolescence. Rigo introduced me to Eduardo Ariza Aguero, his surrogate father, who introduced me to his oldest son and writer daughter at a birthday party.

My friendship with the Arizas was based on a slow-to-develop trust that never quite matched the intensity of my interest. I am a curious person in the sense of having two measures of curiosity. And perhaps in the other sense as well. That may explain why I am in this country in the first place. It helped that my farm was once part of the land owned by the Ariza family. Still, no amount of trust could have elicited the anecdotes that comprise their story had the youngest daughter not been a writer. She wrote a well-received and thinly veiled novel about some of the same happenings, including a character based on Rigo. She is a "born feminist," as the saying goes, and Rigo, I came to suspect, told his side in part to balance the version presented in her novel. She was modern and atypical which goes a long way in explaining why she came to tolerate the idea of a foreigner writing stories about her family.

I'd written a few stories based loosely on Rigo's tales and showed them to her. For the usual reasons, and in spite of her own brazenness, she insisted that I wait to publish this story until after both her parents died. Oddly, it was she who initially most resisted my involvement, but in the end, trusted me the most. She agreed that while all three children gave me a lot of facts, much of the story would have to be made up. She also served as the family arbiter of truth and fairness and was my first editor. You should remember that when you get to her part of the story.

Rigo came to work during the time I was building my house. It sits on a coffee farm and he introduced me to coffee farming, to the *campesino* value of humility, and to the local patois. *Campesino* is a general term for country people. It was Rigo who built the *almacigo*, a coffee plant nursery, and showed me how to sharpen a machete by placing the handle into my hip, springing the blade against a tree and using a file, to wear a new edge. He showed me how to use it to harvest a stalk of bananas called locally by the old name, *guineas*, after their place of origin.

Rigo wore the machete scabbard on a string to hold it around his waist. He disdained the "luxury" of wearing a machete on a belt. I did anyway, if for no other reason that my fingers could not manage the tiny knots. It was Rigo who convinced me that no poisonous snake should escape the machete and no non-poisonous snake should suffer from it.

I was the rankest of amateurs but Rigo and I developed a mutual respect as employer and employee. I gave him a good deal of discretion, which he rarely abused, and he responded well to my trust in him. I know he appreciated the fact that I sought his advice on many things. When he injured himself, it was I who took him to the emergency room.

"Peón" survives the Spanish feudal period and at one time carried the same meaning as "peasant" in English. I was still unsure of my right to be on this land, so to speak, and I had not used the "p-word" to the men during that first year, though the locals and even the *peones* used it often enough. My reluctance was in the manner of the country people, who, in their politeness, don't use *"gringo"* to your face until they figure you can handle it. "Gringo" doesn't usually imply a criticism in the *campo* but one never knows what the gringo standing in front of you might think. Nowadays, *peón* means day worker, usually in construction and agriculture.

Rigo and Mento, who years later would replace Rigo as the main *peón,* never hit it off. Both had something of an independent streak and a touch of cussedness that wouldn't allow either to give a centimeter. Still, Rigo was number one and Mento kept his job by remaining dutiful if sometimes sullen. Better than all the others, Mento could unerringly find any stone its proper place in a rock wall. "Every stone has its place," he would say when I would suggest placing one. He was polite but clear that he, not I, knew that place.

One day, I asked Mento if he might consider becoming a mason because it paid better. "*Nunca!*" He spit it out. "Never! I am a *peón!*" The force and deliberateness in his reply startled me. That "*peón*" as it is now used might have cachet, honor even, could only come from someone who lived from a disappearing worldview.

Rigo and the two Ariza kids grew up in a time when the culture was changing almost as fast as the technology that was pushing it. Those changes affected a lot of the choices they made. The oldest son is at the center of their story and he was the first to leave home. When we finally met he surprised me as the calmest, most empathetic person I'd ever known. How he got there is the most amazing part of my story.

Part 1

Querencia

El Indio

Central America, 1970

"Guit...!" The boy's name sucked in with the man's breath. But the boy, Guito, heard and eased his hand from the cavity beneath the tree trunk. A moment later the coiled *tercipelo* was in two pieces and his father jabbed the machete at the dozen or so babies birthing from her eggs. *Terciopelos* – Fer de lance to the non-Spanish world – incubate for only minutes. Guito watched the chop, chop, chopping, of the machete as it methodically killed baby snakes. His father saw the boy's pained, sideways stare. "They come out ready for action," he said.

Guito had held many snakes in his seven years, even a *terciopelo* his father was unaware of. The boy was fearless with animals, but most noticeable was his way with dogs. *Campesinos*—country people—are inclined to fear dogs, but the boy was easy with them. He would approach, whispering to those known to be *brava*, and they would snarl, top lips curled thin, canines showing and pop their teeth, then within moments become calm and affectionate. More than one neighbor agreed that the little boy could be a reincarnation of St. Francis and had it been up to them, he might have been sainted.

Guito spent much of his early years in the *quebrada* that bordered his father's property. It was a noisy stream with a series of waterfalls that stimulated a young boy's imaginary games. He would climb the steep and rocky streambed with his dogs, stopping to play in the pools, throw rocks or use them to make small dams and change the course of one rivulet or another. In time, he could navigate the streambed eyes closed, using only the sounds of the stream and the feel of rock beneath his feet or the one he was touching with his hands. He memorized each scene on all sides and knew the direction he was facing and what his dogs were doing by their sounds. As his childhood passed from innocence to confusion, the *quebrada* became his *querencia*, a safe place—the one, safe place—where his world was in order.

One early afternoon a few weeks after his father killed the *terciopelo*, he found himself resting on a rock in the *quebrada* and gazing at another snake coiled in a patch of sunlight on a nearby log. The snake's head and the first inches of its body were rigid, raised off the trunk, staring directly at Guito. They gazed at each other as the stream riffled and purled by them. As the gaze lengthened, Guito's attention riveted, bliss-like, eliminating all other senses. Time seeped from consciousness through his eyes.

At some point, time returned, peeping in as the boy began to sense the presence of someone else, that he was being watched. His eyes broke the snake's gaze and he looked on all sides. There was no one. He looked up into the foliage. Still, he saw no one. But the forest light had changed.

Rocks and trees snapped into focus as though each were its own vivid photograph. Every nuance of color and fissure in each leaf and twig stood in high relief. A shaft of sunlight illumined a column of a myriad floating things. Its base revealed another world of small beings as it tracked the slow rotation across the streambed. Swirls in the passing water became detailed objects of Guito's attention. The sounds of the stream changed from gurgles and splashes and the roar of the larger cataracts into a hummm, one syllable, a mere vibration, in background of his consciousness. The feeling of another's presence remained strong but there was nothing sinister in it.

When his gaze returned to the log the snake was gone. Guito's vision remained intense and sharp as he lingered on his rock, sensing, without forming thoughts, a connection to everything he could see. A peace settled over him.

Guito felt his dog's nose on his knee and remembered dinner. Rosa remained after the other puppies had made the long trek back to the house hours before. He wondered if Rosa had been touched with the same feeling. It faded after a while but wisps remained for weeks. Those wisps became part of the ineffable cargo he carried into the next phase of life.

∾

Days later, he was helping his mother while his father went to the capital for meetings. "Will Papi be back for dinner Ma?"

"Si Dios quiere, mi amor."

He looked at her. "Does everything God wants, happen, Ma?"

"Why, Guito...what a question *mi amor*...I guess so...yes...." The mop took a decisive swipe at the floor. "Yes, if He wants it to happen, it does."

"Where does God live Ma? Does He ever come here?"

His mother stopped her work, raised up, holding the mop handle with both hands, leaned on it and gazed at him for a long moment. "Well, *mi Amor*, God lives in heaven...but there is a little bit of God in every person, I think. God is always with us but we don't see Him." She stood there, staring down at her son. He seemed satisfied with this answer. He went back to his chores and she to hers.

ॐ

The wonderment of his experience in the *quebrada* stayed with Guito for several weeks, but year seven was momentous for other reasons. It was the year that his father's exasperation arose and that Guito took a secret name.

Guito was born Carlos Ariza Valverde but the name "Guito," had been bestowed on him; it was his first "word" for animals. No consensus emerged as to what he might have meant, but every dog, chicken, horse, cow, or toucan was a, "guito." When the boy's gifts became obvious, his grandmother remembered the name's origin and she avowed that what Guito had been saying was, "*giro*," meaning turn, or change of direction.

As age had its effect, this grandmother had begun to interpret the dreams and "signs" of those who would bring them to her. There weren't many because her interpretations often included a fiendish twist. Still, her reputation grew into something of a good witch. "*Giro*" is pronounced with the hard, "dr" sound in Spanish. "It only sounded like 'Guito', coming from a baby," she insisted. Her theory was that little Guito was trying to turn the animals into humans. Her good eye gleamed; his mother shuddered. His father would not allow the story to leave the house.

Guito's secret name arrived unexpectedly as the family was returning from a day trip to the beach. The name would remain a secret until shortly before he left home. For most of those years, his secret name was also his identity.

Near the entrance to Paso Llano, Guito's mother turned to her husband. "Chico, let's find my old house. It won't take long, we have to go right by it—almost."

"Can you find it?" He looked at her, "Do you really *want* to find it?"

The exchange puzzled Guito. He thought that his mother was from a small village near where they lived. She had gone to high school in a nearby town and had met his father there. The idea that she had a secret life he didn't know about fired him with enthusiasm. His year-old brother caught the excitement and added his gibberish to the clamor until their father drove straight into Paso Llano.

They turned onto an unpaved road that was now lined with houses. "This is a much better road than when I was your age, Guito."

But it didn't stay that way. They were headed up a 2-mile ridge toward the now rear entrance to the village of Yamiya. It became rutted and then overgrown, the two-track just discernible. Eduardo swore once under his breath and then once more, not-so-under. He labored now; the ruts were formidable and the Land Rover did not have hydraulic steering.

"If this weren't a jeep we would be back in Paso Llano—that's for sure." "Sure" exploded from his lips and the wheel spun in his hands as a front tire slammed into the side of a ravine-like rut.

His mother, both hands on the dash, her neck and head twisted to scan the left side of the road, said nothing. Another five jarring minutes passed.

"Stop," the word choked out. The boy heard and looked at her. "This is it," she said quietly.

"What is it?" her husband said. "I don't see anything."

A moment passed, "Look over your left shoulder...at that tree. That Ceiba has been here for over a hundred years, maybe two hundred. Our house stood beneath it."

They sat in silence for a minute or two. Guito sighed audibly and both boys fidgeted; Eduardo said, "Let's take a look shall we." He got out and went to the passenger side of the Rover to help his wife out the way he did on their infrequent visits to church. Guito took his brother's hand and held him in check. He watched his mother walk around the overgrown land until everything seemed normal.

Holding his brother's hands in his, Guito crossed the clearest part of the road. He picked up his brother at the edge of the heaviest growth and went directly to an ancient tree with many small branches from repeated pruning. Three rusted machetes remained in as many crotches in the tree. He showed his father, who pulled out one blade with a wavy edge.

"This one was sharpened on a grinder. Look at that edge, the *peón* could not hold it the same way each time. These other two were sharpened with a file. Alba, how did your family get hold of a grinder?" he asked turning to his wife.

"I don't remember," she said squinting, "there were other men with machetes."

As though he read her mind, "It's not important," and walked over to the old privy hidden in the second growth. The door was gone but the hinges, flaps made from rubber inner tubes, still hung there. The wooden seat with one hole was visible. "Well," he muttered to no one in particular, "This was the good old days."

"The house was here. That big rock was the stoop for the front door." She struggled to make a line in the soil by dragging her foot through the weeds and high grass. "We had a wood house with a dirt floor, that's why nothing is left. I lived here with my mother and my uncle." She turned to Guito. "My name in those days was Alba Yamí."

"Yamí?—Yamiya?" Wide-eyed, the boy said, "They named the town after you?"

"Kind of." She smiled pleased to have surprised him. "Long before the settlers came, my family lived here on the side of the hill that runs all the way down to the river. It was a big family, I think. But when I was born, there was only my mother and my uncle. My mother and uncle were both *Indio-Indio*. Everyone called us Yamí because that was the name of our people."

"You are *Indio*," the boy whispered. Still saucer-eyed, he looked at his father, "I am *Indio*. Did you know that Papi?" Eduardo, indulged a smile.

"Yes, we are Nicarau." She said this with none of the enthusiasm the boy thought she should've had. "When I was your age, I went to live with another family of *Indios* in San Juan. That is how I became Alba Valverde. And now I am Alba Valverde Yamí de Ariza because I am married to your father." She spoke brightly, as though all of this was nothing more than a lesson in civics.

Alba never knew her father. Her mother and uncle had only one name, "Yamí." She had been taken from her mother by the authorities from San Diego, but if she remembered that, she left it out. In those days there were still a few mostly-*Indio* families living in the San Juan area. She never saw her mother or uncle after she left. She heard that her uncle had died but no one could tell her where he was buried. It was possible that he was buried here on this property, but she said nothing of that to the others. Her mother had evaporated. The property was not and could not, ever be hers because it had never been recorded in the *Registro*. She never bothered to inquire.

Guito knew that he was true *Indio*, and he began to call himself "El Indio" in his imaginary games. The woods near the *quebrada*, became his tribal land and his time there became a life apart from life on the farm. His secret lasted until he was 17.

Eduardo's Frustration

In truth Guito was gifted with all living things. The animals were the most obvious but the plants were the special pride of his father. Eduardo, owned a coffee farm and it was just this year that he put Guito, at barely age seven, in putative charge of the *almácigo*, the coffee plant nursery. He had shown the boy how to sprout the coffee *granos* and to bind them into packets of 10 so that they could be easily counted and carried. In May, with help from the *peón*, Guito planted them in neat rows in that special section of the farm where they could be weeded and watered in the dry season. They remained there for a full year before the *peón* replanted them in the spot where they would spend the remainder of their lives.

On the first day of his assignment the boy and the *peón* tended the previous, year-old plants that were about to be moved from the *almácigo*.

"What are you doing, *Chico*? Leave that one alone...it's dry."

"It is still living, there is green at the tips."

"Don't waste your time...it will not survive."

"I can save it."

"Come over here and help me put these in the wagon."

"But it is green!" the boy's lower lip trembled. The *peón* said something unrepeatable and left Guito alone. His father came out a few minutes later to check on things. The boy saw the *peón* say something to his father, they looked at him; his father shrugged his shoulders and walked away.

There were several bitches around the house and one or two litters arrived every year. Most puppies survived to be given away with shortened tails because Eduardo said it looked better and the *peón* wielded a machete to each puppy that looked strong enough to survive. Guito could not bear to see it.

This year Guito noticed milk coming from the nose of one of them when it fed.

"What is wrong with this one?" he asked the *peón*.

The man slowly turned the puppy over and opened its mouth. He showed Guito the small hole in the roof of it. "*Es un defecto, Guito.*"

"Can we take it to the doctor?"

"It will never be right." He turned away and selected one of the several machetes wedged into a crack between the wall and frame of the barn.

Guito reddened, readying himself for another struggle, but the *peón* saw and put the puppy down and walked away.

"That is not how a farm works Guito," his father said. In his father's voice was Guito's first memory of Eduardo's puzzled reaction. The puppy disappeared.

⁊ʊ

Guito had been born nine months to the day after Eduardo married Alba. "Good timing" Eduardo would say whenever the subject came up. His affection for the boy always brought a smile to his listeners though most had heard the story more than once. The father harbored a dream that was rooted in his own youth and Guito's gifts roused his hopes, his ambition of passing on the farm to his oldest son.

Eduardo was a *gemelo,* a twin, and when their father passed on the huge farm had been split between the two sons. Eduardo maintained his part in legacy coffee and it had provided a comfortable if unspectacular existence. His twin had received the larger share of planted land because Eduardo had gotten the family home. With the home came a barn and a small corral that was all that remained from the original homestead, almost 90 years old now. The farm was large enough that locally, Eduardo was known as a "planter."

His brother had succumbed first to ambition, then to women and finally to *guaro*, cane liquor. Over the years that Eduardo watched his brother's life unravel, the brother's farm devolved from coffee to tobacco and finally to cattle. When the last parts of it were sold to settle affairs, an embittered Eduardo would only buy 75 acres of clear grassy land without incurring "imprudent" debt. So the greatest part of the original farm – "the home place," as Eduardo called it—had passed into the hands of absentee owners. The pain of this loss toughened his resolve to pass his own legacy, intact, to this child.

The boy's fascination with plants and animals warmed his father's heart in a manner that he could have never explained to another person. But his affection was for an imagined boy.

෨෬

Guito was desperate to be what his father wanted. He was successful with the *almácigo*. But he couldn't bear to see a plant die from lack of care.

In the summers, especially in the dry ones, many did so. "That's not how a farm works Guito." His father said it so many times. But the boy could not get the idea of making a profit based on the life and death of plants or for that matter, the animals which his parents also raised.

The boy tried to be careful but his struggle was obvious to all. At age eight and one-half, his father began to show him how to keep the books. Eduardo kept careful records of cost and return for various sections of the farm. He would show the boy how more fertilizer was needed in some areas, how insects and fungus were more prevalent in others. In short, he would show the boy how a farm really works. "Seeing is believing," he told his wife, and the boy became an apprentice bookkeeper.

Afternoon followed afternoon; the boy ground away with receipts and orders and harvest records. His father might ask him simple questions about what could be known of production in this area or that. Guito would sit there, or guess, blind to the realities of the numbers. "Right there. On the page!" his father would yell, and then he would walk away. That was the part that Guito feared most. He knew he did not measure up, that there was something wrong with him; something his father could not love.

It wasn't that Guito did not agree with his father; that wasn't his place. He simply did not understand. He could eat the food without qualm. But the idea of making money from it could not penetrate his enigmatic, inexplicable attitude. Guito's inability to grasp the fundamental idea of farming as a business left Eduardo exasperated. Yet he persisted, angrily redoing the books himself at times after the boy had fled to the *quebrada*.

Grass¹

Snip...snip...snip. The large scissors decapitated each twist of leaf. It was 9:00 AM and Guito had been working for two hours. Since he did not like to work on the books his father said coolly, "You'll work with real plants." He had been at it for the better part of a week.

His father's solution to Guito's ineptness with bookkeeping was to assign him to mow the yard with scissors. It was the long school vacation and his time in the *quebrada* or with friends was postponed. *For a little while,* he thought, *maybe a week*. The front yard was a large trapezoid extending from the corner of the barbed wire fence some 50 meters to opposite corner, then another 50 meters up to the house.

Day followed day. Blisters arose, broke, scabbed and arose anew elsewhere as he changed his grip. Soon the corners and pads of fingers on both hands seeped continuously. His hands cramped so that one could not massage the other. Shoulders knotted and kept him from sleeping in spite of his bone tiredness.

At night, his mother made the poultices she had learned from her mother and insisted that he keep them on his hands until they began to dry. She watched him and he could see her eyes redden but she had said nothing to his father and he knew she would not. Her inaction mirrored his own impotence and he recognized, for the first time, the feeling of being totally controlled. He longed for the safety of his *quebrada* but his father felt that blisters were an insufficient reason, "Not to finish the job," he said.

Rains in the afternoons felt initially like a blessing. He couldn't leave the house but they were a respite from the soul-numbing task. The combination of still wet soil and increased sunlight had its effect. After two weeks, as the scissors neared the house, he could see large blades re-emerging in the initial corner. Another fear began to build in his chest.

In the third week, when he finished the first circuit of the yard, he asked his father if he could go to the *quebrada*.

"Papi, it's done." His eyes squinted in anticipation of the answer.

"I think not," Eduardo said. His father pointed to the new tall grass in the corner where the teaching had started.

It was punishment. And even in his confusion he knew it was mean. But mostly he knew the feeling of life without options. He began to curse his father in his mind. *Puta! Maldicio! Shit! Damn him!* He ruminated.

With his friends cussing was a great experiment, risky and fun. Now each word rushed from a flood of tears, some of them visible. *I hate you, Eduardo!* His mind roiled with emotions he could not put a word to. Only sullen looks betrayed the feelings. But the anger served to slow his drift into anomie. He never spoke a word against his father who would thenceforth be "Eduardo" instead of Papi.

Within the last week of the long school break, the grass stopped growing.

His friends had long stopped dropping by, so his remaning week passed in solitude. Slowly, some sense of self recovered. Curiously, it was the combination of opposing energies that saved him: his anger and his *querencia*.

&

There were brighter moments in their mutual quandary. Guito attended high school at the *Liceo* for a year. He passed his subjects with little effort. But even, "life sciences," seemed abstract and irrelevant to understanding life. He thought he would go to the university until, at age 13, with little family discussion, he left the *Liceo* and enrolled at the technical high school in Paso Llano where they had programs in agriculture and tourism. He would study both.

The school was 5 kilometers downhill so that he could walk it if necessary. His mother fretted but his father was hopeful. Guito began the more serious study of English that was required by the *turismo* program and found it enjoyable. He loved learning and when compared to their usual student, the teachers in the technical high school found Guito enjoyable.

While browsing a friend's book for a tourism class, in the chapter entitled "The Indigenous Peoples of Central America," Guito discovered that the Nicarau were a Mesoamerican tribe from the north that had settled in the Northwest. They may have originated in Mexico and followed the great dry, climatological belt extending from Southern California to its southernmost end. The Chontal, also Mesoamerican, had settled the Great Valley and west to the edges of Nicarau territory. The mixing area encompassed his school and home.

The mostly *mestizo* colonists assimilated the tribes even more so as they moved outward from the Great Valley. By the time his mother was born, neither tribe had much that remained of language or tribal organization. There was little of interest to anthropologists so not much was known about the original culture of these people. *If this is true,* he thought, *how could Ma be Nicarau? Are we Chontal?* It surprised him that the question upset him so much. He spoke to his mother when they were alone.

"All I can say is what my mother and my uncle knew. They had no reason to make this up. It is possible," her eyes searched upward as though the answer might hang from the ceiling, "that they were a *cruce* of both. The family I grew up with was both."

He believed her. The upset faded and replaced with a more pronounced curiosity about *Indios* in general.

※

The final tragedy, waiting just off-stage, began its irrevocable drift into his adolescence. In a survey agriculture course, Guito heard about the wonders of organic food production. His enthusiasm fired with the words of his instructor, "A way to farm that was in harmony with nature." Guito told

Eduardo that organic coffee sold for higher prices than the ordinary and he knew that would appeal.

He began to lobby Eduardo about changing methods. His father was skeptical. In spite of his errors, and of no longer being "Papi" to Guito, he secretly clove to the dream of passing the farm intact to the boy. It was a straw, however flimsy, and Eduardo reached for it. Even though it would be years before he could sell the coffee as "organic," he set aside some acreage to try the organic process.

Growing crops organically is a system. Success required a more complete reorganization of the farm than Eduardo had the patience for. He realized later that he had relied on the boy's limited insight from a high school class instead of his own research. He had wanted to encourage the boy, to resuscitate his dream. Year after year the organic acreage succumbed inexorably to insects and fungus. After three years he gave up. That he had failed with the way he had tried to grasp his dream added another spoonful of bitterness. He became angry.

‡

Eduardo's anger was rooted in the daily proofs that his dream of passing the farm to Guito would never realize. But this knowledge stayed buried beneath layers of need and confusion. On those rare occasions when Eduardo was clear on the point, he told himself, *"Any farm would die under Guito's hand."* His second son was car crazy, or girl crazy, depending on the day, and already unwilling to settle into farm life. The girl was simply too young.

The organic experiment and his faded dream were turning him into a more difficult man. Alba tried to help him see the problem differently, "Guito is doing his best, Chico. He's just hardheaded like you." But Eduardo and Guito were riding the rails of their own karma and the tracks diverged sharply. Life was going to unfold as it would. Eduardo for some not-easy-to-explain reason began to act as though Alba was taking Guito's side against him and his misunderstood angst.

They were good people as the saying goes, and so they remained civilized. The word, "organic," was taboo at any time and mealtimes became an unwritten truce. But the dinner table was a minefield where an innocent comment might evoke a stony indifference. Guito ate quickly and left the table as soon as possible.

Eduardo was deeply unsettled, a little disorganized perhaps. This state led directly to a perpetual anger with his life and with his wife. It was expressed as a perpetual impatience. And impatience expressed itself in the distraction of another woman.

Flight

December, 1980

The family joke was that his sister started her first full sentence when she was two years old and never finished it. This sister found some of Guito's early stick figure drawings with names and words in big cartoon bubbles. With a little sisterly malice, she revealed his secret at the dinner table.

"Does anybody want to know what Guito's secret name is?"

Sister and brother saw him blush and the two of them jumped at the opportunity like a pack of little dogs, "I do! I do!" his brother yelled, roaring as Guito reddened further.

"It's El Indio!" in her little girl shout. "El Indio," her brother echoed and they chanted "El Indio, El Indio."

Eduardo's dinnertime somberness deepened; the words, *That's enough,* were just forming when he looked at Alba. Her face was impassive but her eyes glistened. He said nothing. She captured Guito's eyes with her gaze and spoke his mantra, "We are Nicarau." And that ended the chatter. The moment lengthened; it was complicated, but the hidden bond between mother and son lay on the table for both to see. The husband and the father saw it also.

The revelation prompted the smaller children to ask about her childhood.

"That's enough," Eduardo said throwing a napkin onto the table. He stood up, knocking his chair over and strode away.

The other woman was married and wished to remain so. At age 41, she was desirable and an asset to her husband's career. She knew this and was quite intentional about it. Her husband was an executive working in the capital. He was upper management and his long hours had contributed to his earlier success; now they had their own momentum. "I'm not a *peón*," he would remind his wife when the subject came up, as though that insight should answer every question. This satisfied her much of the time, for he was successful. They lived in a large home on acreage not far from Eduardo's farm, nor far from where the woman had grown up in a humble setting.

࠾

The caretaker at her home worked until 1:00 PM each day. The housekeeper came four days a week, including Saturday. Her husband's long commute facilitated the logistics of rendezvous. The woman had no children, and since she had known only one man in her life, she was uncertain whether it was she or her husband who was culpable. She assumed that it was herself she told Eduardo, because, "Men make babies all over the place." The danger titillated Eduardo, *she knows what she is doing,* he thought. Like a man in the early stages of addiction, he was sure that he could stop the affair whenever he wished.

Disconfirmation arrived with pregnancy. Dominated by the impending pain, their mutual guilt for the unprotected sex scarcely surfaced. Abortion was unimaginable. Her conventional religiosity and latent longing for a child would have overwhelmed any real consideration of it anyway. She took the familiar way out; she would tell her husband the child was his.

She was clear her husband did not want a child, especially at this point in his career. But the normal forces of pride or convenience might have their effect and he could get over it. And who knew? He might surprise himself with his own fatherly instincts. She was confident.

She put his favorite record of Mexican love songs on the player. "Jorge dear," she said, "Sit down. I have some news." She said this despite of the fact he was already sitting with his evening three fingers of neat whiskey. She had rehearsed the conversation and wives always said this in the movies. He looked at her. "We are pregnant," she said simply and smiled.

His eyes widened...then slowly narrowed...his neck swelled as the blood rose through it to his face. She thought he might choke. The glass struck a glancing blow on her left shoulder. He was still sitting. Her blouse was soaked. He stood and stalked to the kitchen sink to wash his hands. He turned around and from the kitchen and spat, "You slut! You god-damned whore!" She stood there, head down, stunned. But at the names she lifted her head, raised up onto the balls of her feet. She stood straight, glaring at him. Her face revealed a different set of feelings.

The glass struck her shoulder but the words struck a firing pin. A percussion cap deep within her detonated with "slut."

He came out of the kitchen, "I know—I *goddamn know*—god-*damn* you, I can't make babies. Who've you been fucking?"

A new rage arose visibly contorting her face, the words arrived with the tempo of an artillery salvo, "You-cock-suck-er. All those years I tried to talk to you about children—and *you knew*." Her right hand came winging from no-where, the flat of it spun his head and staggered him. "God-damn-you! And you're right, I met a real man!"

A lot of cruelty passed but not much information for the remainder of the evening. They stopped the hitting but fought well outside the boundaries of their civilized life. She found out that he'd been tested years before and kept it a secret, and he found out some details of the affair. Actual words mattered less than mutually assured destruction. What he did not find out was the father's name. He would have to pay for that. The next day, he went to work later than usual.

But it was he, after a consultation with his lawyer, who came up with the solution. He would not accept this child as his own in spite of any damage to his *machismo*. And she realized the child might not be raised safely in this house. The choice was either that she would go to Panama for an abortion or someone else would raise the child. If one of those options sufficed, they could stay married. If not..., he was both powerful and knowledgeable and it would cost her a fortune to get any part of what he had. She knew he would hide (or had already hidden), whatever part of his assets he could. She might prevail but, "at what cost," she told Eduardo.

Neither she nor Eduardo could veto the solution. He was not willing to have his child raised by anyone else, although it was not his decision. The woman might still be the natural mother and perhaps see the child, and she would wear the scarlet A inherent in the arrangement. It was more humiliating than she could have imagined. But she agreed. Hoping beyond hope that Eduardo could make it happen.

Eduardo noticed her coolness with the proposal. *There are not many women who could handle it this way*, he thought. But her husband's suggestion of abortion kindled more anger than he had known in years. She had teared at Eduardo's fierceness when she told him the options.

Eduardo's turn: They were sitting on the porch for the breeze. It was hot and even in the shade and they sweated.

"Alba," he began, "You know we've not been getting along for months. You've been complaining about me with Guito the whole time and you've pulled away from me." Sweat rolled down the side of his face; he brushed it away and it ran onto his shirt. "You've been yelling at me for months."

The afternoon sun dropped below the roofline and began to cook them. Alba's brow beaded as

Eduardo spoke. Her face changed from impassive to quizzical to something else as she listened to his opening. "You are making this up Eduardo. What are you trying to say?" She leaned away from him, her confusion changing to disbelief.

"What-have-you-done?"

He stared at her, trying to find the easiest way to put it but she'd caught him, and her steely manner left him mute.

She stood and turned away from him. "There's a woman. Isn't there?" She turned back to him, her hands wrung the strings of her apron and her face blazed.

"It doesn't mean a thing," he said. "It doesn't mean anything."

"It's Adele, isn't it?"

He had desperately wanted to understand the affair, and to have her believe it as partly or even mostly her fault. But now she sat there, her face a stone. Once started, he laid out the facts plainly, but his guilt and anger worked against him from the start. In his miscalculation, he had left out the essential formula, which was his remorse–to ask for forgiveness–to let her hear him say, "I'm sorry." This omission, the importance of which eluded him in his angry confusion, caused a big problem to become immutable.

A short, cool breeze refreshed his face and neck; it was the measure of his confusion that he thought he had succeeded.

For the first time in 18 years of marriage, her hurt spilled over at the dinner table. Plates and pots slammed the table. Her eyes were perpetually red. "Leave," she yelled at Eduardo, "go eat with your girlfriend." The children fled their parents' presence. His brother sobbed in the old barn while his sister and Guito held him, both of them weeping.

Eduardo's approach, which appeared to everyone to be nothing more than "Just give her the facts and she'll get over it," required rethinking.

⁜

Guito's antipathy exploded. He was the only child old enough to appreciate the crime. This new injustice re-fired—with acetylene—the accrued resentment of his father's disappointment. Guito knew he wasn't deficient this time and he wanted to strike, to smash Eduardo for the senseless destruction of their family. Instead he withdrew, even from his mother. *"Damn him! Damn him to hell!"* he ruminated every time the situation came to mind, which was often.

⁜

At the time his sister revealed Guito's secret name, he was in his last year of high school. All of his classmates were in their required internships. His teachers and the school Director pushed him to find an opportunity. Finally a notice came through the school system that a botanical team would be working in Aguas Calientes and was looking for interns to help in their study of rain forest plant life. It offered a shared room, two meals per day, no stipend, eight to ten hours daily.

The notice arrived the few days after his parent's fighting began. Asking no one's permission, Guito applied formally and by telephone from the school. The call turned into an interview, partly in English. The interviewer asked to talk to a teacher or the director.

Guito's acceptance arrived in the next mail. The first his parents knew about the decision was the day he asked for bus money. He held his mother in a long goodbye for the first time since her rage began. He held her; she clung to him. She handed him an additional 40 dollars in *pesos* when he stepped back. He said, "*Adios*," and otherwise ignored Eduardo and trudged uphill to the bus stop with full backpacks slung over each shoulder.

છ૭

Eduardo's guilt surfaced strongly for the collateral damage. The cheating itself remained curiously insulated from guilt. He could not blame himself for the fall in spite of its predictable results. He was still confused and verged on depression. He finally left the house after several days, and for several more weeks stayed with his brother's family while he thought it over.

His twin brother, who was no one to give advice in such matters, said only, "Chico, think about what is really important." It was a subject on which he was an expert. Eduardo called the woman, Adele, and asked if they could talk. They met in her driveway.

There was some empathy, a little tenderness, no embrace. The turmoil overrode any affection that may have remained. She did smile at him, *playfully*, he thought. *Maybe she loves me; maybe she is already missing what might have been.*

"Every time I talk with Alba it goes crazy, we both go crazy. You are so cool with all of this. How do you do it?"

The smile left, she sighed, looking at him for a long time. "Eduardo, I did what I did...we did what we did. Life has delivered us a package, it's not just the baby, it's the whole situation. I have some options, but I can't change the package. Neither can you."

"But she expects *me* to take all the blame — "

"Oh for God's sake!" she slashed him. "Listen to yourself. There must be something you're sorry for. I have to work my life out, you work out yours!" Tears sprang unbidden, "Just work it out!"

It started as a yell but stuttered to a sob. "*Que vaya bien*," she managed to say and retreated into the house. They would not talk privately again for another 16 years.

A few days later Eduardo asked Alba if they could talk.

᠄

Sexual betrayal is common enough in marriage. Alba and Eduardo found a way to resolve it in a manner not dissimilar to others. Eduardo was remorseful and grateful, acknowledging to himself and to her how great his loss could have been. He did love Alba. Her emotional temperature cooled and she came to see his sincerity and recognize the man she had known for 20 years. The other woman *was* beautiful. If they had known his state of mind then, as did Alba, most people could understand how Eduardo could have fallen. For her part, Alba would never again bring herself to speak to Adele. It would be a mutual estrangement.

In the private hospital, Adele named the child after her own mother, Aurelez[2]. Alba's anger flared briefly, "The *puta*! And she expects me to raise this child!" But the issue had been overlooked and the woman had her rights. Aurelez legally became the child of Alba and Eduardo. Alba, shrewdly,

---

[2] Pronounced *Ow-ray-lez*

insisted. There would be no recanting. To get her way, she agreed to allow the child to know and to visit her natural mother.

Part 2

Aguas Calientes

Prólogo

During a Great War

Juan Carlos Torquemada y Torremolino the third bore an unbearable name. The oldest crones claimed to remember his great grandmother, *who thought she was Spanish,* they would say when the coven convened on fiesta days. *Imagine! The "y." She was arrrogante.* The r's roiled in malice. This grandmother was *chocante,* striking, which did not help matters, and when she announced her son's name she sealed her own demise in the river of *chisme. She murdered her politician lover in the capital,* the gossips said.

The *Rurales*, who might have testified to her identity, preferred to visit her instead. Soon, other men did as well. She had come to the volcano with her boy child, Juan Carlos' grandfather, and whatever her tattered pretensions, they did not survive the life that followed. She died with them before the newest Juan Carlos was born.

She bequeathed two things to her rustic neighbors. The first was the line of eye-fetching Juan Carloses and the second, a small plant that made a fruit. "It is a *fresa,*" she told Juan Carlos' grandfather. "Keep it in the family." But the latter proved impossible.

The crones spotted the Devil immediately. *That fruit causes good Catholics to do unmentionable things,* the coven gleefully reported. Indeed, the average morality of the average *Católico* did appear to suffer after tasting the fruit. When some noticed that the new generation seemed to be less of "something" than the previous, the crones purred knowingly.

Like his father and grandfather, each a "Juan Carlos," Juan Carlos the Third gratefully accepted the nickname, ToTo. In fact, he was known as ToTo Tercero. Like both his ancestors, ToTo[3ro] prospered as a hunter and as a grower of the little plant, which his neighbors envied. This year he attained 17 years and had already learned to amuse himself with a local widow. *To be expected,* the *chisme* said, *he brings her fresas.*

⁊

Today ToTo Tercero waited at the top of the long unforested slope called the *rododendros,* or sometimes the *flores,* whenever a name was required. Just beyond he could see the hamlet of Palo Seco where the original squatters gathered for consortium and security. The *rododendros* was on the western slope of the saddle between the great moribund volcanoes, a place of some mystery to the original squatters. The area was an oval some 1000 meters long and 500 meters wide surrounded by primeval forest. A few skinny junipers grew in the oval but the wild rhododendrons flourished in great patches. They formed a low landscape with natural trails through which game and men must predictably pass.

Late morning and dense clouds from the sea gathered to the northeast obscuring the coastal plains below. To his right and southwest the weather was clear and he could see the tectonic lake that dominated and drained Great Valley. The stiffening trade wind raised the fogs ominously to eye level, then higher. Within the half-hour that same wind would roll fog over the great saddle for the remainder of day and most of the night.

ToTo[3ro] awaited the foreigners who had purchased a great portion of ancient forest and the *rododendros* between the volcanoes. They seemed nice enough. He had "No complaints," he told his neighbors. "They are refugees like us, religious but they are not *Católicos*. We will see." Since the neighbors were squatters and had been treated fairly by the new owners, they agreed to wait and see before squatting once again.

He saw the newcomers emerge from the forest below. They led horses that, like the men themselves, were short of breath at such an altitude. His perch on the crest of a massive and mostly buried, volcanic outcrop offered the only full vista of the peculiar landscape. The newcomers had not yet seen him and it pleased ToTo Tercero to coolly gauge their progress through the narrow trails in the great swaths.

These people were new to the country, but they were not greenhorns. They had science and they did experiments with the soil. They even chewed the grass in the area of *rododendros* where the few thin trees grew. They told him they wanted to raise milk cows. *Milk cows! Sure. They will thrive here, but what will they do with the milk?* He and the other settlers lived by hunting tapir and deer and eating potatoes and the fat strawberries. *Vamos a ver* he thought, they would wait and see. If the milk spoiled, there would be plenty of meat for everyone.

It took the company 20 minutes to cross the expanse of wild bushes and volcanic rock. When finally they saw him they shifted to his direction. The clouds billowed over the great gap between the volcanoes, but the sulphurous odor from the soil would not reach them until the vapors had steeped the ground for a few hours. Early on, visiting hunters had established that the smell was *diabólica* and it explained why no one had built a dwelling in the otherwise obvious spot.

"Ho-la, ToTo Tercero," the lead Gringo said in accented Spanish. "Is there any water close by?"

ToTo[3ro] pointed toward the Eastern Sea and down, to the hot water spring. "*El grifo alto*," he said.

The men trekked another fifty yards to the first of several steaming springs feeding a stream.

"Whoa!" one said to the horse that backed suddenly. "That'll scald'ya."

"Muucho caw-lor," the leader said to ToTo[3ro].

"*Si señor, aguas calientes,*" the taciturn youth said and offered a wry smile, mouth bent in the corner, lips pursed. "*Aguas calientes.*

"Ag-guaas cal-lentes, hot water." the man repeated thoughtfully. "Ag-guaas cal-lentes. Sounds like a name, it'll be our refuge."

❦

"And that is how the Aguas Calientes Rain Forest got its name," ToTo[3ro] would tell researchers in their own language years later. And in one of the curious accidents of naming history, the foreigners became known as "refuges" instead of refugees.

In the intervening age, life changed for ToTo³ʳᵒ. It happened that a couple of years after the *Refugios* arrived and years before he became Don ToTo, he rode his horse just before full daylight among the rhododendrons. The faint odor of sulphur still lingered near the ground from the long, soaking night. He was looking for his milk cow that had joined some *Refugio* cows headed in for the morning milking. *That milk is mine,* he thought and he was annoyed at having to track the cow before his first coffee. He had just risen in the stirrups to remain vertical as the pony lay into a steep incline when the unmistakable feel of a lariat settled over his shoulders, pinning his arms. *Rustlers!* was his last thought as the air burst from his lungs and the back of his head bounced off the ground.

He awoke to a smelly sock, redolent with sulphur, cow dung and fermented strawberries, nudging his nose. "*Uggh!*"

The word had just formed when someone said, "Watch yer manners, Upperian!"

A throbbing cloud packed his head where his brain should be and it took a moment for him to focus his eyes. A portly but diminutive man stood three feet away; a coil of rope hung from his left shoulder and dragged the ground. He pointed with his left hand cross body to his right, his elbow remained high to keep the coil from slipping off his shoulder. Triumph irradiated his countenance.

ToTo³ʳᵒ rolled onto a shoulder and stared where the man pointed. A small group of similar sized men watched him, their hands clasped solemnly behind them. Each wore a floppy, colored *lona* with the widest brims ToTo had ever seen on a hat. His surprise was so great that he failed to notice a group of women and children until the man in front of the group snapped his fingers and they melted into the rhododendrons. Then he knew. *OH Nooo,* his mind groaned.

"Do not be afraid," Fingersnapper said, "you are probably not in danger."

"Probably?" ToTo said weakly.

"Probably." Fingersnapper replied. "Most likely not."

"You are the Little People?" In a still weak voice, perhaps with a trace of hopefulness that he might be wrong.

"Calling us names will not help your cause," Fingersnapper said. Then in a more pleasant voice he added, "I apologize for Samo but you insulted his feet. You do understand that, do you not?"

From the corner of his eye, ToTo saw Samo's diffident nod. Abruptly, ToTo's entire self mobilized with the intent that "probably" should become "definitely" not. "How may I serve you?" he said in what he hoped was his most gracious manner.

The council of Little People murmured, some nodding approval at what was obviously the correct approach. They looked among themselves nodding and shaking heads so that it appeared to ToTo they were having a discussion. This went on for a while.

"You may sit up," Fingersnapper said. And ToTo did, crossing his legs. "You are Don ToTo are you not?"

"I am ToTo Tercero. The Don ToTo is my grandfather." The council began to cluck loudly, their consternation clear. In the slightest of moments, ToTo went from the beginnings of confidence to despair. "But I will do what I can. Perhaps, I may leave to go get him. It will take just a few minutes to get to the village.' His voice faded to silence as the roper, Samo, moved closer, stopped only by Fingersnapper's glare. *Samo got the wrong ToTo,* ToTo thought. "People make that mistake all the time," he said hoping to avoid Samo's anger. "I'll go right to Palo Seco now."

Fingersnapper pointed that he should stay, "Omelas,[2]" he said.

"What is omelas?"

"The name of the village."

ToTo was confused and more than a little anxious, "Why do you call it that?"

"Because there are elements in that village that find happiness in the pain of others." He held up a palm indicating no more questions.

His answer did not seem propitious to ToTo and he was even more confused. He knew that this was a good time to change the subject but nothing came to him.

Fingersnapper turned to his little council, then back to ToTo, "You will have to do," he said, "we've lost the element of surprise."

"I will help if I can."

"You will help, period. There is no second chance, ToTo Tercero. If you can't help, perhaps your grandfather will to save his grandson from adjustment."

ToTo did not know what 'adjustment' meant. Vague or not, he knew he had been threatened and his dread-o-meter needle swung closer to the panic point.

"This is your task," Fingersnapper said. "You must stop the *Refugios* from raising their cows."

That's it? He thought, *that's all they want?* "I don't understand." But what at first sounded trivial, now began to take on complications.

Fingersnapper humphed with exasperation, 'They eat the strawberries and crush the plants when they roam. We are practically out!"

Suddenly ToTo knew why a third of the *fresa* crop disappeared every year. It wasn't the rabbits. And what Fingersnapper said was true, *fresa* prices had rocketed upward since the cows arrived.

"Strawberry wine, man!"

Wine. This is serious business. ToTo understood fully now. Everyone knew that the Little People loved their wine nearly as much as they loved mischief. But he understood the *Refugios* too. They came to make a living and cows were what they knew. With this understanding came an inkling of a problem to be solved. But the opposing needs of two groups would have to be met. *Surely there is a way,* he thought, *everyone needs to eat...or drink.* The necessary steps began to form a mental list.

"There is a problem," ToTo said, "they speak another language. I only know a few words.

"Humph."

He tried again, "They only know one way to make a living."

"Show them another! And quickly! The growing season is upon us," Fingersnapper said.

"But—." ToTo already had a list of objections to bargain with the chief but Fingersnapper waved, really, a mere flick of a couple fingers at ToTo³ʳᵒ.

ToTo had tired from the strain of arguing with the Little People, he could hardly keep his eyes open and soon he slept like a milk-fed-puppy.

❦

"Where have you been?" his father, ToTo the Second demanded, "The horse came home by herself yesterday. Your brothers and I went looking and your mother did not sleep at all." He paused, "What is that smell?"

Suddenly exhausted, ToTo³ʳᵒ plopped himself onto the bench that served as a couch in the living room. "Pa, what is adjustment?"

ToTo Segundo's jaw dropped like a broken tailgate. In slow motion he walked to a chair, pulling it up to ToTo³ʳᵒ. ToTo Segundo sat without taking his eye from his son. "Tell me what happened."

ToTo³ʳᵒ told him of the encounter. "They thought I was grandpa," he ended. He took a deep breath as his father sized up the story. Then he remembered, "What is an adjustment?"

ToTo Segundo took his own deep breath and metered it out. "It might mean a lot of things but rest assured, you will spend the remainder of a short and miserable life grubbing for roots and nuts in the forest."

Suddenly ToTo³ʳᵒ remembered a sight he had seen while hunting in his early teens. He had surprised a naked, hairless creature with a grotesque, protruding face digging in a deer trail. The thing hopped rapidly into the deep brush but not before the boy had looked into its wretched face. Now he wondered why he had never said anything to his family, *How could I have forgotten that?*

His father must have seen the terror in his eyes. "It is serious, for sure." He turned away from ToTo³ʳᵒ and looked at his grandmother's ancient pendulum clock. "Was one of them named Samo?"

ToTo³ʳᵒ nodded.

"Let's go talk to Grandpa."

Grandpa ToTo was equally somber but he said nothing that might further agitate his son and grandson. They agreed that the only solution was to find another source of income for the *Refugios*.

"The Little People will not put up with failure, and it will not just be ToTo³ʳᵒ," the older man said, "Everyone will suffer, even the *Refugios* but they will not believe it until it happens."

"I'll just tell them what happened."

The two older ToTo's snorted.

"We'll help where we can," Grandpa ToTo said. "But you have to take the lead, grandson.

ToTo³ʳᵒ saw the chairman *Refugio* standing outside the school cabin in *Rododendros*. The four men awaited him in a circle of homemade school desks. The circle parted slightly at the one saved for him. ToTo had asked for the meeting to broach his proposal. He had prepared his reasons for a request that he knew would cause consternation. *Our neighbors*, he would say, *cannot benefit from all the additional milk now and their primary living is from sending the berries into the lowlands and it is threatened. We could all grow strawberries, they are so much easier to store and transport, we could all grow them and be the center for fresas all over the country.* His list was long and his father had urged him to shorten it and to put reasons on the table all at once so that they could be discussed in total.

All the Toto's were certain that the *Refugios* would give consideration to a request from their neighbors. Most of these men had tried to learn a little Spanish so it would be a struggle, *but not impossible,* he thought, *not impossible.* "Speak slow and give them time to talk among themselves," ToTo Segundo had said.

The *Refugios* had already learned that pleasantries preceded business in their new country but eventually one of them said in Spanish, "So, ToTo Tercero, you called a meeting. What's up?"

Deep breath. "Well," he said. "I've been asked to point out that, as you know, the cows are destroying much of the *fresa* crop each year." He knew that these fair-minded men would agree with his opening statement and he paused to let the heads nod. Instead, the men stared at him. Shock contorted the faces of two of them. *What's wrong?* He thought. "I mean, you know that it's true, we've spoken of it several times." Blank faces gaped without speaking.

Then he knew. *My God,* he thought, *I'm speaking English.*

His English was perfect. And is until this day. The fact that he had obviously been studying diligently spread around AC carrying his request with it. People talked about it for weeks and one day the chairman *Refugio* came to ToTo³ʳᵒ and told him that they would sell the extra cows to everyone at good prices, cut back the rhododendrons and grow the *fresas* in the acidic soil. "All the family cows will have to be fenced from now on," he said. "Everybody has to do it to make this work."

Years later, ToTo Tercero's grandfather's soul had already passed through the largesse of sacrament into the Ether-of-the-Eternal-God. His father became Don ToTo but he died and passed in the manner of his father, just a few years after that. More than one saw his earthly vapor ascend into the thatch and hesitate before swooshing to Heaven. ToTo³ʳᵒ became Don ToTo.

With his father's passing descended an invisible mantle, *El Español.* Only the crones had ever spoken the word in regard to this matter and, in truth, ToTo³ʳᵒ could not have expressed it himself. Any vestige of whiteness bequeathed by his great grandparents had evolved to the swarthy mocha of his neighbors. But the oily *chisme* of the crones had polished the lineage of Juan Carloses with irony. People began to treat the new Don ToTo, the Spaniard, with the respect due a paterfamilias.

In 1982, Los Rododendros

ToTo the fourth, ToTo Cuarto, leaned his chair back, appraising Guito. Guito's expression remained in its hung-jaw-raptness for several long moments. "How did he learn English?"

ToTo[4to] gazed at him. After a moment he said, "Think about it."

Guito's expression contorted. "That cannot be true."

"I'm telling you it is true." ToTo[4to]'s face showed no emotion. His eyes bored into Guito's so that he could not escape the obvious conclusion.

Guito expelled the long breath he had been unconsciously holding. He swiped his brow with trembling fingertips and glanced again at ToTo's unrelenting gaze.

Still struggling with the story, Guito said lamely, "So that's why the community shifted from dairy to *fresas?*

"That's it. And that's why you never deny the Little People in front of the ToTos."

Xochiquetzal

Late December 1980

Guito walked five kilometers uphill to San Diego, county seat of Asturias. He took the bus from there to the capital at the head of the tectonic lake Great Valley, then another from there, skirting the lake that dominated the center of the Great Valley. He had only been on this road once before and it had been an amazing adventure to see so much water then. Today he was lost in thought and was surprised when the bus pulled into to Pinto, the capital of Pinto Province. He had gotten lost walking from one bus station to the other in the capital and hailed a taxi so, along with meals, his cash had begun to decline. In Pinto, he had to run to catch the dilapidated school bus to Fresa, a small village about two-thirds the way up the volcano. He got to Fresa after dark and there would be no bus until the next day at noon. The señora in the store that served as the bus stop, let him stay in a room in her house for a dollar. He slept fitfully throughout the coldest night of his life.

ॐ

Guito spent much of the next morning walking around the village of Fresa, stopping to pet and talk with the various stray dogs. He walked up a loamy trail, through a living fence of *itabo*[3], into the surrounding mixed forest of pine, fichus and oak. *Not a strawberry in sight*, he thought, *where did the name come from?*

The thought had no sooner arrived, than his special connection to the forest settled in. It had been years but his normal, low-level anxiety displaced upward, wedged out by a peacefulness pushing up from his center. It pressed upward like a cloud filling his chest yet clearing his mind. His special vision returned and the pine needles and bark furrows arose once again in high relief. A large leaf of the speckled *lotteria*[4] caught his eye.

---

[3] Ee-TA-Bow (A yucca plant).
[4] Lo-ter-RI-a

He stared at it, *It looks like a face,* but as the thought arrived the leaf faded into the foliage. The dogs started forward, then stopped, sniffing the area. He stood wondering after it for a while then began following the trail deeper into the forest.

₭

The trail comes to a clearing that once held a cabin then angles away to the left. A sawed log still lies in the crook of it. Guito sits on the log and thinks on the disappearing *lotteria* plant. The dog pack settles in around his feet. Across the trail, a large aloe plant flourishes in a remaining sunny spot. Its stem, centered in its spiky nest, suspends flowers, long and narrow tubes enfolded by succulent red petals. The stem leans into a mote-filled beam of sunlight. From his peripheral vision, Guito's eye catches the wing flurry of a single hummingbird. The Hermit hovers on his side of the path. At the same moment the flower and the bird sense each other, ambient light assumes a saffron hue; time drips, puddles.

The flowers waggle their seductive red, lips pursing to reveal orange and yellow, their stigmas swell in anticipation. In a blur of wingbeat, the bird moves slowly, seductively toward the flower, sinking low on the stem to position its curved sabre beak. Rising now, the beak dips, its tip finds the opening, slides smoothly into the flower brushing the anthers in its search for the stigma. The stigma reaches for the bird and its beak thrusts into the sugary nectar of the ovary. The long stem undulates with the thrust of the bird and low orgasmic rumblings stir Guito's libido. For a moment, bird and flower rock in raucous lovemaking until he withdraws leaving a precious trace of pollen. The throbbing life of the forest now resonates like a tom-tom in Guito's temples. A tingle of longing ripples through him. His mind attempts to put a word to the feeling then surrenders to non-thought as the bird reprises its love play with awaiting flowers. Time continues melting, unnoticed.

᠁

The path returned Guito to the main road where a small girl sat selling strawberries from a table sliced from a mango trunk. Yellow seed packets enmeshed in red pulp glittered like jewels. The fruit seemed to fairly levitate out of its wicker basket. He ate a whole container while standing there.

"Have you ever had a *fresa*, *señor*?" She asked shyly.

"A few times" he said. "But never any like these."

She grinned. "These are special," she said.

In her smile he saw that she was older than her years. Guito stared at her for a moment then said, "Thank you," paid her and started back up the road.

When he returned he met the *señora* at the entrance to her little store. She was wide-eyed and holding a broom at the ready. It took a few seconds to realize that she was staring at the pack of dogs trailing him. They were in a playful state and by the time he had shooed them off to her satisfaction, the bus to Palo Seco was ready to leave.

The Fresa to Palo Seco bus was a faded yellow that said, "█████████ School District," on the side. About half of the passengers were going to the two intermediate hamlets called Bajo and Alto, lower and upper. The rest went on to Palo Seco. All were *nacionales* except for one, older foreigner. Everyone carried multiple sacks or boxes, which took some time to load. The bus had been built for paved streets and the trip took a painful three hours over the deeply rutted road. Guito's sublimity from the hike into the forest faded after the first jolty mile. It was the windy season but today there was none. Dust, boiled up by the lumbering bus, hung head high. The dust moved away far enough to coat the trees and bushes, but most of it settled back to the roadbed. Except for the frequent rocky sections, the road suffocated in it.

After the latest debacle Guito was no longer sure that Eduardo's cruelty was unintentional. But whether intentional or not, Eduardo's exasperation had tattooed the boy so that even his father's resignation was a sign of his failure. The reaction to his father's affair had changed Guito's shame to anger but the anger did not change anything else.

Like his *querencia* and his anger, his studies had been part of Guito's salvation. In truth, he had an interest in learning for its own sake. He was naturally curious and school met most of those needs. But this adventure was different. He was sure he would learn from his new duties and the English-speaking foreigners. But his usual concern about whether he could please them rode with him for the rest of the trip and muted his excitement. He would have to write a paper detailing his learning from the internship. Handing in assignments, on time, had always been a problem and as he thought about it now he realized that he feared the inevitable judgments that came with the completion of anything. But the end of the internship was a lifetime away. He was able to store the anticipation on his mental shelf and avoid the paralyzing panic that made him delay such assignments. Only the tingle from the forest stayed with him.

৪০

Six passengers remained when the bus arrived. Guito waited as the others unloaded their sacks and boxes. Clouds had settled thickly for the evening and a man walked out of the fog towards him with his hand outstretched. He was shorter than Guito, but with broad shoulders, long arms and a big smile.

"*Buenas tardes,*" he said, "I'm Sochi. Are you Carlos?"

"Yes, call me Guito, Sochi. *Buenas tardes.* How did you know?"

"Oh, I don't know, Amigo; must be the fancy backpacks...*Mucho gusto,*" he added. He was smiling and slung the largest of Guito's packs over his shoulder. "People call me Sochi; it's Indio but everybody uses it. You speak some English."

"A little," Guito said. "You are not *nacional,* are you?"

"That's good...you noticed," the man laughed. "Up north, but most of us are *Indio* like me. I grew up in Atlanta, U.S. God only knows what I am now." Still smiling, he got it all out in the open right away.

"*Caramba,*" Guito said, "I am too...*Nicarau.*"

"Excel-lent! *Q'echi,'* myself. We'll have to catch up on all of that." They high-fived off to a good start.

The pension where the male interns stayed was a 20-minute walk uphill. With the packs and little sleep, Guito was tired but Sochi was wide-awake and talking. They had a large room set up with single bunks because of the long stay. There would be just Sochi, Guito and Pablo who was expected the next day for a couple of weeks only. Sochi took a beer out of his ice chest and held it up. "*La cerveza* is not good with either my folks or the *Refugios*. If Brian and Sharon weren't so liberal I'd be doomed." He paused, "Do you know about the *Refugios*?"

"They are the foreigners who settled in this area, that's all."

"It's enough for now. One of the interns is a *Refugio*, I'm sure you'll learn more."

They went next door to the *soda*. He ordered coffee and a *casado*–a full plate of country food– for Guito without asking. Sochi said that he and his family were members of a Pentecostal Baptist church in his home country. This was during the 1960's when the insurgency, then led in part by left wing army officers, held much of the eastern mountains. The rebels, realizing that the war could not be won with just ex-soldiers, union members and intellectuals, enlisted the aid of the peasants, comprised mostly of the long-suffering Maya. In 1966, *Operation Cleanup* had begun with American support of kidnappings and assassinations. The unpunished and decades-long violence against the *Indios* occupying desirable land was increasing.

Sochi's father was an indigenous schoolteacher and a lay minister in his church. He spoke some English and the Church leadership relied on him. But being a liberal, indigenous educator and leader put him at risk. Informing—being an *oreja* for the government—became a viable way to manage one's personal safety. Sochi said that patrols of soldiers would enter the towns, usually to arrest someone, which predictably meant rough treatment. "What was unpredictable was whether they would ever be un-arrested."

The Church helped to get the family into the United States and they were located to a Southern state. His father's favorite Gringo story occurred when they got off the plane in Atlanta. "Are the Indians down there, Cominists?" the man had asked in his North Georgia patois, not knowing that he was transporting Mayans.

"*Are* they communists, like the papers say?" Guito asked.

"Some of them at least. But they are really fed up with the exploitation. Right now they will take any help they can get and the Cubans have been 'helpful.'" He made the quotes sign while keeping his fork-full of food balanced.

"So, what now...are you going to go visit now that you're down here?"

Sochi waited, longer than Guito expected, to answer. There was no smile flitting about the edges of Sochi's face. Guito considered repeating the question.

"I don't think so. The war ramped up fast after the Americans got involved. He breathed deeply, "Honestly," he exhaled, "I don't think I have the guts to do it. Maybe some day." And his face broke into the Sochi smile. "Anyway that's heavy. We've got things to do here." Sochi freely laced his speech with American aphorisms and Guito tucked "heavy" into his stash of English sayings.

Sochi had gone to college in South Carolina on scholarship and had now finished his first year in the graduate botany program at the University of Richmond. "It helps around here that I speak a little Spanish," he laughed easily. Guito succumbed to Sochi's unrelenting good humor and, for the first time in a week, his polite smile grew into a chuckle.

"Remember to sign for your meals each time. If you want something else you pay...theoretically." Sochi ended dinner with another grin.

Guito tried to call his mother from the office before turning in, but the service was down. He had some knowledge of the civil wars in Central America, but Sochi's story was too personal and Guito went to sleep mulling what it meant to be *Indio*.

The morning came as early as on the farm. At 5:00, just early light, Sochi slapped the side of Guito's bunk and said, "Let's go, *Amigo*." Sochi was good-natured in the morning, a skill Guito had never mastered. He insisted that the room be picked up before leaving for breakfast and gave Guito a key, "This lock can be a little cantankerous," using the English word. Guito figured it out.

By 5:30 AM, the little *soda* blazed with a wood fire in the *fogon*, a raised, rectangular fire pit with a narrow channel, which funneled the heated air to three burner eyes. In the back was a small domed brick and clay oven that used firewood. Three yellow-shirted, "*Fuerza y Luz*" electrical linemen munched empanadas and drank coffee. Guito's morning priority was always coffee. The cook also offered eggs with cilantro, peppers and onions if he wanted, but Guito could not eat eggs early in the morning, so the cook gave him a huge portion of rice and beans, a piece of fried cheese, and an extra empanada. Sochi ate big portions of everything. "Eat well," he said, "the team doesn't take the long 9:00 o'clock break that you are used to."

"The team must pay a lot for breakfast."

Sochi smiled, "Its part of my job to handle these mundane affairs," he said. I also work with the *pension* and do the buying of other supplies. You gotta' learn to speak English, my man." He said with a grin. When they left, the pretty waitress gave each an extra empanada for later.

ℬ

The team met in the main room of the leader's wooden house. The house was halfway between Palo Seco and the cluster of houses called *Rododendros*. From there it was a 30-minute walk to reach the Aguas Calientes forest. Atthisnpoint, the forest had been ceded to the government but the administration was still local. The team leaders, Sharon and Brian spoke some Spanish. They had been to the AC on other occasions and had studied the language at home as well. But they loved the science more than administration. "We are delighted to have Sochi as our graduate assistant this year." Sharon said.

The other two interns Tessa and Pablo arrived. Both were light skinned but Pablo was the whitest *nacional* that Guito had ever seen. Pablo had arrived late in a private car and had spent the night in the only hotel because his driver could not find the pension. Tessa, who lived in the *Rododendros* and had gotten to the meeting early, had been sent to track him down. She caught up with him him on the road walking towards the house from Palo Seco.

The team spoke Spanish and English interchangeably. Team leaders introduced themselves and heads turned to Sochi but the new intern spoke up. "My name is Pablo Lorenzo Calderon Salazar," began Pablo. "But I'm called Lorenzo. My mother is also on the team but she only comes by sometimes to consult. She is a Professor of Botany at the University. My father is an engineer but he owns a big trucking company," he said, beaming. Sharon shifted her glance from Sochi to smile at Lorenzo. "I just finished high school, The American School actually, and I'm starting University in a month. I'll get a Ph.D. in Botany as soon as possible. I've been on several field trips already. I—," Sharon cut in.

"Thank you Lorenzo. So, Lorenzo it is, not Pablo," looking at the group. Speaking to everyone she said, "*Professora* Salazar is a key part of this team. She helps us with early classifications and keeps our contacts with the University in good order. You'll meet her later. Sochi, you're up. Sochi is your first point of contact. He will give you assignments and solve your problems. He also pays the soda so you better stay on his good side." Sharon smiled broadly at him and spoke in Spanish except for the, "You're up."

"Let me start with the most frequently asked question," he said, "The 'Sochi comes from my ignorant classmates in the USA who couldn't pronounce, 'Xo-chi-quet-zal,' seems easy enough to me." The interns snickered. He said only that he was originally from "up North" and had majored in biology in the university. He hoped to take a Ph.D. with an emphasis in "ethno-botany" which was the cultural use of plants for food, medicine, dyes, construction, and "so forth." Lorenzo looked away and covered a yawn.

Sharon pointed to Tessa and said, "Your turn Tessa. Tessa's people are, in the final analysis, the main reason we are in the AC and not some other jungle."

"Well, my people," Tessa began, "are members of a religious community that originally came from Germany back in the late 1800's. We come from the same stock, if you go way back, as the Amish and Mennonites if you've heard of them, and we had some of the same problems in Europe that they did. Many of them left also and went to other parts of the world. But we are not them, even though some of them are in Central America also. We just share the same distant roots. Then we went to Oregon and lived there for a few generations until we moved here in the 1940's."

"Why?" Guito asked.

"We're different in some ways. We don't believe in war and we sure don't like being taxed to pay for it." She opened her hands as though deciding what else to say. "In the U.S. we lived a more communal life. People called us a cult. Ma says that in the 1930's people started calling us a Communist cult. We weren't but things got nasty and we pretty much decided to start over after that."

"Are you still Communists?" Lorenzo asked.

"No. Never were. And we certainly aren't here either but we do live kind 'a close together up in *Rododendros*, closer to the AC."

"What do you believe in?" Guito said.

"We're *Christianos*, kind of conservative." She glanced at Sochi, "No drinking for example. But we have a lot of tolerance for others. Ma says that's what people understand the least. We try to live plain and simple. It's a lot easier to do that in these mountains than it was in the U.S.—even in Oregon."

"No priest sounds like asking for trouble," said Lorenzo.

"So tell us about you," Sharon said.

"I've just completed high school and I want to go to university, soon but maybe not right away. I work in the packing plant retail store. My mom is from one of the settler families, and she happens to be the store manager," she chuckled along with the others. "My family is very active in the *fresa* business here. My father is pure *nacional;* that's how I got to be so brown. He works for the coop too."

"I don't think you are so brown, and you've got green eyes," said Guito.

"Well, maybe not me so much, but you should see my brothers." She studied him.

Guito opened his mouth to say something else but shut it on second thought. Tessa saw it and laughed at him.

"Thanks, Tessa, OK Guito, your turn." Sharon turned to face him and spoke in English.

"Well," he began in Spanish, "In truth, I have not completed high school. One of my areas is agriculture and my father has a coffee farm in Asturias, on the other side of the Great Valley, but I don't think I'm cut out for farming. I can say that I have a lifelong love of plants – and animals. I hope to learn a lot and do what I can." His look to

Sochi said, *I'm not saying anything about Indios
if you don't.*

"What a modest bunch of interns we have!
Guito is the star pupil in his high school and is
only this internship away from finishing. He has a
reputation for his skills with plants, farming or no
farming." Sharon was emphatic. "I wouldn't be
surprised if he can find new ferns better than any
of us." Guito felt his heart jump at the
confirmation then shrink in fear of disappointing
her.

"OK, let's take a little break; then we will go
outside for some training." Sharon and Brian had
chosen the two study areas from two distinct
environments of the five that had been so far
indentified in the AC. "The AC is the Aguas
Calientes Rain Forest," Brian said, "But everybody
calls the whole area the AC."

They found two contrasting sites that would
offer an opportunity to complete the study within
the four months of the dry season. One section, at
over 6000 feet mean sea level, less than a
kilometer from the entrance to the AC was about a
hectare of rain forest under dense canopy. They
marked the main path with an arrow trusting that
the unmarked entrance would be ignored by the
birdwatchers and other eco-tourists that were just

beginning to visit Aguas Caliente. The other site was about three kilometers to the east down a maintained trail that followed the saddle between the volcanoes. There was an area that dropped steeply down towards the Eastern Sea to about 3200 feet and offered a practical opportunity for comparison with the higher, less open, site.

"The type of vascular plants of interest to us are known as ferns to all of you. Vascular," explained Sochi, "means that the plant has a plumbing system that moves water and nutrients up the stem. For example you can look just up the hill a little bit to the right and see that large tree fern *Acrostichum danaeifolium* – here it is called *helecho macho*. It must be 15 feet high. It is different from most other ferns because its rhizome grows vertically rather than horizontally. Sochi passed out a handout to explain the use of fern presses and how to count, collect and press plants so that they could be carried back for further study.

"As time goes on, I'll show you how to use the lenses, clippers, compasses and cameras," Sochi said.

It was almost dinnertime when the Meeting broke up. They all went to the soda for the first of many team meals. "Tomorrow we learn how the sites are different," Sharon said.

"And how to move about in the study area without ruining it," said Brian.

"Exactly. It will take at least another hour to reach the second site. Sochi will carry a machete, but we also have other equipment. We'll all share the load and we can change off during the day. A local guide who knows this trail will take us out the first time. There are some steep and muddy places so wear your rubber boots and bring a knapsack for your lunch, water, whatever. Just remember Hiking Rule # 1: if you bring it, you carry it. Questions? *OK compañeros, hasta mañana.*"

Readiness

The Internship January- May, 1981

"ToTo Cuarto," Tessa grinned. "I didn't know you were our guide."

"I'm just full of surprises, cousin. I heard you were on this team. I came to see you do your stuff."

Tessa blushed. "I'm just an intern, ToTo."

"Just teasing," he said. His affection was patent. He was older than Tessa by several years. His father, ToTo Tercero, was her father's much older brother.

The hike began immediately after introductions. ToTo^{4to} led followed by Sochi, Sharon, Lorenzo, Tessa, Brian and Guito. The elevation was over a 3000 feet higher than Guito's home and that, with the presence of clouds spilling over the Divide from the Eastern Sea, created a very different plant habitat than he was used to. The visit to the first site included tying some yellow string from side to side of the study site to help maintain orientation. It was also useful to identify the quadrants in which plants might be found. During the hike to the second site Guito noticed the manner that the team walked through the forest. At the lunch break he spoke to Tessa about this.

"Why don't you say something to ToTo Cuarto?"

"Not me. He's your cousin."

"Oh, talk to ToTo and see what he thinks...go ahead, you do it. He's a good guy." She gave him a smile so he didn't feel bad about being pushed out of his student role by a girl. He noticed her looking at him as she had during introductions the day before. *She is pretty*.

"Thanks Guito, I was whacking away up front and didn't notice." ToTo gazed at him with an appreciation. "You know," he added, "we don't have any up in the *Rododendros*...too high."

"No *terciopelos*?"

"Nope...but there are plenty of them down here."

During the rest, ToTo spoke to the group, "Folks, it has come to my attention, when you come to fallen logs, some of you step over them. That is not a good idea when you are this far down the mountain, even with rubber boots, it takes a little extra work but it is best to step up on the log, then step away on the other side. You never know what might be coiled next to it. Up in Aguas Caliente we don't have much in the way of poisonous snakes, but down here it pays to keep your eyes open." Then he repeated it in Spanish to make sure Lorenzo understood.

Sharon seemed surprised, "That's the first time someone has told us that, ToTo. Thank you."

"Amen," Brian mumbled.

The visit to this site followed the pattern of the first. Sharon's comment in the introductions proved prescient. The climate of this site was similar to Guito's home and he spotted a fern growing in a deep bark crevice. "Does anyone know this one?"

Sochi, who was close by, nodded "No."

Sharon came over, "Could be new."

I don't know it," said Brian, "Let's take this little guy just in case. Sochi, get the coordinates from the northeast corner and I will write it up," taking out his notebook. He showed the interns his field notes on the plant which included the date and time, a coded "name/number," the type of tree, "ToTo, what do you call this tree?" he asked about the *guachipelin*. He made notes about the depth of the bark fissures, the height from the ground, the directional side of the tree and the concomitant location of the sun, and notes on the other surrounding epiphytes. "Epiphytes," is the same in English and Spanish," he said, "although we say it differently."

"We do know a few things." Lorenzo smiled weakly, too late to avoid the blunder. Brian ignored him.

With help from the leaders, it became broadly apparent how plant life varied between the two areas. They got back about 4:00 PM as clouds began to settle in. Before they left the team house, Guito asked if he could borrow one of the plant books written in Spanish. Sharon asked him to sign for it, "This is for all of you," she said, "The books on this shelf may be borrowed, but please don't take them anywhere except to the *pension* – or your home."

It took Guito a day to look through the book. In the first time he leafed through it, he found a small bookmark with a quotation. He went back to the team house to use the dictionary. There was a small handwritten note below quotation.

Daily Scripture

I call upon God's Name…. [But] God has no name. His Name becomes the final lesson that all things are one.

No one can fail who seeks the meaning of the name of God.

Guito assumed that the reason he did not understand this passage was because his family was not religious except for attending Mass on the major holidays and funerals, and perhaps a confession every year or so. He was sure he never heard anything like this in Catechism class. With the handwritten note it seemed personal and he was uncertain what to do with it. He wanted to talk with Sharon or Brian about it but he knew he could never do that. He copied it into his diary and replaced the bookmark where he found it.

The book itself was a technical description of tropical plants with good, if small, photographs, and he recognized many that he had seen on the farm or studied in his tourism program. For the present time, the book served to orient him to what a technical description included and to introduce him to plant families and the naming protocols. He resolved to go back to the book as he learned more in the internship.

Two weeks passed quickly. Guito enjoyed Sochi and liked Lorenzo, but there was a tension present whenever the three of them were together. Lorenzo rarely failed to point out whenever he thought Sochi's explanation or instructions were deficient. At times Lorenzo did so to Sochi's face, but Sochi always seemed prepared to let a comment pass. It was odd because with Guito he never let an opportunity go to apply his good-natured banter whenever Guito didn't have something quite right. Guito learned to give as much as he took and the two of them became close.

On the day that Lorenzo left, he said his good-byes at the end of the workday and was waiting at the *pension* with Guito for his car. Fog was already skulking through the trees under a dense overcast. The outside light from a nearby house flashed then muted as the miasma passed through the area. As the car pulled up Lorenzo reached to shake Guito's hand.

"Enjoy the rest of your summer, Guito and watch out for Sochi."

Lorenzo saw his surprise. "He's *Indio*, a communist, Guito. Do you know what they are doing in his country? Ordinary people like you and I are not safe there. They are the cause of all the trouble there, in all the civil wars. You can't trust anything Sochi says, Guito. Anyway, *mucho gusto*, have a great summer."

He closed the car door and waved again and was gone. Guito had no opportunity to say a word, even if he had been able to. It was the first negative thing about *Indios* that he had ever heard and it left him speechless.

Guito stood in the same spot for several minutes sorting his feelings. Without going back to his room he started walking to the team house when he ran into Tessa carrying a bag of groceries.

"Can I help you with that, Tessa?"

"You *can*, Amigo, my arms are about to break; help me carry'em home and my Mom will feed you dinner."

Without answering, Guito took the bag and they started walking again, "Tessa, I just said goodbye to Lorenzo and he made a comment about Sochi. Did you know he felt that way?"

"Was it about Sochi being *Indio*?"

"Yes–and it wasn't nice."

"I'm surprised you couldn't tell Guito. I think Sochi must have been warned in advance; I never saw him take it personally. At least he never acted that way. We could turn him into a pretty good *Refugio*." Her humor eluded Guito.

"Tessa, I'm *Indio*."

"So what? It doesn't matter to me or to any of us. To us all God's people are equal in His eyes. Actually, I've always assumed that most people here are part *Indio*. Come to think of it...*I* may be part *Indio*. I'll have to ask *Papi*. Why is it so important to you? Anyway, we just take people the way they are, and you, my amigo, are one of the best." Her question, for the moment, was lost.

He blushed and couldn't think of anything to say for a while. "Well thank you," he finally got out, "I like you too." And he blushed again. They walked quietly for another minute or so.

"How do you feel about Lorenzo now?"

"He is a very sad person, Tessa...and I feel sad for him. I can forgive him for myself, but I wish I could help him. I am sure he would not listen to me."

They walked in silence for another few moments, "That is very kind of you, Guito." She turned to look squarely at Guito, her expression partly quizzical and partly respect.

"Maybe." He almost added, *I wish I could forgive my father*, but realized with a shock he did not really want that at all. "Tell me some more about your people."

"Well...we are a famous bunch of nice people."

He looked at her but she looked straight ahead, her face indecipherable. A moment passed before Guito smiled. "OK, I get it. Is there anything else important?" They both chuckled. "Are there any others besides here?"

"Not many, maybe a few who stayed in the States, maybe some. There are some other groups scattered around Central America but we are not related to them. What you see is what you get."

&

There were three brothers and her parents, all laughed easily. After the grace, her ten year-old brother started things by addressing the guest. "Guito, thanks sooo much for carrying my sister's groceries all the way here; you must like ugly girls."

"José David!" his mother began, but she was soon caught up in the laughter. Even Tessa was smiling as she jabbed her bother's hand with a fork.

"You little twerp!" she said in English.

"It is one thing to tease our guest," her father said solemnly, "but at least let's do it in Spanish." More laughter.

The raucous ice-breaker led to as much dinnertime fun as Guito had known in years. Everyone participated in talking about his or her day. Although an English and Spanish mix was the usual language in the house, they spoke mostly Spanish to include him. He did manage to pick up a half dozen new American words during dinner. As soon as the family saw that he was trying to learn, they began to offer new words as part of the conversation.

The discussion of the school captured Guito's attention. Unlike his high school, it sounded like the expectation of students was that they would go to university. All courses were taught in English. There were several *nacional* students enrolled. Some were on scholarship. The news was that one of them had received a scholarship to a college in Oregon.

Guito was quietly enjoying the banter when he felt himself leave his body and rise near the ceiling gazing down on everyone. He could see the serving bowls and the food; except for his, all the plates were clean, napkins folded carefully or still in laps. People gestured as they spoke but he could not hear their words. He saw his own body from above, relaxed, laughing sometimes, commenting and receiving their laughter. There were these lives playing out below him. Lives were just happening with no purpose than to just be alive. He remained there, observing, until Tessa suddenly remembered.

"*Papi*, are we part *Indio*?" Guito found himself back in his chair.

Her father's head made a small, surprised jerk; he looked at her, "Why...I don't know of any *Indio–Indios*...as far back as my grandmother. The others, I'm not sure about. It's very possible that we have *some Indio* blood...we've lived in the *campo* since the early 1900's as far as I know. Our family...your grandparents...came over from the west. My father's side came up from the Great Valley. They claimed to be Spanish. But maybe, who knows."

"Out west means *Nicarau*; I am *Nicarau*."

"You are?" he looked at Guito, "You are very tall for an *Indio,* Guito...although, I hear that *Nicaraus* do tend to be taller."

Guito paused; he had never thought of his appearance in relation to his self-image. "Yes...well, actually it was my grandmother who was *Indio-Indio*. My mother was raised in an Indio family."

"That's not *Indio* Guito," said her second brother. "You're a *nacional*... like me."

"Well, dear ones..." Her mother spoke up. "Where our family comes from, one fourth will let you be a full fledged member of most tribes. And one *cuarto* of the wrong blood, would have kept you riding in the back of the bus—or worse—in some states." she said, She paused, "If Guito thinks of himself as *Indio*, he is more than entitled. And that's good enough for us."

Her pronouncement assured that Guito was now *Indio* for this family. But the brief conversation had already had its effect; his identity as an *Indio* began to loosen. By the end of the summer, the charge that had been associated with El Indio had fled, "*se fue,*" he told Tessa.

The conversation shifted back to the height of *Indios*. Tessa said that a visiting researcher had made a presentation to an assembly in the school last year and had said that height was almost purely a "function of nutrition."

"Yeah," her second brother had been there also, "especially when the kids are real young and when they are teenagers."

"You mean there are no differences from the *Conquistadores*?" her father said.

"Nope, just how much food when."

"Not exactly," Tessa said, "there are genetic differences but among different groups, but it's the food that counts."

They are taught very different things than we learned in my school, Guito thought.

Tessa's brothers rarely missed an opportunity to point out the humor in their activities or those of others and the meal recollected to Guito the fun that his family had shared at dinner when he was younger. As he walked back to the *pension*, he smiled at the thought that her family – the brothers at least – probably thought that something was going on between him and Tessa.

৪০

The light was on in the room when he got back. *Sochi must be worried about where I am*. Sochi was standing over his bed. All three mattresses were on the floor.

"You left the room unlocked Guito; someone came in while we were gone." He spoke quietly, each syllable dropped with a thud. There was no hint of a smile. "I put all my travel money under my mattress. It's gone...all of it." Money was the only thing missing; it was for Sochi's personal living expense. The thief could not have known that his passport and the money to pay for services were being kept for safekeeping in the leader's house.

Guito dropped, sitting on the nearest bed. The scene with Lorenzo replayed instantly. His mouth went dry, "This is my fault Sochi." They were quiet; Sochi sat down. The implications slowly seeped into Guito's awareness. "I have some money that will help for a little while, my folks can send more. I am so sorry, *Amigo*. How much do I owe you?" He stood up and took the remainder of his mother's last minute gift from his pocket and gave it to Sochi– it was just over 20 dollars.

Guito's response, and the prospect of some cash, reoriented Sochi's prospects and attitude. He relaxed a little. "I'm sorry, *Amigo*. I was being hard on you. The University is paying me so I may be able to get an advance. Here, keep half; we will figure out how to do with what we have." He moved on to problem solving.

"Sochi— it was my fault; tell me how much I owe you."

They talked about the incident in the team the next morning and something was worked out to keep Sochi solvent.

Later, Guito called home and talked with his mother. She wanted to know, "When are you coming home?" "When are you going to finish school?" "Are you well?" "Are you enjoying yourself?" When satisfied, she told him that she would help with the money.

"Eduardo," she said, "is staying with his brother, but I am doing OK; it would help if you called more often." He said he would call every week. She added that she was sure that Eduardo would want to help him also. His brother and sister were well.

"Tell them I'm thinking of them." They said goodbye with mutual *"Te amo's.*[5]*"*

He spent much of the afternoon reflecting on his feelings of being jerked from pillar to post the previous day. The shock of Lorenzo's prejudice,

---

[5] TAY A-mows (I love you).

the pleasure of the dinner with Tessa's family, the anger with himself for having jeopardized his friend's security. His thoughts moved on to his family and how their world had been destroyed by his father. It occurred to him that nothing might be permanent, that the day might just have been a microcosm of life. The thoughts depressed him and it made him long for his days in the *quebrada*. *Fortunately, this probably won't last long either.* He was right about that.

The summer was progressing; the steep part of the learning curve declined for the interns and the team was largely focused on getting the work done. Guito's language skills and his plant and environmental knowledge had improved by a couple orders of magnitude. Guito called his mother at least twice a week to assure that he made contact at least once. He found out that his father had moved back to the house and his mother told him that things were much better between them.

He learned about his new sibling when she told him, "The baby will be born in August, Guito." He said nothing and she offered nothing more in that call. Guito knew he would not be there for that event. But his mother did not back away from the topic in subsequent calls. It was as though she knew that he had to come terms with the baby and that it was something that he could not do with his father. These calls left him quiet for a while and Tessa began to inquire. He told her what he thought would explain things, but he stayed away from his sharing feelings and she did not probe. They had become good friends but he was not ready to explore this with her.

After work, Guito and Tessa usually spent time with Sochi. When Sochi was unavailable, the two of them talked everyday. Guito often ate with her family and occasionally helped her father and brothers with big tasks. His relationship with her was confusing. He liked her and he respected her. She aroused him. He felt encouraged by her in the same way. They often sat close together and from time to time touched each other in conversation. Sochi once tried to provoke him, "She's pretty isn't she?" watching for Guito's answer and expression. Sochi got nothing for his curiosity.

Guito had not tried to kiss her and when he did hold her hand he was tentative. She had not backed away, but had not encouraged him in a romantic way either. They shared a pleasant little confusion but there was no sense of urgency about what might be happening between the two of them.

In those first weeks Guito had been bombarded by new experience. He'd made a weak and unsuccessful effort to consolidate what he was learning into a personal theory of something—anything. He knew that what he understood about life was changing. What he did not know was that he had three other discoveries that summer, each of which would weigh on the balance of his life.

God?

The human life has only one purpose and that is to know God.

Soon after Guito found out about his new "it," too early to know his sibling's gender, Sharon announced that the whole team had been invited to dinner with a new pair of researchers in the area. They were Hollanders but both spoke good English, she said. One of them was on the botany faculty of a university the other was completing his doctorate in ornithology at another. "That is the reason they are here," she said, "Rajiv needs a topic for his research and they are here for three months to explore the possibilities. They heard about the *Refugios* also, and that is a draw for them as it was for us."

"Good!" Tessa said, "Would you ask them if they would make a presentation at the school."

"I'm way ahead of you, Tessa, and I've already warned them about you." Laughter all around. Even as he was enjoying the repartee, the thought came to Guito, *This is what I love about this work...these people; anything can be fun.*

"Anyway, it's tomorrow night if everyone can make it; if not, we'll pick some night when we can all be there." The next night was fine. "Just a little warning, Guito. Rajiv is an Indian, like from the country of India; the food may be a little hot."

"Thanks be to God!" Sochi grinned.

The team finished early before the dinner to clean up. Tessa came with a dish of chicken and rice and rice pudding for desert. "This may save your life, Amigo," she whispered. Sharon, Brian and Sochi brought wine and some beer. Guito cut a bouquet of large hanging heliconias from the garden of the pension. The group was festive and ready for a party.

The cabin was one large room with a bedroom area and enclosed bath in one corner, a kitchen in another, an office desk and a homemade bookcase in the third. Just off center was a large round table. There were five chairs and two upturned boxes to sit on. Their hosts insisted on the boxes.

In the remaining corner was a wooden box turned over to make a small table with a candle, a photograph and cushion covered in an ethnic style that could not have come locally.

The house billowed with smells but for garlic, there was nothing Guito could identify. Their hosts were exuberant. Rajiv was working at the two-burner gas stove and both men kept up their hosting responsibilities with easy-to-enter conversation.

Wym was a tall blond man with the confident air of athleticism in spite of a left arm missing at the elbow. "From my experience keeping NATO's idea of the peace, yes." he smiled broadly at his own humor and the stump of an arm disappeared for his visitors. Rajiv was younger and shorter. He was of Indian descent and one of the most handsome men Guito had ever seen. He was also athletic. Wym's sport was soccer. "Luckily," Rajiv smiled wryly, and said his was cricket. Wym grinned and shook his head as though Rajiv was just something he had to put up with.

The visitors laughed politely, still not used to the edgy banter between the two men. They were obviously good friends and that awareness soon eased everyone into a light conversation. Within the first half hour, Guito realized that only Sochi was subdued. In one of his frequent glances at his friend, Tessa caught his eye and her glance told him that she also noticed. She held his gaze beyond the intuition however and Guito felt his heart began to beat in his face and forced himself to look away. When he looked back, she seemed to have lost interest.

Only Wym spoke much Spanish. Rajiv said he would try but that he was, still, "struggling to understand my own mother." His father spoke "rather good" English and spoke that to him as a child. Rajiv was born in Holland to Indian parents and was a citizen. "I'm going to stay there even though I think my parents will probably return to India to die," he said. His matter-of-factness about their death startled Tessa she told Guito later. Guito was intrigued with it.

Guito found that the only thing that he absolutely could not eat was the spicy chicken that had been grilled outside. Rajiv also did not eat the chicken, "Too hot for me too." Guito noticed that he ate fried plantains instead of the potatoes. Everything else was wonderful, vegetables, lentils and the most delicious grilled flatbread he had ever tasted.

With the wine and beer people were into the party. Guito was having his third beer of the summer and the first of the evening. The beer was imported from India and named in English after a bird also found locally. It was perfect with the spiciness of the food. Tessa had her first ever, raspberry iced tea. She had told Guito that the Community did not drink alcohol, but said nothing more about his newfound taste.

The science would not wait forever. Brian asked Rajiv how he was thinking of his project.

"It will be an autoecological design. That means that I will be looking at the interaction between birds–probably a single specie–and its environment. Since the environment is a seasonal thing, it will take me at least a year of regular observations. I may have to stay here all year or I may be able to commute for extended visits. The design I settle on will determine that." His attention had shifted to the interns.

"Unfortunately, that's all I know right now. We are here to look for locations, specie, weather, all the practical matters. There are lots of research opportunities here and it looks like a lot of fun."

"That's been our experience, but you may want consider involving a *nacional* scientist."

"I would love to, but this is my dissertation. It would require special permission to involve someone else."

"Sorry, forgot about that. Well, if it's of any interest to you, you are welcome to tag along and visit our study areas. Who knows Wym, maybe you could come up with a study for yourself – we've also been known to take free advice." Sharon smiled. "Besides, Guito here is an untrained-diamond-in-the-rough-Central-American-bird-expert," she added in one breath. "I'm sure he would love to help and soak up your knowledge as much as he does ours. But he is ours for another six weeks."

Rajiv stood, "*Jai Bhagwan*," he said with a mock formality and slight bow, his hands in prayer form; he stuck his hand across the table to shake Guito's, "I accept." Their friendship began there.

As people were getting up to leave that evening, Sharon went to the small table in the corner, "I'll bet you are the person to ask about this," she said to Rajiv.

"Actually, both of us are followers of that saint. The cushion is mine though." Rajiv smiled. "We are always happy to talk about it whenever."

"I'm interested too," Guito said.

On the way back to the *pension* Sochi was quiet. As they approached the room, he sighed, "*Huecos*,[6]" as though he were setting down a weight. His shoulders dropped.

"What?"

"Queers... *playos*, he added using a local term.

_____

[6] HWAY-cos

"Yes." They went in; Sochi said nothing more.

❧

Rajiv and Wym went with the team for two days. On the section of path to the second site there was an area open to the northeast. The Christmas winds were still blowing as they did off and on for the summer. Strong today, they blew at a speed Wym called a "fresh gale," and gusting into hurricane range as it crested the top of the Continental Divide. The bank was steep on the north side and the team had to assist each other to pass the area safely. Rajiv helped Wym keep his balance.

"I said Wym was a soccer player which is true," Rajiv said when they were safely through. "But he was also champion dingy sailor which is where all this 'fresh gale' talk comes from."

"You have to be a better sailor than me to hold a tiller and trim a main sheet with one hand. *C'est la vie*. Life happens, yes." There was none of the lightness this time.

❧

After that, the two Hollanders hired ToTo Cuarto to show them around other parts of Aguas Calientes. ToTo[4to] stopped by the afternoon team meeting to thank Sharon for the referral. "We are happy to help," she said, "But you better thank

Tessa and Guito; they are your public relations firm."

ToTo smiled at both of them, mouthed a "Thanks," and turned to leave. At the door, he turned back, "Guito, I know your weekends are all tied up nowadays, but a week from Saturday I'm taking a group of serious English and American birders out all day. This is the second time some of them have been here and I could use your help finding the birds. I would split my tips with you. And you might like it anyway."

Guito blushed at the, "weekends, all tied up." He recovered, "OK. What do I do?"

"I'll meet you at the soda at 6:00 AM that morning to go over the map and some possible spots. But be thinking about birds and locations you've spotted in the past week or two. We'll talk more then."

჻

Sharon ended the afternoon meeting. "Guito, Rajiv has invited us to come by some afternoon and follow up on our questions about his little altar. How about today?"

Guito looked at Tessa who nodded and smiled. They expected that they would climb the banks of the nearby creek to an abandoned mill, where they could talk and be affectionate in private. The last time they were there, the top button on her shirt had mysteriously appeared open and he had kicked himself since then for his timidity. He had been thinking of her firm little breasts all day.

"Go on, Guito," she said obliterating his opportunity to refuse. "I've got stuff to do."

"Okay. I guess I don't need to bring anything?"

Sharon and Guito walked to Rajiv and Wym's cabin. Rajiv met them at the door and gave them the slight, hands-clasped-in-prayer bow again. He was wearing a loose fitting white shirt and trousers. "Welcome friends. I have a slight request. This is my normal meditation time and I thought it might be well if we sat quietly for about 15 or 20 minutes before talking. Okay?"

"It's fine with me. I meditate myself – have you meditated Guito?" Looking back at Rajiv she said, "Guito is up for anything."

"I don't even know what it is." *Sharon is making that up.*

"Not much to it, we are just quieting the mind and going into ourselves before we talk." Rajiv explained to Guito a little about how to focus on his breath and brought a chair over. "I sit on a cushion, but it is easier for most in a chair...just keep your back straight and try not to fall asleep," he smiled.

"If you are going to light that candle...I normally meditate with my eyes open," Sharon said.

"Sure – lots of ways to do it."

Guito was fascinated now.

"In meditation we just remain quiet. But I begin and end my sitting with an *Om*. I'll explain about that later. Guito, just focus on where your breath tickles your nostrils as it goes in and out."

The '*Om*' sounded more like, "A-ummmmmm" to Guito. Rajiv drew out the sound until it just vibrated in a long hummm. It felt familiar. They sat quietly, Sharon gazing at the candle, the others with their eyes closed.

"A-ummmmmm."

"So, are you a Hindu or a Buddhist, Rajiv?" Sharon asked.

"Jain. Have you ever heard of us?"

"No, what's the difference?"

"The Jains are rich." He smiled, "Just kidding," he added.

He is not kidding, Guito thought.

"Jains have beliefs similar to the Buddhists," he said. "Some people think that Gautama may have been influenced by Jains because of his early emphasis on asceticism...Gautama was the Buddha," he added seeing Guito's question. "In general, Jains believe that everyone has a soul and that each is potentially divine. Like the *Refugios* we believe in non-violence. In order for us to 'be' that way we teach non-attachment to material things, forgiveness of others, and respecting the views of others."

"That's what Tessa says about the *Refugios*," Guito spoke.

"Yes. Jains take a vow of non-violence so...we are a little like the *Refugios* in that way... you won't find many of us in the army. The *Refugios* are one reason that Wym and I feel at home here. I should add that I am the Jain. Wym is just some white guy who wandered into my clutches."

The "ahem" behind them signaled Wym's arrival. He was smiling at Rajiv's joke.

"*Ja*, I certainly hope that the two of you don't suffer my fate. I'm doomed to listen to the 'guru' forever. Get out while you can, yes." Laughter.

The Meeting broke up. Sharon thanked Rajiv and said that she was going to restart her meditation practice while she was here.

But Guito wanted more. "Would it be all right if I came back to meditate with you again...maybe we could talk some more?"

"Sure, I'll set the time at 4:30 so I won't start without you. If you drop by fine, if not, that is Okay also. But," he held up a finger, "please don't be late."

Four o'clock was the time at which the team broke up on most days. Guito was sizing up the trade-off: meditating and learning, or having fun with Tessa. *Maybe we will have some time afterward.*

Guito's sense was that he had a lot to learn from Rajiv. There was something about Rajiv's approach to life that was strange enough to be interesting and oddly familiar at the same time. In the meditation, his mind had been all over the place – mostly on Tessa's boobs. The question "*Why do they do this?*" was still lingering when he got to the soda. His mind was filled with such questions, but Sochi was not in a mood to talk "religion." Tessa was more curious, but like Sochi, conversation did not go far.

Two days later, Guito was back at Rajiv's cabin.

"You seemed to be comfortable enough for 15 minutes. I wonder if we might sit longer this time. We Jains have a tradition of meditating for not less than 48 minutes," his hands flew up, "don't ask me why. It's a tradition. I'm sure someone must have told me at one time but that was then."

"I can do that." Guito went over to the table for a chair.

"Good, have any questions from last time?"

"Well... I cannot be doing this right. I cannot focus on my breath for more than a couple seconds."

"Yeah, that's the way it is to start. It's the 'monkey mind,' jumping around out of control. Think of it as training the monkey to be still. Meditation," he added, "is not doing it perfectly. When you catch your mind wandering bring it back to single-pointed attention on the breath. You will be able to train yourself if you stay with it." They sat for almost an hour.

"A-ummmmmmm."

Again, the 'Om' resonated with Guito. "Why do you say the 'Om,' Rajiv?"

"Well...we believe that 'Om' is a sound that makes the same vibration as the universe...all that is or ever can be."

"Is that like God?"

"Sort of...it's like calling God...although God has no name."

"So you call the name of God by making the sound of the universe."

Rajiv pondered this, "You can think of it that way. Another way is to think of the universe, all that is, and God as the same — they are both 'ineffable' as the Christians say."

God lives in heaven I think, but there is a little bit of God in everybody. The words tumbled from their memory bins like marbles onto a stone floor; they popped and bounced, denting the walls of his mind. *No one can fail who seeks the meaning of the name of God.*

"Is he a Jain saint?" he asked, nodding at the photograph.

"He is a Buddhist saint. His body died in the '50's...it doesn't matter anyway. He teaches that if you want to know reality you need only ask the question, 'Who am I?' By asking it, and by looking inside yourself for the answer, you will eventually realize your true self."

"Why don't they just tell you what your true self is? That's what they do in church. According to them you are pretty bad but it seems a lot easier to start with something. What is reality anyway?"

"Buddhist believe that you must discover reality for yourself. The way that you find it is to live an ethical life and practice concentration through meditation. When your mind is purified, you will be ready for the final step, realization."

"Sounds like work."

"It is. You have to do the work, but the Buddhists promise it is the best chance for realization in this lifetime." Rajiv smiled; he took a breath and sighed, looking out the open door of the *cabina*. Beyond the long yard a group of teenagers were passing by, pushing at each other and laughing loudly. A gust from the newly arrived wind slammed the bathroom door. His gaze returned to Guito; he studied the boy's face intently for several moments. "You amaze me, really. I love your questions, but I have not prepared myself to answer them in a way that might make sense to you." Rajiv cocked his head at Guito and smiled, "Actually, I'm pretty sure I don't have the answers but we can learn together. If you would like to know more, why don't we plan several sessions a week? We can meditate to focus our minds and then I will give you a little lesson on how Buddhists understand the universe. We can talk about the Jains too."

Over the next several weeks Guito meditated with Rajiv. At times Wym joined them although he said his best time was mornings. Guito's mind seemed to focus for more extended periods, "still only seconds, but more of them," he said. Rajiv explained the basics, realization as best words can describe it, the Jain notion of non-absolutism, and karma.

Guito's sense of justice resonated with Wym's description of karma: "The great accounting system in the sky," he said, "you can't get away with anything. Even your past lives follow you around until you settle up." Guito was awed that they could joke so easily over something that seemed so *life and death*, he thought. *What is Pa's karma?*

The obvious question about his own karma was too threatening, it became: "How important is all this re-birth stuff?"

Wym looked a Rajiv. "Well," Rajiv began, "The most important thing is to do the practice, the meditation. My father says that you don't have to believe in the cycle of birth and rebirth. He does, and so do I but we grew up in a culture where that was part of cosmology so it was natural for us. It's like the Christian cosmology, that the earth has a creator who still intervenes in the life of humans...Christians anyway. For the Buddhists there is no creator of the universe. The Buddha said that we are reborn over so many lifetimes that we are almost certain to have been our own mother or father in one life or the other."

The thought stunned Guito. The idea that his father and he may share a common *soul*, was the word he put to it, opened a small window of empathy in Guito's mind. It closed rapidly.

"How did you get involved in all of this Wym?"

"We-ell," Wym looked at Rajiv, "I was beginning to feel that everything I had done was not giving me anything that looked like happiness. I had tried my whole life to be a good boy; get good grades; be nice. Maybe you are like that too. It became really clear when I was a teenager that I was in trouble." He shared a smile with Rajiv.

"Me too!" Guito blurted, blushing. "Different reason."

Wym and Rajiv chuckled, Rajiv gave him a friendly punch to the shoulder.

"Anyway...I tried to prove how worthy I am by getting as many prizes and credentials as I could. I even have two master's degrees, the other is in philosophy...for all the usual reasons...you know, if I have degrees, I must be a worthwhile guy." Wym's mouth pursed, wryly, "But none of it worked; I still had this nagging fear that I could never measure up. Soo, I went to hear a free presentation by a swami." He smiled at the word. "After that I went to his meditation workshop and met Rajiv."

"In the eastern traditions, that feeling that something is not quite right is called *dhukka*." Rajiv said.

"Jeez," Guito said, "I'm loaded with dhukka."

"Don't feel rained on, everyone has it." Rajiv continued, "Even when things are going well, we are inherently unsatisfied because we know that it is going to change. We all *know*, that we can't keep life perfect even if we ever get a glimpse of it." He looked at Wym, "We Jains tend to be very tolerant because we look for the truth in all points of view. As a result we tend to remain open-minded. It makes us good researchers."

"*Ja*," Wym spoke from the kitchen, "That's what he says *before* he does the dissertation, yes."

Rajiv just smiled broadly and shrugged without looking up. "We see everything as relative. Your intention is more important than the actual outcome of your actions."

Guito took this back to Tessa as he did everything. She was curious, especially in what seemed to be the parallels between the Buddhists and the *Refugios*.

"I've got to get you to Sunday school before Rajiv does something to your brain."

"This stuff just blows me away. Is it okay if I go to your Mass?"

"Well," she drew it out, "my guess is we are at least as tolerant as the Jains. You can use the service for one of your meditation sessions. And it's definitely not a Mass."

"Well, I do not think that in *my* church, *you* could *partake* of The Holy Eucharist." The pompous church language left them giggling.

"Then you are coming with me on Sunday. Ma has been on me to get you there ever since she heard about you and Rajiv."

"What about him?"

"Not what you are thinking. She is just being a Mom and looking to take care of you." She raised her right fist, "*Refugios* to the rescue!!!"

They kissed goodbye and Guito began walking back to the pension. He walked a few yards then turned, "Tessa."

She turned back to face him. "Yes?"

"Is it all right if I talk to your Pa?"

"What about?" A suppressed smile tippled the corners of her mouth.

He felt himself color. "Ah...oh, you know...about us."

She hesitated, perhaps to keep the charade going, but seeing his difficulty, she grinned at him. "Okay, but no more kissing until he says Okay."

"I wasn't going to say that."

"Oh," she flipped her hand airily, "you men have *such* secrets. You better remember every word he says or there will be no more kissing." And she walked off, swinging everything—to good effect.

Guito was encouraged. He began sitting by himself in the mornings, a practice that would continue for the rest of his life. When he told Rajiv about his practice, he said, "Okay, then I need to alert you to a possibility so you don't freak out. When you begin to sit a lot, after a while there is a possibility that you will have an 'experience.' Its normal but sometimes you may feel like you are in an altered state. Once, back in Holland, I was taking a morning walk along the quay—a long dock. Suddenly I was overcome with feelings of love...just pure love...love for everything and everyone. I began to cry and couldn't stop. I didn't want to stop really; I was so filled with joy. It lasted for two or three hours until I finished a long meditation out at the end of the pier. I have had other experiences but I remember that one especially." He took a deep breath and sighed. "But the difference between you and me is that I come from a long line of meditators so I *knew* I wasn't going crazy. I just wanted to warn you."

"What do the experiences mean?"

"Nothing."

"They don't mean anything?"

"Nope, they just happen. My father thinks they are a glimpse into reality, but nothing more than a glimpse."

They were silent for a while as Guito absorbed the story. "I have had experiences."

He told Rajiv about his experiences in the forests and when he had seen with such clarity and without thinking about what he saw. He spoke of the presence of someone else, someone who could not be seen. He shared the experience at Tessa's house and the other times he had left his body. He said that he had never been frightened and that, in some ways the experiences did not feel new to him. It was as though they were, normal, just not, usual.

When he finished, Rajiv was looking at him through soft eyes. "My friend," he said, "That clarity of seeing is the experience of bare attention. It is the mindfulness that we train ourselves for by meditating. You've seen it already. You know what

it is. I think there is no turning back for you."
Silence returned.

"But...isn't the experience what I should be looking for?"

"The Buddha says not. They are just states that come and go. The fact that they aren't permanent means that they are not reality. When you realize your true self, it stays with you."

Guito went quiet thinking about this.

"Wym was just kidding when he called me, 'guru.' I'm neither a master nor a guru. The truth is I'm no more advanced than you, Guito. We are just two people doing the best we can to free ourselves from suffering in this lifetime. Might work out. Might not."

"I do not know about this stuff; we Catholics have getting into heaven pret-ty-well-nail-ed-down." Guito pronounced every syllable of his new American expression.

Rajiv laughed, "True, true, the churches do have the answers," he chuckled more.

Her father's face darkened as he took Tessa aside. "*Cariña*..." he said, "Guito spoke with me." He paused, watching her confusion emerge, "I said yes." The grin split his face. "We are happy for you."

Love

To love without knowing how to love wounds the person we love.[7]

Tessa was not a pretty girl in the popular sense, the way so many teenagers are. She did not make up her face and did not dress in a provocative manner. But she also did not cover her head as was the tradition among the older women in her church. Those facts did not prevent Guito from being provoked. She was handsome as some people say of women, and that had its own attraction. She was as tall as Guito, who was somewhat above average for his age, and both of them were still growing.

---

[7] Thich Nhat Han

Tessa had the "buzz." Guito couldn't say exactly what the buzz was, but he knew it when he felt it. A couple of the girls that he had known in high school had it too. In an unsettling way, a teacher in his high school had had the buzz. Later in life Guito would be able to put more words to it. For now, the "buzz" felt like a reaction to him personally. And it was sexy. Perhaps there was really something there, or perhaps he was just projecting his hyperactive libido onto attractive women. Regardless, he always felt encouraged by the girl when he felt the buzz.

The girl who served them their morning rice and beans, their *pinto,* had the buzz. This girl was luscious-pretty. She was very short and brown and had a full mouth that reminded Guito of his mother. She always wore tight jeans and a blouse that one could look into when she bent over. And Guito, bless his heart, took every opportunity. She worked at the soda next to the pension since before the team had started its work. The girl talked extra with Guito and he enjoyed her attention enough to spend time at the *soda* other than at meals. But for Guito, the buzz ended early, the day he saw her in the grocery store.

An older man leaned next to her, into her, attempting to nuzzle her neck. His hand was touching her tummy. She looked embarrassed and was fending him off. That scene evoked another that slammed from memory into mind as he watched. In the earlier scene he knew that the woman he was watching had taken money from men, probably the one she was dealing with at the moment. The girl saw Guito and tried to smile. He felt sad, tired, and perhaps a little old. He stopped spending extra time at the soda.

℀

Tessa asked him to go with her to a "mitsingen," as she called it, smiling at his blank stare. A "sing-a-long." "Para cantar," she added still seeing his confusion. It was the anniversary of the coop packinghouse and the *Refugios* were planning a party. Since he announced his desire to learn English, Tessa would only speak to him in that language. "Mitsingen," she said, was "the only word she knew in German," and that was because she liked to sing.

The sing-along was a tradition going all the way back to Germany. The crowd of 50 or so of the *Refugios* and local families gathered on the slope a little above the packinghouse. Young boys tended a huge bonfire off to the side. Guito found a large tree stump in the back. *Amigo, I'll bet you have been here since time began,* he thought.

Tessa joined him after saying hello to her friends. "Working the crowd," she said as she sat down. She eased the left side of her body along the right side of his. Her leg was pressed close to his and he rested his forearm on her thigh. When he put his hand between her knees and began to caress her thigh, she took his hand in both of hers and held it. She looked directly at him and smiled in a way that, he hoped, said, *this is not the time or the place.* She kept hold of his hand, massaging his fingers with hers.

Tessa's father and a much older local man were playing guitars in front of the crowd.

"That's ToTo Cuarto's father, Don ToTo," she said, "Papi's older brother. He's kind of the unofficial mayor." Guito could see the resemblance. When Don ToTo smiled, one side of his mouth twisted like ToTo4to. Seen side-by-side, Tessa's father also shared the family trait.

"Was he ToTo Tercero?" She nodded. "And he's your uncle?"

She looked at him, "Duh."

They played some *rancheras* and *salsas* to warm up the crowd, but the music drifted into English and Spanish folksongs and a couple German hymns that a few people seemed to know. Everyone else hummed along. The players would shift lead depending on who knew the melody best. From time to time Don ToTo picked up another guitar-looking instrument that Tessa told

Guito was a mandolin. It made an ecstatic sound in the man's hands and Guito felt happy just watching him play it.

Someone called out a birthday for someone else and they sang it in Spanish and English. They sang "Greensleeves" in Spanish and then in English, to the mandolin. Guito could hear ToTo⁴ᵗᵒ's *basso* above the crowd as though it were leading people in the words. Here and there, there was laughter as some misremembered the stanzas. It was a long song with many refrains and soon, Guito was joining in the chorus. He knew the meaning of the English words, but wrapping his tongue around them in a song was difficult.

The last of the logs placed on the fire signaled the closing of the evening. Don ToTo looked up into the crowd, "Tessa," he called. She raised her hand and he motioned her down. She stood up and made her way to the front. He surrendered his guitar and his seat.

Tessa strummed a few chords, smiled at her father and then looking out, above the crowd, began a ballad about a woman named Alfonsina, a Chilean poet. Love gone bad, she had killed herself by walking into the sea, Tessa told Guito later. "At least that's the government's version." Her face had changed from one just on the verge of a smile or a joke, to that of a woman with intention, focused on singing her mind. Guito liked the song, but he loved hearing Tessa's voice, which was as strong as her father's.

She finished the ballad; without hesitating, she struck the opening chord to another song. She smiled directly at the crowd then shifted her gaze to Guito. The song delivered slowly, each word arrived to its hearer, "*Gracias a la vida, que me ha dado tanto....*" The crowd had heard her sing it before and when, "*Gracias,*" opened onto the night air, they broke into cheers and applause. Her voice was in the alto range and it became husky, gritty, in the lower register. She sang only in Spanish but the words were, "Thanks to life that has given me so much...." Like a stiletto, the words penetrated Guito and halfway through it he teared up. Sitting as he was in the back, he could hide it from the others, but the boy discovered that he had brought the rest of his life with him to Aguas Calientes.

Later, as they walked home together she said, "You cried with my song." But he felt emotional again so he said, "*Sí,*" nothing more, neither did she. As they neared her house, they paused in the moon shadow of a large tree and began to kiss, more passionately than before, savoring each other deeply for a several minutes. "I have to go in." He released her, and she pulled away still holding his hand. Then came back, kissed him on the cheek and said, "Guito, I'm virgin," and went inside.

Guito and Tessa were making the same hajj. The next two weeks were less like a seduction than a stroll through a new and magical wood. Neither was trying to convince the other to do anything. Tessa had opened the door and both of them stepped through with intention and without hurry. They explored their affection by giving each other as much pleasure as they knew how. Without rushing or fumbling, they practiced each lesson until the next revealed itself.

In the middle of that second week Sochi left for an errand in the capital. Still dressed for her interview with a college rep from the States, Guito and Tessa went to his room. He sat down on the bed and pulled her to him. Standing over him, she pulled his hands under her skirt, and coaxed them up her thighs until he found the edges of her tights. She dropped her skirt over his head and he eased the tights down, kissing her as she hugged his head into her.

They spent two hours in his bunk. Once, then again, and would have again had Tessa not checked her watch. They rested for a while. Guito watched her, he ran his hand over her head, face, and breasts as though she might be a dream from which he would awake. She relaxed under his hand, looking at him in her own wonderment.

His father's debacle had created a deep-seated revulsion in Guito, which produced an equally deep commitment. He swore to himself he would never be like his father. On the morning after, he awoke to a conscience screaming for him to make good on the pledge. As soon as he could make his excuses to the team and to Tessa, he found himself in Palo Seco on the sidewalk in front of the pharmacy.

Guito hesitated outside the pharmacy door. Only moist beads gathering on his upper lip belied his demeanor. He was sure that this was where they were sold. A woman busied herself behind the counter. Another at the "*caja*,[8]" where they took your money, watched a soap opera on a small TV. They have not noticed him and he is trying to remain invisible until, *exactly the right moment,* he thinks. How that might be known is unclear. Once in, he knows he is committed and his imagination is playing closed-loop scenarios of what might be said, or who might come in while he is in there. *If Sharon...or Tessa's Mom!...Ohhh God!* His mind groans and he leans against the wall.

The mind movies keep him paralyzed and in the end, he cannot bring himself to step inside.

---

[8] KA-ha

They probably wouldn't sell it to me anyway. His open hand wipes his face beginning at the forehead, slowly squeezing both eyes and nose, and finishing at the chin. His hand is wet. The surrender to failure offers just enough relief for him to step away from the store.

Determination revives itself overnight and the next day he is again outside the pharmacy. This time a man wearing a pharmacist's white over-jacket is behind the counter writing with a marker. He walks out from behind to tape a handwritten notice for a "*Promoción*" for suntan lotion in the window. It is not selling well. He smiles at Guito and opens the door, "Can I help you, *muchacho*?" Hunkering his head into his shoulders, staring straight ahead, whispering through his thick throat, *"Buenas tardes,"* Guito steps through the door. They go to the counter; the pharmacist scowls with concern.

His tongue is swollen, he is hoarse, but the words make it out the dry tube that is his mouth. "I want to buy a condom."

"I see," said the pharmacist relaxing, looking at Guito as though sizing up his age, "Just one?"

Guito is stumped. As though the possibility of doing it twice has not occurred to him. Or maybe he thinks they are reusable. The words, *I think three will be enough,* are trying to form but they

dry up somewhere between the "I" and the "th...,"
so he holds up three fingers and shakes his head
"yes." His eyes search for some sign of man-to-
man understanding in the pharmacist's face.

The pharmacy carries a variety but the man
pulls up a strip of blue plastic packages connected
with serrated edges. He tears off three. They are
the plain ones, and although he has others with
"features," he does not discuss these with this
particular customer. He writes out a small slip of
paper for the *caja*. The *caja* lady smiles at Guito.
Her long red nails click on the Formica counter as
she pulls his money through the half-round
window.

Guito takes his neatly taped package and steps
out into freedom and the fresh air. His breath
comes in short choppy gulps and his knees wobble
as he steps off the curb, but he stays upright and
moving. Walking downhill, relief soaks into him as
though he was walking in a warm shower but he
cannot stop to enjoy it. He is past the coop and
uphill to the next intersection. The climb forces
him to take deep breaths and the relief morphs
into bravado that approximates, "master of the
universe." He leans against on a large rock and
pulls out his package to read the instructions.
There are none.

ဆ

The AIDS threat had not yet emerged, and *campesino* men of the time were not given to using protection. Most of those that did were irregular in their purchases. Guito was determined however, and he showed up at the pharmacy almost every week for a supply. If one extrapolated his use to those of the average man, Guito's buying, and other presumed habits, began to take on a heroic dimension.

To his credit, the pharmacist did not talk about his customers, but within the pharmacy Guito's reputation began to swell. The lady at the *caja* smiled and found a way to touch his hand as she gave him his change instead of pushing it through the half-moon window. As the internal pressure of the story increased, a few insiders began to talk to others. Some joked; some were awed. A new channel developed in the *chisme* river. Within a few weeks Guito became, "The boy who buys condoms," around Palo Seco.

Sochi, who was known to everyone, heard and treated him with the greatest respect. For the second time, again unknown to him, Guito had become a local legend. The talk, this time, was of manhood rather than sainthood.

One can only guess how mothers know, but this one did. Tessa's mother walked out of her bedroom, "Tessa come with me for a minute." When they were outside the house, she looked hard at her daughter for a moment, "Tessa are you and Guito having sex?" She spoke in English. The breeze blew a lock of her hair that had fallen over her forehead. Her arms folded below her bosom.

Tessa returned the gaze. She took a breath and sighed. She looked at the trees over her mother's shoulder and then back to her face. "Yes...we are." Her voice was low but she did not back away from the question nor look away from her mother. They were still for a moment.

Her mother's arms unfolded, her right hand went to her face then clasped her left hand, wringing it. "Do you know what can happen? I assume you love him, don't you? And he loves you? Are you protecting yourself? Do you even know how?" Her voice and tempo rose in spite of her rehearsal. Anxiety convulsed into interrogation.

"Yes, Mom, yes...Yes...YES to all of that." Tessa caught herself. They were quiet again, then they reached for each other and they stood there, holding on, for several moments. And it was over.

Her mother told her husband in bed, while turned away from him, "Tulio, we have a son-in-law."

"Yes," he said chuckling, "'El Indio.' He is a good man. We should thank God for that." He rolled over and pulled her to him.

"Men," she whispered.

"What did you say *querida*?"

"Nothing," and she turned over to him.

By the time Tessa and her mother had their talk, it was already clear to many people that Guito and Tessa were an item, "*novios*," to the locals. In local culture, the issues were more practical than moral. No one was more practical than Guito.

Fourteen years later mother and daughter were standing near the same spot discussing Tessa's daughter, how fast she was growing up. Her mother mentioned the talk of that day; it had occurred just a few meters away. Tessa told her mother the story of Guito, the pharmacy, and the "boy who bought condoms." She had heard parts of it from Guito and parts from Sochi who had given her his own version with improv conversations and animated gestures. Her mother started to laugh, and then both of them; they laughed, sitting, then lying on the ground and laughing until they teared. "Oh daughter...Lordy, Lordy," her mother said over and over, still laughing, "Who can know how life will go, who can know." Or perhaps she was weeping, who can know at such times.

Work

The privilege of a lifetime is being who you are.[9]

Guito waited at the soda for ToTo[4to] to talk about the birding hike later that morning. He was sipping hot coffee and eating an empanada when ToTo came in. "Welcome to the family Guito," ToTo pulled out a chair. Guito wasn't ready for this but he managed a "Thank you" without blushing. *Is nothing private around here?* He reminded himself, *people know everything at home too.* ToTo had a telescope and lightweight tripod, probably a first of what would become standard for guides in the AC. "We probably won't need it

---

[9] Joseph Campbell

for this crowd. I bet they'll have at least a couple with them." ToTo said the scope had cost him "a half-dozen cows." He was a strawberry farmer in his day job and kept a few milk cows. "Have you ever had strawberry milk?" He asked but Guito missed the joke.

"So, what would you like me to do?"

"You have the best eye for birds in Aguas Calientes. And I'm not the only one who thinks so," ToTo added. "These birders are experienced, some of them have been on a number of trips to South America, Guatemala, Mexico; you name it. What I hope is that we can get the Bell-Bird and the Buffy Crowned Wood Partridge identified before we get into the AC. Maybe a Quetzal. That will make the trip for some of them."

They spent the next half hour going over the trails. Guito offered names of birds he had heard or seen in the areas ToTo suggested. ToTo was re-folding his map as they finished, "Do you know the Tapaculo? You don't see them often but you can hear them, makes a kew, kew, kew sound."

"I don't think so. Have you seen one?"

"Actually, I haven't seen one but I've heard it. They are supposed to nest in a hole in the ground – I don't think anyone knows for sure. Anyway...," he took a breath, "I think I've found a possible nest right near where you turn off to go to your team's site. I'll point it out to everyone when we get there, but keep an eye and an ear out for the bird. Look in the dense undergrowth – they don't like to come into the clear. They say that there are several species in the world, but there is supposed to be only one in this country. If we see or hear one, it will for sure be a big find for most of these folks."

A thin overcast kept the temperature pleasant and reduced the glare from the sun. A light breeze made Guito glad he had brought his rain jacket. The group spoke an English that sounded like Rajiv's and Guito could understand most of what they said. The group leader had to repeat a question twice to Guito, but then he added,

"Sorry, I'm from Leeds." Guito had no idea what that meant but it felt like he had been let in on a secret; it felt...sophisticated, as though he now knew something special about people from "Leeds." The birding was going better than they had imagined. The group leader told ToTo that the day was beginning to feel, "successful," already.

It was an altogether pleasant group and Guito was enjoying both them and the walk though the woods. They were serious and patient and he was engaged with them, concentrating in the manner that left one mentally fresh at the end of a task. ToTo and Guito alternated finding new subjects with the group so there were no long gaps between spotting's. Almost all members of the group had the satisfaction of adding at least one life bird and some of the newer members had substantial lists. ToTo's smile flitted frequently across his face.

They were over an hour later than planned when they reached the turn off to site one. ToTo was in front and Guito behind the group. It was past lunchtime and the group decided to rest and eat. ToTo pointed out the hole; it looked like a small cave in the side of a bank where the turnoff to the site began. Either there was a turn in the hole or it was so deep and dark that one could not see into it for more than a foot. The mouth was about 6 inches in diameter[3]. Several members of the group took turns looking into the hole, but there was no Tapaculo to be seen.

Guito knelt by the hole and listened for the *kew, kew, kew*. Nothing. "Cht, cht, cht." He spoke softly into the mouth of the hole for several minutes, "Cht, cht, cht, cht, cht, cht." The rustling of the breeze made it difficult to hear; he couldn't be sure. "Cht, cht, cht, cht, cht," Guito kept talking; he shifted now from a squat to kneeling to rest his thigh muscles. The group ate sandwiches quickly, most not bothering to sit, and moved on and set up to view a North American migrant about 10 meters away.

Two different migrants consumed the full attention of the group now. They were taking turns looking through the scopes and moving slowly around to get a better view with their own glasses. The overcast thinned further and then parted, and the sun warmed the area. Guito heard something now, but he couldn't be sure what it was that he might be calling. He leaned back, but kept up a, "Cht, cht, cht, cht," calling out the fear of the animal, what ever it was, and speaking directly to its curiosity. ToTo was standing back, arms folded, alternately observing group and looking to see if Guito had found the next subject.

"Shush!.... Shush!" The already quiet group heard the startle in ToTo's voice. They turned as one to look at ToTo. He was wide-eyed, staring back at Guito. "Don't move." He said it in a hoarse whisper. They were 30 feet or so away. They stared, jaws drooping as Guito held the flat back of his hand to the mouth of the hole. Within a few seconds a small bird put its head out, turning it from side to side. It looked cautiously at Guito. It came to edge of the hole, about half its body could be seen.

Cameras began to click; the feet that moved, did so quietly. Another minute passed, the bird appeared to be satisfied that all was safe and stepped onto Guito's hand. It was less than five inches long and stopped at the row of large knuckles, the breeze fluffed its feathers; its tail cocked up like a bantam rooster. It stayed there, looking about for, perhaps, a minute. As though sensing that the tension could not hold, Guito used his free hand and index finger to gently prod the bird's silver grey breast, to get it to turn around and reenter its nest. He wanted to say, *go back Chiquita, you did good*, but all that came out was "cht, cht, cht." The bird turned and moved deliberately along the back of his hand to the entrance. The long moment of silence continued.

"That friends, was the *Tapaculo Frentiplateado*." ToTo, literally, had nothing else to say and he said this so quietly few heard.

Everyone except ToTo had gotten a view of the bird through binoculars or telephoto lens. Some captured images of Guito, with the bird or resting, knees on the ground, hands out, or folded in front of him. The group came to the mouth of the nest, talking quietly, some looking again into the hole. Many patted Guito's back; a couple offered him a hand to stand up. No one tendered a theory of what they had just witnessed. "I don't think we are going to beat that," said a hoarse voice in a heavy Yorkshire accent. With an uncanny reverence, they began the hike back.

❦

ToTo insisted that they take the evening meal together at his place to avoid being disturbed. His house was about half way from the AC to the *Rododendros* center. It was large and spare; it was obvious that he lived alone, though the furnishings still projected a woman's sensibility.

An unfettered pygmy owl, recovering from a broken wing perched on a solid log ledge above a fireplace hearth in the big sitting room. A couple of charcoals were on the walls. One of them might have been of a younger ToTo. He served leftover deep fried pork, with rice and beans and cornbread with small pieces of bacon and cheese inside. It was the first time Guito had had cornmeal in this form and it was delicious hot with honey and butter. They drank cold whole milk.

"Well Guito, someone told me that you had a way with birds." ToTo's sense of humor was recovering. On the way back he had said, "I may never be the same, Amigo." But his awe did not last long. "How did you do that?"

"I'm not sure. I thought I heard something and so I decided to talk to it. My Tapaculo is improving, don't you think?"

ToTo smiled then stared at Guito. "I'm serious now...and this has nothing to do with Tessa either." Guito felt his scrutiny like sandpaper. ToTo paused and started over, "We are talking with the government about protecting the forest with a government agency. They have a vision for the AC in which they open it to what they call 'eco tourists.' They come to Aguas Calientes from all over the world. We are already seeing it happen just from the scientists and birders who go home and tell their friends." He paused again. "What I'm getting at is that there is a need for people who know Aguas Caliente, who know the plants and the wildlife, to guide them around, and who can speak English. I'm a farmer; birding is fun and I get my spending money from it, but my plants and livestock are my life. But you" his head wobbled as if to say, *it's just too obvious*. "You are perfect for it."

"Don't you feel funny taking money for this...."

"Tessa told me you would say that." He sighed deeply, "Guito...honestly, you can be such a twit sometimes." They both grinned. "This is the fundamental problem with life. If we want it, we have to eat. The *Refugios* have gone to some trouble to live out our values but we have found a way to *try* to be the people we should be, and *eat* at the same time. Think about it."

Guito knew this was true. He had known the truth of it even when his father had tried to make the same point, but now he wanted to hear it.

៩៣

Two weeks later the two of them were working with a less experienced group of birders, all

Americans this time. ToTo insisted that they work as equal partners. One of the least experienced members was dead set on seeing a Crested Caracara, an eagle-like falcon that hunted from the ground.

"Do you know it?" ToTo asked. "I've never seen one."

"I do. There was a nesting pair that lived somewhere along the road down the Fila de Asturias. Common as dirt. They have a juvenile every couple of years. But they are from over in the West, the open areas of the *sabana*. Close to the woods on the edges of pastures...and much lower down. I think this man would better off renting a car and driving along the highway over there than hiking around here."

"There is some open land like that further down the trail to your team's second site. It was opened up by squatters but it's considered AC now."

"Okay, but if you haven't seen one, I will bet they aren't there."

ToTo took Guito to explain the odds of finding a Caracara to the birders, but the man was adamant. He did not, "have time to go chasing around the country." He agreed to go with only those who felt like the hike and who were willing to pay for an additional outing. The terrain was not easy and the guides would have to re-clear some of the trail.

They started walking at 7:00 AM. It was unusually cloudless and warm. ToTo and Guito took turns on point. They stopped only for birds that could not be immediately identified and reached the clearings by about 11:00. People were tired and already hungry; they had lunch and several rested before serious looking. Some napped. A black hawk hunted just beyond a still-standing dead tree, its shadow skittering over the ground. Several buzzards sailed above the group, checking their readiness to be lunch.

The hazy view east was the Eastern Sea. It could occasionally be seen from points around Aguas Caliente, which was nearly 2500 feet higher, "above mean sea level." Guito knew the concept well enough, but being able to actually see the ocean made the idea tangible. The sea was golden, *make that peach*, he thought, from the frequent but peculiar rays of the sun through the clouds. *Here we are, 3500 feet above peach level*, he smiled.

Just below the steep side of the ridge, a *quebrada* with a six-foot falls gabbled in the background. Guito went off to find a place to relieve himself. Walking back, he saw a large rock with a shallow concave bend that looked as though it was made for a back. He sat down and leaned back against the sun-warmed stone. About 10 feet away, a large, sawn tree lay where the previous squatters had left it. A large *terciopelo* rested close to it. She preferred the cool of the shade. He closed his eyes again, *You had best be careful, amiga, ToTo[4to] doesn't care for your type.*

The sun pressed down, palpable, with the weight of a thin blanket. It went behind a cloud, a breeze sprang up, he closed his eyes and felt the toastiness of the rock embrace him.

The breeze was desultory, rising and falling. When it was up, the murmuring trees blocked the sound of the *quebrada*. But when it slowed, the sound of the water and the wind in the trees melded into one low sound. He had begun thinking on the question that Rajiv's guru claimed would lead to the realization of his true Self. *Who am I?...Who is asking?* He repeated the thought, trying to imagine what it would be like to no longer have a stake in this life, to know that he was not this anxious person residing in a body. Rajiv had said that we are all, each of us, already enlightened but didn't know it. "The day will come when you will laugh, and that day is exactly the same as this day." *What does that mean?* He closed his eyes, the breeze rose and fell several times, then he heard it.

"Aumm," said the water and the air together.

"Aummmm," *so this is how I knew*.

"Aummmmm," the sound absorbed his whole attention. Some time passed.

❧

"*Hey* Guito, we are ready to go." ToTo strode toward him. For the briefest moment Guito considered saying nothing, but his friend would pass too close to the log.

"Careful, Amigo." He cupped his right hand and made a pointer of his index finger.

"Whoa!" ToTo took a step back. His machete unsheathed. He was too experienced to fear the snake other than merest respect, but this was a big one with a long strike radius.

"You wouldn't consider letting her off this time would you?"

"Sorry, it's against my religion when it comes to these bad girls." ToTo severed the snake's head with an arm's length slash.

That is an odd way to put it. As she died, one of Wym's karma metaphors flashed before Guito, "The Americans have a saying," he said. "'There is no free lunch.' They don't know how right they are."

❧

There was no Crested Caracara that day. In addition to the usual Aguas Caliente fare, they saw a Red-throated Caracara and ToTo's sizeable snake. The big falcon turned out to be an exceptional find as within the next few years it would disappear, unexplained, from Aguas Caliente and many of its Central American habitats.

Guito was ready to see that doing what you love for a living might work for him. "Worse things could happen," he told Tessa.

Querencia

End of the Internship - May 1981

They walked carefully, picking their way through the mud and ruts, helping each other in the slippery parts. The rains had begun two weeks before and Tessa and Guito walked together under an umbrella, wrapped in jackets against the clammy coolness. Party or no party, the weather called for rubber boots. Tessa carried her good shoes. It was a little after 5:00 PM but thick fog and the overcast above had brought night an hour early. This was the last team party, potluck, at headquarters. ToTo said he had some work at the farm but was planning on coming.

"I'm not going home next month." Guito said.

"I think I knew that."

"I want to stay here with you."

She smiled to hear him say it. "I know, and I want you to be here. But don't you think you should go for a visit and work things out with your Pa."

"Not yet. I don't really know how he and Ma are getting long. I just don't want to be back in it yet. Buh-ut," he made the two syllables over a deep breath, "I need something to do and a place to stay. Ma will keep on helping, I think, but I still need work. Do you think the families will give me work as a *peón*? Maybe some guide work if there are any tourists. Do you think they would take me in the high school?

"That's a lot of questions, *mi amor*." She chuckled, "I'm sure you can find enough work to keep body and soul together. But a place to stay– don't get any ideas. We are a tolerant family, but until and *if* we are ready to get married–I mean really married—we're not living together."

"Don't worry, I wasn't thinking that." Living together was an expected solution among *novios* but it annoyed him that she might have thought he expected it.

"Well...*are* you ready to talk about it?" He said.

"No."

The bluntness stopped him. He hadn't thought of it before this moment, but he assumed that marriage could be discussed. In fact, he *assumed* that marriage was decided, awaiting only the right time to happen more or less automatically. Suddenly, those assumptions were off the table. "Well..." he said, composing himself, "what about school?"

"I'm sure there is room if you are willing to take the subjects required for graduation, I know they would be glad to have you. One of my cousins is the director."

"You people are all cousins. It's a miracle you have all your fingers." He flung it out with an edge, not all that funny. Tessa chuckled anyway and saved the moment.

"ToTo isn't married and I think he has a new girlfriend. I'm dying to find out who," she said. Tessa was ready for a party and Guito knew she would not allow any sulking to spoil it.

"I hope he brings her." His statement was detached, rote, embedded in worry that something had changed with Tessa. As the day of departure had drawn closer, Guito, like the others had begun to pull back. He felt remorse and a need to protect himself from the loss of friends. Distance had replaced the intimacy he'd felt all summer. He sensed this and was hoping that the party would re-bind them just one more time like the *old days*, he thought and wondered just what old days he might be thinking of. His arrival at the beginning of the new-year, felt like another lifetime. It was only May. And Tessa had rattled him more than he wished to admit.

"What are you thinking, *mi amor*?"

"Oh...a lot has happened since we joined the team." She squeezed his hand. "I have never known a group of people that I like more than these. It seems like everything we do–did–was fun."

He was thinking; she waited. "I don't think I've ever felt as accepted for who I am as with these people." She waited.

"For that matter, with your family as well...this has been the best time of my life." He squeezed her hand and pulled her to him; they held each other tightly for a moment. Hope revived itself in Guito's chest.

"I want to teach, now, " she said. "More than ever...but I have to go to university for that."

"Yesss." He sighed it out. University meant separation. *So that is what this is about.*

The room was bright. Sharon had turned on all the lights and opened the doors to each room. She had borrowed a table lamp that threw a glow over plates of *pakoras, samosas* and little snacks called *bocas,* and pitchers of *refrescos* made from local fruits. The inevitable clay dish of tortillas sat front and center covered with a Melmac plate. There were a couple boxes of wine and Sochi's ice chest.

Standing next to it was the big-smile Sochi, and the girl from the soda.

"Guito and Tessa, may I present Marisa whom I think you know. Marisa may I—"

"Sochi, you *chico malo*! *Mucho gusto* Marisa!" Tessa did not let him finish and she took the girls hands in hers. "Welcome to our team."

Marisa beamed. *"El placer es mio."*

Neither of us knew her name all these months, a light shadow of shame passed over Guito.

Beaming was not the right word for it. Marisa radiated pleasure, perhaps with the joy of inclusion. Guito could literally see a warm aura surrounding her. She had had a perm so that there were little black ringlets draping either side of her face and from the tips of her long dark hair. Her face was made up, her lips full with a bright red lipstick that matched her fingernails. She was wearing a dress that none of them had seen before.

Guito was touched as much by her effort as by her sexiness.

She held Sochi's hand with her right and had placed her left over both as though he might try to pull away and leave her alone with the foreigners. Tessa's mother hen stepped out of her nest and took the little chick, at least as old as she, into her protection. Between Tessa, and the others repeating things in Spanish, Marisa was never left out.

Wym and Rajiv were already there. Rajiv wore a towel as a turban in honor of the occasion. "I have a Sikh great-grandfather that we were not allowed to talk about," he was grinning.

"*Ja*, I have a Celt in my family but you don't see me wearing a skirt." Wym winked.

Sharon said that Profesora Salazar and Lorenzo had sent their regards to everyone.

The party settled into normal for the team. There was more storytelling, talking about things that had happened over the summer. ToTo⁴ᵗᵒ, alone, said only, "What girlfriend?" when Tessa challenged him. The emotions below the surface did not appear until ToTo told the story of Guito and the Tapaculo.

Sharon watched Guito closely as ToTo told of his shock when he "...turned around and saw Guito holding that little chicken. I may never be the same." He repeated the phrase to laughter. "If we had been with a group of amateurs, they would have scared the bird away, but this group knew they were seeing something special."

"ToTo," said an awestruck Sochi, "I can't believe that we are only hearing about this now." He grinned, "I have a Guito story also." With two beers already, he may have been about to launch his story about condoms when Sharon saved Guito.

"Friends," she began. All heads turned, everyone could see her eyes were filled. "Friends," she began again, "You are so special to me...." She didn't finish whatever she intended and began to go from person to person, hugging each of them to her and being hugged in return. Others teared, watching and then hugging her, even Brian was damp eyed. They all began to hug each other. Little Marisa was weeping for, perhaps, her own reasons, and hugging along with the rest.

The party did not end with this but people became subdued. They used the openness of the moment to talk quietly, making their goodbyes and pledges to stay in touch. ToTo, Wym and Rajiv left the team to its closure, "Don't be a stranger, Guito."

Brian said that he and Sharon had been planning their "write-up" of the summer and thought that they had three, possibly four publications from it. "All the interns will appear as co-authors." The party was over.

കാ

The Americans left the next day and when Guito returned to the pension he found two books lying on his bed. One was the team's Spanish-English dictionary and the other was an autobiography of a famous naturalist. It was the story of the man who had spent 35 years studying the birds in Central America. The author had signed and dated it, "1973." In the top right corner of the page was Brian's name. A note on the back of a bookmark was in Sharon's handwriting.

Dear Guito,
The life of this man may resonate with you – as you do with all of us. Please stay in touch – we hope to see you next year.

Affectionately,
Sharon, Brian and Sochi

He found an old book review folded behind the back cover and read that the author trained as a botanist but that his greatest contributions had been to ornithology. "...[H]is observational skills, and his capacity to reflect on the nature of life, led to writing numerous books on his philosophy of caring for nature, and his personal meditations on animal and plant life." Guito turned the bookmark over.

> Daily Scripture
>
> *Thoughts increase by being given away.*
> *The more who believe in them the stronger they become.*
> *Everything is an idea.*
> *How, then, can giving and losing be associated?*

Guito found a room in the home of one of the local families with a child in the school. If Tessa's family had helped, it wasn't obvious. The room was a former storage barn that had been attached to the house by extending the roof and the concrete floor. A single bed made from rough lumber squatted near a window with an even rougher wood shutter. There was a small table with a drawer. A single bulb hung at the end of a black wire. On the fresh painted wall hung a watercolor of a fichus tree.

With a horse and homemade packsaddle, Tessa's older brother Tomás brought over two blankets, a four-inch foam mattress and a small chest so that Guito could empty his backpacks. The room was larger than usual for a bedroom. It had a new door into the house, but it also had the original outside door. Privacy wasn't perfect but it was good enough for the lovers.

Guito helped the children with their homework. The youngest boy in fourth grade, asked a lot. Except for the frequent generosity of his landlords and Tessa's family, he continued to take meals at the *soda*. She gave him the same deal as the team. Marisa's presence there had changed. She dressed the same and Guito still took peeks, but now he felt kindly toward her and protective.

Wym and Rajiv left the following month. In their last meditation and discussion, Rajiv told Guito that since there were no teachers in the area, he would leave a handout with a description of the Buddha's "Eight-fold path" to liberation from suffering. "This is all practice and no theology, Guito. He tells you in detail the obstacles you'll run into and the steps you take to overcome them. Read it more than once."

Guito did. He read through it every week to help him focus his mind before meditating each morning.

Rebellion

8 August 1984

Guito was hungry. He had smelled the small *Refugio* bakery on his way to meet his last nature group before leaving for Asturias and home. He hesitated outside her door allowing the smells to wash over him.

"*Integral!*" he yelled so she could hear him.

She laughed and yelled back, "*Barra Blanca!*" It had been their joke for several weeks that he would try to guess what was in the oven. He rarely got it right but a friendship was forming and he was treated well when he could afford to buy there.

His favorite was the stuffed pastry that she made from her special dough and he had been imagining it all morning. She embedded a *salchicha*, a hot dog as he now called them, with cheese and herbs. Her pies were different too, with thick doughy crust, covered with raw dark sugar, and filled with mango and syrup. The visiting foreigners were her primary customers because her food was expensive for locals. He ate there only when he felt he had extra money.

The building was of wood, small, with hardly room inside for the small case facing the door. The oven was back a few feet but close enough to keep the space too warm. She had surrounded the little building with plants. A thick, long log formed a low wall along the ground to prevent the occasional car from pulling into the flowers.

A small boy sat on the low wall next to the bakery, elbows resting on his knees, the heels of his palms pushed into his eyes, not moving. As Guito entered the walkway to the bakery door, he saw and sensed the boy; he sensed pain. The pain followed him into the bakery.

He paid for the pastry and a huge vanilla cookie with cinnamon on top. She looked for the largest in her selection. Passing the boy again, he reached the road before the shock of the thought, *I feel this pain*, came to him. He turned around.

"*Hola chico*, is there room for me on that bench?" He sat down.... "It's a beautiful morning. Why aren't you playing before the rain starts?.... I live in a cabin over in Palo Seco....It belongs to Don Efraín, do you know him?"

Mumble.

"I don't think I've met you before...I'm called Guito."

"I know who you are."

"*De verdad?* Maybe I *do* know you...how are you called?"

"Juan Carlos."

"Ahhh...Juan Carlos...the King of Spain...of course, I heard he was a *chico*."

The hands came down, the boy looked at Guito, "I'm not the King of Spain; I'm Juan Carlos Garcia Daza."

Guito thought he heard some indignation. The boy's eyes were red. "Well your Highness, would you care for some of my *salchicha*?" He broke off a small piece and held out the most of it to the King. The boy grabbed the pastry and bit off a huge piece, stuffing his cheeks, making it impossible to speak. His jaws worked a while to get the lump down.

"Thank you Don Guito, *mucho gusto*...I'm really not the King of Spain." And he took another bite. The pastry had almost disappeared.

"Welll... my mistake...you sure look like the King." This time the boy smiled, perhaps realizing that Guito might be teasing him. "So tell me, your High..., forgive me, Juan Carlos, why aren't you playing with other kids?" The boy told him that he and his older sister had been given money for a cookie each but they had met an older friend of hers on the way. When they got to the store she had bought a cookie for the friend and they left him there.

"She is mean to me," and he started to tear up again.

"Well, " Guito said, "Juan Carlos is a famous name around here. Are you one of the ToTos?"

"No," the boy grinned, "not my family. Lot's of kids are named after the mayor."

He just finished saying this when his sister came back alone. Consternation writ large over her face, a wary look in her eyes, as though her crime may already be known. But her worry, and her need for friendship, were as present for Guito as the boy's angst. He smiled at her. He found out that her name was Aurelez. "Aurelez, *mucho gusto*, that is my little sister's name. She will be three on Sunday." He smiled again. "*Amigos*, I have a cookie in this sack. Would either of you care to share it with me?" He broke it into three smaller cookies.

Still cautious, she took it. "Thank you, *señor*." Then she pushed her piece at Juan Carlos who took it.

"Thank you Don Guito," she said.

They nibbled for a minute or so. The girl smiled at Guito.

"So, Aurelez, what would you say to Juan Carlos?"

She hesitated, looking into Guito's eyes. Seizing the opportunity, taking a deep, deep breath; "I'm sorry, Juanito."

The boy stopped chewing, he looked at her, his face unfolding, his mouth swelled into a smile, "That's okay Relez." A few moments passed, the cookies were gone. The sky clouded quickly.

"Well," Guito said, "I do have to go. It has been very nice to meet you Juan Carlos and Aurelez. Watch out for the rain," and Guito walked back to his cabin.

Everything is an idea, even the salchicha, he thought, *giving and receiving are the same thing*.

☙

A lot had changed since Tessa left for university. She had finished three years and had been home each summer except for this one. They had, "for all intents and purposes," she said, lived as though they were married when she was home. But, "The scholarships don't cover everything," and she had written that she could get a good job and a place to stay with her mother's relatives in Oregon, "Just for this summer. I need to pay back some loans," by way of explaining why she was not coming home. She would miss him dearly and write often. But her letters had gotten fewer and shorter. *I'll see her for Christmas*, he thought, *that's enough.*

Now, "out of the blue," her mother said, she was coming back in September. "She is trying to get a student teaching assignment approved for the *Refugio* School," she had said just two days ago. "It's a little like an internship," her mother explained. But the questions in his face were mirrored in hers.

The changes did not sit well with Guito, in spite of his usual equanimity. First came the adjustment to her staying in the US for the summer, and now this. *Maybe I should have insisted that she not stay up there for the summer, she doesn't know how much I miss her....* But he resisted making futile requests and it would have been futile with Tessa.

He imagined her stepping from the bus. He could see her face, she had her mother's features and father's color. Her face would look as if she had been thinking something funny, and he loved everything about it.   He would be happy, more than happy, to see her, but something felt undone. *Maybe I'm just worried about going home.* He was right about that also. He began to think on how the three years had passed.

⁖

January, 1983

Sharon and the research team had not been back. It was right after New Year's, and the beginning of the tropical summer of 1983. Tessa was back in college in the States when Sochi showed up to stay for a week. It was as if the "old days" had just dropped from the sky.

Sochi was winding up a bus trip through Central America, partly vacation and partly visiting locations that might serve as research sites for his dissertation. "Just like Rajiv," he had said, "but without a 'boyfriend,'" as we walked back to the cabin. He grinned, but Guito saw nothing funny in it. The humor felt forced anyway. Sochi said he would fly back from the capital and that he had stopped drinking beer. "I got re-religionized," he said, but Guito did not get the joke. The walk back to the cabin was the template for the entire week. Guito tried but they never connected in any way that felt like before.

Still, they did have some nice time together and Sochi went with Guito on his tours, yet he knew that something had changed. Sochi's "old self" came through only in spasms, as though he was making the effort. But neither his sporadic somberness nor his sobriety kept him from sniffing around Marisa, his old girlfriend, who was now living, *juntados,* or as they say, in a "free union," with a man from up north.

It was unlike Sochi to be so aggressive and it caused a stir. The man came around to the cabin to "require" that Sochi stop saying "pretty things," to Marisa. He worked as a *peón,* older, and wearing a machete, which may have been coincidence. According to him, the *unión* was not so *libre.*

"Sochi," Guito said, "that guy was upset. I do not want angry *muchachos* with machetes showing up at my house."

Sochi forced a grin, "OK, amigo." His expression changed; it might have been contempt and it shook Guito. But Sochi said nothing more to or about Marisa.

Sochi said that he was far enough along in his program to be thinking about a research project, still, ethno botany. "Would it be possible to find

Indigenous in this area?" Guito knew there were not, but he also knew they had been coming to the area up to the "'World War," after families began to move into the area below Aguas Calientes on the northeast slope looking out onto the Eastern Sea.

All *campesinos* know something about medicinal herbs and edible wild plants. Even the holiday drink, *chicha*, of fermented corn, is an *Indio* concoction. In those days, everyone in the area still collected wild plants for many reasons. Guito took Sochi to meet the patriarch of a settler family on the Eastern Sea side of the cordillera, and on the banks of the Rio Calientes.

Sochi had a research committee and he had talked about projects with them, but he had only begun to outline his dissertation proposal. Even so, he went back to the potential site by himself and took detailed interviews, searched for plants with one of the brothers, and took samples.

It was after dark when he got back to the cabin that day. He said the people there had come from Colon, on the slope of the Eastern Sea, in the early 1900's. They had lived initially as hunters with a few crops, much like the *Indios,* but they themselves, were not. They had not seen Indigenous in the area since the first few years after they moved there. But the family had a lot of knowledge about local plants and had invited him to come back and "stay awhile."

"I may, amigo," he winked, "There is a pretty school teacher down there, and I think she likes me." But his eyes had a wild look.

The last evening of the week, the weather had kept them mostly inside. The wind had been gusting with passing storm cells all day. There was an intermittent rain as happens at times even in the dry season. Sochi bought some *tamarindo* and made a pitcher of juice and sugar water. They sat at the table and he began to talk about his trip. He had said little to this point, avoiding the topic it seemed but time was running out.

"What time is your—" Guito began but Sochi started talking. He said that when his bus had arrived in his home country, some soldiers at the station had given him a hard look and checked his "papers." He was traveling on a U.S. passport. A gust slammed a shutter twice against a window frame. "They scared the shit out of me, just like that did," he said. His mood darkened. It was the first oath Guito ever heard from him.

"You are just being paranoid, Amigo," He smiled to take the edge off, but Sochi's face darkened more.

"Do—not—tell—me—I—am—paranoid."   He was looking down and each word came out hoarse and separate and with equal force. "I *know* a hard look when I see one. *Indios* from out of town are automatically 'persons of interest.' Do you know what really, *really pisses* me off?" The words came with specks of spit, saliva formed a large bubbly fleck in the corner of his mouth. "I'm sure those soldiers were Indigenous! This-*damn* war is tearing the people apart... and the 'people,' are *Indios*!"

Tears, pressurized by the unspoken story, sprang from his eyes, rolling down his face, his nose leaked, unstoppable. "*El* Presidente, el General is an *evangelico*...an *evangelico*...like me! And, he is a friend of a leader in my own church. He is being a Christian with death squads." Shaking now, Sochi said, "His philosophy is —this is a quote Guito — "A Bible in one hand and a machine gun in the other." He rested again, breathing in, exhaling deeply, looking at the ceiling, "If I had any *guts*, I would still be there." The story came out in lumps, as though working its way through a grinder.

Guito could feel it coming; *he is going to explode.* He was weeping with Sochi now; Guito felt everything his friend did. He reached for him but Sochi flailed at his arm.

More moments passed. The story of what he had seen hovered above their heads, in between them, all around the cabin, awaiting its voice. Sochi began talking again, quietly at first, looking down and wiping his face. Heavy sweat now added to his tears and phlegm; it soaked his shirt and streamed down the sides of his face and head, his words were barely understandable.

"I took a bus to our old village in El Petén," he began and he told Guito the story of his sister, of his friend Chaco, now a priest and the village. "The soldiers were killing everyone they could catch...smashing baby's heads into rock walls...raping the girls and women...they filled the well with bodies...." Guito watched his face, Sochi had leaned as far back as he could and stay upright, legs extended straight out, his face unrecognizable, arms rigid, hands clasped tightly in his lap. For a moment, Guito plumbed the depth of Sochi's anguish, he could feel his own face twist under the weight of it. Sochi made no attempt to clean himself, everything ran, dripping off his chin. A groan gurgled and escaped his throat. He keened. "Ayyeeeeeee...Ayyeeeeeee," for several minutes in the manner of Guito's mother at his grandmother's funeral. Sochi became quiet.

"*Auumm.*" *God be with us now. Oh God, be with us.* Guito was pleading. His prayer and presence were all that he could offer Sochi.

They were quiet, both of them seeping. More minutes passed, maybe twenty. Sochi, body rigid, leaned his head as far back as he could, hands over his face, his voice now modulated. "Guito," he sucked a ragged breath, "God save my soul...I will never look at another woman until I kill someone...God save my mortal soul." The last words came out in a calm whisper. Guito would never forget those words.

Sochi fell asleep in the chair that night. When Guito found him in the morning he was curled like a newborn on the floor.

He took the early bus. There was nothing to say, no niceties, yet Guito felt equally closer to and further from him than he ever had. He wanted to hold Sochi, but he felt like a bar of cold steel.

"Maybe I will see you in a couple of years," he said and they shook hands.

"Take care of yourself, Sochi," He managed to choke it out. But Guito never saw Sochi again. *He is not Sochi*, the thought crushed his spirit to the ground as he walked away. He wanted to hide somewhere, curl up in the bushes nearby. Guito called Sharon and left a message to call him at Tessa's.

She did a day later and left a message for him. "It was urgent," Sharon said; "Sochi has not shown up for the second semester." She sobbed when he relayed Sochi's story. She would call the family and the embassies. Tessa's family gathered to listen in on the call. Grace at dinner that night was devoted to Sochi and to all the people caught in the civil wars. Guito wrote the entire story in three letters and sent them to Tessa, Sharon and Rajiv.

At a professional meeting later that same year, Lorenzo's mother, *Profesora* Salazar brought up the, "Sochi caper," she called it, and had, "tsk'd, tsk'd," knowingly in a manner that visibly infuriated Sharon. Caught off guard, she turned away and then turned abruptly back, but Brian stopped her before something was said–or done– that she might have regretted. Neither she nor Brian ever returned to Aguas Calientes.

Chisme

Morning, 9 August 1984

Guito climbed on the bus to Fresa at 6:00 AM for his trip home for his sister's third birthday. It was the same vehicle he had arrived in almost four years before and the one that Sochi had left in. He had taken it a few times and knew the driver by sight. *"Buenos Dias,"* they exchanged. A family operated the bus service and there were only three drivers, the father, oldest brother and oldest daughter. Guito had heard that only the daughter had an actual driver's license. He had fallen earlier in the week. Stepping backwards off a bank of earth, he fell and hit a branch of a log, hard, on his left side. Although his usual window on the left side allowed him to collect the better views of the line of volcanoes that formed the horizon, today he leaned against the right side of the bus where there would be long views of the dominating Lake of the Valley and the river that drained it.

The prospect of going home for the first time in three years left him ruminating on how it might go. He had been that way for a week, since his mother's call had convinced him to come home for Aurelez' third birthday. "You missed the first," she censured him. Lightly, but enough to trigger his postponed sense of obligation. He knew that the baby would have been dressed like a princess for that first birthday. The entire neighborhood and all the close relatives from out of town should have been there for the traditional celebration of the child's survival of her first year. There would always be a birthday party in the *campo*, but they became decreasingly intense as the other children arrived and as it became more likely that the child would make it to maturity.

Now, on the bus from Palo Seco to Fresa then to the capital, was a good time to sort and settle himself to reengage with his father and his new sister. He worried about Tessa, *what was going on there*, but her arrival was at least two weeks off. It would have to wait. His remembrance yesterday of Sochi dropped him even lower. It might have been simple sadness, but it felt like guilt; he could have done more to help Sochi. *I thought I was over this*, he sighed. *I could have insisted he stay longer*, and such thoughts, filled his mind.

An off-and-on-again diarist, Guito kept a thick one, of the type that had no dates, a stiff binder and a ream of creamy pages, expensive. His mother had bought it for him on impulse while he was in high school. Unusual for her, it *was* expensive, especially for a book without any words. He had been intimidated by its sheer luxury. The thought of marking its pages with a mere pencil or ballpoint pen made him anxious, as though nothing in his life could warrant defacing it. But the reluctance disappeared when he got to Aguas Calientes.

The things that happened to him there were important enough to sully its pages. Most of the early ones were filled with thoughts about the team, Sochi and Tessa, mostly Tessa. Under the influence of the scientists who kept detailed journals, he began to use it to make notes on his fieldwork. Nowadays it included a hodgepodge of personal entries, lists of groups, sometimes contact information, and notes on plants and wildlife with locations, dates and times, etc. He did not make entries every day, but when he did he often used more than one page. Only 5 or so clean pages remained. Guito saw it on the table and picked it up as he left for the bus.

Waiting for the bus to finish loading, Guito opened the diary to the day after Sochi left, the day after his "radicalization," as Tessa called it. She said she had studied the "role of radicals" in social change and, except for war, radicals now seemed to fit her definition of how to get things done in a democratic society–"As long as there was no violence." He remembered something that had confused him, "Compared to the rest of the world, the *Refugios*," she said, "are radicals in their own way." After that, he wasn't sure what a "radical" meant. He reread the painful entries he had made the day Sochi left, it took all of three pages, front and back. The last sentence read, "Talk to Rajiv!" He remembered, Rajiv had returned for another three months of his research two weeks after Sochi's departure.

February, 1983

"Wym and I aren't together anymore." He got it out within the first five minutes of meeting. Guito had moved back to his old rental room to give Rajiv the space he needed in the *cabina*. Rajiv promised that Guito would inherit the cabin when his research finished, but between visits, Guito sub-leased it at a reduced price to keep it available.

"That is, if you can work it out with the landlord. I know he is charging us foreigners double what anyone else would pay."

Don Efraín will be one disappointed dude when that conversation comes to pass, thought Guito. "So…what happened with Wym?"

"Well…you know how we used to tease each other. After a while the teasing came to feel hostile—not fun. It was the same for both of us. We got into a pattern where it felt like we had to attack the other person just to stay even."

"Yeah, it feels like Tessa and I get into the same place."

"It isn't fun."

"No."

"Anyway, we tried counseling but neither of us put our heart into it—So, we decided we liked being friends and we quit while there was still a chance that we could be." Neither spoke, Rajiv sighed. "It was the right thing but I miss him."

"It seems like nothing good lasts. It scares me sometimes to think that Tessa and I are not permanent. I do not see enough of her as it is."

"Well, Amigo—what does the Buddha say? Experiences don't last; only one thing is permanent." Rajiv was smiling now; he poked

Guito's shoulder, seemingly back to his old self. "How are you getting along with the *Refugios*?"

Guito smiled also, "What is not to like about them?" He cringed at his use of another Sochi expression. "I really like it here and Tessa says that I am a good fit."

"What does she mean?"

"Probably she thinks that because I am committed to non-violence and I am pretty accepting of people."

"Yes—*and*, I think her sense, as is mine, is that you allow the spirit of God to speak to you my friend. You listen for the Holy Spirit, as you Catholics say."

"Perhaps, maybe so. I guess I don't feel much like a Catholic anymore. Anyway, she has given me instructions to get you to church and to try and save your soul before it's too late."

"I'm too far gone for a new religion, Amigo, but—."

"You know I am kidding, so was she."

"Yes, I know. But I would like to go to church with you. How often do you go?"

"At least one time a week. There is one this Sunday. Tessa's mom will be there. I'll get some points for dragging you in."

Rajiv shook his head, grinning, "You've been hanging around Sochi and Tessa too long."

"Oh my God." Guito was stricken. "I've been so caught up in seeing you again...you didn't get my letter." Rajiv's face darkened.

He tried to shorten the story of his last visit with Sochi, but Rajiv wanted every detail. So Guito left nothing out. He spoke of the "tone" of the week with Sochi, his changeable attitude, of Marisa and her husband, the trip to gather plants, Sochi's exact words to the best of memory, of the last night, and the call to Sharon. "No one has any idea where he is now. I assume that he is in the war." He hesitated, watching Rajiv's face. The concern remained, no change. The silence lingered.

Rajiv breathed out, audibly, "I always felt that he had something bubbling inside." Long pause. "You know...he is on his own path, there is no alternative. There was nothing you could have done."

The quiet held as Guito absorbed the words.

"I have a new guru, Guito. I turned to her after Wym and I parted. You know how you may hear something once, or twenty times, and then the very next time, you *really* hear it? It is no longer just a fact or a piece of information; it becomes something you know. And you know you know. A few months ago she said that, '*In the end*, you don't really *want* to change anybody.' There is no 'should' in this; it isn't another concept to aspire to. It's just...*in the end*...you just don't want to. We have to deal with each other of course, there are people you would rather spend more time with and others less. But Sochi is going to live out this life with the hand he has been dealt. As are you and I, and Wym, Tessa...everyone. If I were to see him in pain, I would try to help ease him in anyway I could, but I know now, I am ultimately indifferent to how Sochi lives this life out."

Rajiv's "indifferent," caused an almost visible gasp, Guito's blank face, wide-eyed stared at him, but Guito said nothing, letting the words sink in. As the moments passed, his certainty that Rajiv was neither callous nor uncompassionate reasserted itself. But the conundrum remained, *what does he mean?*

"I feel sure we will want to talk more about this, but let some time and thought pass before we do so." Standing up, Rajiv said, "I think this is a good time to give you your present." He rummaged through his duffel and withdrew a small volume of his guru's collected teachings in Spanish. "I found this in a used book store. Have you been keeping current with the Buddha?"

Guito nodded, "He sure knew what he was talking about."

"Yeah. When it comes to purging yourself of bad thoughts, he's the best. Let's go back to sitting together and talking like we used to."

୨୦

This was Rajiv's fourth trip to Aguas Calientes in two and a half years, and the next to last of his project. In each trip after the first, Rajiv had come prepared to make presentations to the school. He was well known not only to the teachers and students but to many of the adults in the community as he made presentations of general interest to everyone. Around the edges, it felt like a homecoming. The traditional service included preaching and ended with a pulpit call responded to by several people. As people rose to leave, some of the kids, yelled for Rajiv to speak. He walked to a corner of hall and was immediately surrounded a fair sized crowd including the minister whose duties at the door were shortened by so many remaining inside.

"My friends, I am Rajiv Gupta from the Netherlands. You may be interested to know that my guru has recently given me the name *satyahimsa*," he glanced at Guito, "I tell you that just in case you Spanish speakers think you have the corner on syllables," laughter. "I answer to either name nowadays. Actually, my new name means 'knowing non-violence,' it emphasizes the interdependence of Truth and Non-violence. We Jains share some things in common with you *Refugios*. So...that's my lesson in comparative religion for today."

There were a few chuckles but people were paying close attention. "I've been here several times and it is difficult to tell you just how happy I am to be back. I will be here for about three months and I am 'informed,'" making the quotes in the air, "that my soul needs to get itself saved in this Church." Tessa's Mom led the laughter among the few people who appreciated Rajiv's slightly weird humor. She wagged her finger at the sheepish Guito. Blushing, he looked caught by Rajiv's outrageous candor. "Actually...I agree with that judgment...my heart feels good to be among you and I do need to be here." He started to move away but stopped "Oh, an announcement. I'm looking for a car, preferably a cheap jeep if anyone knows of one." He sat.

A week after Rajiv's announcement, an old Land Cruiser pulled up in front of the *cabina*. Its owner drove across the patchy grass to the door, and called *"Upe!"* several times.

"I've just put in a new clutch," the seller said. "They are the first to go in these mountains."

And the truck may have been the oldest one in the province. It had a three-digit license plate that remained with the vehicle for its natural life. The truck became a gift to Guito after Rajiv's last visit to the AC, as did the opportunity to rent, then buy, the *cabina* at a good price. The two gifts put Guito years ahead of what his earnings as a guide would have permitted.

But this last visit with Rajiv would be as turbulent as the one with Sochi.

ဢ

The bus's horn blasted for a full 5 seconds, and then again. An ancient pickup truck, attempting to turn around in the middle of the highway, stalled for the second time. A cacophony of impatience arose as horns traveling in both directions joined the bus. The three men in the pickup got out and pushed it to the side of the road. They were a block from the large bus stop in Pinto and Guito could see the next bus already loading. It was full; his large backpack went into the cargo compartment and Guito stood until a seat became available. He returned to his diary.

ဢ

The three months with Rajiv had had its own potential tragedy. Correspondence and talk about Sochi had been heavy for the first month or so, but slowed when it became clear that no one knew anymore than anyone else. An angst-filled letter from Wym brought them back into memories and discussion, but that also faded.

With Sochi gone, possibly gone forever, Guito found himself relying almost exclusively on Rajiv for friendship. He reciprocated strongly in the absence of Wym, and the two of them began a regular meditation and discussion. Often they ate dinner together. The amount of time that they spent together confirmed to Guito just how much he had organized his life simply to avoid loneliness. He had friends, but not people he could talk with in the way that he could with Tessa, Sochi and Rajiv. The three were very different, each a foreigner of one type or the other, from his other friends.

These thoughts came with a kind of low-level rumble as though some-unknown-thing was not right. His image was that of riding in a neighbor's ox cart back home, with one wheel slightly off center, *athump.......athump......athump.* Just enough to create a small discontent when he wasn't otherwise distracted. *Dhukka, more dhukka*, he thought, *more dhukka. It never ends.* When these thoughts entered his awareness he condemned them, and himself, for not being happy.

The big things he could deal with. At least he could identify them; Sochi's disappearance was, somehow, in a different category from the small dissatisfactions that inexplicably plagued Guito. The panic attacks that he once suffered when an assignment came due had largely succumbed to his practice of examining fears as they arose in meditation. It was the little, *something is not right*, that caused him a degree of suffering that could not be explained by his loving, satisfying, and otherwise successful way of living. Such ruminations usually ended with, a *just get over it,* or, *stop whining*, or some such thought.

"OK Rajiv, I have thought about it. How can you be 'indifferent,' to what happens to Sochi?" Guito was back at the cabin. Weak sunlight came through the afternoon window and formed a fuzzy trapezoid on the table between them.

Rajiv did not hurry to answer. "The...or *my* answer...lies in the meaning of compassion...what some people call unconditional love. You've heard that term before."

Guito nodded, "It means, a love that is accepting of everyone and everything."

"Close enough. The word 'compassion,' literally meant at one time, simply *being with* the feelings, the 'passion,' of another. One can only love in the manner of simply being with another when you are not attached. That is when you understand love as something other than simply an *emotional* attachment, which is of course, how everyone *does* understand it. When I was in university in New York, I went to a Protestant church and the minister preached a sermon about, 'Worshiping money.' The sermon was an allegory for the Christian mandate not to worship false idols. You may have heard that kind of talk when you were growing up."

Guito smiled, "Nope. If I heard it didn't register."

"Worship, used in that sense is an attachment. It's an emotional attachment that we can make to any 'thing.' The 'thing' itself doesn't really matter, this is all about the emotional nature of the attachment. Sometimes it is called grasping. The 'thing' could be money, a person, a pet, spirituality, a concept, self-image...it doesn't really matter. We grasp for it; we put on a pedestal and worship it. One can *only* love unconditionally, and be truly compassionate...no strings attached...when one has no *emotional* attachment. For most people, this is a hard point to understand."

He paused, "Questions? It is hard to explain anyway, but all the more so because I cannot speak directly from personal experience." He paused again but Guito just shook his head, "No."

"If one were realized, that is personally knowing the world as a unity, then the lack of attachment would have already been achieved.'

"What comes first?"

"Actually you can go a long way towards non-attachment with your meditation practice."

"So meditation leads to both?"

"Yes. It can get you right up to the cusp of enlightenment. But something has to happen to push you over the edge of the abyss so to speak."

"I do remember a priest in catechism class saying that you get to Heaven by grace, not by earning it."

"That's a great analog—grace. Anyway...there are thousands of years of people experiencing the universe in this way. There must be something to it." He paused, "We scientific types would call that 'empirical evidence.'"

"Obviously the science does not help much if you are not already liberated."

"My point exactly. Science, logic, words, scriptures—they only point you in the direction. None of them will get you where you want to go...where you *think* you want to go," he smiled. You must personally experience the doctrine of non-duality –all is one-through meditation and ethical living. But in the end, it is the spirit of Buddhism that tumbles you over the edge into an ineffable experience of the non-dual world."

"Sometimes you make my head hurt."

Juan Carlos and his sister came to Guito's mind. It was the day that he felt the little boy's angst outside the bakery. He remembered the girl also, he had felt her feelings as well. *Maybe I glimpsed the non-dual world,* he thought, *maybe unconditional love is like that.* "It is a lot Rajiv, I need to think on it."

"Yeah, it's different, overwhelming maybe, but back to Sochi...I do feel an attachment to him and his friendship, yet in another way, I know that his life is going to happen as it will. I can let him go, trusting in the will of God. The *Christians* have another saying, 'Let go and let God?'" He said it as a question, as though it might be familiar to Guito. "Few Christians really surrender to God on a permanent basis any more than Buddhists. It's just their talk. Same as it is with all religions. It's all talk until it happens. That's what you and I are trying to do in this lifetime. Less talk and more do."

"I guess that's what I'm trying to do. Since I met you and Wym, I realize how far from it I have been, all my life. You sound like *you* know more about Christianity than I do. It is almost like you have a problem with it."

"Sorry, I don't. The reason that I went to that church in New York was because I had a friend who went there. He was a little like Tessa, out to 'save my soul' so to speak. So, I went with him. In his church being gay was all right but I knew that in some churches it is not. Wym was a Dutch Reform Christian and being gay also had something to do with his leaving the church. "I don't know why Guito, but I have wanted to know God and to understand how the different religions do it since I was a kid. My father was open-minded, even for a Jain, and we had some books about most of the religions in our house. How did you get interested?"

It was the first time Guito had heard him use the word "gay;" it arrived with a noticeable jolt. "I do not know. We did not have many books in our house...not just religious books...*no* books except the Bible...my mother had some pamphlets from the Church and she used to read them...and newspapers. But I do not think I knew I wanted to know God until I met you and Wym."

Discussions like these were compelling. More than just interesting, they felt supportive to Guito and he valued them. He showed up at the *cabina* almost every day. He stopped taking meals with his landlords or with Tessa's family.

The logic of Rajiv's explanations did have some effect. Guito meditated daily and occassionally he could sense that his mind had no boundary. It was as though these glimpses had a life of their own, as though they were "teaching" him, as it were, compelling him to look with even more discipline. Rajiv told him that there were eight levels of consciousness but no matter what level you obtained by good effort, there was still a discontinuity between what you had achieved and the final experience of realization. "That is where grace comes in," he said.

Time passed and Rajiv and Guito were continually in each other's presence when not working.

৪০

About two months into Rajiv's stay, they took advantage of bright day to combine a walk into Palo Seco to food shop with a little birding. Rajiv had been reviewing his notes and doing some preliminary writing. He said his results would support his initial hypothesis but there might be an additional publication from his work. He was pleased with himself, and playful. His mood was infectious; both of them joked and kidded during the long walk. They passed a young couple walking with arms intertwined. The girl stared at the two men until they were just past, then turned her head away and tittered into the cup of her hand.

The owner of the little market often had a selection of fresh meat, all of it locally slaughtered. Guito pulled out a package of an entire cow's tongue and put it, in the basket. He knew the sight of the entire organ would turn Rajiv's stomach. "Ugh...put that thing back." He took Rajiv's poke to the shoulder as a fitting end to the joke. Still chuckling, Guito saw ToTo[4to] at the far end of the aisle just as he stepped out of view behind the end cap.

"ToTo... ToTo." *Did he see us?*

ToTo reappeared, a surprised look marked his face, "Guito, hi... hi Rajiv.... Well, have the two of you come up for air?....We haven't seen much of you this past month." The words might have been better chosen in any case, but his deep blush assured an awkward pause.

Rajiv filled the space, "Yes, I'll put together a dinner soon...I hope you'll come."

"I'm looking forward to it; just tell me what I can bring. Gotta run, you'all have a good day." ToTo bolted to the cashier's line.

The walk back to the *cabina* was cloaked in a different mood. Guito's mind bounced around inside his head. Rajiv said nothing.

"What was wrong with ToTo?" Guito did not expect an answer. As he walked, the feeling of some small-wrong-thing grew into some-big-thing. A fear welled slowly from his center, filling his stomach and chest. Discussing was out of the question.

At the *cabina*, Rajiv asked, "What do *you* think is wrong with ToTo?"

"I have to think about it...something is not right."

"When you do, let's talk...sooner is better than later."

"This feels bad."

"Yes...it does. Do you want to talk now?"

"No...no dinner tonight...we can talk tomorrow."

For the first time in years, Guito ruminated uncontrollably. Wym had said that, "Ruminating was what passed for 'thinking about it,' for most people." But for now, it was the only 'thinking' he was capable of. The meaning of ToTo's behavior was uncertain but sinister. He dismissed the possibility that ToTo was simply having a bad day and let the tightening in his gut, his shallow breathing, dominate his awareness. *I am afraid*, was his final thought before sleeping. He awoke an hour or two later with the moon full in his eyes. Or maybe it was the dream that brought him awake. In the dream, two parts of himself were talking. One part seemed to see clearly, the other was caught, as in a net of fear.

"Do I have to spell this out for you? ToTo thinks you are having sex with Rajiv."

"But I am not, he is just a friend. ToTo is a tolerant man; it will be OK."

"It is bad enough that you are acting in an unexpected manner, but he thinks that you are betraying Tessa... betraying Tessa... betraying Tessa...with a man."

"It is my fault, I made it look that way. Life will turn out the way it will. I don't care if some people think I'm gay."

"Look, you have to control this, it is going to be bad if you don't. What about Tessa's family? What will they think?"

"Oh God, but they are tolerant too, it...."

"Not of betrayal."

"God...this is not fair...."

He returned to a troubled sleep.

Guito awoke early, tired but clear. He rarely remembered a dream but the conversation had seared itself into his consciousness. *Life will work out the way it will*, he thought, *but this time, the way it works out...this time will depend on me.* Guito put some coffee on the single burner and began to clean the room. He sorted, picking up and rearranging things that had been put off, refolding and replacing things that did not need arranging, waiting for the space between when ToTo would finish with his early morning farm duties and when he would leave for Church.

℘

"ToTo...can I talk with you." Guito stood on the steps of ToTo's cabin.

"Hi Guito...come in ...there is some coffee on...you take it black?"

"Thanks," he took the coffee, "I do not want to sit." ToTo stared at him, curious but not unkindly. "I need to say this for myself. I am *not* saying that it will make any sense to you. I am.... ToTo, I am afraid that you think that I am involved with Rajiv in some way that betrays Tessa." He blurted it.

"Guito, I...."

He held his hand up. "Just let me get this out... I am not doing anything with Rajiv except being his friend. I just need to know that you understand that." He looked squarely at ToTo. "I am not." The pause held. ToTo stared at his own cup, turning it in his hands, holding it with both, as though to keep warm. Moments passed.

"You've got guts, Guito...I understand what you are saying, and I trust you." He breathed deeply, sighing and looking at Guito. "Forgive me."

Guito nodded, "Thank you...forgive me for being so thoughtless." They stood there a moment, "Do I need to talk with Tessa's family?"

"I think you should...just her mother...I'll take care of the boys."

"Thank you, ToTo." He turned to leave, at the front steps he turned back, "Rajiv may be the best friend I have ever had except Sochi. I am going to try not to lose his friendship over this."

ToTo nodded, "Don't do that, Guito. He is a good friend. Leave it to us ToTo's, we'll fix this with people."

&

The bus arrived early into the capital. Guito waited impatiently for his backpack to emerge from the cargo compartment then took a cab to the station for buses to Asturias. He made the early connection.

Little Sister

9 August 1984

Eleven-thirty AM. Guito was hungry but felt lucky to have caught one of the express buses to Asturias. The little package of sugar-coated peanuts, his favorites, would have to do. Hopefully there would be a little more time between buses at the next change. He had turned down his father's offer of a ride from San Diego to the house. "There is a bus shortly after I get to San Diego," he had said.

Being around his father was the most uncertain part of the visit. Thinking about him felt prickly, although he knew that his mother was expecting that things could be patched up. "If you can do it...," she had said several times but the idea of having to work actively at making amends made him cringe. What he wanted in return for coming home at all was just to be left alone, to muddle through the visit as best he could. Coming home was at his discretion and the idea of her agenda angered him.

He had put up with ten years of his father's relentless disappointment. Stardom in that family drama was over for him and he would not get back on stage in the boy role again. At this point, he could think of no role he did want, not even Mother's Successful Boy appealed. The role of Big Brother was scarcely conceivable. He realized that he didn't know what he wanted and he didn't know what they wanted of him. The two uncertainties made him feel like staying on the bus and returning to Aguas Calientes where such things were known. *Or not*, he remembered Tessa.

Making up with his father was the one relationship in his life that he was not open to. "You know that you are fearing something about him, or yourself," Rajiv had said, and he guessed that Rajiv was right about that. But, it did not help, *so here I am...same ole, same ole*, he thought. The expression reminded him again of Tessa. She brought it home after her first year in college. *As though I do not have enough to think about.*

He knew that Tessa thought he was pathetic on this point. Her tolerance with his despondency on the subject of his father had its limits; when they were reached she was merciless. "I pity you," she had told him when he last saw her. The "pity," drove him away for a day. When they got back together, a tacit agreement not to talk about his home, ruled.

ভ

The two of them were working in the kitchen, Eduardo helping Alba to put last minute touches on things. Steam rattled the lids of pots. "Eduardo, can we talk about Guito." She waited for Eduardo to stop puttering and look at her. "I think that Guito may be still upset with you. You haven't spoken to him in three years. Somehow, I think things can be all right if we don't push him."

"Jesus, Alba," he sighed, "do we have to do this right now. I'm sure things will be fine." But he didn't really think so. He had considered apologizing to Guito but he could not imagine how to do that. The pressure to talk from Alba was too much when added to the pressure he was placing on himself. As usual, using her as a coach or a sounding board, would not occur to him.

She walked away, as though it was over, but Eduardo followed her. "I'm sorry *querida*. But I don't know what to expect from him. I'm sure as hell not ready to hear any criticism from him. It feels like I don't even know who he is anymore." It was the most he had said about Guito since the time he first told Alba about the other woman.

Alba waited for him to go on. But after a few moments, "Eduardo," she said, "I love you."

"I love you *querida*," he looked at her, his shoulders lowered a little. "Maybe we should just let him take the lead."

"Maybe so. But he may need some encouragement too. Can we keep talking after he gets here?"

"Okay," he said. "Okay."

The trip thus far had been good; bringing the diary had been a good idea. Thinking about Rajiv had been like sorting and putting away a pile of papers that had been accumulating on his table. Yet as Guito had gotten closer to San Diego his thoughts increasingly rankled him. As though getting closer to the source of his disquietude had its independent effect. He had a shelf in his mind where he put stuff so that he could focus on other things. *Like, going home, how is that going to go? Why can't I be different with Eduardo?* He hoped it was an honest question.

He knew that he was one blessed human being with the way his life had gone in Aguas Calientes. He was happy there. But his thoughts about his father were frustrating; he was sure that the answer—the solution to angst—was sitting right in front of him, waiting for him to open his eyes and see. But he couldn't, or didn't, and when he thought of home, anxiety displaced satisfaction with his life.

The bus discharged passengers on the west side of the plaza in San Diego. It had to pull around three sides of the park to get to the unloading point. The first thing that Guito noticed was the new trees planted in all quadrants, the result of a recent burst of civic pride and a big donation. Then he saw Eduardo sitting on a bench a few meters from the bus stop. Panic leapt into his chest.

Ok...here we go, the image of some soldiers getting ready to jump out of an airplane in one of his childhood movies came to mind. The thought relieved the panic and brought a smile to his face. And it was that smile Eduardo saw as Guito jumped, both feet together, from the last step.

His father walked toward him, both arms outstretched. Guito kept a distance as they embraced but the long silence of the bus rides broke.

"You look good Guito, we are glad you are home. You're taller – added a little weight. It looks good on you."

Indeed. Guito saw that he was a full three inches taller than his father. But his hands were exactly like those of Eduardo, large, square, powerful. *I'm his son, no doubt about it.*

"Thanks, Eduardo, I'm glad to be here. Do you have some work for me? I feel like getting very tired and very dirty."

"That can be arranged," his father smiled. The horse stalls had not been cleaned for two days and there was unlimited opportunity on the big farm. If he noticed the "Eduardo," it didn't show.

"I hope you're hungry Guito, your Ma has made a lifetime supply of *bizcochos*." Guito's favorites included the little cornbread empanadas filled with farm cheese and baked on banana leaves in the wood fired oven. Her recipe included small bits of onion and a touch of *picante* hot sauce in the dough. Eduardo did not say that he had spent the morning deep frying pieces of pork into *chicharrones*, another Guito favorite.

"I'm going to eat until I can't walk."

The idea that Guito was looking forward to the big family meal encouraged Eduardo. He tried a few starts at conversation but the ride to the house was mostly quiet.

cg

Rosa broke into a limping run as soon as Guito stepped out of the Land Rover. She was a little gray around the whiskers and held a hind leg in the air from an untreated horse kick, but she was still Rosa. His little sister Louisa ran after Rosa and leapt into his arms as he leaned over to pet the dog. She was eight and had last seen him when she was five. Guito swung his oldest sister in a circle and covered her head with kisses. When he put her down she held his hand tightly and clutched Rosa's fur in her free hand. One of the challenges that Alba had faced after Guito's departure had been Louisa's fear that she had driven Guito away by revealing his secret name. He wondered if the little girl had really gotten over it.

Alba was holding the baby's hand, at the top of the steps. "Hello Ma."

"Oh Guito...*mi amor*. I am so happy to see you." Her eyes filled and her words muffled in his chest. Her hands found both his then she wrapped her arms around him. They held each other tightly for a long moment. Wiping an eye with her free hand, her other firmly clutching his shirt from behind, she turned sideways to the baby. "Guito this is Aurelez; she is going to be three tomorrow. Say hello to your brother Aurelez." The little girl was holding his mother's skirt, a forefinger in her mouth. She was round all over with a pretty face and dark eyes that looked directly at Guito.

"I am pleased to meet you Guiiito." She spoke in the way that children are taught in the school she had not yet begun. But she drew out the first syllable of his name. It might have sounded mocking were she not on the edge of babyhood, and had she not been so serious, looking at him square in the eye.

"It's Guito *mi amor*, call him Guito."

"No. It's Guiiito. Guiiito will you give me a ride on your shoulders? Please Guiiito, I'll give you a big kiss...two big kisses," she bargained, smiling at him.

He looked at her and resistance slipped away. His shoulders dropped. He lifted her up to those shoulders and she planted a big kiss on the top of his head and wrapped her arms around his forehead. "The pleasure is all mine," Guito replied formally, "and happy birthday Aurelez." Guito had been prepared to be indifferent to his youngest sister but she broke his heart, right there in front of God and everybody. There would be no diffidence with this little girl.

His mother gave his elbow a squeeze, firm and clinging, she kissed him on his bicep as he settled Aurelez onto his shoulders. "Giddy'up Guiiito!" and they walked into the house, careful of the door jam, hopping a little here and there, and stopping whenever they came to a picture on the wall. "Whoa horsey."

His mother nudged Eduardo by leaning into him. They both smiled and Eduardo sighed. Still dealing with Guito's coolness, he slipped his arm around Alba.

ᚩ

Eating his usual portions was out of the question. Food was always in front of Guito and after the first dinner he succumbed to his mother's unwillingness to hear, "But Ma, I'm full...." He looked forward to physical work as a way to manage the deluge. It was a relief when Eduardo gave him real farm work.

Unlike the old days, Eduardo worked side by side with him; there were no *peones* to distract them. Their talk was limited to the work and the farm, but both would have acknowledged privately that it was successful in the sense that no disaster, was a success. Slowly, they regained a passable rapport so that by the time Guito left on Monday morning, he could authentically thank Eduardo for the visit and wish him well. His father would be visibly moved. Guito would have children of his own before he would sense the loss that the father already knew.

On Saturday after the morning's work, Guito walked the half-kilometer downhill through the coffee to the *quebrada*, his childhood *querencia*. He had anticipated this walk for hours and now the memories of his youth made him smile as he wove his way through the coffee, scrambling at times, grabbing coffee branches to stay upright in the steep spots. He thought of how his energy for being "El Indio" had dissipated. He felt a kinship for *Indios* but he also knew that he was not El Indio anymore. The melancholies of the thought surprised him, and even before reaching the *quebrada*, he missed El Indio.

There were changes in his relationship to things around the house because of his new size. But food and the emotion in seeing his family had kept them on the periphery of his attention. Here in the quiet the changes were everywhere. The highest waterfall that had been his "cliff" was a mere ledge. He could climb it in three big steps instead of the hand, over hand, over hand effort that he remembered. At the top he sat on that same rock, now smaller, where he had had his encounter with God, years ago...*13 to be exact*.

God did not show up this time. The log from which the snake had stared at him was gone too, rotted, perhaps, washed away in a big storm. The *quebrada* appeared to him as a chaos of tumbled boulders and white water and he knew that as a child he could have recited a story for each rock and its spot on the face of the earth. It was as though the rocks had had their own stories to tell in those days. They were just rocks now and although the sounds, the vistas recollected to him with a faint familiarity, the feelings were not the same.

He had hoped that the rocks and the water would remember him, that they would somehow recover the old days. He tried, reaching back, trying to pull some reaction up and into consciousness. But no matter where he looked inside, there was nothing there. When he looked at the scene in front of him he felt that the rocks and the water knew this. *Are they laughing at me?* He was disoriented, even with his eyes open, and it made him tired. He stopped trying and just sat. "*You can't go home again,*" came into his thoughts. It was something that Tessa had read in her lit class. But then, she was talking about herself and he did not understand what she meant. *Maybe this is like that,* he thought.

There is magic in the AC. How did it get there? The thought struck him hard enough to bring him into meditation. He sat quietly for half an hour. No answer emerged. Remembering Tessa here in his childhood *querencia*, he had the irrefutable sense that he was no longer a boy. After a while, he began the long climb home. *Querencia* was elsewhere.

His eight-year old sister Luisa took him to the porch for a "private chat," she called it. She brought him up to date on her school and her friends and asked him questions about his girlfriend. "She will be my sister you know." She asked him if it was okay if Rosa became hers and she told him she loved him and asked him to come see her more often. His heart filled with her earnestness; she reminded him of his mother and he held her for a long time. She did not want to separate when he finally let go.

His brother arrived later that afternoon. He was in a technical institute to learn automobile repair. He proudly reported that he would get a "paid" internship next year at age sixteen. His school was on the opposite side of the capital and with transportation being so infrequent in those days, he stayed with the family of a high school friend of his father's. The man was a lawyer, married well and living in an urban area. Guito could sense the boy's ready enthusiasm for city living.

But it was Aurelez who made the impression.

All *campesino* children are a little spoiled, but this one had an irrepressible aura going well beyond childhood willfulness. She was independent and able to amuse herself, but when she wanted Guito's attention there was no denying her. And she was smart. Taken with her directness, he saw a young Tessa and the thought moved him even closer to his little sister. When Monday morning arrived, she and Guito were bonded in a manner that he could not have imagined in Aguas Calientes.

Guiiito would remain her name for him for life.

The Letter

12 August 1984

He saw the letter before he turned onto the long path up to the *cabina*. It was a long white envelope like those the lawyer sent to his father. Someone had wedged it into the space between the door and the jam. It waited for him, cocked at a rakish angle; taunting him as he walked towards the door.

It was from, or about, Tessa, he was sure of that. *But why now...why a letter?* The answer came to him in his body, his throat began to dry, his tongue thickened. Step by step he made his way to the door, eyes riveted on the envelop. On the stoop he could not bring himself to reach for it.

This is stupid, he told himself. He unlocked the door allowing the letter to fall. He picked it up, dropped his pack just inside the door and walked to the table, opening it as he went. "Guito" was written in Tessa's script on the face of it.

"Guito," He spun. She was standing in the door. "I called to you as you were walking, but...."

"Tessa? ...Tessa, oh Tessa." She stood there as he walked to the door, took her hands and pulled her inside. His arms encircled her and pulled her close. Her hands reached only to his sides. "You are home early." He sensed the resistance but he could not pull himself away. The embrace ended when she pulled back, her face a misery.

"I do not want to hear this."

"I know...." She took a deep breath, her shoulders squared, looking into his face but avoiding his eyes. "But it is true, Guito. I've been with another man."

༄

All of her rehearsals took over; she spoke as if on automatic. Only the tearing in her eyes revealed her feelings, anguish in this case.

"Is that why you are back?"

"She shook her head "yes," and put her hand up to stop him saying more. "I'm back...early...." Her voice broke, the tears flowed, "because I thought I was pregnant." She gulped a breath, "And, he dumped me." The sobs came openly. One could not know if her anguish was due to her betrayal of Guito, or from being "dumped." She turned, sobbing and stumbled away from the cabin.

He stood in the doorway for a long time, the numbness left him unable to move. He held to the jam as if he might fall. In the morning, after a long night, he arose and called a number he had seen on the bulletin board of the grocery store. He bought the puppy for the asking price.

❧

Tessa picked up the puppy while she waited for Guito to open the door. It was an unthinking act, but its loving persona comforted her a little, as it did Guito. He opened the door, she took another deep breath, "Guito, I left yesterday without giving you an opportunity to say what you need to say…I'm ready."

"You are ready? Tell me what happened, Tessa." Dry lips clung together and his words caught in his throat. She hesitated but did not ask to come in; she put the puppy down. "I was working in a state park as a summer ranger. So was he. He is a graduate student in botany. We had a lot in common; we talked a lot. I was lonely...too lonely. There was a staff party...it just happened, Guito. We spent about two weeks together before he went back to school. He had a girlfriend there."

She hesitated; it looked as if he might speak. "I would give ten years of my life would it never have happened. I'm prepared to take the consequences."

"That's damned convenient for you. I'm not quite that ready...I wish I could brag about it." He placed both hands on the door jam as though blocking her entrance to the cabin.

"I'm sorry. I didn't mean it that way." Her little remaining confidence fled.

"Do you love him?"

"I thought I did...might have...at the time...I'm ashamed...I've shamed myself...and I'm sorry."

"I don't think forgiving is in the cards right now." He paused, "I don't know what to say...I can hardly think" The silence held, his thumbs flipped wildly back and forth on the door jam.

Perhaps it was her anger at herself that projected itself onto Guito. Perhaps it was simply an intuition, but she took his non-response as an angry stonewalling. In those peculiar ways that people find themselves responding under stress, this was not acceptable. *I deserve better* she thought, *you are not entitled to stonewall me.*

"God, Guito! Don't you.... *Didn't* you even love me enough to get mad? You always just *sit* there. Yell! Throw something. *Do something*!

"You are mad at *me*! Jesus, Tessa...you whore around, and *you* are mad at *me*!

"Whore around?" She whispered. Shock blanked her face.

"It's hard to love someone who dumps you...as I am finding out."

Their words stopped both of them. They stood there, glaring, for the short while that felt like an hour to each. She turned and left.

ಬ

Guito focused. In some ways his guide work was not dissimilar to the play he had used to distract himself from his father's disappointment. Work became a solace of sorts, as time in the *quebrada* had been. It was something he could *do*, something that could absorb all his waking time. Guito was something of a lead guide; now, perhaps he might have been called an informal "Dean" of the guides, as the corps of people doing so had increased each year with the increase in opportunity. He called a local young man who had expressed interest in learning to guide and began a series of discussions and co-guided tours. He found the man's enthusiasm and questions to be a comfort. The evenings were longer than ever; Rosa, the puppy, became his best friend.

He went to the homemade bookcase holding maybe thirty of Tessa's college paperbacks. All novel's and short stories, "Literature," she called it. On every trip home she brought five or six, sometimes more, books that had floated around her dorm or were assigned for classes. "I'm going to teach English she had said, "I have to read it. So should you." He selected one by an American writer from up north where they are snowed in all winter. *Maybe that accounts for the darkness,* he thought.

The book was about a man who had a successful career but had lost his wife. It caused Guito to rethink how he had spent his life. The man's thoughts so mirrored his own that he found himself sweating as he read it. Sometimes terrified, other times so caught up that he couldn't put it down. He began to dream about Tessa who was always with another man in the dream, and always laughing. Her image was always fuzzy but he knew it was her and he would wake up sweating and would tell himself over and over that it couldn't be her, *she was not callous*, and eventually he would fall back asleep. In other dreams he saw his father, with a younger man.

Guito would be there but they would give him tasks and both would shake their heads at his work. He left the book, unfinished, on the kitchen counter and one day it found its way back to the shelf.

Guito put the puppy on the floor of the *cabina* and turned so that his body was square with the table. He had drunk his last beer, the one that had sat in his refrigerator for months awaiting just the right moment. *This was that*, he was certain. Elbow on the table, his left hand supported his tilted head and his right played with the glass. His anger had taken on a life of its own, sitting side by side with an equally strong sense of loss. And the loss: not just Tessa, it was as though he had become unhinged from his life in the AC.

He had not gone to church for three weeks, certain that he would have to see her there. *Have I made a mistake? Was she trying to tell me she was sorry? That she had made a mistake? That she loved me more than anything?* But then the anger would makes its move and check his self-doubt into self-righteousness. *How...how...could she have done that?* The two feelings struggled for his full commitment. *It would be petty if she simply made a mistake.*

The beer did not help his ability to think, but it probably did not hurt either; such is the nature of the pain and anger twins. His attitude toward his father lingered near the front of his mind and it surprised him that he could sense irony. He had, to that point, been unwilling to accept any explanation for his father's behavior. *I'll come back to that if I ever get over this*, he thought. The three weeks had been one long struggle and he was vexed with his inability to get on with something...*anything other than this*. Vexation gradually took its place alongside the anger and the longing, competing for his attention.

Tessa's family reacted strongly but in different ways. Her oldest brother Tomás, refused to speak to her for a week, until his father took him for a walk. "We all make mistakes...she is your sister, and she has a lot of remorse. You don't have to like what she did...none of us do. She is your sister," he repeated. They could all see her sorrow even though she was often defensive. To outsiders, as a family they hung together; inside, they avoided testing her. At times she felt that they were avoiding her altogether. Only her mother would not relinquish.

"From the sound of it Tessa, you haven't given Guito a chance to get over it; he needs time."

"*He* needs time? He doesn't want *time*; he just wants to beat me up. I'm the one that needs time."

"What?"

"Not that Ma, you know Guito better than that…. He is mad at me and he can be…mean about it." She choked for a moment, "I don't want it."

At other times her mother would say, "I'm proud of the way you've been honest with this Tessa, it takes courage; we are all proud of you for that, but…." There would always be that "but," and Tessa would back away again.

She would leave the house and go to the little clearing that had been a playhouse, a fort, and club house, depending on her age and the friend, as she was growing up. Her confession to her family and to Guito had the odd effect of exonerating her to herself, so that she now directed her anger at others. But time passed and she became clear that what she had done was unacceptable to the Tessa she truly was.

It did not help, *didn't solve anything*, to realize that, and she remained in an angry, guilty confusion for weeks. As her anger transmuted itself, *I have ruined my entire life,* she thought, *Guito is a good man and he is gone. He said that he wasn't ready to talk about it. Did he mean, not ready yet, or never ready again?* At such times, and for a short while, she would allow her heart the freedom to ache with a pure pain, *pura dolor, for my stupidity*, she thought. During one of these times her mother found her.

"Tessa, I've been calling—Oh Honey." Her mother sat next to her and let her daughter cry in her lap without speaking.

                      ဢ

Tessa increased her efforts to get work at the school and accepted a volunteer position as an assistant teacher to try to get her mind "off it." *Hopefully, this will qualify as supervised teaching*, but that was just something she told herself.

No one, including herself, ever doubted that she would be a great teacher. She wanted to be influential in the lives of these children; she wanted good things for them. She had an impressive patience and could signal when the kids approached the end of it in a manner that affirmed them. She asked to make lesson plans and threw herself into subject matter. She looked for ways to make it fun. That was easy because she saw humor in almost every aspect of life except her own situation. The school saved her, as she later thought about it. It provided an emotional base, an equilibrium that served her in the following months.

꽃

In the fourth week, impatience with his state finally took over. *I can't live like this. I'm giving up my life.* Guito sighed through these thoughts and resolved to go back to church and recover his life, or to at least to find out what was possible to salvage. It was on that Friday that he met Tomás, Tessa's older brother and his girlfriend walking home from Palo Seco. Tomás said something to his *novia* and crossed to Guito's side while she waited. He offered Guito his hand,

"*Hola,* Guito... I'm sorry *amigo*...honestly...we all are. How are you doing?"

Guito considered passing it off as *Okay but it isn't, I'm not going to pretend about this*, he thought. "*Más o menos*, Tomás, it's hard...but I'm making it."

Tomás seemed to consider his answer. "I am disappointed Guito. All of us are, about everything." It was as close as he would come to being disloyal to his sister. "I hope we can be friends...that's true for our whole family."

"Thanks Tomás," Guito offered him a smile. They shook hands, "Thanks," he said again; he waved at Tomás' girlfriend and continued on. *What does that mean, 'true for our whole family?'*

Getting ready for church he had the same image as the day he got off the bus to meet his father, like he was jumping into a dangerous situation. *Buck up Guito,* he told himself. But it was one of Tessa's expressions and it had the opposite effect. But there was no turning back and as he trudged up the driveway in a misty rain, Churchgoers greeted him warmly. Some went out of their way to shake his hand and welcome him. People smiled as though glad to see him. Tessa was not there but her Mom was. She embraced him with moist eyes and for the first time he sensed that others may find the situation as hard as he. *That can't be; nothing for them could be this hard.* But his feeling was that the congregation folded him into itself, including her Mom. *How could I have thought anything else? I wasn't thinking at all,* was his answer.

The congregation was the first to know there was a problem between the two of them. But the community of *nacionales* was also small and word spread.

৪০

Her name was Flor. She smiled a lot and when she did, it made her ordinary face rather beautiful. She was in her mid-thirty's with an unusual shape for a woman. She was short. Her shoulders were broad and level as though she wore pads. They tapered down through an indiscernible waist, through her thighs to short but thin legs, her ankles improbably well formed. Stout, perhaps, but one would not call her fat. She was simply her unique, triangle self.

When he was feeling generous she reminded him of the tapered, stainless steel bottle stopper he had seen in a gift store. And at other times, a midget football running back. As far as anyone knew, she had never had a serious boyfriend. Those same "anyones" would agree that she was quite a nice person, a hard worker, and very protective of her younger brother who lived with their mother nearby. She spoke good English and the mystery of that intrigued Guito though he had never inquired.

Guito had seen her over the years at the soda where she worked occasionally, or at various stores around town, also working. The two of them were friendly; they even kidded each other and laughed from time to time. "Your English is *pachuco*," she would say. He had suspected that she was sweet on him, but people are often attracted to each other *without any complications* he told himself. *This is one of those things*. If she was flirting she did so in a deniable way.

He saw her unmistakable form on the side of the road as he drove Rajiv's Land Cruiser to the grocery store. It was almost dusk, no headlights yet. He slowed the car and eased up behind her so that she sensed his presence and turned around. A big smile illuminated her face. She stuck out her thumb, American style, for a ride. He reached over and opened the door from the inside. She, hitching up her short skirt to make the big step, climbed into the Land Cruiser.

"Hola, caballero." She said it with a faux elegance and a warm smile.

"Muy buenas tardes, senorita, to where may I deliver you?

"Now that you ask, how about my place?" And she turned half sideways to him, pressing her left knee against the back of the seat; thighs spread wide, her eyes bright, searching his face.

He looked at her, understanding her. He pulled the car forward ten meters and off the road into the parking area of a closed store. Both hands held the wheel, he looked straight ahead, then with measured breaths he looked at her. "I am sorry Flor...I can not do this. It is too soon."

Nothing was deniable now. Her only apparent choice was to withdraw, or to try to deny her offer, but his demeanor stopped her. He had not said "No" in a mean way, in a brusque way. He had said "not now." And he had said it with respect, as though he had given thought to her and really, for good reasons she could not know, could not love her now. A look of concern for him replaced the embarrassment that flashed across her face.

"Well Amigo, this is the story of my life."

She shifted in the seat, gave a little smile and tried to make it light but he knew she was speaking the truth. That knowing cracked his heart a smattering, as had hers; they sat there, open and frangible. He reached over and placed his hand on her shoulder; she draped her left arm over his arm, entwined and they sat for a while longer without speaking.

"I feel like a beer; maybe 20," he said finally, looking at her.

"Okay, cowboy," she said in English. "I just got paid, you're on."

In a small bar on a side street in Palo Seco they sat and talked for two hours. Most of the patrons were foreigners. Guito drank three beers, one more than he had ever had in a day. Flor matched him, paying for her own. She told him that she had lived in California where her father found work applying his trade as a backhoe operator.

Her younger brother was born with Downs's syndrome three years later when she was 15, and about a year after that her father and mother separated. "I guess he just couldn't handle the baby's problems." She said this matter-of-factly as though some people can handle them and some can't, no blame. *She is no victim*, he thought. Her mother had tried cleaning houses and waiting tables but eventually gave up and they returned. Flor, her mother and brother came to Palo Seco to get work. As far as she knew, her parents were still married.

She listened to his story about how he got here and about Tessa. She said only, "You still love her."

The fantasy began during his second beer. He remembered the way she got in the car and he began to imagine what it would be like to love this little woman. Everything about her was responsive and vulnerable. Her need for companionship, for touch, for sex, for all the things one calls love, stood in high relief for Guito. It called to his own longing, his own fear that he had been deprived forever. *God knows, I'm entitled,* he thought. *What would she feel like? How would she taste?* Flor moved her free hand so that the tips of her fingers rested on, and then played on his arm.

His fantasy ended as though the fingers flipped a switch. In a few moments the hand returned to the glass, then to a purse. It searched inside and withdrew a small pack of cigarettes, the stiff kind that holds ten *cigarillos*.

"You are surprised?"

"I haven't seen you smoke before."

"You've only seen me at work. And I only smoke when I'm drinking beer."

"The evil twins." He raised his glass.

"I won't if you don't want me to."

"No, suit yourself, everyone else is." It was true, a low smoke haze hung just above their heads. "I have never tried it; never been interested."

She fingered the little pack and left it unopened. They left after some less intense conversation.

He got out of the car when he took her home that night and held her, pulling away only when she began to rub the small of his back.

"Never hurts to ask," she said with a little smile.

"No, it does not...and has not."

She turned around to go in. He saw a small movement ahead then she stopped. Her back square to him; she looked straight ahead.

"I'm sorry, Guito."

"Flor, we are—." Her hand shot up flat then crumpled into a fist, he heard the in-breath.

"I don't know how to act around a nice man anymore. I am very sorry." She walked into the house.

ജ

On the drive back to the cabin, the car chose its own course. He scarcely watched the road; the jostling of the pothole strikes did not register and he made no effort to avoid them. Near the boundry of Palo Seco and Rododendros there was a clear view to the southwest and he pulled the car to side of the road. The engine stopped of its own accord. He realized that it quit after a few moments and turned the switch to douse the dashboard lights, then the headlights.

He could make out the glow of the capital and the smaller towns of the Great Valley stretching from east to the black hole of the Lake of the Valley. The villages and small towns that surrounded it continued west forming a tail along the Rio Vallejo. The river formed a highway of lights gradually disappearing somewhere out near the Western Sea He got out and walked around to the front of the truck and leaned against it like a man who had got to where he was going. Pleiades was headed toward the western horizon and he could see it clearly without lifting his head. He stared, remembering his surprise to learn it was a galaxy in itself and wondered about what things he didn't know, what things waited for him to discover them, and whether he wanted to. He felt the urge to descend to the lake and follow the light road to anywhere but here. After some time he got back in the land cruiser and headed it for the *cabina*.

He saw her almost as soon as the group emerged from the trees. She leaned, legs crossed against a large log in the area that would become parking spaces in a few years. Normally Guito made the trek with the group back to Palo Seco where most of them stayed. "Folks, this has been a real pleasure, I've really enjoyed our conversation but I need to leave you here today." This was true; his groups were always a pleasure, even the ones that had a "misanthrope" or two, as his college-student-girlfriend called them. *'Former' girlfriend*, he thought, watching her from the distance.

The group was disappointed and some said so but they gathered around thanking him, saying nice things about the experience. Several pressed money into his hands as they shook, mostly dollars. Guito slipped the money into his empty pocket without looking.

"Hello, Guito." She attempted to stand upright but one foot did not quite make it from behind the other, she stutter-stepped to catch herself; he reached to help her.

"Hi Tessa. I am sorry about the 'whoring' comment. It was not right." He spoke too quickly, while reaching for her. It felt awkward, uncool, and he blushed.

She hesitated, staring at his color, "You meant it though."

He expelled a breath and paused, "That makes it even less right...I am trying to apologize."

She looked at him as though gauging his sincerity. "Okay...we've been down enough rat holes already. I didn't come here for more of that."

Thank God, he thought.

"I'm sorry for what I said also. But... I'm through apologizing for the rest of it. What's done is done...I need to get on with my life."

"You have not had any trouble with that so far." He was grim. She said nothing; another few moments passed.

"I would like to take that back, I am sorry too, no more rat holes."

They started walking. He kicked a large clump of dried mud that turned out to be a rock, "Ow." *Not going well, at all,* he thought, *who cares? I don't need to impress her.*

"I went to church."

"I know. I'm going to start going Sundays again...Mom said I should speak to you."

Her Mom never gives up.

"My Mom never gives up."

We've been married too long. Unbidden, his mother's words simply filled his head. She never failed to say that when his father said something she had just been thinking. In spite of himself, he relaxed a little. "I was just thinking the same words." They both smiled. They walked in silence until near her home. "They still like me at church."

"That's a surprise? Lordy, Guito...what a dumb bunny thing to say." She shook her head, he looked flustered but smiled.

"'Dumb bunny,' he began a low chuckle, "*that* is funny."

She smiled and murmured, "I'm glad you took it that way, I didn't mean to criticize." She paused, "Mom said that the pastor asked her if he might be of help—between us—let's not make this that kind of problem."

"Okay with me.... What would he do anyway?"

"That's a topic for another day."

At her house, her Ma was sitting on the stoop shelling roasted peanuts. She smiled at both of them and leaned to one side so Tessa could go in.

"Goodbye," she said.

"Hi," Guito said, over a long exhale, to her Mom.

Guito watched her mother deftly removing the peanut from its shell. She squeezed the end opposite the stem so that the shell split neatly in half.

"You've done this before."

She smiled at him again and dumped her two most recent prizes from their cradle into his hand. "Once or twice."

"Did you get them here?"

"These came from some visitors."

"Is that legal?" But he saw that she was tearing.

"I'm sorry Guito." She gathered her apron full of shelled peas and went into the house.

∞

As his impatience with his condition grew, anger and longing receded into the background. One or the other would poke its head up to torture him from time to time but he was focused usually, looking for a way to get on with his life. They saw each other at church. Guito, when he could, began to go to the Wednesday night praise meetings also.

They ran into each other at other times. Neither ever had a partner. She was an assistant teacher and sometimes substitute taught social studies. She told him that it amazed her that some people were just not interested in history and geography. The anger faded first, followed not long after by the self-righteous stories they told themselves. As with the first time they got to know each other, there was no rush. Had they been thinking about what was happening it might have felt like forgiveness, the good kind, the kind that forgets or ignores any harm to themselves. Within the month, the only posture left standing for either was the longing.

❧

It was early fall in North America and the southward migrations were in full swing. The weather this Sunday was promising even though it was the height of the rainy season. Guito took his binoculars and notebook to church. Afterwards as he looked for birds uphill, towards the AC, Tessa and the two younger brothers approached from behind, on their way home.

"Hi, Guito," they said. They passed by him a few meters but Tessa paused and turned back. Her second brother took the youngest by the arm and picked up the pace. "Ow," he said but speeded up with the older boy.

"Hi, Guito," she said again.

"Hi, Tessa."

"Mind if I walk with you?"

He pursed his mouth; his head wobbled as if to say, *"Makes no difference to me."* They walked quietly, Guito pausing to check the trees from time to time.

"Mind if we talk?" She was looking at him sideways with a smile that said, *People do that you know.*

"Okay," he said and smiled at her.

"Is it possible for us to talk about 'it?'"

He had not seen this coming but now that it was here, it felt ordinary. He became less interested in birds. What little charge was left went promptly onto his mind shelf.

"Okay... what do we need to say about 'it?'"

"I don't know but we need to finish...be done with it."

"Amen to that." *This is pure Tessa.*

"Would you like me to go first?"

"Yes." *Pure Tessa.*

"I would like to tell you what happened…now that we are a little calmer…we are calmer, right?"

His look said, *you must be kidding*, but his dry mouth said, "Okay," with an audible sigh.

She heard it and paused, then went ahead. "I told you that there was a staff party and that he and I had talked a lot before that." She paused again waiting for his nod but he just kept plodding forward. "I had my first—and last—beer. We were dancing. All my loneliness and needs just came to the surface. There is no other way to say it." She paused again. "I told you before that I was through apologizing…but I was wrong about that. I *am* sorry, Guito. I am really, really sorry for what I did to us and to myself. What ever else may happen for us, I am asking you to forgive me."

"Needs," arrived with a bit of a jar, but it went quickly onto Guito's shelf. An image of Flor replaced it and the image stopped him until he realized that what he was seeing, was reminded of, was Flor's honesty and her courage. His heart opened a little. He turned to Tessa, his hands went up as though they might take her and then dropped to his sides. They went up again, he took her arms and pulled slightly, she came forward and they stood for a few moments, bodies closer. He turned to walk, using his hand on her arm to ease her forward as they moved on. She did not resist. "Is there more?"

"After the party I tried to recover myself, I tried to think of you but I couldn't get a clear image. It was like television snow. I had gotten myself confused and I told myself that I must have been confused about you and me. I told myself that we had been...just, some 'first love' kind of thing. But the confusion was in my condition...it *was* my condition." More distance passed beneath them. "I was trying to excuse myself." They walked further.

"It seemed like we were always apart...." Guito began, "When you said you were going to stay up north for the summer, I thought then that life would be good enough if I just had some of you...not too much, just enough to get by. I always knew that I loved you more, but I told myself that the holidays would be enough. It was my secret deal with you. So secret that I couldn't see it myself...and you couldn't know."

They walked a few more meters without speaking. "When all this happened...when you told me, I realized, I needed more than I thought." They walked on. "It wasn't fair to either of us, I'm sorry for that. I should have given you more of me, I should have insisted on more, risked more... to hold onto you."

"Please... please, don't take this on yourself." Her voice, grainy, flooded him with the image of her singing. "Even with all that has happened, even with all that I have just told you, I don't know how you could have ever thought that I didn't love you as much as you loved me...I loved you." She took a breath, intensity blanched her face, "I'm afraid I still do."

❦

They were married in the middle of the tropical summer, four months from that day. The country, with its official tolerance of religion, also has an official church and they were married again, two weeks later, by a priest. Eduardo and Alba came with Aurelez and Luisa to the first wedding. Their gift was a home automatic coffee maker, the first appliance of the type that many guests had ever seen. By the time the marriage was official, the couple was pregnant. They would have three daughters: Salome, Elizabeth, and Anaís. Guito was to name the boys "when and if."

It was residue as he thought of it years later. What had happened flamed brightly then burned itself out leaving a fine ash. It would seep into the spaces in and around the two of them, packing them tightly together as though their marriage was a container. More ash from other stresses accumulated, sifting, settling, becoming tamped down as they worked through those episodes. The ash, he thought, had enriched their marriage as it might the soil.

News

1987

In 1985, an insurgent leader of the UNRG, one of their several *comandantes,* nom de guerre: *Cólera,* shortened from, "Wrath of God," and supposedly an American citizen, made the news for alleged atrocities in the slum suburbs of a major city. He and his men were trapped in a building with hostages; their death or capture was imminent. The U.S. State Department issued press releases throughout the Americas to shore up support for the current policy.

There was no way to know if it was him, *not likely*, Guito thought, but the reminder put a lump in his throat that lasted for days. There was no follow up in the news. Tessa read the news also; she teared as she did. Guito thought the tears were for Sochi but they were for him.

In 1987, on a visit to her in-laws, Marisa went with them to the nearby refugee camp to bring blankets that had been collected locally. She said she had seen a man that looked like Sochi. In fact, she said she was sure it was him, "He scared me...but I did not run away." He had flat scar sweeping from his left ear under his chin. His beard almost covered it. Either she was mistaken or he ignored her, even when she had tried to grasp him.

Guito's feelings for Sochi, or whoever he might be now, resurged with the story. He focused. Glad at last, to have a clear mission. He found replacement tour guides for his groups and drove Rajiv's truck, now his, to the camp in the same week Marisa returned. He carried some extra clothes and a pillow for him to sleep on during the ride back. And, at the last minute, some beer, *just in case Sochi has changed back,* the thought made him smile.

The camp, designed only to intake people and determine their status, was full to overflowing at the time, nearly 1000 people. The national police patrolled and guarded it, loosely. He and his car were searched thoroughly and the camp administration required him to have an escort, "But everyone is busy." Guito solved that problem in the manner that "busyness" is handled in Central America. On the second and third days he was searched but no escort was required.

No one had been registered under a name that could be Sochi. He searched for as far back as the administration still had records. It took the whole first day to find and talk to those first. Afterwards he branched out, following leads from them. Walking, looking and talking for another two days, he saw no one that could have been his friend. Not everyone, he noted, could, or would, speak Spanish.

Displaced people from all over Central America had made their way there. He found some Xochiquetzales, no *Cólera*, not even a man with the scar. Some thought they may have seen such a man, but...*quien sabe*. Some people recognized the name, *Cólera* and tried to help, most of them trying to help themselves to a life outside the miserable camp.

He listened to the stories. Stories of violence, revenge, oppression, revenge again. There was no shortage of vengeance on either side. Most of the refugee stories were, in some way, self-serving.

They were no doubt true, but usually only what, "*They*...did to me, (my father, my mother, my sister)." From a female victim in another ethnic conflict years after, Guito would hear the expression, "The soldiers came and they...." *Yes*, he would think, *those days were like that*.

After the three days it felt finished. There was no Sochi. He went home. Marisa wept on his return and said that she could *not* have been mistaken. That night, Guito wept, for his friend and for all that he had heard.

Part 3

RIGO

Prólogo

Late 2004

It was far from the first time Rigoberto had met the *terciopelo,* and one would have had to know him well to detect the ruffle in his studied composure. It was the last snake he would kill before moving on to be a security guard in an upscale office mall. The pay was much more than what he was earning as a *peón*. Two, possibly three times as much with overtime.

This snake was *mansa,* he would tell his employer—passive—awaiting your approach rather than seeking you out. The *terciopelo* didn't move as he worked his way up the hill clearing the former pasture with the sun at his back. Laying aside the high grass with his *gancho* — a branch cut to an "L" shaped hook – he chopped it with one swing of the machete and tossed it aside in a single motion. The snake didn't move, blending with the brown-ness of the grass stubble and his shadow. When he did see, it coiled between his feet. The first throb had just reached his temples when a downward thrust of the machete ended the snake's life. He had killed countless snakes in his life and, at one time or the other, had found them in every room of his home. This was not a large viper but even with his rubber boots he knew there were no guarantees with these ladies. *That's how it is for the peon. Working the hillside with machete and stick,* Rigo thought, *machete and stick and snake.* He sighed, *It's not for me.*

I have been in this country approaching 20 years now and my use of the language is still inelegant, if even that is not bragging too much. But it is humbling to remember that Rigo worked for me for well over a year before I sensed that he was talking about two families, his birth family, about whom he said little, and his surrogate family. It is to this day, embarrassing to remember how long it took to figure out that Eduardo and Alba were not his real pa and ma. After I understood the basics, things came together and theses stories emerged, anecdote by anecdote over the next few years. I asked to meet his real family several times but he never found that convenient. He did tell me about his Aurelez experience, and when I told him I was writing stories, he became my primary supporter in talking with Eduardo. It was utterly obvious that the Eduardo trusted Rigo like a son.

Family

1994

Rigo grew up in the province next to Asturias. The province bordered the Great Western Sea but his home was in the foothills closest to Asturias. At 1000 feet above sea level with the combination of high humidity and low 90's, just standing up made the sweat run. The town, Paso Llano, had a plaza and a soccer field, with the church across from the eastern goal a part-time government clinic across from the other. The local police station, the municipal *palacio* and public telephone dominated one corner, and at the other three were bars. Almond and mango trees, the local crop, surrounded the plaza, with massive benches in between. A cop and an old lady talked on one corner, three unemployed men lounged around the bench at another. A single worker moved slowly around the square sweeping the sidewalk and picking up trash. If there were a competition for sleepiest town in the universe, Paso Llano would be a contender.

At 9:00 in the morning, one week before his fourteenth birthday and after having worked for three hours, Rigo found his father lying in a raked up pile of leaves, hay, and dry cow manure. Caught in the never-land of not quite asleep and not quite awake, his body was working through the homemade *guaro* from the night before. Rigo paused and stared at his father on his way to the front door. He paused, one could see his shoulders rise and fall with the breath. Like the final drop in a supersaturated solution, the certainty of Rigo's life on this farm crystallized. In that moment, his life, here, with these parents ended. He walked into the house, got his lucky cross, a plastic coffee mug with a picture of Harley motorcycles, his underwear, several shirts and his one sweater, and stuffed them into the tied off legs of another pair of jeans. He squeezed his mother's hand and said, "*Luego*." She teared. "*Te amo Rigoberto*." He tied his sweat-darkened leather machete scabbard, *lima* and knife to his waist with a cord and started walking up the mountain road toward San Diego.

Rigo's oldest brother, who had a small farm on the way up the mountain, caught up with him on horseback near the highway. He and the horse were breathing hard from the climb.

"I want you to go to Eduardo Ariza's farm, Rigo. Luisa just got married and left so there is room and work. Do you want a ride?" Jesús hesitated, drawing more air. He looked directly at Rigo trying to catch his eye as the horse backed a step then lowered her head to crop the grass. Rigo shook his head, started walking again, and then stopped and, looking for the first time at his oldest brother, said, "*Gracias,* Jesús."

The encounter left Rigo softened. *Jesús was trying to help me. No matter what happens, Jesús is family.* Bolting the house rode a wave of adrenalin that precluded reflection. Now, he thought of his good-bye to his mother—one could scarcely call it that—and regret pushed aside some of the gritty resolve.

He had, at least in recent months, defended himself from his father. It had been less than a year since his father had sought to strike him—again, but as the hand drew back, Rigo grabbed it and threw the man to the floor. No one present was shocked. He stood over his father for a moment, daring the man to get up. He didn't. The hitting stopped.

His mother had never struck him. She never even criticized him. It was what she didn't do. Without knowing the correct word for it, he understood her standing by, not defending him when he was smaller, as complicity. *Did she want him to hurt me?* Over time her passivity answered that question in his little boy mind. His reaction, which turned first to confusion, resolved itself in hurt and anger and grew into a barrier. And yet now, after all these years, he felt regret. He wished it had been different. *I must still love her*, fleeted through his mind before resolution reasserted itself.

Rigo could not believe that everything in life was good, but he was inexplicably an optimist. That optimism re-fired itself with his leaving. Something better was up there. He was sure of it and his stride resumed.

Years before, shortly after Jesús made his own stand, he had gone to work for Eduardo Ariza. After a few weeks of positive experience, an impressed Eduardo made Jesús the same offer he would make today to Rigo. Although Jesús often got home late or spent the night in Eduardo's barn, he could not fully break with his family. And he felt a responsibility to his younger siblings. It was Jesús who spoke to Don Eduardo about possibilities for Rigo after he heard of Rigo's stand. He asked if his youngest brother could work there,

"Should Rigo need to leave the house," he had said.

₹ා

Eduardo Ariza Aguero lived halfway between Paso Llano and San Diego. He stepped out onto the large porch as Rigo trudged up the flagstone walk, bordered with small flowerpots set in gravel, alongside the walk. The house was large with white stucco and set well off the road. It had a clay tile roof in the Spanish fashion. A deep veranda paved with shiny red Mexican tile graced the entire front and two sides. Sitting across the porch were brightly painted, chairs with a floral design on a white background. Large pots of flowers and small palms lined the edge of the porch.

Rigo did not notice any particular aspect of the setting, but the size, the color; the *neatness* of it all stopped him. He paused, looking at his feet.

When it appeared that the boy was not going to come closer without encouragement, Eduardo stepped off the porch and extended his hand.

"*Buenos días*, Rigoberto."

"*Buenos días*, Don Eduardo. My brother told me to...ah...stop by."

"We need some help, Rigo. There is a vacant room in the back– *la señora* will show you – put your things in there," he said pointing to the house. "She has some breakfast."

Rigo had left his home without thinking of food and his angst had propelled him for the two-hour walk up the mountain. He was hungry and wanted the food, but he felt too vulnerable to accept a room in the house. He struggled with the moment and, with an independence he didn't feel, independence fueled by the very fact of his unworthiness, he asked to make a space for himself in the *bodega*. Eduardo nodded, not quite yes or no, but said "Okay." Relieved, Rigo walked over to the barn. "Let me know when you are ready to eat, Rigo," called Eduardo.

Rigo had spent many nights in *bodegas* in his short life and this one had a familiar feel. He would spend three nights in the barn until Eduardo repeated his invitation.

"You can't work without a good night's sleep, Rigo."

" *Si señor*." So Rigo accepted his own room, a regular bed and the first hot shower he had ever had.

The house sat in the lower part of the farm. Further up the mountain towards San Diego, Eduardo's coffee farm bordered about 200 meters of the big fault. The whole area was unstable, and he rebuilt much of the house after a big quake. Eduardo Ariza owned over 350 hectares in mature plants and another 40 hectares of grasslands. By local farm standards it was huge, big enough that he felt he could afford to insist that his children finish high school and to allow them to move away if they wished. All except one had. Eduardo and his wife, Alba had four children, their two sons worked in other parts of the country and their eldest daughter was married with one "on the road," Doña Alba explained happily. The other, Aurelez, was in high school and lived at home.

Rigo ate every meal at the table with Eduardo, Alba and Aurelez. The meals were a revelation for the boy. The family ate slowly and talked about anything anyone was interested in. When Aurelez spoke her parents looked at her and listened as they did to each other. His own gobbling left him so embarrassed he resolved in that first meal to copy everything he saw. In spite of the respect shown, or perhaps because of it, he could not bring himself to enter the conversation.

During the first evening meal after Rigo moved into the house, Eduardo spoke to the boy.

"Rigo, I saw you carrying water to the horses today. Is there something wrong with the line?"

"The water is not arriving to the faucet, *Señor*. Perhaps...there is air in the hose...perhaps." Rigo took a deep breath.

"Most likely, can you fix it?"

"It is quite long, Don Eduardo. I think it will take two people to clear the line. Perhaps when the other *peón* comes in the morning, we can work on it, Don Eduardo."

"Very good...thank you. If you need help, let me know. I really need to replace that hose with a pipe, don't you think?"

Rigo again fell silent, struggling with a blush and the warmth of what felt like a compliment, yet unnerved by the open gaze and direct questions of his *patrón*. He tried, but could not remember ever being asked for an opinion.

Eduardo did not coddle the boy. He did what he said he would do, which was to work him for six to 10 hours per day depending on the rain. Rigo got no favors and worked as hard as any other man. Being treated equally with the other men felt good and an in-seeping pride began to overtake him. After three months Rigo was earning more money than he ever had, even with some for room and board withheld. In spite of his innate humility, he began to feel like the master of his own life.

Eventually Rigo became accustomed to the evenhanded directness and with having people pay attention to him. Over the next several years he would incorporate paying attention to others into his life repertoire. Eduardo would remain *"Don Eduardo"* to Rigo for his entire life, even after the older man sat insensate in a home for *ancianos* in San Diego de Asturias. For their part, Eduardo and his wife may have come to love Rigo but they never said so.

⟡

Aurelez was 13 when he arrived, and only a few months younger than Rigo. In high school she was thought of as a super-smart and unconventional student. Her birth mother had been available during a period that Eduardo and Alba were having a hard time. The two women still ignored each other. Aurelez inherited the steady gaze and directness of her father. Her fearlessness in saying what she thought, to almost anyone, often stunned Rigo.

In the *campo*, the time it takes for girls to become women can be short. In the tradition of isolated communities and a subsistence culture, no one paid much attention to the laws unless force was involved. Before the departure of her sister, Aurelez had been privy to the details of Louisa's two-year old, off and on again love affair. And she often imagined her own, yet unknown boyfriend. She had been pubescent for almost two years when

Rigo arrived and somewhere in those first months she fell in love with him. In her adolescent enthusiasm Aurelez judged his quietness as "macho," and there was nothing that Rigo could do or say that did not gain her rapt attention.

Everyone seemed to know except Rigo. The 20-year-old bus driver neighbor who had his own agenda for Aurelez sensed her attraction to Rigo and had become wary of the new *peón.* The neighbor started coming around the house in the afternoons about the same time Rigo retreated to his former bedroom, the *bodega,* for his alone time. There were some partly open hay bales among the larger stack that Eduardo kept for his horses and Rigo would often lie back to gaze at the rusted underside of the tin roof.

He was not melancholy, though a casual observer could easily think so. He alternated his time imagining he owned a farm like this one and a house with a deep porch and a rocking chair, with thinking about the work that needed doing on the farm. He had his anger. But his natural reticence to express any strong feeling and his unwavering acceptance of life as it came kept the intensity tamped down. In these moments he sensed that his life was in his mind and he believed that he could make life what he wanted just by changing his mind. In his optimism, the poor hand he had been dealt was just a problem to be solved rather than a life sentence. It was an odd confluence of prospects. In spite of his unlikely chances, he still thought at age 14, he could make what he wanted of his life.

"Leave Rigo to himself," was her mother's injunction. Aurelez did understand Rigo's preferences, but after a short period of leaving him alone, she had begun hanging around the *bodega* talking about anything she could think of. Rigo was always polite and sometimes conversational. When he got to know someone, his smile was quicker than most. Rigo did not dislike Aurelez—most of the time he enjoyed her visits—but he was consumed by a desire to do a good job for Eduardo and in thinking of his own future. Being nice to Aurelez was expected; it was respectful of his employer.

A couple of weeks into these visits the bus driver neighbor showed up and found Aurelez at the door of the *bodega* talking to Rigo. At first, she was coy with both of them, talking first to one and then the other. Suddenly mindful of her new mission, she stopped looking at the bus driver at all, focusing only on Rigo. It took the neighbor a few minutes, trying to reenter the conversation, to realize what was happening. Glaring at Rigo, he hesitated, but the boy did not rise to the challenge.

And then the neighbor not-so-lightly slapped Aurelez on the butt, turned and walked away laughing. She winced, looked at Rigo, blushed, and kept right on talking.

She looked at Rigo and blushed as though they shared a secret. The boy understood now and he reddened at the thought of it.

Rigo saw—and felt—the blush and warmed to the possibilities, but he sensed a threat to his new life. Still, he could not get over his new arousal regardless of any potential danger. He forced himself to make small talk until he recovered his normal "manly" composure. An hour passed and eventually Aurelez said "good night" and "*luego*," touching his hand lightly, and walked into the house alone. The loss of any opportunity that might have arisen with a less ambivalent boy did not dampen her enthusiasm. The touch, then watching her walk away, hips roiling, her neck curved and presenting her profile, fired an intensity the boy had never known.

Rigo was still a boy, but he was sure that loving Aurelez meant leaving his new life and the thought terrified him. When he returned to the house at dark, he was flooded with a danger-tuned lust. That night he kept imagining Aurelez' butt. For a youngster, hers was large but it accentuated a waist that otherwise might not have been there. Imagining Eduardo's reaction to his feelings frightened him and fear alternated with his visions of Aurelez and his uncontrollable arousal. He relieved himself imagining her and fell asleep in the early morning. He awoke still agitated and unsure that he had actually slept.

Rigo ate his usual warmed-over *empanada* and hot coffee and was at work before Eduardo's other *peón* arrived. Their work that day was to build a small calf corral, at some distance from the house. Rigo knew cattle. Although the other *peón* was a grown man, he, like most local men, was primarily a coffee worker, and he knew little cattle lore that Rigo did not already know. Except that the other *peón* acted like a know-it-all, Rigo liked the man. He made the effort that he knew Eduardo expected.

At 9:00 AM they walked back to a wooden table in the shade of a fichus tree near the house to eat the big breakfast of eggs, rice and beans and to rest. Rigo looked at the house and smiled broadly at Aurelez' waving from the door, then glanced at the other man to see if he had noticed. He had, but chose not to meet Rigo's gaze. He spent the rest of the workday in his nighttime fantasies except for tasks where paying attention meant keeping the fingers on one's hand.

Although younger, Aurelez had slightly more hands-on experience, as they say, than the boy who had none until meeting her. During the last Independence Day celebrations, following a lunchtime performance of traditional dances in the lobby of the National Bank, she had stood next to her older partner leaning against the high wooden sides of the pickup truck. She did not stop him when he nuzzled and kissed her neck and touched her breast with the back of his hand while he held on to the truck with his other. She gripped the sides of the truck tightly, closed her eyes, and smiled. Just before the truck pulled into the parking lot, he twisted his body and pushed his face into hers with an experienced, full mouth kiss. It made her happy, excited, when she thought about it. But nothing more happened until Rigo.

After a few months, Rigo had began taking weekend walks to the lower part of the farm where there were several small waterfalls in the creek. It was a strong stream that gushed from its clay bed just a kilometer uphill. There were deep, hidden pools even in the summer. Aurelez began to accompany him in the increasing desire for privacy that both felt. Except for watching for the snakes that also liked the coolness in hot weather, they were as carefree as Rigo could ever remember.

They held hands, nuzzling and giving each other little pecking kisses. When alone, they found ways to bump into or touch each other. The touching became familiar. One day, Aurelez splashed him from a pool and began a playful game that left her t-shirt soaked and her two small titties with their prominent round aureoles as visible as if she had no shirt at all. The boy was dizzy; he reached for her but she was already moving strongly towards him. They clung to each other through their soaked clothing and began kissing in a manner both had imagined for weeks. His hands found her butt and pulled, but she had already jammed her sex hard into his.

Sunset found them still walking uphill through the coffee. A brief rain delayed them under a tree and provided the excuse for wet clothes.

Rigo clasped her hand before resuming the climb, "I think I should talk with your father."

"About what?"

"About...us being...*novios*. It's time...*past* time, to get his permission; he *is* my *patrón*." That she did not immediately know his meaning unsettled him.

"I owe it to him," he said.

"I know you do...I guess. Let me think about it some more...you know, the best time." She shrugged off his hand and began to stride ahead of him.

She entered the house alone, through the back door. Rigo entered the front. Eduardo did not notice the late arrival. Alba, from the kitchen, noticed the time and the T-shirt but said nothing.

࿇

Aurelez showed up the next afternoon wearing lipstick, little faux gem earrings and a frock that hung loosely from two straps over her shoulders. The frock made a walk through coffee impractical, but the urgency of the moment made it irrelevant.

With her greater sensibility to such things, Eduardo's wife, Alba, alerted him to "developments" when he returned from his errands.

"Eduardo," she said, "I think you should go out to the *bodega* and see if everything is okay."

By the time Eduardo peered in the *bodega* the straps of the frock had dropped from her shoulders and Rigo was vigorously massaging Aurelez' left breast in his mouth. His still-in-his-jeans erection undulated firmly against her extended leg; his left hand under her dress. Seemingly unsurprised, Eduardo stood in the doorway saying nothing for several seconds. Aurelez noticed first, swallowed a small shriek and grabbed for the straps. Rigo rose to an elbow so quickly he slammed backward against the wall of the *bodega*, still too caught up in lust to be properly terrified.

That night, Rigo feigned lack of appetite to avoid the dinner table. Subsequent dinners were strained affairs in spite of the parents' lame attempts at conversation. Both Aurelez and Rigo left the table as soon as it was possible to do so. Unsure how these things might be handled, Rigo waited for the firing. He called his brother from the public phone on the highway to ask if he could stay there. His brother agreed but would not comment on the predicament. "It's up to you, Rigo," he said.

After a week Rigo began to relax, and after two weeks he could engage Eduardo in normal if less familiar conversation. Apparently Eduardo had said a lot to Aurelez because she avoided looking directly at Rigo. He at first imagined that she might fly to him and that they would leave the farm for an unknown life together. But that thought so filled him with dread that he became cold. His life long fallback was to accept that he had done something wrong but now that it was done, he didn't know what it was. Part of him was relieved at being ignored and part of him cried out for her to look at him, to tell him she loved him still.

Rigo had unknowingly leaned against the secret panel of childhood. The wall of life gave way and he fell through into another reality. Nothing he knew for certain now made any sense. He wanted Aurelez and was afraid of her. Although he thought he might still have his job, for the life of him, he didn't know why. He had given his heart to Aurelez in spite of the danger and she broke it by ignoring him. The boy was on his own. And he was thoroughly lost.

Aurelez had her own epiphany. Suddenly life was complicated and threatening. Safety required stratagem and deceit and standing up for your self. To figure it all out, she fled after school to her natural mother who seemed to understand life's complexity and what one's options were. She always returned at night but she came back having learned to keep her thoughts to herself, to anticipate the motives of others and not to bare her heart.

And Aurelez acted. She stopped speaking to her father at all and became diffident with her mother. She only saw Eduardo's single-minded blame and in mounting resentment of her father's attitude, her imagination shifted from the loss of Rigo to thoughts of the proper punishment for Eduardo and Alba.

Revenge

Late 1994

"Eduardo, you are being too hard on Aurelez. It takes two to tango" Alba said. He knew this, but he could not help himself. His reactivity arose every time he was in Aurelez presence and he remained critical of her to the point that she talked as though she hated him. The perversity was that Eduardo felt remorseful when he thought about his behavior. In moments of clarity, he did not doubt that he would pay for his unfairness. Guito's reaction to him flitted through his mind but to no effect on his behavior.

"It takes two to tango." That was as close as Alba came to suggesting that Eduardo's hypocrisy was showing. Neither she nor he wanted to revisit those days. But Eduardo persisted with his daughter. Three months into his unreasonableness, Alba heard him say something to Aurelez and a door slam. He came into the kitchen.

Alba put a cup of hot coffee on the table, and pointed to a chair. He looked at her and sat down.

"Chico, this has gone on long enough, too long...."

"Alba...." Looking down, he shook his head in disagreement.

"No-Eduardo-this-will-end."   Each   word threaded onto a steel rod. His head jerked up, mouth agape, staring at her. Threat filled the space between them. They were quiet for several minutes, his index finger played with the handle of the cup. He looked at it, and the door, and back to the cup. He took a sip, then a deep breath. Only a small portion escaped. She leaned backwards against the counter and gazed at him, not with hatred.

"Eduardo, Aurelez is a teenage girl. She did what girls do; don't you remember us? Me?" She said this in earnest, as though he might not. He gave a little snort and his head jerked again, as though the image had slapped his head. He pursed his lips; the corners turned up slightly. He glanced at her. "Aurelez would never be denied, even as a baby...remember the day she met Guiiito?" She drew his name out. "She has always been different." Eduardo's smile developed.

"Yes...but I asked your Pa for permission."

"The expression is 'to ask to enter.' It means the house, not me. You were a little devious." She smiled. He stared and then laughed. Alba laughed. She had an earthy sense of humor but the bawdiness surprised both of them.

"Your *papás* were not born yesterday."

"Neither were we." They were silent again.

"And Rigo?"

"Rigo is almost a man. God knows he works like a man. And men are," she gave a little sideways nod, "men." She took a deep breath to get it out. "If only he had talked with you first, things might—." Eduardo's face blanched, he looked away. "Things might have been different." She finished, her voice quieter.

"Rigo is the son I should have had." He said hoarsely.

The other *peon* had noticed the drop in interaction and was mouthier, teasing Rigo in an unwanted manner when they were working alone. It stopped when he grabbed the man's arm and holding it firmly while looking in his eyes said, *"Esta bien,"* as though to say, *"That's enough."* The grip lasted only a moment, then Rigo relaxed and gave him a little smile.

During the month after being caught, Rigo spent a lot of time in the *bodega*. As his fear of losing his new life subsided, another fear flooded him with a dull and confusing ache. He guessed that he loved her. He missed her affection, physical and otherwise. He thought he was lucky anyway to have loved her and to have felt her love in return, and to still have his new life.

It could be understood simply as, "So close and yet so far." But when one understands his certainty that he had missed his *only* chance for love, that no one would ever love him again as Aurelez did, the boy's angst becomes vivid. The alternate pain and relief left him jumpy. Anything unexpected now created a sense of panic. He watched Eduardo when the *patron* was not looking, trying to anticipate what might come next.

He was certain that this girl's love was more important to him than he had known and that added to his confusion. He found himself staring numbly at the rusted ceiling of the *bodega*. Near the end of that month, Rigo saw Aurelez dressed up in the frock on a Saturday afternoon headed, he assumed, to meet young people in the local square. That sub-second intuition stopped his breath as though he had taken a blow to the chest.

It took the entire afternoon in the *bodega* to resolve the fresh anguish by reminding himself that what *had* happened was what was *going* to happen, and that that was the end of it. There was no going back. Over several low hours—the nadir of this particular passage—relief returned to him as a slow-rising tide of warm water, lapping at his feet and legs, rising over his chest. His heart quieted. He became settled again. Within a couple of days the cold sore that had plagued him off and on throughout childhood, disappeared.

A few days later Rigo was in the *bodega* making a rope halter when Eduardo approached him with a paper in his hand. He waited for Rigo to look up. When Rigo noticed, he glanced at Eduardo's face and looked back to the knot, his hands still.

"Don Eduardo...I'm sorry."

Eduardo cleared his throat, "It's over, son," he said, turned and walked away.

Rigo continued to live at the house and eventually they became friends. Once the shaming stopped and Aurelez had made her own decision about Rigo, she became tolerable. She became pregnant at 16, with a man, whose name and marital status remained unknown to her parents until too much *guaro* loosened his tongue at a neighbor's Christmas party.

She continued high school and finished that same year. Her parents accepted the child into their home without question, and they loved and cared for the little boy as she continued school. The father paid a minimal child support and paid it on time for a few months. Payments became uncertain after that, but Eduardo refused to speak with him.

When Rigo heard that the child would be a boy, he asked her to name him "Rigoberto," but Aurelez laughed at him, certain that he was joking. He wasn't, but he forgave her and let it go. Rigo became "Uncle Rigo" to the little boy and he gave him as much attention and affection as any member of the family.

When she heard about the impending birth, her birth mother scolded Aurelez in a manner she judged as hypocritical. "A little strange for the mother of Aurelez, don't you think?" were her exact words and her mother said nothing more about pregnant girls without husbands.

Carmen

1998-2004

By the time Rigo met Carmen, his first real girlfriend, he knew a lot about cattle from his first life and a lot about coffee from his second. He was slender with broad shoulders and gentle, even delicate hands. He was still quiet and mostly stayed away from girls except for a couple of local *señoritas* who knew how to make shy men less so, and about whom he was free to talk if the other men got into talking about women. In those days, an open, informal kind of prostitution was an accepted solution to a number of rural pressures.

Carmen was 15 and he was 18. They were off and on, but when they were on they were inseparable. Carmen had a strong religious conviction that would eventually return Rigo to the Holy Mother. Although he was now the experienced partner, she placed limits on how far she would go and later could truthfully say–and did–that she was a good girl until she was married. When she turned 16 they married in the church. With moral support from Eduardo and Alba, she had insisted on a real marriage. Rigo did not object, although he knew that his friends rarely bothered. His main reservation was a remnant attitude from adolescence that a real *peón* never married the mother of his first child, even though he knew that this wasn't strictly true. In truth, he loved Carmen; he was sure of that. But marriage would unexpectedly change his reticence with women. It was as though finding a permanent solution to the problem of being loved had created a perverse license.

Rigo was determined to live a better, more predictable life like Eduardo. It was an attitude that matched Carmen's and she loved him for it. He saved his money, lived on little, and was the key to the local soccer club offense. He took a job with the Gringo and with his new wealth, he bought a motorcycle and began to wear a bandana tied over his head like the riders on his plastic coffee cup. The bike terrified Carmen, but she would ride with him when he asked. "It is economical," he told her. That argument sufficed because she also wanted to save for a more secure and better life. And her trust in Rigo was total.

It was to Don Eduardo and Doña Alba's house that Rigo brought Carmen and introduced her to them like family. After the wedding, he bought, with Don Eduardo's help, a small piece of property sufficient to qualify for the government subsidy for a house. Rigo and Eduardo's other *peón,* with Eduardo's help, built it.

Even though Rigo no longer worked for Don Eduardo, he and Carmen often visited on Sundays. With Aurelez studying in San Jose, the couple split Sunday visits between Eduardo and Alba and Carmen's parents. They met Aurelez' next oldest brother and sister, but the oldest brother lived too far away, and Alba always told Rigo when Aurelez would visit so Carmen never met her.

Their first baby died in the womb at six months. Carmen's heartache turned to agony when she delivered the stillborn. It was a boy. Church became an even greater part of her life and she confessed weekly. For months she refused sex with Rigo or was merely compliant. In exasperation, Rigo became angry, accusing her of frigidity. His frankness was often brutal and she responded with her own self-righteous attacks. Her response often took the form of blame for his Christian inadequacy. He was not yet reconciled to the Church but her attacks stung deeply. After a few years of off and on distress, he took a job on a ranch on the western coast. The distance meant that he had to stay in a barracks provided by his employer.

Five nights a week, every week, away from Carmen was enough for Rigo to discover girlfriends. The nearest large town was a port, at one time quite important. Nowadays the economy revolved around local fishing but the love-for-cash tradition of the port still thrived.

Rigo's ethic was that he was above buying sex directly. His preference was to seduce a woman, even speaking to her parents if necessary, so that she fell in love with him. Carmen met his larger need for being loved, but it could not requite his constant, daily requirement to be cherished, and to be told every day that he was indeed, lovable. Sex was important but Rigo's love deficit was deep and misunderstood by all, most especially him. It was as though Carmen's love was the backstop, a safety net that allowed him to take chances with other women—and their ex-boyfriends and their fathers. The practice, once begun, continued even after Carmen's pleading brought him back to Asturias.

❧

At age 20, after the health problems and just poor timing, Carmen delivered Anna Rosa. She immediately became Anita. They had two other babies in quick succession before they decided that three was family enough.

As Rigo settled into the life of a man with a responsibility-filled future, an old resentment about his lack of opportunity to go to high school returned to haunt him. By the time his oldest sister had been born, home finances had deteriorated to the point that there was no money for uniforms or books. He had often thought of his play with the soccer club as a consolation prize for not going to high school. Quitting the team had held a special pain for him and he put off his departure for far too long. Carmen had also been taken out of school after the mandatory sixth grade, and while she had her dreams, she seemed to find her life more complete than the deficit that dogged Rigo.

He, with great effort, read a self-improvement book loaned to him by his aunt, who bought used books in the capital. It was she who found the lot on which Rigo would build their house. Rigo could barely remember having met her before, but she became an important neighbor and source of books in the years to come.

The unfamiliar words in his aunt's books slowed his reading but what Rigo found hooked him so thoroughly that he managed to find a half hour or so on most days. It was tiring although he occasionally came across passages that thrilled him with their familiarity. When Paulo Coelho wrote that "There are no tragedies, only the unavoidable," he knew that he had believed this all of his life. The recognition left him wanting more and more confirmation. He was sure these books contained the solution to some yet unknown obstacle to achieving his dreams. In his searching through one of them he discovered the book's index, an "aha" of no small proportion.

His Aunt was in their house several times each week. When she left she always said, "Peace be with you." To Rigo, this was just the way his aunt said goodbye, but Carmen, with her much greater time in Church, knew that it was a shortened form of "May the peace of God be with you."

They sat down to dinner as soon as she had left. She asked him, "How did your aunt get so religious? She's not even Catholic."

"There is a story behind it." Rigo knew the story and he was certain of Carmen's reaction; it would be one of the few ways that she could be upset. He had learned the story from his brother who had also reminded him to "let bygones be bygone." But the story persisted. He turned in his chair and draped his free arm over the back of it. Carmen folded her hands and leaned on both elbows, waiting for him.

"Jesús is the one who told me this. She is, or was, my father's "pretty" sister, younger than him.

When she was 19, a neighbor spread the rumor that she went to a bar in the capital on Fridays and sold herself to foreigners."

"No...oh no." Carmen dropped her hands flat to the table, her mouth gaped.

"That's what people said Carmi. I can't say if it's true or not, neither can Jesús. Anyway, it was bad for her for a long time. She finally decided that what the neighbors were saying was a problem with the Church."

"De-ver-dad?" He glanced at her but returned his gaze to window. The Christmas winds gusted outside; he spoke more loudly.

Don't ask me how...or why. She went down to the evangelical church in Paso Llano and never came back."

"She is going straight to Hell unless she can find her way back!" Carmen leaned back and crossed her arms, still staring.

Rigo smiled, looking at her for the first time, "Maybe so. But no one in my family seemed to care since my mother was the only one besides my Aunt who ever set foot in a church. It made a fuss because my Aunt used to teach the Catechism."

"Well, she's wrong," her voice flat, "but I trust her, especially with the kids." She began to eat.

Rigo's reading surprised Carmen who was not interested in such things, but she found in it a new source of respect for her husband. She once spent the afternoon in bookstores near the hospital in the capital looking for such books, but only found new ones that would have cost a week's earnings. That was too much for a book even if she was sure that she could have picked one Rigo liked. She did try but she could not get interested in his discussions of what he had read, especially when they seemed to contradict the Truth that she felt she did understand. In these moments she heard herself saying, *"De verdad?"* and soon Rigo stopped talking to her about the books.

Part 4

Aurelez

Prólogo

1997

"Welfare mother! ...Welfare mother!" The words choked out through a shriek. She picked up the baby and stalked from the house.

Her anger lasted for days, but Aurelez knew what her natural mother was talking about. Aurelez and a few other girls with babies, remained in high school, at least in part, to get the stipend, the *beca* as they called it, from the government. Aurelez got it also even though Eduardo saw to it that she and the baby wanted for nothing. One of the extra bedrooms was turned into a nursery.

Most mothers did not surrender the *beca* to their parents with whom they continued to live. They spent most of it on the baby and the rest went to a combination of savings and self-indulgence. Combined with the generally small support *pension* that they got from the fathers, it was good money. But it was the most that they would ever get as the *beca* ended with termination of high school and the father's support could be uncertain. For some, drawing out the length of attendance had become an art form. Her girlfriends had explained the facts of life, as they understood them. They told Aurelez that the money from the baby's father, would become uncertain if she ever stopped having sex with him. *Why doesn't someone tell you these things sooner*? She fumed. When she was feeling strong she could see the humor in her own rumination. This was not one of those days.

She had hidden from her self-inflicted reality until her mother lashed her with "welfare mother." Now she saw her future searching for someone to take care of her, as were the other mothers of her age. By the twenties, thirties at the latest, they were either desperate or resigned. Some worked cleaning houses or in retail; good career jobs were uncommon. Some found a real marriage; very few found the love or the security that they wanted. None, not one, of these options was acceptable to

Aurelez now that she was forced to think about it. Understanding her own needs this early had required that her natural mother slap her with a prognosis for her life. Her reaction was anger, which yielded to depression, yielding to determination. *Not me. Not this girl.*

She applied for admission to the National University. She was accepted in the fast track admissions program and began early, as soon as she graduated high school. Eduardo and Alba cared for the little boy.

Roommate

1998-2002

Aurelez bolted out of the *campo* and into University. By her own admission, she would be a somewhat less than excellent mother during those first few years. But things were changing faster for her than for the usual student her age. Her roommate was Luisa, a girl that had gone to a private international school taught in English.

"Well hello, girlfriend." Luisa was already in the room and stuck out her hand as Aurelez appeared at the door. "I'm Luisa Ciani Marin, and you are...?"

"Aurelez.... Ariza Valverde." She added as she took Luisa's hand.

"I took the bed by the window, hope that's OK with you."

"Can we speak Spanish, my English is not too good."

"Sure, so we are new best friends; put your stuff down and let's talk."

"Whew! Are you *nacional*?"

"The Marin part," Luisa grinned, "but half of me is New York, and that half is pretty much Italian."

"Well, I'm from Asturias and it's pretty much coffee and cows."

"You think?" Luisa grinned.

"What do you mean?"

"With a name like Aurelez? I grew up in Pinto and I never even heard that name before."

Aurelez dropped to the empty bed. She put her hands on her knees and looked directly at Luisa for a long moment. "Can we slow this down...*girlfriend*?" They looked at each other and began to giggle.

"Yeah sorry," she looked not quite sheepish. "Did I mention New York?"

The two talked until lunch, then left and went to the student cafeteria together. Aurelez told Luisa about her family, except about the baby. Luisa said her father had come to the country with the Peace Corps. He had met her mother here and after brief return home, came back and they married. Her New York family's business was importing and her father said it was too, "dog-eat-dog" for him. The family agreed and financed a small but fancy hotel on the slopes of one of the Aguas Calientes volcanoes. She "just loved" her American aunts and uncles and went to New York several times a year. Luisa's mother's family was already in the hospitality business and provided training and support so the hotel had prospered.

They talked as they were going to sleep that first night. Luisa told her that she had stayed in high school an extra year to get her grades up. The university that the women members of her family attended was "one of the Seven Sisters." But she had not been accepted.

"That's why I'm starting early, to try and get some grades. Have you got a boyfriend?" Luisa asked.

"Not anymore."

"Me neither."

It was as though the Gods that put people in each other's lives had offered each of the girls her match.

Tomorrow was registration.

❧

"Guito, I want to talk with you about Aurelez." He had just walked into the *cabina* and was sniffing, following the coffee aroma, when Tessa stopped him. "I just put a pot on."

"What about."

"I'll get to that. But I've been thinking a lot since we got back from Mother's Day at your folks. You know, Aurelez was the baby; she never got to see her mother raise a child like me or her older sister."

"That's right—."

"Well, there's a lot she never learned. I was seven when José David was born, I got to help mama with my younger brother."

"You think she is not a good mother."

"Not as good as she needs to be, *mi amor*. She's going to regret it someday.... I think you know that." The pause held.

Guito sighed as though releasing a held breath. "I know it, honey...It pained me to watch last week. Ma is raising Chiquito all by herself. It is not good.... I wonder why we are just now talking about it."

"I want to bring her and the baby here for the long Christmas break"

"It would be pretty tight in this house."

"We could do it. But my folks have lots of room in their place. Only one of my brother's will be back. My Ma would be great. Even when I was finishing university Ma insisted that I spend as much time as possible with Salomé."

"You did not need much coaching Honey. How do you think Aurelez will get along with your Pa? She can be kind of ornery."

She smiled. "I needed more coaching than you remember. That last year of college was hard, back and forth all the time. You know how many times I put Salomé off on you. You loved it and you're blocking on the way I was then. Anyway, Aurelez and Papa will be either a raving success or a raving disaster, I'll speak to him about the teasing."

"I put it at fifty-fifty." He chuckled, "This is a good idea. I could go down and get her, the ride back would give us a chance to talk."

"It would, but I've been thinking about that too—."

Guito gave her his "duh," look.

"You know most young mothers would have to take the bus—baby, bag, food, the whole nine yards. It's a pain and something *could* go wrong, but I think it would do her good to really have to look after Chiquito, to be thinking about what happens to him every minute. She might learn something about herself."

"She might do it but she would be tired and upset when she gets here."

"For sure," she searched Guito's face, "but it's time for her to grow up, just a little more quickly." She put her hand on his. He was calm, watching her face. "Anyway, she's got a phone card if she needs our help. I'm sure big brother will be on standby while she's traveling."

He nodded "Okay. Her grades should come out over the break. That should tell us how serious she is." He paused, "Who makes the call?"

"I'll invite Aurelez so she knows I really want her here. You make sure your folks are okay with her making the trip alone."

જી

Aurelez did agree. In part, to have a reason to refuse a holiday visit with Luisa's family. She liked Luisa—really liked her, but she had not told her about the baby.

And she was tired when she arrived, disheveled, the baby sound asleep and a dead weight. The trip was hard: changing shitty diapers, dragging the bag between busses, keeping Chiquito fed and happy. He was already crawling and being in the chest-carrier all day made him cranky. The odor from the prolific little boy was just below her nose. Her seatmates looked distressed and that made her feel guilty and incompetent—until it made her angry. And that made things worse. But the trip turned into a good story and she told it many times to herself and others. She would often referred to him as the little 'poop king,' and while the story got exceedingly old by the time he was a teenager, it was one of the many ways the little boy learned how much his mother loved him.

Aurelez' relationship with her brother's father-in-law was a raving success. Dinners became a repartee between the two that no one wanted to miss. And her English improved. Her first semester grades turned out to be three A's, a B+ and a B. "I'll do better," she told them.

※

"Luisa, I have a baby boy, I'm sorry I didn't tell you sooner." They weren't the first words out of her mouth, but pretty close to the first.

"De-ver-dad."

"Ver-dad."

"So...that's why you go home on weekends, why you didn't come visit. Well, girlfriend, what's my little nephew's name?"

"You're not shocked?"

"Oh girlfriend, you don't know 'shocked' from a chicken empanada. What's my little *sobrinitos* name?"

"Eduardo, but we call him Chiquito." Aurelez had her father's wide mouth and it tried to split itself with a grin.

"Okay, girlfriend...it's come-to-Jesus time." She hesitated, "I should have had a baby." She watched Aurelez.

Aurelez watched her back, expecting more but there was no more. It took a moment for the locked eyes to communicate. The grin fled; she dropped into a chair, "No."

"Yes. Remember? New York? I told you you didn't know 'shocked from an empanada.'" The moment resulted in a closeness that neither expected.

❧

With Luisa's family's recent response to a capital campaign, she might have been accepted to Barnard at the end of that first year, but she did not apply. The two women shared an apartment thereafter.

By the time Aurelez entered her sophomore year she had established herself as an A student. Her advisor heard her ambition and encouraged her to think of medical school. The sheer audacity of it fired Aurelez' imagination. After several weeks of thinking about it she riveted the goal to her vision of the future. She would be a doctor. That same advisor approved her request to take a junior level psychology class out of sequence. There was no suspense in the approval; her advisor routinely approved all but the most outrageous requests from her ward. The class was taught by Jack Cochran, a tall, spare American who once told his students that he, "hailed from the state of Montana," during an unusually candid lecture. His wife was Central American and his idiom was polished yet un-stuffy, sounding more upper class Mexican or perhaps like a Castilian businessman. He was often the object of his student's transference and he knew it. He maintained a scrupulous distance.

She was hustling to take an armload of overdue books to the library. Passing an outdoor Mexican restaurant that served as a café in the day and a bar at night, she saw Jack Cochran reading the paper at one of the outdoor tables. "Dr. Cokran, hello."

He looked up, smiled and said, "*Coch*-ran, with an "Ahh" sound. Good day Miss Ariza. Headed for class?"

"No, the library. I have a question for you, if you have time."

He nodded tentatively; the smile left. "Perhaps."

"The other day in class you said that the big, the first, distinction between belief systems was the nature of reality. What does that mean exactly?"

He hesitated, the smile returned, he gave small chuckle, then folding his paper and placing his hands on the armrests, he scooted himself more upright. "Okay Miss Ariza, I do have some time. Care for a coffee?"

She sat down placing the stack of books on the table between him and her. "They might be safer on the floor." She put them down, dropping them the last four inches.

He smiled wryly at the gesture. "Have I explained what a paradigm is to your class?"

She shook a no, "But I know what it is."

"The reason it is important to your answer is that, the difference lies in two different paradigms, which as you know are broad sets of assumptions about what the world is really like. If you live in one paradigm you can't see the other and vice versa. One paradigm is rooted in the belief that reality is what we see – the material world. Another is that the material world is created by, for example, projection, and is therefore not real at all. So the first cut is, what 'reality,' is one's beliefs based on. The choice can lead to very different cultures, rules, behaviors, actions etc."

She had never met anyone who talked like this. "Who believes the second idea? The Church? They are always talking about the 'mystery' that nobody can see." She had little use for priests.

"No, the Church is firmly grounded in the material world in spite of dogma. The big problem for the Church is trying to explain how they can be grounded in materialism and yet purport a reality that is spiritual or non-material. The religions, most of them, end up having to use a device called 'faith.' And that faith has to be faith in an external entity that can do unusual things like God can. Otherwise, the story falls apart." He took a sip of coffee and watched her.

'And they need a Devil to explain the rest."

"Yep. Both are real yet both are mysterious. It's a kind of highbrow materialism. They have to insist that the non-material elements of dogma are observable fact, in other words, material, like the virgin birth, the resurrection, the earth created in seven days—that sort of thing. The same is true of most religions by the way, not just your Church."

"Well, who believes in the other reality then?"

"You mean, whose reality *is* the other reality?"

"OK, that." *Small point— very small*, she thought. He acted as though his job was to teach her the questions she should have asked, *annoying*. The discussion continued a while longer until she realized that she was running out of time to drop the books off and get to class. *Not likely this is going to be on the exam...still, interesting.* He had said at one point that one cannot be convinced to change paradigms by "intellectual understanding alone." *What's the point of going to university then?* He was a curious man.

In addition to becoming aware of her own transference in that class, Aurelez was so enamored of Jack Cochran's presentation of psychology that she began to form the possibility of psychiatry as a specialty. Cochran, as it turned out, was a clinician rather than the more usual social psychologist, and he did not often teach at the undergraduate level. It was an onerous duty

within the department and all full professors
shared the burden. Some, like Cochran, saw it as a
renewal or a re-grounding opportunity. She
undertook his extra credit assignment to write a
personal "theory of personality," and was humbled
by both the difficulty of the project and the B
grade. The assignment resulted in a mere A for the
course. Dr. Cochran was helpful by giving precise
feedback, he was even sympathetic yet unrelenting
in his grade when she wheedled him.

Jack Cochran provided one other boon to
Aurelez before she entered med school. In that
same year she took his class she wrote a short
story for a literature class. The story obtained her
usual grade but it continued to nag her. She asked
Jack Cochran to read it and an outline she had
prepared for a book based on it. His feedback was
as usual, precise, and in this case, supportive of the
idea for a book. "Psychiatry," he said, looking at
her as he terminated their last discussion.

She picked up her books to leave, "Is there
anything else I should think about?"

"You might try to be a little less solipsistic."

"What does that mean?"

"Look it up Miss Ariza." He turned back to his
desk.

At the door she stopped and looked back, "You
are really not going to tell me are you?"

She saw his shoulders rise and fall; he looked at the wall and then half turned to her. "Your protagonist, Laura, she is all tied up in her underware, so to speak. We know nothing of César, how he sees the world, women—nothing. Laura is interesting to a psychologist, especially if he were billing, but if you write the book you will have room to develop César's character more. Try that." And he turned back to his deskwork.

"Thanks Dr. Cokran." He shook his head and sighed.

Later, after she was a licensed psychiatrist, he would tell Aurelez that he had loved her from the first week of that class. Not, "love-love," he said, but the "affection and respect that only a Montana cowboy in a foreign country can have for a smart, soul-mate cowgirl when she walks into his class." Aurelez understood this. She understood it because she held him in similar esteem and affection. And she loved being called a, "cowgirl." "Besides," she confided to Luisa, "I had dated one of his sons by that time."

As a life marker, the short story assignment was life changing. She came to think of it as, "The Assignment." It was mandated in a literature course, not creative writing. Yet one of the assignments had been to write a "10 page short story in the style of_____," one of a list of assigned authors. She had chosen Gabriel García Márquez, based on her reading of "Love in the Time of Cholera," which she felt was so pathetically unrealistic that she would easily be able to write like that. *(I mean really, 600 plus lovers, and we are still holding out for the one true love?).* She would be a published author before she realized how 600 plus lovers might signify a single intense and true love. And she would be an experienced therapist before she knew why the choice had turned out to be so evocative. "An artist does not observe anything any differently than anyone else," Garcia had said in interviews, "But you need 'innocence' to really see." She read that he had described art as "layered" so that it would last for generations. *Layered,* she thought, *like my life.* And her search for her own innocence in order "to see" was stimulated more by the art of García Márquez than by any therapist she would ever meet. It would add humility to her practice and her writing and although she came to know this, she would never be able to explain it.

Easy assignment she thought; *first love is perfect.* As is often the case, the first love story was so compelling that many students came to the same conclusion. It was a standard assignment for the course regardless of the instructor, and it typically resulted in stunningly frank stories that even if poorly written, would reveal the degree of student understanding of the author. It also served the departmental purpose of identifying students who may have the gift of expression. Aurelez stood out.

But the assignment had another less predictable outcome. She re-experienced the "immersion," a word she used in her introduction, of herself into this unrequited affair. It was the recall of the intense feelings that her first love had evoked. *What had happened to them?* She wondered if that was something that children did and then got over. To her mind, her "loves" since then had been rather rational except for the anticipation of, and the too few moments of sex. The intense commitment that she felt with Rigo had "gone missing," and her judgment was that it was gone forever. She was too mature now.

She had seen Rigo a few times since she left for the University and not at all since he married. She knew that her father had given him the money for his house lot. At the time, the idea resurrected a bitter memory of Eduardo. She was certain that he loved Rigo more than her, and the "why" of that was a painful and unanswered question in her life. Rigo was her first love, even without consummated sex. There had been nothing like it since him. For months, he, was her whole universe, no second-guessing, just unequivocal, committed emotion.

She had not counted on the resurrection of the intensity of her love for Rigo. Not, strictly speaking, the love, that was well over. But she did re-experience the sense of being torn from him. That was how it felt at the time, a physical pulling of her flesh from his. She had been ripped from his side before she could ask the questions. *Do you love me? I told you I loved you. Why didn't you ever say it? God!* she thought, *I've got to stop this.* After the separation came the shaming. Her mother was at first upset with her, but with her father's unrelenting blame, Alba became supportive, trying to lessen the effect of Eduardo's unreasonableness. *She saved me, if she hadn't,* Aurelez thought, *I might have become unhinged from them altogether.* The pain and confusion of that time returned in doses large enough for her to relive the experience for several short episodes while The Assignment birthed itself.

Her anger during that earlier period had led her into several adolescent mistakes, of which her understandable, if erroneous, belief about her father had been at the root of all the others. The topic she had chosen required that she reenter this past. And, although she found that creating a story from the loose set of misremembered facts was as satisfying as anything she had ever done, it was also personally compelling. It was as if the story had chosen her, had roughly shouldered its way onto her life list of "to do's," and would not leave until it became a book a few years later.

❧

By the time of The Assignment, Aurelez had known love with several men. She had matured in such a way that love had become a need she met, "as required," and for which she had developed a distinct preference for the uncomplicated. Luisa tended to serial monogamy and was, as often as not, at the residence of her current love. Aurelez usually chose those who were not in danger of falling in love to sleep with.

The Spanish language version of Erica Jong's 1973 attention grabber was still making the rounds of college students and the concept fit her needs exactly, *for now,* she told herself. Yet, she was not promiscuous, if that means easily available. *No time for it*, she thought; which was unquestionably the truth of the matter. But she did enjoy the sex and "consortium," another lover would call it, of a man in her presence. *Consortium*, she thought, *what a lovely word, it even sounds sexy*. She sought men to provide a more complete experience, even if complication was off the table.

Her "uniform of the day" became the pantsuit. She had heard the phrase from a couple of youngish Marines attached to the American

Embassy. They were seated in the Mexican restaurant and bar that catered to collegians, which was of course, their purpose for being there. "Saturday night trolling," they told themselves. Luisa did not connect with his partner and went home alone and annoyed. But the man, Frank, had a pleasant yet vulnerable look about him sitting with his buddy. His smile when she passed close carried a quasi-not-at-all-offensive sexuality that intrigued her. She wondered what he made of her smile. In spite of the implicit bravado, the man was shy and when he later went with her to her apartment; there was no question about who, had picked up who. She liked his directness, *honesty*, as she thought about it. His last name sounded Slavic. "Ukrainian," he corrected when she tried out her theory.

It was a nice evening but, "I've had a very nice time, Frank," she said after breakfast, "You are very nice, but I can't see you again so please don't try to call me."

"As you request, Ma'am," he replied with a non-smile. The slight formality masked what she thought was disappointment. It was the first and last time she would sleep with a stranger and she was uncertain why she did it at all. She annoyed herself briefly, *I will be just another barracks story about local women*, she thought. It surprised her that Frank respected her request.

Luisa was more effusive over dinner. "*My God, Girlfriend*, you had that guy twisted around your finger. I bet he would have married you before sex."

Aurelez laughed. "I'm too busy for that. Besides, I like them a little unpredictable."

"Hey, when you find a trainable one you better snap him up and start the program. That's my plan. So far, they haven't been as smart as my dog."

"*Girlfriend*...love is more than just spending your life getting someone to do what you want."

Luisa stared at her, "What?.... What are you, some kind of psychologist? Where does that come from, Miss Prissy?"

Aurelez just shook her head and smiled but her mind left the conversation. *Where did that come from? Was that smart? Is that what I think?*

In Aurelez' fourth year her natural mother's husband retired. He had a sequence of heart attacks and a small stroke. Her mother's loyalty resulted in more control over their finances and she sought to reenter Aurelez' life with money. Aurelez could have entered medical school after her third year, but didn't. In addition to science courses, she took more literature and creative writing. With the new financial help, the roommates moved to a larger apartment with three bedrooms so that Chiquito or the occasional friend could visit and maintain some sense of privacy. Shortly after they moved in, Luisa placed a square, embossed envelope on the table when Aurelez arrived from morning class. The addressee stared at them in a precise, calligraphy.

"Don't you have class now?" Aurelez asked.

"Yeah, but you're crazy if you think I'm leaving before that envelope gets opened.

Aurelez slid her finger under the top flap and it flew open with a little pop of wax at the tip. "Fancy."

"I'll say, read it."

"Well," she hesitated, "I am invited to a dinner party at the home of *Doctor y Señora* Jack Cochran. In three weeks....*Caramba*."

"*Bastante caramba*....I'm already eating my heart out. We are going shopping, girlfriend; we got to get you in shape."

"What does, 'RSVP,' mean?"

"Oh, girlfriend," Luisa stared at her, "You've come to the right roommate."

Aurelez' life in college had been the social life of a student. She worked harder than most and her love life was ragged and undemanding, a little consortium now and then sufficed. She smiled again at the thought of the word. "Cocktails at seven," was new. *Bastante nuevo*. Luisa was impressed and her, "*bastante caramba*" made Aurelez chuckle every time she thought about it. Every adjective got a "*bastante*" in front of it for the next few weeks. Those weeks were filled with discussion of one scenario after another completed with a weekend visit to Luisa's house for supplemental training in table etiquette. Luisa's mother held the invitation and its envelope to the light of a table lamp, "This woman grew up rich," was her verdict. She made a place setting at dinner with every conceivable utensil. By the end of the weekend, Aurelez had simplified the instructions to 'start from the outside and don't drink too much.'

But by the middle of the second week of Luisa's unrelenting enthusiasm for teaching, Aurelez was annoyed. She felt mildly inadequate and she could see that Luisa was enjoying the disparity. Still, Aurelez had a goal not to embarrass herself and if it took playing inferior for a while, so be it.

❧

By the time she got in the cab to go dinner in Barrio Argentina her confidence had returned. Any slip would be handled the way she always did it, with some kind of acknowledgement and immediate release. She knew how to do that. Still, at the door, when Sra. Cochran welcomed her with, "Ahhh, the famous Aurelez," she found herself disconcerted. Jack Cochran appeared in that moment and her aplomb recovered. As she shifted her gaze to him, she realized that the greeting had had its intended effect.

She was the sixth of what would be 10 guests. The seventh to arrive, from another part of the house, was the host's son. "Finally. We could use your help, Rojas," said Jack Cochran.

"Rojas, may I present Aurelez. Aurelez, Rojas has just started his second year of medical school; you two no doubt have something in common."

The two shook hands with the mandatory cheek buff and *mucho gusto'd. He is interested*, Aurelez thought. She certainly was.

It is said that among those who are open to a romantic encounter, it only takes a few moments of eye contact to decide to pursue the matter. Those seconds grew into twenty minutes as the party organized itself and gained some momentum. Jack Cochran and his señora were busy hosting and as one introduction was made, Aurelez turned slightly to her left as the last new arrival moved away. She noticed an almost two foot bronze flanking the entrance to the dining room. It was of a North American indigenous rider.

"My God. That's the saddest, tiredest horseman I've ever seen, and that horse. Look at that thing."

"Beaten, might be a better word," said Rojas. "It's some of Jack's cowboy art. This is the only one I like. Most of his art is paintings of a bunch of yahoo cowboys raising hell."

"'Yahoo?'"

"It's American...can refer to almost anything...I use it like redneck."

"'Redneck?'"

"Well...*campesino*, but in the rough sense. You obviously didn't go to an American school. Tell me about you."

"I think not, I'm the guest. You go first."

The cheek of it stopped him; a hand went to the corners his mouth; he smiled after a moment, eyebrows arched. "I guess that's true. Well," he said, "I started out as a child."

She found out that he had been a *nacional* since he was five years old. He came in 1979 from a neighboring country with his mother and second brother and that every male in his family was a soldier, beginning with his grandfathers.

"What army?"

"My older two brothers are in the US Army the other in the Guatemala Army."

"What happened to you?"

He hesitated then plunged dutifully, "I don't hold with it...courtesy of Jack Cochran."

"Sounds like your Ma has changed her tastes."

"Ma?" he smiled at her. "Not really, my mother, likes—," he saw his mother approaching.

"Time for dinner, my dears, your name is by your place." She looked intensely at Aurelez. *What is wrong with this woman?* Aurelez smiled and said, "thank you."

The ten guests sat the largest table Aurelez had ever seen. There was a huge, low spray of flowers in the center with an oval of flanking candles and dimmed overhead lights. She sat between Jack Cochran at the end on her right and Rojas on her left. Rojas held her chair and she slid easily into it thanks to Luisa's training program. Jack Cochran held the chair for a woman professor on his right. Her husband did the same for a visiting professor in another department. The party was in honor of Jack Cochran's old friend from college, the man at the opposite end who held the chair for his hostess. His name was Paul.

"This week marks 30 years of friendship," said Jack Cochran, raising his glass to Paul, "It began in ROTC at Michigan, continued into the Army and has survived a number of, shall we say, *mutual* girlfriends."

"Here, here," said several guests; they sipped, someone snickered.

"In my defense, I would just say that all these mutual friends were sequential." He paused, looking at Jack Cochran, "That is true isn't it, Jack?" Laughter.

"Paul is not the one that needs a defense ladies, in the Army he had the reputation of being able to read the enemy like a book, so stand forewarned."

During her training program Aurelez had gotten the impression that this might be a stuffy affair and Luisa's mother suggested that she might watch the amount of wine she took. *So much for that theory*, and she joined easily into conversation with Cerise, the woman professor across from her whose interests were in political behavior.

"Where do you teach?"

"In Virginia, but I'm on leave for as long as Paul has this assignment."

"He is with the embassy," said Jack Cochran in response to Aurelez' expression.

She caught herself, mouth open, staring, remembering Jack Cochran's welcoming toast.

"I'm sorry," she said, "I thought you two were married," nodding at the man next to the professor.

"Nice recovery," said Cerise. She smiled at Aurelez, then looked squarely at Jack Cochran. "Jack, you must change that toast, it gives people the wrong idea."

"That is what you said the last time, my dear."

"Yes, and the next time is the third," as she looked at Aurelez. "Something is supposed to happen on the third strike isn't it?"

Plates were being taken before desert when Rojas and Aurelez finally talked again. "I think I've earned the right to hear from our guest," he said.

"I think so, what would you like to know?"

He started to speak, and then smiling said, "Well, what about boyfriends?"

"Apparently, I don't do boyfriends."

"Whaat?" His look flashed from confused to incredulous.

Her laugh exploded. "Not that, *ha, ha, ha,* not *that* dummy, *ha, ha, ha, ha.*"

When she regained some control and wiped her eyes. "Oh my, I've read the word 'aghast' ever since my first year in college but I never knew what it looked liked until now. *Ha, ha, ha, ha.*" She realized that she was getting too much attention and regained her composure.

"Forgive me Rojas...this is the wine speaking. I just meant that I haven't had a real boyfriend for years."

"Okay, let's say it's the wine and I'll pretend like I'm not offended. I'm afraid to try another question."

"No, do, really, I apologize for being rude."

In contrition, she told him about her life in Asturias, her plans, even about Chiquito." They made plans to meet the following Friday.

"Jack likes your book but writing it seems too complicated with school and a baby."

"You know," she said after a long pause, "it really isn't. Writing this stuff down is like subtracting from my life, not adding to it. It simplifies things, if that makes any sense." She paused again. "But thank you for saying that."

As she was making her goodnights Jack Cochran said, "It looked like the two of you did okay together."

"Is that what this was about?"

"Of course, but we all hope to see more of you."

"All?"

"Don't worry about that."

After the first date she realized she was right about Rojas. He was present in conversation and could talk without always taking the lead. She liked it that he seemed not to have a possessive 'bone in his body,' as Luisa said. He said that he liked to, "Screw on Fridays," and the easy directness of it got her past the crudity. Fridays became a regular date. Those evenings ended early because both like to work on Saturday mornings.

Aurelez remained in university until graduation. She had been accepted to medical school after the third year, "But," she said, "I wanted to finish it," without being more precise. She did spend more time with Chiquito and finished a complete draft of the book in that year. She and Rojas lasted until the summer after she graduated when each developed another interest. The separation left them still friends and occasional lovers.

Motherhood

August 2002

Both Aurelez and Luisa eschewed the graduation ceremony in favor of time away from school. Luisa went to New York and Aurelez, with Chiquito, visited Guito and Tessa following a week at the beach. The trip was a gift from her natural mother, Adele. Luisa remained in the States to get a graduate business degree at a little known college west of Boston. In her "org behavior" class she took a personality inventory and sent an email saying, "I know you'll find this hard to believe girlfriend, but I'm a raving extrovert." Her family had a "dream job" waiting for her taking care of business in Latin America. "I'm supposed to learn Portuguese," she said, *"sem problema."*

By the time first year classes began at the medical school Aurelez was antsy. She had her own apartment now, smaller but with a part-time housekeeper and babysitter for Chiquito, also thanks to Adele. Her natural mother fancied herself as computer savvy and kept Aurelez in whatever technology she required. There were no grades *per se* in those first two years, but the courses were otherwise in traditional format and focused on medical science. It was a milieu in which she was used to excelling, but more often than not her results were "pass" or "high pass" in lieu of "honors." Her class of would-be doctors was full of high achievers and she no longer stood out.

That fact instigated a peculiar change; she would put in a good effort she decided, but she cared more about taking time with Chiquito than being the smartest person around. She had men friends but they never stayed over when the boy was there. Chiquito was in an accelerated *kinder* program in an international day school and that, plus his increasing demands on his mother, filled any time left in her days. Rojas was beginning his residency in emergency medicine and his schedule varied. They saw each other from time to time and he would take her to parties at his parent's home. "Jack is still hoping that I'm going to 'lassooo that heifer.'" He would drag out the "ooo" in "lassooo" and chuckle on the verge of losing control. He repeated it to her more than once. She saw the humor but it never felt really funny and her mirth was more from the pleasure of seeing Rojas laugh. Rojas was good with Chiquito and sometimes brought him a present or took him for ice cream, although they did not often date. The friendship felt good to Aurelez and her respect for him increased although she knew, and thought that he did also, that they would never be more than that.

       \}

"Dr. Cokran —...."

"Caahkran," he said, smiling. "Nice to see you again Aurelez."

She blinked at him, his fussiness over the name was suddenly hilarious; she began to laugh. The student who came in with her, backed away. Jack Cochran had had lots of opportunity to laugh at himself for riding his fences around his name since he had been in the country, especially with Aurelez. He joined the laughter, sheepishly, but grinning broadly nonetheless. The student returned to Aurelez' side.

It was the first year of her residency. Jack Cochran's seminar was required and both had anticipated being in a professional relationship again. He saw her name on the student roster and was looking forward to her penetrating questions and guileless repartee. There were too few students like Aurelez, smart and who could sometimes be outrageous, that made up for some of the dreariness of day in and day out instruction. Graduate or professional school was better, but the drudges who over-focused on the grade tended to concentrate in those places also. "Someday," Cochran told his colleagues, "I'm going to make a study of that."

This seminar was a detailed look at the theoretical underpinnings of several therapeutic strategies. The content was co-selected by the Department of Psychiatry and the Department of Psychology and the class included a predictable 6 to 10 advanced students per semester. This year only Aurelez was from the medical school. She was surprised at the extent to which the clinical psychology students anticipated doing research. All of the students had been exposed to these bodies of knowledge in at least one other class. But this was the class, along with their clinical work, where they developed affinities that would focus their personal approaches to therapy. The reading list was huge even by graduate school standards and the seminar carried an extra hour credit. Performance was determined by two large projects over the course of the semester and Dr. Cochran's office hours were often filled with students. One of those projects was exactly the same assignment she had done for extra credit in his undergraduate class. He said, "You got a 'B' last time Aurelez. Show me what you've learned," when she pointed that out to him.

This year he began the course with a reading of the second edition of a book that challenged the idea of "mental illness." It is nothing other than a "metaphor rooted in the history of medicine," the author wrote. He was an American psychiatrist[4] and the first edition of his book had created a serious call for his removal from his university. Aurelez resonated with the audacity it required to challenge the idea that the medical profession was "over-focused" on the treatment of disorder to the exclusion of authentic "health," mental or physical. The author referred to "the rule of medicine or of doctors" as "pharmacracy," and she was excited as much by the metaphor as she was by the ideas. Jack Cochran's stated purpose was to challenge his student's minds with the notion of, "what *is* mental health?" before plunging into the course; hers split wide open. *God*, she thought, *I am so glad to be back in his class.* She had deeply enjoyed her rotations and had given thought to changing to pediatrics. Now she was delighted to have stayed with psychiatry.

This year, for the first time, Jack Cochran exercised his discretion to include gestalt therapy even though it was of little academic interest.

"Hard to research, using accepted methods," he explained, "but conceptually rich in theory and intervention." Most of them had heard something of it. Aurelez had been excited in previous courses, both in psychology and anatomy, about the relationship of the unconscious to the conscious. As a corollary she discovered that the unconscious was much more important to observable, effective functioning than was previously understood. She was excited by the directness of the therapeutic tools, "bringing the past and the unconsciousness, into the now and into consciousness, so that patient and doctor could work together." Jack Cochran said that the therapist should allow what would emerge from the patient to do just that, "emerge rather than be excavated."

That was therapy, but an aspect that seemed of equal importance to Aurelez was the possibility raised by one writer of "holding two opposing ideas simultaneously." It was the idea of the polarity.

"Suppose," Jack Cochran said, "that there was no perfect solution to any of life's problems. Suppose that choices ran on a continuum from one pole to the other. That would mean that an individual or a society would be looking to manage itself so as to provide what it *deems* to be appropriate." Aurelez thought, *If an individual can understand her choices as movement between either of two polar extremes, why couldn't a nation also?* The idea she concluded was that most problems weren't solvable in the ordinary sense. They had to be managed somewhere in between the polar extremes. She could see that the language of polarities gave society, like an individual, a more productive way of thinking and talking about the choices it faced. It was as intellectually exciting as it was practical. The idea became her subject for an independent study that provided two missing hours of credit. Jack Cochran, as always, was supportive. "You can publish that he said," but she was too involved in her novel to bother.

"You've relaxed some," Jack Cochran said at the end of an engaging semester for both of them.

"Yes, I have. What do you make of that, Doctor?"

"I think it's time, Doctor."

Jack Cochran read the draft of "El Campesino," pointed out a couple of areas to expand or cut, and recommended an editor.

Swami

November 2002

"I'm in the swami business."

"Hah!" and a spurt of tea exploded from Tessa. "Oops," wiping her mouth, "I always thought you were up to something." The table broke into laughter.

Guito had picked up Rajiv at the Airport in mid afternoon. It was a long, four-hour ride back and it was dark when they got to Aguas Calientes. Rajiv queried Guito on his practice and nodded when he heard that Guito had been meditating on a sign that had come to him. "It's a little oval shiny stone," Guito said, "it seems to loiter near my nostril where I pay attention to my breath."

"You are ready to shift your concentration to that, Guito. Now you can focus on any event that keeps you in the moment." He grinned at Guito, "Congratulations."

Rajiv hurriedly put his stuff in a rental *cabina*. Tessa managed to keep supper ready though the meatless lasagna had gotten dry. None of that mattered to the three friends. The girls enjoyed Rajiv but, with a little prodding from their mom, they left the table after desert and amused themselves in another part of the house.

"Well...," Rajiv finished a chuckle. "My mother died eight years ago, quickly, of cancer." Concern passed over the faces of his listeners, but he showed no emotion. "A year later my father decided to return to India to a life of asceticism and seeking. It is a little old-fashioned now, but it used to be really common when a successful person got near the end of his life. So...he made me his attorney and left all of his assets for my use. I still teach as an adjunct, but I no longer need to work."

"So what's with the 'swami business?'" Tessa pressed. The phrase brought another smile to their faces. Guito remembered Wym using the phrase to refer to the numerous practitioners of the "spiritual arts," as he called it when he was feeling irreverent. It wasn't a compliment.

Slowly, as though remembering events, Rajiv or "Sat" as his friends now called him, continued. "A few years ago just after Mother died, I saw Wym at a conference where he was presenting. He seemed genuinely glad to see me. But he was with a partner and the partner was not happy with me being around. It was awkward...*really* awkward, and it reminded me how caught up in the world's illusions I still was."

"How is Wym?" Guito broke in.

"Huush."

Rajiv smiled at her, "I'll be quick. He's a big success. After we separated he took a leave to learn more about DNA manipulation and then took a research job in agribusiness. Now he is a bigwig vice-president. Anyway...back to my story. The Conference was in Geneva so I walked out of the hotel, downhill until I found myself in a park at the edge of Lac Léman," he gave the French pronunciation. "The sun had set but I wasn't hungry so I sat on a bench and meditated.

The night was cold and clear, and out over France, the stars were brilliant even with the city lights. As I sat, the thought came to me that the light from the stars was energy; it was coming to *me*, touching me, literally, *photons touching* me from all those light years away. The star was *touching* me with this energy…it was an amazing thought. The light, the energy was just washing over me…I sat in it for a long time. The moon appeared and added its energy. Light, energy, was swirling about me. I felt a presence," he glanced at Guito, "but as I looked around, all I saw was me. Not my body, now everything was *me*. Everything," he paused, "It did not last long, just a few moments, no more than a glimpse really." I had dinner in my room that night and left the conference the next day."

His listeners stared, unspeaking.

"So what do you make of it?" Guito asked finally. "Do you think it was God?" Tessa's mouth gaped, her eyes wide; she looked from Sat to Guito and back to Sat.

"Maybe," Rajiv smiled. "Or maybe it was just that… it is those kinds of experiences that gave rise to the idea of 'God.'" Leaning forward, elbows on his thighs, "I've thought about it a lot, of course. Then I remembered something that a guru said when people asked him about the cancer that eventually killed his body. He said, 'Where would I go? I am here.' I never quite understood that answer. But now…I'm sure he meant it literally, not as 'I am here in this spot,' but I am HERE. I am THIS. I am everything." He paused again.

"But what…," Tessa hesitated, "what about the presence?"

"The short answer is that I think what I experienced as 'something else,' was me. You could call it the Real Me, or the True Me. But it was simply me. I wouldn't even capitalize the 'm' in me. Reality is just reality. I have gone through my life living the lie that I am my body, my life, and then all of a sudden I get this glimpse of reality. I'm resisting my tendency to make up a new theory to explain it. It is just *me*." He paused again, a slight smile, allowing them to take in this idea. "It was just a glimpse; it lasted for just a short while, but it was enough for me to know that for once, I had seen my answer to, 'Who am I?' I left the University at the end of my contract and spent as much time as I could looking at 'me.'"

"But what does that really mean?" Tessa was into it.

"Well, I have always felt, as most of us do, that who I am are the thoughts, the beliefs, habits, behavior...body, he added totting his list. All that tangible of stuff; I have always thought that was "me." You know, like. 'who **I** am'." His cupped hand touched his chest with each word. "What I glimpsed was a presence, the 'me' that was none of that. Just empty, yet...everything." He lowered his head. Looking up he said, "Who you think you are is nothing, who you really are is everything. But, that, and a two bucks will buy you a cup of coffee." Rajiv beamed his *isn't that marvelous* grin.

Both his listeners smiled at his joyful state but neither spoke. Finally, Guito said," I know there is more to this," but Sat remained quiet.

"I've said this many times," he began again following a prolonged sigh, "talking about it doesn't help much. But perhaps there may be a clue or a hint in there that will be helpful."

Tessa's eyes were large, "I don't know if this is helpful to Guito or not, but it is like he used to say, this stuff just blows me away. Tell us the rest of it,"

"Well, as time went on I spent more time looking, in meditation. The looking did it. Just spending time looking at the source of these thoughts. It was so gradual that it took a year or so to realize that the struggle was over. My body was going to live itself out to its appointed time, but 'I' am here forever."

"It didn't happen like...you know...*Shazamm*! Like with the guys who write books?"

"No. Gradual, over time...just looking and more looking...after that first glimpse...that did it."

"Would that work for me?"

"Not so fast *El Indio*. I'm not sure I want someone around that I can't get mad at." Laughter, the spell broke.

"Anyway...that's why I'm here, to share this with both of you. I hope we can get back to our talks and meditations. And yes, if it will work for me it will for you also."

"But you still haven't answered the part about the Swami business," Tessa said.

Guito held up his hand as though to stop her, still struck by Sat's statement about coming back for the two of them. Sat glanced at each of them but focused on Tessa.

"I'm sorry. You're right, Tessa. After things became clear for me some people began asking to meet with me. And there were a few that my teacher recommended. The group grew and I began to hold meetings. We Jains call them *satsangs,* but I think I'm going to stop using the term. It conjures up an image of 'sitting at the foot of a master who can transmit the wisdom of the ages.' That's not *me* and that's not *it*. Anyway, I do this for donations to cover the cost of Meeting places and any food that is served. It's my new mission in this life. I want the whole world to rid itself of the internal warfare that comes with living in the lie that you are this life, this body. I'm lucky that I don't need to save for retirement or to buy a Rolls Royce." Smiles all around. "And," he added, looking at Guito, "I still want to go birding with you."

Guito stood up with a small bow, hands clasped in prayer form, "*Jai Bhagwan.*" He reached across the table to shake Sat's hand. "I accept." Sat remembered.

Later that evening Rajiv called to ask if he had left a leather satchel in the car. "I could have sworn I put it on my porch but it's not here or in the house."

"I hope it's nothing important," Tessa said.

"Just papers that I might need here plus some reading material. I can live without it but it was my father's case and I don't want to lose it."

"Guito says we don't have it," she said, "but while I've got you, Raj, or Sat, I just want to say that I don't think all this stuff is for me." Tessa explained why she would not go with Guito to meditate with Sat. "I told Guito once that my people are so tolerant that some people think we don't stand for anything. But we know what we stand for; I know, and I am happy with that."

"Then I am also," said Sat, "You don't have to give that up...but... well my door is always open."

"Thank you, I know that."

꧁

"Only one million twenty-four thousand, five hundred twenty-six to go." Sat smiled. "In our tradition, it takes one million eighty thousand Oms to achieve liberation. I'm not sure even my father believed that."

"Funny, but...." Guito's folded hands parted, in a, *why?* motion.

"It's my introduction. I'm going to tell you that a lot of the stuff about Jains that we talked about over the years, I no longer think is important...it doesn't hurt, but isn't important. I hold a simpler view of how one achieves the experience of reality. I'm not the only one who sees it this way but most say it is for advanced practitioners."

"That is you for sure."

"Maybe...but I think they are wrong about that Guito."

"You don't trust your own saints?"

There was a long pause. "I suppose that if it had happened in a single experience I might believe that it is only for the spiritually advanced. But it didn't. I got this little glimpse, nothing more. All I did after that was to concentrate my medititation on 'who am I.' He made the air quotes. "Like I said before, you have to do the work. I have discipline but so do you, so do lots of people."

"You make it sound easy."

"You know...it is easy. You can make it hard by believing it's hard...as virtually every spiritual adept on the planet does believe. You know a million Oms ain't chicken feed."

Guito laughed then subdued. Years before the expression had come to Rajiv from Sochi via Guito. "Did you put jokes in your research also?"

"Yeah but my editors take them out." Sat was chuckling. "Seriously," he said in a manner that did not sound serious, "the difficulty is in letting go of the view that you are this life, this body. The ego doesn't want you to...it doesn't want to fade away. You aren't the ego but nothing I can say is going to make you experience that. Nothing that any of the scriptures 'say' is going to make you experience it either. You have to see it for yourself. You have to let the light in...the light of the truth of who you really are...repeatedly, that is what does it, and you can do that."

"I remember that story, about some guru saying that one day you will laugh, and that day will be like today—."

"Yes exactly...I have my own story, and I will share my sense of the most direct path, but the truth is that it is just my story. I tell you to help you keep your motivation up, but you are on your own. That part still holds."

They both waited, thinking, Sat said, "I have a friend who spent a number of years in India in an ashram. She says that it is commonly believed that only one seeker in three million achieves liberation. Forget about the fact that you don't have either a numerator or a denominator. The statement itself reflects a belief that realization occurs as an accident or fate. Just so you know, I don't think that is true."

It already felt like a full session to Guito, but Sat said, "Ready to start? I want to begin where we left off."

"Why do you think this kind of stuff is not part of Christianity?"

"I think it is. Part of the tradition if not part of the belief."

"It's not taught in church."

"I know, but the churches have theology, a world view that is rooted in the worldview of the Bible. Some are more open than others. It was a Christian poet who said, 'At the still point of the turning world. Neither flesh nor fleshless; Neither from nor towards; at the still point, there the dance is.' Awakening cannot be nailed down with concepts or theology. It's fluid, a process of opening that never stops. It's alive, living."

"How?"

"The traditions attempt to prescribe a series of beliefs, practices, ethics, a whole way of being in the world that is supposed to help us see reality. They often use the phrase "ultimate reality." But Guito, reality is just reality; just plain old, small 'r,' reality. It is part of the human condition. We don't have to reject the condition, our humanness, to find something we already have. Something we already are, which is very, *very*, ordinary."

"But honestly...even the word 'ordinary' is confusing. It is hard to take ordinary at its 'ordinary' meaning."

"How can something so extraordinary to our experience be so 'ordinary,'" Rajiv said.

"Exactly. How?"

"I don't know." He grinned. "It is what you are seeing and experiencing right this minute. It is hard to understand. In fact, you can't understand it in the mental sense."

"So that's what the guru meant when he said you would laugh."

"I'm sure of it." He paused, "But he also said that you have to look at what is experiencing the ordinary. And I say now...that if you just get a glimpse of the seer...and you keep coming back to glimpse...again and again...over time you will experience reality so deeply that you become aware of who you are that this ingrained belief that you are this life just evaporates."

Guito cogitated on this. "Often...when I meditate, I get this sensation that there are a lot of unformed thoughts churning around somewhere. I cannot tell what they are or where they are, sometimes they feel like they are coming from the back of my head, sometimes they are just there....I cannot say for sure, but they are there, waiting to pop out. It is as though focusing on the breath is the lid that keeps them in. That is when meditating becomes work."

"Your meditation has become quite subtle Guito. Focus on the churn. Sooner or later you will see that it is nothing, just a thought...yet, there you are, anyway. Just you." He paused, "Let's stop thinking so much and meditate for a while."

"You know how people say that you can hear the ocean when you put a conch shell to your ear?"

"Tell me later. Let's meditate."

They sat for an hour. Finally Sat made the "Aummm. Okay," he said, "tell me about the conch shell."

"Well a few weeks ago I had just finished a glass of water and was holding it up, near my head. I could hear that same 'roar' you hear in a shell. So I tilted the glass and I heard that same sound louder. It occurred to me then that the body was making this noise, and the body was hearing its own noise, and...but...I was apart from all of that." They both waited. "It was like the body was doing its thing, but I was not that."

"Yes."

"All this will take some getting used too."

"I know, I fear your previous teacher was something of an amateur."

"How do you know that you aren't still an amateur?—That didn't come out right."

"It's valid." He smiled and paused. "In the past few years I've become a person for whom the fear of life has fled. The fear has gone because I know I'm no longer this life. I mean it the way the guru did when he said, "I am this, I am here...that everything I see is me."

"In a way, that is what you've been talking about for years."

"It hasn't helped much has it?"

"No."

"It is like I said before...many times. Describing reality gets us nowhere. The Buddhists say enlightenment occurs beyond words and beyond scripture. Get your first glimpse and keep on looking whenever you think about it. It's 'Who am I? Who is asking? Who is the seer?'"

"You wear me out, Sat."

"You're the one with all the questions."

Someone Is Here

October 2002

"Papi, someone is here." Anaís woke him at 4:58 AM. He rolled over and looked at the clock, *time to get up anyway.* "A horse is eating our grass. She is still wearing her saddle."

"OK. Honey."

Guito rose quickly and walked into the main part of the house. The family's new "Rosa," a black lab puppy, got up from her bed near the wood stove and followed him to the front door. She sat and waited, she hadn't scratched the door since the first "NO!" Guito had administered. *Good puppy Rosa, you are the only dog in the whole county that sleeps inside.* He glanced at the horse in the yard. "Some guard you are Rosa." He opened the door and she, ignoring the horse, went directly across to a patch of trees to, "do her stuff," as Anaís said. Tessa's family had kidded him for years about his habit of talking to his dog. "The dog whisperer," Tessa named him after the novel about horses found its way to Aguas Caliente. Anaís also spent long hours brushing and talking to whatever animal they had at the time. "I am too Papi," she would console him whenever the bromide made its appearance. His agreement with Tessa had been that she would name the girls and he, the boys; the same accord her mother had with her father. *Bad deal*, he thought, *all girls*, but it made him smile as most thoughts about his children did.

He pushed the start button on the coffee maker and tossed the pile of remaining raw *chicasquil* leaves into the sink. The first half had been cooked yesterday. His mother would strip one of their trees whenever he came home and he had just returned from there two days ago. She trained Tessa to cook them the way Guito liked. But the deal was that Guito had to chop the tough leaves. In Aguas Caliente, only he, Tessa's father and Anaís would eat the *picadillo* with any relish. While awaiting his first cup of coffee, he walked back to the window.

The mare grazed outside. She looked old and bony, but Guito could not see more than that because she was the same color as the low light. Part of the saddle skirt had been made with a swooped gap in the leather, *a macleta saddle* he thought, *not many of those around, Paco*. Paco, one of the local drunks would sometimes stop at the house on the way home at night and ask for food. *This is the first time he has stayed over*. He smiled at his own humor. The family never turned anyone down who asked for food so Paco dropped by every week or two. Guito went back into the bedroom for his jeans and shoes.

"It is just Paco, go back to sleep, dear."

"Pull the covers over my back."

Guito stopped in the kitchen and poured himself a cup. His morning, less-than-ebullient mood resolved itself with the "cure," so coffee was step number one, every morning. Anaís had gone back to bed. *What was she doing up this early?*

The grass was wet. He walked over to the mare and picked her reins off the ground. She was fractious in spite of an obvious infirmity and she whinnied with half a heart, backed feebly and rolled one eye. *Maybe she only has one good one.* A plastic bag draped from the pommel and the left stirrup was twisted outward, it would not return to its proper attitude when he twisted it. *He must have fallen off...where is the body?* Another smile. Guito led the mare over to a bucket of water from last night's rain. The only sound was the squish of their footsteps and the light clink of her tack. He snubbed her to the drainpipe with enough lead to crop the wet grass. *I'll bet this is her last year.* He slid while walking back down the slight incline. He caught himself but in the process his gaze swept across the yard past the *bodega*.

The door was open. *There he is...boots?* Paco never wore shoes, he hadn't since childhood, and yet here unmistakably, was a leg and one rubber boot in the doorway. Paco put in a full days work in the woods, in cane, and with the clearing crews for the AC, barefoot, *pata de suelo* as they say, and had never been seriously hurt. Guito, fully alert with the near fall and aroused curiosity, strode to the *bodega*. He paused outside, the man was curled, fetal-like, one leg extended, in a patch of old hay. His machete flopped across his body. *Not Paco.*

This man had a full and unkempt beard, *Good lord*, *never shaved*. He looked about 60 maybe 70 years old, maybe older. He eyes were open but glazed. There was a stick firmly clamped between his teeth, his hands clasped tightly together. Guito knelt, his knee smashing a currycomb that had been jostled from its nail on the wall. *"Amigo,* give me the stick."

The man rasped for breath. *"Saco,"* he whispered, *"medicamentos."* Alarmed now, Guito went back to the mare and found a small plastic sack within the larger one. It had maybe 20 round white pills with numbers stamped on one side. He brought the bag and a ladle of water. The man could not move, even his head. Guito lifted it, pushed two pills into his mouth and tried to give him water but the man could only manage a couple of sips. "Do you want more pills?"

"Sí."

Guito pushed two others into his mouth with more water then walked back to the house.

"Tessa, there is a very sick man in the *bodega*...I may need your help getting him into the car."

"The *clinica* is not open this time of the morning," she reminded him, getting out of bed anyway. "It's not Paco?...what's wrong with him?"

"It is *not* Paco, ...and I don't know. I will call Rojas. He will be up, I hope." *No meditating today*.

౪౨

Guito had met Rojas about eight months before. Aurelez had told him to keep an eye out for the doctor's arrival. His name was Félix Anastasio Rojas S. but she called him "Rojas." "He picked the Aguas Caliente area to start his practice after obligatory service with the Health Service. "You two may have some things in common," she said. After a few months Rojas had called Guito a, "humanist's humanist," *maybe that was it*, he thought, *maybe we are both, 'humanists.'* Rojas finished medical school two years ahead of Aurelez and was, perhaps, more than just an acquaintance. That was a guess; but this was the first male friend of hers she had ever suggested he meet. Of the two doctors serving the government *clinica* in Palo Seco, only Rojas made his home there. The other doctor lived over an hour away near his hometown. The talk was that he would be gone as soon as his debt had been paid to the government.

Rojas answered on first ring, Guito told him the problem, he said, "I think he may have fallen from his horse but he does have some pills."

"I'll be there. Don't move him until I do. Call the Cruz Roja ambulance."

Rojas arrived in 10 minutes driving his ancient Defender. Guito showed him the pills. The ambulance had not arrived.

"Morphine, 60 mg...how many did you give him?"

He cocked his eye at Guito's, "Four. My God, are you trying to kill him—not really, *don't worry*," seeing Guito's alarm. "Can you talk to me Señor?"

The man may have said, "Si," but it was too low for either to hear. He gave the slightest nod.

The tablets appeared to have some effect. Rojas took the man's pulse, listened to his heart and lungs. "What are the tablets for Señor?"

"The cancer."

He examined, probing, squeezing, "Yes" and "No," questions, about other injury.

Rojas said the *clinica* would be open soon; he had the keys anyway. "Who is he?" he asked Guito on the way in. Guito was sitting in the back supporting the man on one of the benches. They passed the ambulance; Rojas waved and motioned him to turn around.

"I don't know. I've never seen him around here."

At the *clinica* the first nurse to arrive helped undress him. She searched his pockets for identification. There was no identification. "He said his name is, Déthios?... a foreigner?" She asked. There were a few coins. In the bag of tablets they found the label with instructions; it had the ID of the Health Service pharmacy in the north part of the country with another name on it. The man had no more than about three dollars in *pesos*. Rojas, had a call placed to the other *clinica* and waited. The new doctor there called back promptly but said he would have to get the man's file, "Déthios, how do you spell it? I'll call back after I make a dent in this line of patients."

"How long have you had the cancer, Señor?"

He thought for about two years. It was the prostate; he had been told and that it "was going to be my death." Early on, it had burned like fire when he sat, but now, it burned all the time unless he took the pills. But the pills were not strong enough to sit astride a horse for long, and he told them that he had ridden all night draped over the saddle holding himself with one foot in the stirrup, and his left arm crooked around the pommel. The other held the edge of the blanket.

Rojas said, *with admiration* Guito thought, "This man wanted to get to here...*that* is real pain." Fortunately there was no one else needing to be sequestered because the clinic had only one bed in a separate room for temporary observation.

The hallway was already filled with the front of a long line of patients. Tessa arrived with Anaís about 8:00 AM. She brought a covered plate of *chicasquil* and some tortillas. She spoke to him as she unpacked the food.

"I unsaddled and fed your horse, Señor. She is in our bodega."

"Gracias, Señora," he whispered.

"She has a cracked hoof, on her hindfooot. She could use some rest."

His head drooped, perhaps a nod.

His eyes still glazed, she fed him small mouthfuls of the *picadillo* rolled in the tortilla while Guito walked Anaís to the bathroom. The patient was able to lean upright against a pillow but he kept his eyes in his lap.

"This is *picadillo de chicasquil*, Señor, all that we had ready, have you ever had it before?"

"Sí, Señora."

"My husband loves it, he is from Asturias. Have you been there also?"

"Sí." He chewed tiredly, eyes engrossed with his lap.

Tessa turned away to find something for a napkin.

"Related to the itabo family, *Euphorbiaceae*." He said quietly, in English.

She jerked upright, staring at him; his eyes closed.

&

Guito and Anaís returned to the doorway of the observation room.

"Mamá!"

Guito had already seen her. Her lips disappeared into a thin twist, her mouth held tightly shut; she shook, sobbing without sound, tears flowing freely; she held the man's hand. Guito's gaze followed hers, searching for the first time. The noise from the hallway faded into white; Anaís winced as his grip spasmed.

&

"Different," was Guito's impression when they met. He had stopped by the *clinica* on a shopping trip into Palo Seco and had asked for "*El doctor* Félix, tell him I am Aurelez' brother." The receptionist looked upward, thinking for a moment until his request registered.

"I'm Rojas," he said, "So you are Guito. Nice to meet you." They made an appointment to meet for coffee in the afternoon. Guito's first impression was that Rojas was *not unfriendly*, not even particularly quiet. He was, reserved, as though his participation in conversation were determined entirely by the person he was talking to, always just a little less. He looked older than Guito expected for a new doctor. *Maybe Aurelez looks older too*, he thought. Everyone called him "Rojas," even the nurses and receptionist/clerk at the *clinica*.

The more senior doctor had spoken to Rojas, and the nurses, about protocol in the Health Service, but his practice did not change. He did not want the title, disliked the name Félix, and "hated" the name Anastasio. Rojas said he was from a surburb of the capital and the home of The University, and that his father was a professor there. But he preferred the *campo* and had served a few months at another clinica, before his request for Palo Seco had been approved.

He thinks my sister told me more than she did. "Well Amigo, if you think that was the *campo*, you have now arrived in the *campo-campo*."

Rojas smiled. Guito still thought of Aguas Caliente in that way.

In an unusual move for a new doctor, Rojas had opened a private *consultorio* in a building near-by. He told Guito, "Sooner or later the Health Service will want to move me; I want an option when when I've done my time." *He is definitely different*, the thought would cross Guito's mind more than once over the next few years, usually with a chuckle.

The first impression held. Rojas remained on the margin of all but a few relationships. Guito liked the man and they became good friends within the month.

୨୦

Guito told Rojas the story of Sochi. He held nothing back including their friendship and the allegation that Sochi, nee Cólera, had committed atrocities in the war. "That was an allegation by the Government of the United States," Rojas said this as though he already knew. His open hand went to his mouth and slowly dragged down his chin and neck. The thought that Rojas may have heard about Cólera stopped Guito for a moment, then he refocused on his story.

The return call from the doctor confirmed only the diagnosis. "We have no file. But some people know him, our nurse and receptionist both have some special knowledge of the case, he may be *Indio*. There are several groups of Indios close by...but they, now, have I.D. cards. Somehow...," he breathed it out over a long breath, "he got

diagnosed with prostate cancer. It will end soon....
I'm not sure that treating him is...uhh...legal."

"He has no health care card." Rojas repeated.
With no identification, normal, sustained care
through the government clinic is impossible. Then
speaking to Guito, "I may need for you to collect
some affidavit's that he is a refugee, but we will
find a way to provide palliative care regardless,"
Rojas told him.

He talked with the other doctor at the
reception desk. The senior doctor resisted at first,
but, upon agreeing that Cólera was short-lived,
said, "I guess we can treat him under the
emergency care provisions. I understand the rules
have changed; see if they can get him a temporary
carnet." He winked at Rojas when he said this.

"I like him better than I thought I did." Rojas
said. The obstacles to prescribing morphine
disappeared.

Guito could not remember if he had ever
spoken to Aurelez about Cólera.

※

"Cólera de Diós, Wrath of God, Sochi," Tessa
asked, "What should we call him?"

"I don't know... I'm guessing that he hasn't
been "Sochi" for a long time." Guito stuttered a
little with the thought.

They tried, but he did not respond to Sochi, "Cólera," seemed to serve. They also tried English but he never spoke it again.

They put him in Anaís' room and set up a bed for her in their bedroom. "You can let Rosa sleep with you," Tessa relented. Anaís was thrilled with the arrangement and interested in her parents' friend. "He is very sick, but he is also our very old and dear friend," was all they told her.

They had added on to the *cabina* so that now the girl's room had the original bathroom. Tessa hired a woman to help clean, feed and move him. She was there 10 to 12 hours every day. "It won't be for long," Tessa told her.

Cólera lived for eight more days. The last three he was unaware of anything, to the best anyone could tell. In the five days of off and on awareness, he told them that he had been captured and imprisoned at an air base with several of the men in his unit. They had at times, been forced to watch each other tortured and to tell what ever they could remember or lie about. About him, he said only, "I was abused in many ways." They had been released by an attack for that purpose.

They were fed rice and beans twice daily. There were no clocks except in the interrogation room. It had a large white face with a prominent sweep second hand. Cólera would glance at it when entering but was unable, or could care less, when leaving. His impulse to know things, to measure things, came out. Upon waking he would look out the window covered with steel mesh that blocked most vision as well as escape. He would notice the sun, or the length of shadows. In the exercise pen he would notice the sun's location over the edge of a building. Thus Cólera made his own clock and became competent at predicting the very predictable events of prison life.

What Cólera did not say, and what controlled his life from that point forward, was the nature of the abuse. Except for the, "moments of stark raving terror," as he had once heard something described, existence acquired the feel of waiting in an airport closed for weather. He knew, or assumed, that if he could keep his mind active he could avoid the peculiar dementia that came upon some incarcerated people.

Shortly after capture, an American from the Embassy came to talk to him. This man was different. He spoke Spanish but did so only to establish rapport with Cólera, then switched to English. He gave his name, "Mike Garcia," and said that he had been raised in Miami. "We're both southerners" he parlayed. He was one of the "good" Cubans. He offered that as part of establishing rapport, or perhaps testing Cólera, but that simple little statement became the last time that Cólera would ever experience anger without abasement. He said nothing. "Mike" was more interested in Cólera's family and friends in the United States than his activities in this country. When, and how, did he become a Communist? Who did he know in Atlanta? The interview lasted for hours but there was no abuse, no threats even. Mike never lost patience and returned again and again to questions that Cólera could not answer and sometimes to questions he thought he had answered. Cólera saw no reason to withhold or lie and by the time he left, Cólera thought that Mike liked him.

Before leaving, Mike assured the prison *Capitán* that Cólera was an American but had forfeited protection of the US Government. Mike insisted that the prison administration take a detailed life history from Cólera. It could be in Spanish. In the course of that they discovered that he had been called, "Sochi," and perhaps intuited that he held a special fear of homosexuality. When he turned out to be too resilient to the usual mistreatments, they turned him over to a couple of guards who repeatedly subjected him to his nightmare. They thought the nickname "Sochi," was funny. Cólera stopped checking the sun. His interest in time slipped away, as though it had never been invented. He broke soon after and became a so-so source of information as he had little new intelligence to give them by this point.

The treatment continued in the search for yet more.

Cólera broke completely. He stopped caring. Nothing mattered, food, friendship, loyalty. He became trustable to his captors. They could see, as could his co-prisoners, that Cólera was no longer capable of putting up a fight, or even of being devious, of doing anything other than what he was directed to do. He became the epitome of prisoner's despair. Like Kafka's prisoner, his docility masked his ever present desire take God's hand and leave this world for that better place, the place he had been told of all his life, the place he had tried hard to deserve. He had surrendered, or became oblivious. The difference between defeat and surrender no longer held meaning for him. In the same manner he surrendered to God as well, *Thy will be done,* he thought. It did not occur to him that now, given his own excesses; it might be too late. What was once a human with ambition, love, fears and ego had been squeezed into an inert cube, in the manner of junk cars. His former second-in-command told his *compañeros*, "It is over for Cólera."

The survivors were released in a guerrilla attack, he thought about a year after capture. The attackers were a larger than usual group, temporarily assembled for the attack. The *comandante* was a former army officer as were several sub-commanders. They drestroyed several of the dreaded "Hueys" and got one "dragonfly," the *commandante* called it, a US A-37 small jet. The rest of that squadron was parked on the opposite, heavily defended, side of the airfield. For guerillas, the group showed surprising discipline and skill. The main group broke into its component units immediately after the attack to escape the expected massive response. The former captives were spread among these units.

It became obvious during the retreat that Cólera was useful only as a mule. They gave him a weapon, an antique M-2 carbine with a single magazine and helped him to get out of the immediate area. "Head south for the border," their *capitán* told him. A week later a civil patroller for the army found Cólera, showing symptoms of dengue, lying in a ditch. The militiaman might have ignored him but lying halfway down the bank was the carbine. He was too feverish to fight, "and I could not reach the gun to kill myself." For the undisciplined patrol, an armed *Indio* was fair game for whatever sport came to them. They hauled Cólera out of the ditch, cursing him for not being more helpful. They could see he was so sick that a simple beating would be no fun. One of them, eschewing his bayonet, flipped open a switchblade and whetted it in front of Cólera's face. He began to wave it, then slashing a little coming as close as he could to Cólera's nose. Dizzy, yet seeing, Cólera tried a head feint to avoid the knife and the soldier yelped with joy for the challenge. He brought the knife from right to left thinly slashing Cólera at the left ear and continuing under the chin. It looked fatal but it had missed the carotid.

The patrolman should have informed his leader about the find as soon as possible. But now his sergeant called the group back, urgent, "on the double," he signaled. With some yelling and much scurrying, the squad had almost formed when fire opened from behind the houses. The grouped patrol was down within a minute of the assault; no fire returned. They were finished with machetes.

The rescuers were another group of guerillas, unrelated to the larger first group, and not as disciplined. They distrusted Cólera's, story but kept him for a week while they sent a runner to check it out. That week saved his life. They treated the slash with antibiotics and the dengue with clean water. Their homegrown *Capitán* was apologetic when they learned the truth and sent a man, still a boy, along to help him get to the border. "Thank you for your service, *Comandante*," the young rebel had said when he left Cólera on the opposite side of the river. He took Cólera's weapon but left him their bag of food and a canteen of water.

It took another month to get to this country. He moved on roads within groups of people headed south. A few miles before reaching the border, two men joined him on either side and tried to recruit him into the local guerrillas. It may have been an entrapment but he was beyond suspecting such a thing, "I'm not a fighter," he said. The truth of that statement was so apparent that they left him alone. He *had* been in a refugee camp but had left with another *Indio* who knew about a nearby reservation. Cólera lived thereafter with an *Indio* family, working as a *peon* for 12 years, and, looking only at his hands, did not respond when asked, "Why didn't you contact us?" Nor did he respond when Guito told him, "My friend, I went to look for you at the camp."

Rojas was the only person other than Tessa that Guito could turn to during those eight days. He used both of them well. Rojas said, "What are we here for but to help each other *amigo*; there is no shame," when Guito wept. Later he said, "It is likely that Cólera broke completely Guito. People...we...all have our limits."

New Badge

November 2003

Rigo had been thinking about the design of the worktable all week. His Gringo *patrón* was building a separate house on a lot that he had sold to another foreigner. Construction would start soon. The table would be used to bend a lot of rebar into frames to reinforce the cement columns of the house walls. It had to be large enough to rest the six meter pieces of steel bar, and sturdy. It would be at least 10 feet long and would be super stable with six legs of *guachepelin*; those posts were already cut and waiting. The rest of the frame and top would be *cristóbal* boards, which the Gringo had bought and would arrive with tomorrow's delivery. This table would be substantial – heavy. *We build it where it is going to be used*, was Rigo's plan.

The house site had already been cleared. It was a large area but would be jammed with stacks of rebar, piles of sand, gravel, bags of cement and block. Delivery trucks needed space to reach the area and to turn around. Actual workspace would be limited. Rigo enjoyed imagining the sequence of events that had to occur for the house to go up. As far as he could tell, there was only one place where a table might possibly remain for the duration.

It was 2:00 PM on Friday afternoon. Rigo was alone. The Gringo might be back for the sunset. "There are some clouds over the Nicoya, if I don't get back tonight I'll come tomorrow. Enjoy your weekend," the Gringo had said. The portable cement mixer had just been delivered that day. The owner deflated the tires to make it stable, and harder to steal. It inhabited the spot Rigo chose for the table. The ground around it was muddy but level, and he decided to move it. He had done so at many times in more difficult circumstances.

He broke the bond of the tires with the earth by putting his shoulder to the machine from behind and pushing it a few inches. Then, from the front, he took the steel towing bar with its round hand hold and began to pull. Leaning backwards and extending his body to add weight, he pushed his left leg until fully extended, then right leg stretched out, then left leg, then right, the machine was moving. Left leg and then right leg, it was moving well and he decided to put it where he thought the builder, his father-in-law, might want it. The right leg began to ache on one pull; on the next a sharp pain shot from his hip to his knee. *That's enough for today*, he thought.

Rigo left the mixer near the entrance with enough room for the trucks arriving early in the morning. He grabbed his backpack and walked to his *moto*. There was a small muddy drainage ditch running across the face of the entrance that kept water away from the worksite. His practice was to get enough speed in the 15 feet he had to accelerate to pop over the steep side of the ditch onto the driveway. A sharp pain fired through his leg as he bounced over the bump. As he approached his own house he slowed to find a path through the water channels of the deeply rutted road, the front tire struck then slid sideways down a rut. His leg extended automatically to keep the bike upright.

If one were standing within 20 feet of Rigo, one would have heard the crack. But the pain, then the fall as the bike lay down on top of him. Then more pain flooded in to block any sound that might have reached his ears. He was on his back, arched, gasping, trying to make his lungs work. Instinctively, with the help of massive adrenalin, he moved the damaged leg, only to lose consciousness. He could not have known that his last effort would complete the break, making it impossible to knit in the usual manner. Rigo's autonomous system took charge.

His eyes opened. Not fully conscious he struggled to understand what he had to do. He tried rising one elbow but the flood washed over him again, and again he lost consciousness. Perhaps a few minutes passed. He opened his eyes again. He could not see this but his right leg was turned outward at an odd angle. There was no blood. The thought, *cell phone*, passed wistfully through his mind. It was unreachable in his backpack. He rose to his other elbow. The bike was lying at an angle to the ground, next to him. With his raised arm he pushed himself up and over with his chest resting on the back wheel, face down but off the ground. The flood returned; there was nothing to do but to survive it. Out of his sight, two of the frequent buzzards watched him from the ground. The rain began. An hour passed.

He did not lose consciousness again but a kind of delirium came over him. In the dream he imagined that he had called Carmen on an expensive cell phone with a big screen. She told him, "I will arrive very soon. I am bringing some medicine that will help you." Carmen borrowed a *moto* and arrived with a large white pill and some clear, delicious water. He drank and took the pill while she knelt beside him, talking quietly. "Is that better?" she said.

"Yes, much better. I think we can go now," and he stood up to get on the *moto* with her.

My phone rang. It was Carmen. "Rigo has not come home." I left immediately for the construction site. No Rigo. Then on the their house, as I approached the house I saw Rigo's bike at the end of his driveway. Carmen was kneeling over it.

Rigo is not looking up. "He's hurt!" I lunged from the car.

There was no moving Rigo. He delivered a hoarse "NO!" as loudly as he could muster. The fear in his voice was palpable, I was near panic. Cell phone service was mixed and they had no telephone so I drove to find a reception area and called the *Cruz Roja* for an ambulance. Bad phone service mixed with bad Spanish is a guaranteed misunderstanding, I needed clear reception.

Carmen seemed paralyzed, caught between her need to care for Rigo and to care for her toddlers back in the house. "Go back to the house," I said and I put a rock with Carmen's towel so that Rigo could rest his forehead; it kept falling forward as though he was passing out. I put my hand on his shoulder and kept up a stream of meaningless talk.

Two buzzards stood scarcely moving about 20 feet away. I yelled at them to no effect. I threw a stone and one of flapped his wings, sidestepped a little, and settled back to await his meal. Carmen came back carrying one toddler and trailing the second. Forty-five minutes passed, the ambulance had not arrived, 20 minutes after it should have been there.

"Get in the car and drive the highway," I said to Carmen, forgetting that she could not drive. Then the klaxon sounded. We both started yelling and Carmen was blowing the car horn.

"Jesus Mary and Joseph!" the paramedic exclaimed when he saw the leg flop loosely in its bag of skin. He took a deep breath and blew it out an extended lower lip. "This will take all of us," he said to me and the driver. My stomach roiled.

The ambulance ride on the mountain road was in a stiffly sprung, 15-year-old Toyota Land Cruiser. A paramedic rode in the back with Rigo, but there was no way to keep him still in the stretcher, even with an improvised strap. No painkillers were offered. By Grace, Rigo spent some of the time unconscious.

Rigo's aunt came to take the babies to her house. Carmen wept as she assembled a backpack of clothes. We caught up with the ambulance just beyond San Diego and spent another hour following the twisting mountain road to the hospital.

The emergency room at the big city hospital in the capital was packed with the normal outcomes of nighttime accidents, crimes and parties. There were about 50 people in the waiting room. Most were talking quietly and then standing up when a patient's name was called. Some wandered as if lost, some looking over the half-wall down into the triage area. Rigo was triaged as soon as we arrived, but then left on a gurney in a packed hallway with about a dozen other souls. Carmen was directed to wait with us and the other families.

Rigo was in real pain, he was stoic but one can sense it. *Why doesn't Carmen insist that someone give Rigo something for the pain?* She said simply, "They are very busy," with a shrug. I took this to mean, *I don't have the right to ask,* and my first reaction was, *We'll see about that,* I thought. Summoning my cultural best effort, I decided to ask for her. *This is no time for an incident.* My Spanish is hard enough to understand when someone wants to, and the busy receptionist didn't seem to meet the minimum qualification for "wanting to." I by-passed the desk and went directly to the young doctor.

"Forgive me Doctor, but *that* man, my friend, is in great pain. Is there something you can do?" It was rehearsed and halting and, though annoyed, he got it.

Jerking his head, as though I were a nuisance, the intern hesitated before answering, looking in the direction I was pointing.

"Si señor," and he requested a syringe from a nurse. It appeared and was dispensed into Rigo within seconds.

"Muchísimas gracias." Relief. I'm not sure what I might have said had the man refused.

Before we left that night, Carmen kissed Rigo's forehead, then kissed the tips of her clustered fingers and made the sign of the cross over him as he lay on the gurney.

ဆ

Rigo had learned long ago how to deal with pain of all kinds. Close your eyes and say nothing. He didn't move, didn't sweat and with great will, did not moan. This was not his manly act; it was how he did it. He had been on the gurney in the hallway for almost two hours before the initial diagnosis was rendered. It was obvious even to the harried intern that the leg was going to require serious surgery, and serious surgery was not available right away. It would be another week as it turned out, although he was seen by the bone doctor for a more precise diagnosis the following Monday. He spent those weeks with inadequate painkillers and would wait until the very last minute to ask for help to get to the toilet, sometimes to his embarrassment. His wife visited daily, even though it took two dollars each way for the buses and a long nighttime walk back up the bad road to their house. She brought him toilet paper, sweet snacks and small bottles of red pop that could be hidden in her purse. She put up with a half-crazy patient who leered at and tried to touch her from his bed at the entrance to the eight-bed *salon*.

Carmen suffered a quiet terror in these trips because she had heard for her whole life about the crime in the capital. She'd never been there before and had no experience to know otherwise. She was certain that every poor man she saw was an illegal immigrant—doubtless a drug addict—and she kept her purse tightly bound under her arm and always tried to walk in a mixed group of men and women. The bus station was a tense three-block walk through a poorly lit parking lot. The fear was bad, but the logistics required to get her to and from Rigo's side were formidable. Rigo's aunt helped with the babies most of the time as it was her Christian duty to do so, and other than her pious recounting to the neighbors of her "unwavering support during Carmen's travail," asked nothing more for her substantial help. Carmen kept going, and in the month it took Rigo to recuperate, she missed only five days for problems with her own health. Almost seven weeks had passed since the accident.

As his pain eased and some composure reemerged, Rigo began to take note of things around him. He was in an orthopedic ward, and some of the patients had problems far more disabling than his. Many of them were verbal with their discomfort, but Rigo was too caught up in his own fear to become involved with them. The man across the aisle from him told a joke to the two men on either side. Quite by accident, the three of them looked directly at Rigo as they laughed. He told himself that it was coincidence but his sense of isolation increased.

Carmen seemed to be there all of the time. He allowed himself to become dependent on her visits and was visibly agitated when she could not make it. The cold sore was back, overnight and with intensity he had never known. What was left of any sense that he could control his life had evaporated. He tried to find solace by imagining that he was out of the ward and back in Eduardo's old *bodega*. But the old stratagem would not work. Fear overwhelmed all options. He began to imagine the other possibilities. He well knew that a lame *peon* was worth a lot less than a healthy one whether the lameness was from addiction or a bad leg. His not irrational fear that he would not be able to support

Carmen sat on his shoulder daily like an apocalyptic rider. He knew that she was still good-looking, and his accrued guilt racked him with images of her opportunities while he was gone from the house. His dreams were not immune. After a day in which she didn't come, his fears coalesced into a bottomless angst for the entire night.

His brother, Jesús, who visited him shortly after that bout, told him he was silly and that it was unfair to put such pressure on Carmen. Jesús' opinion caused him to reflect deeper on the meaning of Carmen's attention and support. He never talked to her about his fears so the usual result obtained and there was never an opportunity to deepen their understanding. Still, Rigo felt himself shifting inside. The grip of his illusions about love – being loved – not loved – how to love – or *something* about love – was loosening. He couldn't be sure what it was. The book that his aunt had sent said that "confusion" was requisite for personal change – *Probably a good thing,* he told himself. But he could not figure out if the change was something he might want or for that matter, what the book meant. In this state of pain and uncertainty, his desire for personal growth had disappeared from his list of wants. The only thing he could be sure of was that some important belief no longer felt true. The ground on which he stood was shaking. But unlike the many earthquakes he had known, this one did not stop. In his perpetual, unbalanced quandary, he failed to notice the extra-attentive smiles offered him by a new nurse on the ward. Carmen noticed.

"The Campo"

Early 2005

The book was published well before she finished her psychiatric residency. It was called simply, "*El Campesino,*" or, as the American translation later called it, "The Campo." The editors and publicists had quibbled over the Spanish title but decided that the Spanish word was more "Allende-like," and more sellable. It was unabashedly set in the life Aurelez knew in countryside and both Alba and Eduardo struggled to read it. To Alba, the protagonist, the "hero" as she called it, was unmistakably Rigo. The story was fiction of course, but the feelings evoked by her reading were as familiar as the heartache she had gone through with Aurelez.

The book had grown out of the short story she had written for a junior literature course. The assignment had been life changing. She discovered "writing" and would write several other novels. She became better known as an author than as a psychiatrist and remained so. The story was "provincial" as some reviewers noted, but her client list remained full as her rich, female clientele discovered they had more in common with the *campesina* than they had imagined.

Aurelez usually gave a good interview. She had her "accepting" persona as a result of her years in training and therapy. But except for a couple of particularly reactive interviewers – *particularly neurotic*, she thought – she was able to relax away from her professional role and be Aurelez. When she spoke from her non-therapist self, the edginess of her answers to certain types of questions made her quotable; she added color as sportscasters say, a lot of it. Her interviewers were mostly feminist journalists. Those with honest questions, and the skill to put them so that she could talk on her own terms, were rewarded with interesting interviews.

The reactive few that had a version and a "significance" of her book they wanted her to confirm, were left to quote themselves. With these, Aurelez would retreat to her professional self, bothering to correct only the most egregious of their misunderstandings. But the better interviews resulted in a good deal of free publicity over most of Central and South America. She became a sought-after subject because of her colorful commentary on culture. The edgiest of these comments would challenge some feminist truisms and she became known among some as an uncompromising intellectual.

For others she was an uncertain political ally who could not always be trusted to say the right thing in politically charged settings. But "uncompromising intellectual" was invested with a kind of moral capital within the University, of which she was still very much a part. It threatened to place her onto other university faculties even though she was not yet completed nor licensed.

Aurelez was born into a *campesino* generation that had only seen the electrification of their homes within their parent's lifetime. *I'm lucky*, she thought. As a result she had one foot in the eroding culture and the other in the still indistinct, emerging one. She detested the word "global" used to describe culture, but there was no gain saying that this culture was becoming pasteurized, region-by-region, following the introduction of television and the Internet. The resultant consumerism and the desire for "next," and "more," paved the way for the narrow acceptance of the various free trade agreements. *"Rico y Famoso,"* was the name of a local bar, and while most would settle for less than fame and fortune, they were hungry for what world trade would offer them. The agreements that they signed demanded internal changes that accelerated the erosion.

In some ways, without knowing so, Aurelez and people like her were leading the movement into a different way of understanding their world. The more she wrote, and the more she returned to her *campesino* roots, the more she realized this. As her awareness grew, she realized her responsibility. "How do we remain who we are while taking the best that the world has to offer?" And, she would later add, "Avoid the downsides of both."

She was certain that the whining nostalgia and the unabashed acquisitiveness that characterized political debate was not an answer. Her response would be to re-immerse herself in understanding her own culture and then bring that understanding to public discussion through her writing. *It's a dirty job but someone has to do it.* The tired punch line always made her smile when she applied it to herself but it also helped her to realize she was indeed, the one to do it.

❦

Her first new insight about Rigo came surprisingly first hand. Even before The Assignment, a girlfriend from high school told her about him on a trip home during her second year. The girl knew Rigo. They had had a short and torrid relationship until the girl, assuming a certain regularity to his visits, had asked him to help with expenses.

"It's normal," she looked to see if her friend, the college student, disapproved.

"Yes...it is...it really is," was all Aurelez had said. *Yes...it is normal.*

The girl had not reckoned on Rigo's thriftiness and his few calls thereafter were to explain that he was too busy to drop by. The story was fresh for the girl and she related it to Aurelez with the humorless savagery of a woman who had been denied by a man she thought she could trust. The girl's attitude took her by surprise. At first, Aurelez was defensive, unbelieving even. This was not the man that she knew. Rumors began to accumulate and, before she finished medical school, she had heard yet another older, but still first hand, report.

Her protagonist was indeed Rigo, but what interested her more than his evolution, were the stories of the women who spent time with him. The obvious, conventional answers offered by her natural mother as to why women consorted with Rigo were *de facto* banal to Aurelez. And she assumed that there was nothing special about Rigo, that he was just a married man who had had some girlfriends, nothing more. And well before the time the book finished she had heard that he had settled down. But ultimately, the story had little to do with Rigo anyway. He was the foil for an aspect of life in the campo that begged for daylight. The most powerful insights came from her mother.

Aurelez had never met Carmen, Rigo's wife. And she could not bring herself to reach out. But, to her surprise, her mother had been quite willing to talk about her own husband's affair. It was the affair that produced Aurelez and it was obvious that Alba had pent her feelings for years. Aurelez' questions brought the kind of relief that some people waited for all their lives, *just someone to talk to.*

Each time Aurelez thought she had heard it all, another trip home would yield yet another round of discussion. Some of it was venting, but after a short burst of that, Alba would talk about her sense of herself, and others that she knew, as a *campesina*. On this subject, she was articulate. That fact, combined with her views obtained a different respect from Aurelez. The respect was colored with a longing for something missed, a something that had resulted in her being less. *How did I not know this about my mother? Where has this woman been all my life?* That question was followed by her more honest assessment, *Where have I been all my life?* The part about being *Indio*, which Aurelez had heard from her sister,

Luisa, never came up. Her mother was talking about women and men in the *campo*, period.

These interviews had other effects. In talking about her husband's affair, her mother told Aurelez about Guito's childhood and his anger with his father. Aurelez already knew something of that tension and it was one of the things that had brought her closer to her brother as she grew. Her mother also told Aurelez of her father's history, of seeing her grandfather's farm broken up and then wasted through poor farming practices and personal failure. She learned of her father's "brilliant hopes," that Guito would bring his "gifts" to "our farm." She spoke of her husband's years-long descent into despondency with the realization that Guito would never take up his legacy.

She neither glossed over nor excused Eduardo but Aurelez clearly saw that she had forgiven. It was, in fact, the first time that Aurelez could actually see and feel the difference between simple understanding and pure forgiveness.

Alba was clear that Eduardo was too hard, too persistently hard, on Guito as he had been with Aurelez. And she offered her intuition that Eduardo had seen in Rigo the possibility of his dream. That he was "So desperate," she said, he could not bring himself to be hard on Rigo.

"I... *me,*" slapping her breast with a closed fist, "*I* took the brunt of all that...like Guito," Aurelez said.

"Yes, you did." Small tears traced her mother's face for the first time in all of her stories. "But Aurelez, what neither you nor Guito could know, you both were just children...really, just children...is all the ways that your father does love you. That one flaw colors everything. He was, and is, limited to being a man. He failed in trying to make his own dream happen and he created a wreckage of sorts for you and Guito." She hesitated, "Yes, it *was* a wreckage...for you children and your father and for me. *We* failed, and we, *both* of us, love you in more ways than you know." She wept, the just perceptible drops gathering at her chin. "Maybe one person's dream can hurt another person's dream, I don't know about these things."

"I know you love us Ma. So does Guito." They held each other for a long while.

She did know that her father loved her and Guito, "in his way;" just as surely she knew that what was between them stopped everything. But it was her mother's noesis, not just what she knew but how she made sense of it that had its effect on Aurelez. And it began the process of softening to her father. When she thought about it while writing the book, she realized that therapy doesn't just occur when there is a therapist around. She saw the urge to become whole as universal, part of everyone's makeup. The idea would become the theme of a second novel dealing with life of women in the *campo*.

But in the first book, the initial question for Aurelez, had been, why do so many of her women friends in the *campo* end up as mothers without men, and precious little prospect of finding a good one. Indirectly, by her mere presence, her mother encouraged her to look for the strengths, "the intelligence," that these women brought to the reality of *campesino* culture. It would yield a book distinctly different from her undergraduate short story. To Aurelez the conventional answers weren't wrong, they were inadequate to understanding the life of a *campesina* woman. Something important was missing and she, through her mother's sensibility, was filling the gaps.

The change in focus led her to spend more time with her women characters than with her protagonist. Her critics would later call it "fresh" and "original," but to Aurelez, her way of looking at the issue felt natural, *probably obvious*, she thought. She saw her protagonist as the mere screen on which the women projected their lives. By carefully watching the "movie" she developed a perspective that enabled her to question the culture's judgment of the *campesina* woman's complicity in the macho cultural and political forces in play for centuries. Cultural politics kept women in a role, "But it's not the role that is commonly assumed," she was quoted as saying in a Mexican arts magazine.

"Of course," she admitted to a perceptive interviewer, "the same conclusion could be said of men, projecting their lives onto the screens of the women they are with. But *that* is not *my* book." That same, prominent, reviewer concluded that she had written a "journeyman dramatization," of women whose lives had been "cramped by the culture's judgment of their value." She worried about the "journeyman," for a while, but the world understood the assessment as a confirmation of her art.

A therapist had suggested that her search for these answers was a search for the "whys" of her own life. And that possibility put into motion a slow resonance, a gong persisting, reverberating. "A loud temple gong," she would recall, smiling, in an interview years later.

It was the response of women to Rigo's fictionalized life that created a loose consensus among critics that the novel was a "subversive story of strength and independence among *campesino* women." It was the "subversive" aspect that caused some reviewers to compare her to well known feminist writers. A particular comparison, along with her resistance to being labeled, caused the slightest wobble in her commitment to write on her "subject" again. Ultimately, the feminist interpretation of her work prevailed among reviewers and one summed her contribution as,

> ".... The ability to see and depict a strength within an area of Latina life that many of her readers have assumed to be pathetic and even shameless; *sin verguenza,* to the conventional mind. Aurelez Ariza Valverde has demonstrated an instinct for resilience, for survival and quite possibly for heroism in the traditional *campesina* that evokes a deep recognition within the most urbane. It evokes a primal pride, deeper than any conjured up by nostalgia for the national mythology. That type of pride...is supremely superficial when compared to the strength of *campesina* women as revealed by Ariza's unique lens."

The review overwhelmed Aurelez with feelings that transcended satisfaction or mere pride. It was as though the reviewer knew better than she what she was trying to say and the review evoked emotions that she did not understand. The book's commercial success, while never reaching the

American "best seller" lists, made her first effort a triumph.

Life Changes

2005

The operation was successful. Within two weeks from his release, Rigo was visiting the farm with pay to offer suggestions. He accepted rides every day now as the *moto* was still off-limits. He did this in spite of the warning from his surgeon that this kind of hillside work could be a problem for him in the future. I suspected that he was trying to pay me back for the additional assistance I had provided while he couldn't work. But he said "No;" rather emphatically, I thought. In another month he was working alongside Mento and the others. Carmen had developed a wariness of the steep slopes of the farm, with his limited ability to stand firmly when lifting and cutting. Again she pressured him to find other work. Three months later, her campaign to find him a new job succeeded once again. A friend, who had received several calls from her and other members of the family, suggested that he apply for a job as a security guard at the large office center where the friend was a supervisor. Carmen's only doubt about the change was that Rigo would eventually have to carry a sidearm. Rigo applied. He spoke frankly to me and asked for a letter of recommendation. I felt resistance rise in my chest as he spoke, but there was little that I could say. I knew, perhaps sooner than he, that work on this farm was no longer the solution it once was. Rigo got his letter and left after giving three week's notice. "A long time for a *peon*," Rigo said. In the years since, *peones* have come and gone; no one has ever given more than a day's notice.

So Rigo left the life of a *peón* and became an urban worker with a guard's uniform – a new badge with an uncertain meaning. And after five years, my training program came to an end. I visited him with a friend about a year afterwards. He was signing visitors in and out of the marble lobby. He stood in the middle of a fancy faux wood, circular desk with digital everything. His weapon sat high on his left hip in a holster polished bright. *Of course*, I thought.

"I had to learn to write neater." He smiled. I remembered him struggling with his name on payday. I knew that any new learning would have brought a smile to him.

"He is just as handsome as ever in that uniform," I said.

"That's not handsome," my friend replied, "that's dashing."

Carmen's unwavering attention and his own self-inquiry had rattled Rigo's beliefs about love. It had left him without a clear reason to always be on guard lest love be withdrawn. But it was a very old habit and, as it turned out, a hard one to break. Still the discovery that Carmen's unacknowledged love had always been his would sustain the man who had relinquished one enduring identity for another of unproven value.

Not your Therapist

August 2006

The early morning drive along the highway to the capital, crowded with trucks and early commuters, still moved at a good pace. The 9:30 meeting at the government agency responsible for the newly organized rain forest meant that Guito should have come in the previous night. But hotels were expensive and his sister no longer had room at her place. The persistent resistance to his father made a stay over in Asturias an unhappy choice. It wouldn't save *that* much time he rationalized, but knew that that was what it was. For the rest of the trip his mind bounced between ruminating on his father and wondering about himself. *Maybe this is why I have a psychiatrist for a sister.*

It was not a good day for a surprise visit. Aurelez was in her last year of psychiatric residency and she took him to a vacant office, painted in a key lime green from the floor to the height of a wainscot, with a topping of grimy cream reaching to the ceiling. They had to cut into a line of people awaiting new appointments to open the door. This was the only general hospital with a psychiatric ward and it was jammed. She would spend the first six months of her residency here and she would later write about it as a "boot camp," a term she had learned from an American friend.

"I don't know. I think people lie to themselves," Guito said. She could tolerate the conversation until he said that. Aurelez jumped on it.

"You mean you lie to yourself."

"Yes...I mean that. But I also mean that it seems like we make up stories when we have not met somebody's expectations.... I think that also;" he sparred.

"Okay, so *you're* the psychologist. *You* have a theory about why people lie to themselves. How does that help you now?" Regret replaced aggravation as the words shot from her lips.

"I thought that was why I came by, for *you* to tell *me* that."

She despised conversations like this. *Jesus, some professional I am*; her inner voice yammered. She breathed in, sighing it out, her mind clearing a little. They looked at each other. Her day's priorities did a little flip, her eyes softened and she leaned to him and took his hands in hers. "*Guiiito,*" she said, "let's forgive each other and start over."

He smiled also, "I am sorry. I was thinking about things on the way down here...I just thought I might stop by."

"I'm sorry too; tell me the problem."

"Oh, it is me of course. I have been ruminating about Eduardo again. I get into it every so often." She waited. "I used to blame him...I am sure I still do...but lately I have felt like I'm missing something."

That's for sure, she thought, "That is the part about lying to you."

"Yes."

"How long *have* you called him 'Eduardo.'"

"Well...since the...since I was eight or nine."

It's curious how our lives intertwined...I can't be a therapist to everyone, she thought. She sighed gazing at him. "I'm too close to you Guito. I really can't be the one to help you with this."

"I am sorry Aurelez, I did not intend my earlier comment to be mean."

"I know you didn't, brother. It is just...I'm too close to you and to Papa; I love you both and I'm too involved in my own way. I can talk with you as your sister...but that's all you should expect."

"Okay, I understand, when you put it like that. Should we call it a day?"

"I only have a couple of minutes now but I'm going to grab a late lunch in about an hour. Can I meet you at the *soda* across the street?

ॐ

The soda was near empty; most hospital staff had returned to work. A whiff of cigarette smoke lingered. A radio in the kitchen alternated between old American rock and roll and elevator music. *Weird*, she thought, *Jefferson Airplane and 'I did it my way' in the same program*. Aurelez ate a salad and listened to Guito who ordered a hamburger but did not touch it.

"I have this fear that if I don't do something different with Eduardo...the right thing...whatever *that* is...that I'm going to spend my life in hell. He paused, "I don't mean the church-like—."

"I know what you mean, but it sounds to me like you put yourself in hell when it comes to Pa. It's like all these thoughts cause you suffering."

"What?"

"Think about it for a minute."

He took a bite of french-fry and gazed at her. "You sound like Rajiv."

"I don't mean to; I don't really know much about what you guys talk about. I'm saying back to you what I'm hearing."

"I guess...I know that I do it to myself."

"I can see that."

"Are you also saying that it is wrong...that I shouldn't think that?"

"I'm not saying anything, Brother; I'm listening." She smiled at him.

He paused a long moment. "Rajiv says that if I see reality, I will realize that I have nothing at stake here...that I can let life unfold as it is going to. But for most of my life, I have felt like I am doing something wrong. Maybe, "not quite right" would be the way to say it. All that has pretty much gone except for this stuff about Eduardo."

"You are one of the most "on-balance" people I have ever met, Guito, yet when you think about Pa...you lose it.

He nodded, "Honestly...sometimes I feel like I let him down."

"I know the feeling Guiito." She paused, "But you have had feelings about other things in the past that you are not happy about, yet you seem to accept them."

"*That*, is what confuses me. I haven't always done things that I am happy with, yet, I look at them when they come up and I just think something like, 'That's how life was then,' or 'life happens,' or something that enables me to let it go; you know, it happened but there is no remorse. But not with him," he pushed it out through a sigh.

"I have the same feelings, Guito. Pa was just too important to both of us. But you don't have to excavate the history, Guiito. The feelings are just experience. How you relate to them is all that is important."

He stared at her. "My God, you *do* sound like Rajiv."

"Maybe so; maybe Rajiv should be my therapist."

"You should meet Rajiv...he will straighten you right out." He grinned at her. "I spend some time every day meditating and looking for myself— inwardly—trying to see me." "Actually, I *do*, do it. I can spend time with myself and not get caught up in my thoughts...pretty much when I want to now."

"I don't know much about that Guiito." They were quiet for a few moments, "How long *have* you been meditating...looking inside? Has anything come of it?" She leaned back, watching him, her hands flipped up in a question.

"I have been meditating since just before you were born. What I do now has changed, but it's still meditating, kind of.... It is curious, given that I have been whining about my feelings for Eduardo, but over time life has smoothed out. There is really not much to complain about. I have given up being anxious about what people think of me. I do not want my body to die...or get hurt." He paused, leaning forward hands clasped under the table, "But you know, *something is* going to happen to each of us. So, I am accepting life as it comes...I am pretty sure that I am no longer accumulating bad karma, much anyway. Do you know 'karma?'"

"Yes... I had a professor who could get into it pretty deep...I want to talk with you about it, but some other time. By the way," she added, "that professor is Rojas' stepfather; small world, *verdad*?"

"Yeah, I guess so. Anyway, it seems the one thing I have not let go of is Pa."

"Amazing."

"It is...I have not called him 'Pa' for over 25 years."

"Well yeah, okay, but my 'amazing' was about your report. You've just described one heck of a therapy."

"Maybe... if Rajiv were here he would give you his lecture about reality is just reality, small 'r' reality. No point in making it unnecessarily complicated, like a therapy, or a religion...something about a razor, do you understand that?"

"Ockham's razor—the less complicated the theory, the better."

"There is something else. As I understand it, therapy is like a treatment for something that is wrong with you. It is like going to the doctor to make your life better, to fix yourself."

"Most of us think of it as treating a disorder."

"But the inquiry is not that. Rajiv says that inquiry is not about fixing your life. That may be a side effect...and it seems that, in my life, there has been a kind of side effect of making life smooth out...but the inquiry is just about seeing reality. That's all."

"Now you've lost me."

"I wish I could say it better." He hesitated, she began to pick up her things. "Rajiv says that the negative thoughts don't cause suffering."

"Then what does?"

"The basic cause is my belief that I am this life. And that when I see, once and for all, that I am not, it will be the same moment that I give everything over to God." They gazed at each other.

"I want to talk more about it when we can give it the time." She sighed audibly, locking her eyes into his, "Brother, whenever we talk about things like this you *always* amaze me. I'm going to have to leave you this time...still amazed." They stood and embraced. "You'll always be my big brother Guiito."

Contribution[5]

December 2007

In a striking reversal of pattern, the morning clouds gave in to a blue sky so deep Aurelez thought she might see stars in it. She regretted her commitment to the meeting. Chiquito — Eddy, was not in school, *a perfect afternoon for the zoo or the river park.* He was 10 now and refused to allow her to call him "Chiquito" anymore, choosing the American nickname for Edward. A pretty American girl in the sixth grade had told him that his name should be "Eddy," like her college-aged brother in the States. She may as well have branded the name on his forehead.

Aurelez had accepted an invitation to join and present to a large, mostly academic panel to discuss the emerging changes in Central American society. The impending Free Trade Agreements accelerated the changes that had been underway since the introduction of the mass media and the Internet, now a generation old. The panel had been convened and funded by the President of the University at the personal request of the President of the Republic.

"How do we manage the tensions that will come with so much change?" he had asked. Her book had been published and she was known to be concerned about such things and it, buttressed by her academic credentials, no doubt accounted for her invitation to the panel. It is possible that it was her presentation today that accounted for the larger than usual attendance. Additional chairs had been brought to accommodate another ten or so members who attended in addition to the 20 seated around the conference table.

The meetings were held in the University Board Room. They could have just as easily been held in a classroom but the setting added a distinction that communicated the prestige of the group's sponsor. It added noticeably to the self-importance of certain members. Most were professors from this University with a few additions, a representative from the Archbishop's office in the Capital and the Minister of Culture for the government and a couple of *politcos*. The meeting format was largely a discussion of the implications of the anticipated changes following brief presentations. Some of these topics were quite political as the country had several parties, each representing a constituency to defend some existing aspect of the economy. Today's presentations were by an economist with thoughts about coming changes in the nature of employment, a law school faculty member who was discussing the cultural implications of family law, and Aurelez.

The lawyer who preceded her was discussing legal changes to the marital options. He was taller than Guito, angular, with a large hawk-bill nose, *about 40* she thought. A shadow darkened his jaw. *I wonder if he even shaved today.* The lawyer talked faster than most and based his proposition on statistics. "...I think we can agree that the number of unwed young mothers is growing, and the pathetic attitude of the *campesino* towards the institution of matrimony is unlikely to change until we change the laws, the costs and the consequences of divorce." *Yes, of course, let's leave it to the men to talk about the consequences for women....Jesus!....* She stopped herself, *I sound like an undergraduate...of course he should be talking about it...and thinking about it too...thinking a lot about it.* He went on for another five minutes but Aurelez ceased listening. The phrases *"pathetic attitude*," and *"young unwed mothers,"* rolled, basting in her thoughts like so many birds on a spit. And, like many panelists before and since, she found that she had prepared to talk from a perspective that now felt impotent. And, like Adele, her natural mother, on the night she announced her pregnancy, Aurelez also found that she was prepared for the unexpected.

The lawyer finished. He fielded a few questions and the Chairman introduced Aurelez as the author, the *doctora*, and a new member who brings to us her "unique perspective."

She stood up with a tight smile and began her trek from the far end of the table to the little podium. Her face registered her internal process: she was considering, picking and choosing the remarks that she would now make. She did not want to punish the lawyer. His remark was not his central point, *He did not intend a slight... his ideas need to be heard.* At the podium she stalled and for the first time noticed the wooden cabinet encasing, she guessed, a whiteboard on the wall behind it. She squared her thin stack of index cards by tapping them on the table and rested them against the small ledge of the podium. Placing both hands on either side of it, she moved it to her right and turned it so that she could see her notes. She stood there for a moment, her presence now fully visible to the group. She placed both hands into the pockets of her long skirt and breathed. Her first paragraph formed completely; she smiled, engaging the convener.

"Thank you Mr. Chairman. I am very pleased to join with you and I hope I that may meet your high expectations. After listening to our colleagues, I find myself having not prepared in quite the way that I might have. If there is any fault, it is completely mine and I promise you that I shall remain within your very reasonable timelines." She saw a concern gloss his face and received his faint smile in return. She gazed into the group, engaging each person in the room, "I imagine that some of you are aware that I *am*, arguably, a *campesina*," she smiled at the polite titter. "But also I suspect that none of you know just how *campesina* I might be. So I'm going give you a brief reume for the purpose of establishing my rather impressive credentials in this field.... No pun intended." This time the group laughed, more than simple politeness. The look in the lawyer's eyes changed from interest to caution.

"I grew up in Asturias, the land of coffee, cows and *chicasquil*, on a coffee farm. I was into adolescence before I realized that we were actually quite well off, so in that way, we were different from the typical *campesino* family. My father worked in his own fields but he *hired peones*, he was most definitely not one, having grown up in a more-or-less privileged family himself. But my stepmother, the mother I knew best, is one-half *Indio*. She was taken from her birth family as a child for reasons we shall never know. She is the one to whom I dedicated my book." Several heads nodded. "When I was thirteen, I fell in love with a *peón* living and working on our farm." She paused and smiled at those who were smiling, knowingly, at her imagery. "He was an older man, fourteen at the time, I believe. And, had it been up to me, I would have slept with him and had his children." A few smiles now, most faces changed to questioning looks. "Having been prevented from acting on my heart's desire at the time, at age sixteen, I met, slept with, and before the age of seventeen, had the child of a married man. My son Eduardo is now ten, and he is, without doubt, an essential ingredient to the person I have become."

Silence.

"You are forgiven for asking, '*why* is she telling us this?' This is, after all an academic panel on preserving our culture not an encounter group." She smiled, the only person to do so; the room awaited her answer. The lawyer's eyes went from caution to wary, *he is already constructing his counter-argument, 'I didn't mean that…. It is unfair to say this.'* "So let me give you my motives. First, I agree completely with our colleague from the law school, there *are* important changes to be

made in family law. I wish us all the best of luck
with the legislature and the church in this
endeavor." Only the diocesan priest nodded at this.
"But secondly, and this is my real purpose, as a
person who knows something of the most
crippling aspects of *campesino* culture, I would
ask that you hear my remarks as coming from a
person who knows both sides of that life.

I assure you, I am *not*...at all...romantic or
nostalgic about this. On reflection, I see that my
adolescent behavior was authorized, ordained
perhaps, by the very culture we are seeking to
protect from the onslaught of globalization. Back
then, of course, I denied the personal
responsibility that I was later to see quite clearly.
But *I* had options, and *I* had a family that would
open my eyes to them. That is not true for the
great majority girls—or their families—embedded in
such a culture.

I would point out that if we focus *only* on
adolescent behavior of the individual, regardless of
the *age* when it occurs, we may easily come to
conclusions like, 'pathetic attitude.'" She glanced
at the lawyer; he returned an even gaze. "But my
purpose today, is to not only ask that you look at
the downside of a culture that authorizes such
unfortunate behavior. My purpose is to offer a
different approach altogether...one that will help
us see *both* the upsides and the downsides of

competing points of view." The lawyer's face resolved into an understanding smile; his shoulders dropped a little, his resting hand made a quiet, clapping motion on the knee of his crossed leg. But the priest now shifted in his chair, a look of dismay about where this was heading.

"So, let's begin." Holding her arms outstretched, "If you can imagine at my right hand I am holding something called a "globalized" culture and in my left something called "traditional" culture. These are apparently contradictory options—." She stopped herself, dropping her arms, "Let's do better than imagine." She turned and walked to the cabinet behind the podium and opened it to the pristine white board. Choosing a black marker from the full box of new ones, she drew a large cross that filled the board. At the left end of the cross line she wrote "global," at the right, "traditional." Every person sat alert, riveted to her; she had them and she knew it. "Don't take notes, I have a copy of my paper for everyone." The note takers ignored her request.

She led them through a discussion with people offering upsides of and downsides of each end of her polar diagram. It quickly filled.

There was enough remaining energy to have filled the chart to un-readability, but Aurelez stopped the process with, "these are enough examples to make the point."

"What point?" The priest shot back, "This is just a list of strengths and weaknesses. We could have come up with them in lots of ways."

Better economy More opportunity/jobs Fewer poor More resources for those remaining poor	Keep cultural identity – know who we are as a nation Keep values – "La humildad" Family values Care for the less fortunate – social security
GLOBAL	TRADITIONAL
Loss of identity – who are we? Subservient to larger economies Demand for drugs!! Lack of respect for church Greed! Everyone for themselves -no sense of social justice	Slow/no economy Fewer resources for governance Less opportunity – fewer jobs Continue traditional exploitive norms Unable to protect against drug cartels

"That's true. But depicting them in this manner offers us some new ways to use them. I have three more related thoughts that may make this approach clearer. One," her voice became precise, authoritative, pointing to the chart, "Each of these poles has both an upside *and* a downside, that *should* be obvious to everyone. But the fact that there is both 'good news' and 'bad news' about each end of the pole is almost always, overlooked in argument. The presence of both an up and a down side means, that it is perfectly valid...for different groups in society to hold to very different points of view because..." she paused,

"Because...each point of view contains a truth and each truth contains some desirable outcome for society. She paused again.

Two... as you know, there are those, probably people in this room, who prefer the positive upsides of one pole to the positive upsides of the other pole. The people who prefer, for example, the positive aspects of traditional culture, also *disprefer*, and in most cases are afraid of, the negative aspects of a more global culture. Those preferences and those fears combine to form a point-of-view. In this case we might call it a "traditional" point-of-view. She drew a line. Exactly the opposite is true for those people who hold the global point-of-view."

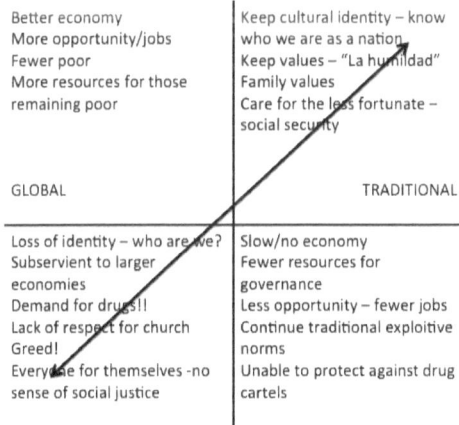

Better economy More opportunity/jobs Fewer poor More resources for those remaining poor	Keep cultural identity – know who we are as a nation Keep values – "La humildad" Family values Care for the less fortunate – social security
GLOBAL	TRADITIONAL
Loss of identity – who are we? Subservient to larger economies Demand for drugs!! Lack of respect for church Greed! Everyone for themselves -no sense of social justice	Slow/no economy Fewer resources for governance Less opportunity – fewer jobs Continue traditional exploitive norms Unable to protect against drug cartels

"Does that mean that people holding opposite points-of-view *fear* movement in the direction to the opposite side?" The lawyer asked. "They must know there are problems with the other side, even if they can't put words to it."

"Yes it does. That is exactly correct. usually, the *downsides of the opposite point of view is all* they can see."

She shifted her gaze back to the larger group, "This is a good time to stop and take some questions. I would add first, that it is the *fear* Don Luis has identified, that drives the rancor in our civil discourse, the willingness to, 'fall on one's sword' as the saying goes, in the service of one point-of-view or the other."

"With good reason," the priest offered, "Those downsides are real."

"Yes...they *are* real...but so are the upsides. Getting people to the point where they can see and acknowledge both the positive and the negative realities of the two points of view is essential to finding and managing the tension that exists between them."

"The political fighting that goes on is just talking about what's good about one side and what's bad about the other." Another member offered.

"That's why nothing ever happens." Yet another spoke up. People were into to it. *These people are smart...it is so much easier to explain when people are open-minded,* Aurelez was listening carefully, looking for those who were picking up on the implications. A few seemed lost, still struggling with the idea of trying to hold two opposing points of view simultaneously. The group shared aha's and asked questions for several minutes.

Aurelez continued, "What is not so obvious is, and this is my last point, if we accept either of the positions at the extreme end of the line, either 'pole' so to speak,... without holding on to the values of the opposite pole, we will sooner or later obtain the downsides of the pole that we are going for." She paused for this to register, *this is not language they are used to.* "For example, if we reach for the benefits of the 'Global' culture and we do not, at the same time, work at keeping the benefits of the traditional culture, we *will* get the downsides of the global 'solution.' The problem is, in this country, so-called political 'dialogue,' as someone pointed out, is exactly that, arguing from the polar positions without acknowledging the opposite reality." She paused.

"Say that one more time...the first part. I get the part about political dialogue." someone called out.

She repeated the point. This time she added, "If we accept either 'solution' that is proposed at either of the poles, and not maintain positive aspects of the other pole, we will inevitably get the downsides of the end that we accept. Those people who *fear* the downsides of movement to either end of the pole will fight...and fight hard...to protect themselves from the downsides that pole. The result is at least stalemate, civil discord, civil disobedience and in some cases, worse. The best that we can hope for is a political compromise based on who has the most votes, *not* what works to meet the country's needs. Notice what is happening today in the free trade debates."

The lawyer half-rose from his chair. "*If*..., that is true, it means that the discussion must be framed...or *should* be framed... as trying to get the upsides of each position... or each pole...each point-of-view, as you call them...and *avoid* the downsides." He relaxed back to his seat; then rising again, "And *Doctora*, for the moment, your point feels intuitively true."

Someone called out for a repeat, "Face this direction if you please señor."

He stood and walked to the whiteboard, looking at Aurelez, "*Con permiso, Doctora.*" She smiled and stepped back. *He's got it.*

Hands on his hips, his coattails suspended behind him, he took a breath and organized for a moment. "If it is true that people intuitively realize that any movement in the direction of, for example, restoring the traditional culture, will bring the downside of that pole, then that segment of the population that is afraid of those downsides, and who prefer the upsides of the a more globalized culture, will fight with all the power they possess. And *vice versa*." He smacked the board to make his points. "In some cases the fighting is simply political, we are all used to that...and the stalemate that comes with it. In other cases the fighting could be actual, as in the civil wars our generation has witnessed. Either way, war or politics, the decision is based on *power*...I would remind you that the practice of politics is the application of power...not the merits." He looked at her for confirmation.

"Don Luis, you take my point." The two of them stood there as though joint presenters. She gazed at him, then directly at the group. "If I may summarize with an implication...it is not that each side, for example in the Free Trade argument, is not right...each side *is* right." She paused. "What both sides lack is the framework to engage the other in a manner that doesn't make the other side wrong...that doesn't make the other side angry... and at a basic level, doesn't make them afraid. The result is fighting, not discourse.

In my judgment, the contribution that this group can make to civil discourse in this country, is to avoid the polemical debate in the newspapers, with the demagogues, the activists, and the legislature. Our unique contribution could be the framework for discussion, perhaps even the process. If we can assist the country to discourse within this framework, we may in effect, midwife more conscious and lasting decisions.... Not to mention, more peaceful decision-making, which, if I am not mistaken, is still a value in this country."

The period for questions and answers lasted well beyond the usual stopping time. The members wrestled with the shift in perspective and the difficulty of seeing beyond temporary polar solutions to the bi-polar management of on-going tensions.

৪১

On the way to the parking lot afterwards she hailed him from several cars away, "Don Luis, do you have time for a coffee?"

He walked over to her car. "Please, Luis...," he chuckled. "Aurelez, I think your presentation has reset the bar for our little group. May I raise your offer to a glass of wine? If not now, perhaps sometime."

"I think you might Luis."

৪১

They did have wine. Thereafter they saw each other with increasing frequency. For Christmas, Luis gave her a book of short stories by Isak Dinesen. He said that he thought she might "See something useful," in Dinesen's use of language. The book had been his mother's. She had been a *profesora* of English Literature in Cuba, and who taught English as a second language in a community college in Dade County, Florida to help support the family in the early exile years. His father had left before Batista fled and got less than a quarter of his assets out, most of the remainder being the large family farms and homes. As a government-connected lawyer with US affiliations he could see what was happening more clearly than most. His mother saw this also but held to a more, "sympathetic," vision of the Revolution, staying until 1962. "Still," Luis said, "I don't think that fully explains why she stayed and he left."

Dinesen wrote in English, a second language for her. At the time the book was published the world knew that Dinesen was a pseudonym, but not that "he," was Karen Blixen. The stories did offer a brilliant use of language. "Perhaps," as the author of the introduction had noted, "It is because a foreigner, writing in English, often falls as it were by accident on inimitably fresh ways of using our battered old words." *Could that be me?* Aurelez thought, but immediately knew that being spoken fluent was not the same as being literary fluent.

Chisme, Reprised

February 2008

The bus from Fresa to Palo Seco made a loud shearing sound, gears gnashing, barely able to clear the road less than an hour from its destination. Guito groaned knowing that it would take at east three hours for the replacement just to reach them. Normally he would wait but today was Rajiv's last day and his sister, Aurelez was visiting. He knew Rajiv would take the red-eye to Madrid that night and it might be years before they would see him again. He desperately wanted to say goodbye. Walking back, the normal one-hour drive would take three, two and a quarter if he took the steeper, cow path shortcut. That is what he did.

Stepping from the bus into sun's glare was like stepping into a shimmering film. *Jeez*, he thought, *already tired and sweaty*. He began a stride that would minimize the time.

Approaching the *cabina*, he saw his mother-in-law leave. He yelled and waved. She looked back, waved and continued on without smiling. *She looks upset.*

Tessa rose from her chair to meet him at the door. Her face was composed and serious. Her laser-like eye contact could sever an arm, *Uh-oh, the bitch face, she's furious.*

Aurelez met him with a buss on both cheeks. "Rajiv waited as long as he could," she said.

"Bad news?"

"Really." Tessa said, "Rajiv wanted to talk to you but he had to catch a flight. Sit down."

ॐ

Aurelez saw the concern on Guito's face and felt a wave of gratitude to the controller-of-coincidences that she had chosen this weekend to visit. *I'm so glad, so glad;* the thought ruminated. The opportunity to meet Rajiv had been irresistible and he had handled it well but even he seemed to appreciate her presence.

"Guito," Tessa began, "Rajiv has been accused of abusing a child." She hesitated, "Sexually."

Guito stared at her. His jaw dropped then his body dropped into a chair. "I don't believe it."

"I don't either. No one who knows him well will believe it."

Guito continued staring, lips parted as though about to speak, but he remained speechless. Aurelez moved her chair closer to Guito and placed a hand on his arm. He looked it and at her as though confused. "It isn't true," he said, finally. "I'll go speak to whoever is saying this."

"It's too late," Tessa said. "She's already built a cons   ensus among her crone friends. They are the ones spreading the story now."

"Tessa, I really don't understand this. I'm his best friend; I have to say something."

Tessa stared at him. "You can't, Guito. They'll kill you." A short, tense breath escaped, "They might try anyway just to stop any defense you can make."

Guito's mouth dropped again, his confusion apparent to everyone now. "What are you talking about? Who'll kill me?"

Aurelez saw his confusion and realized that Tessa needed to give him some of the background. She caught Tessa's eye, "Start at the beginning, sister," she said kindly.

"Okay. I'm a little overwhelmed myself. Rajiv came this morning hoping to catch you before you took off. He waited all day—."

"The bus broke down."

"I thought so. He really wanted to tell you himself, Guito. He says that several years ago, he was in the bathroom at the airport when a little boy came in. He was too short to reach the urinals or the toilets and was peeing himself. Rajiv held him up so he could stand on the toilet bowl in a stall. That's what was happening when an airport cop burst in followed by the boy's hysterical mother. She was screaming at Rajiv and pounding on his back. The cop arrested Rajiv right there." Tessa took a deep breath. "Dragged him outside."

"Fortunately, there were two other men in the restroom and they followed and told the cop what actually happened." Aurelez added. "But the mother was yelling at the cop to do something."

"Anyway," Tessa said, "there was a hearing and the judge found that there was no evidence to hold Rajiv and let him go."

"He never told us."

"No. He probably thought it was done with," Tessa said. "Rajiv is not the kind of guy to hold onto things."

"So, why is it a problem now?"

"The mother lives in Palo Seco. She saw Rajiv and told her friends that he was the man who got away with abusing her little boy."

"Is he here? The boy?"

"No he lives in the States now, with his father."

"You know her don't you?"

"I do, you might also, by sight, she comes to church sometimes."

"Why would she do this?"

Aurelez stepped in, "She's a wounded child, Guito. Seriously wounded and she's been pretty clear with several friends about what happened to her as a little kid. It's why she's so emotional about it."

"So, she didn't believe the judge or the witnesses."

"No Guito," Aurelez said, "she can't. Her fear for her little boy triggered something deep and painful. And now, she's invested in being right. Besides, even if she knew he had been punished it wouldn't matter. *She* has to do the punishing otherwise it doesn't count in her mind. That is the legacy of the wounding."

"I'll go talk to her."

"No, Guito. I'll handle it." Tessa said it in a way that Aurelez had never heard from her. *She's putting her foot down.* "This woman is drawn to Palo Seco because of the *Refugios*. She believed that this was a safe place for her and the boy."

"It is."

"It is but she can't see that now. Or maybe she does and she sees herself on a mission to keep it that way."

"People make up stories that they tell themselves so—," Aurelez started but Tessa broke in.

"We have to deal with it some other way."

"What are you saying Tessa?" Guito's face reddened. "This is a safe place for wounded children."

"But when they act like this they are just mean—filled with malice. She's going to kill Rajiv if she can."

Guito straightened up, "That is not your problem. The universe will take care of that. She cannot avoid the karma of malice. Our job is to take care of Rajiv and not harm her." Aurelez saw the disbelief and contempt in Tessa's face. She knew that Tessa had heard this kind of talk before but she wasn't buying it now.

"I...." Guito could not finish his thought. He looked at Aurelez and she nodded her support. "*I* am here because it is a safe place. Aguas Calientes has been my *querencia* for thirty years." His face reddened more, Aurelez thought he might tear up. She moved a little closer, as though he needed urging to say something that needed saying, but again Tessa jumped in.

"There's a big difference, Guito. You've *never* repeated a hurtful word about anyone. Never!" Tessa voice was husky with emotion. "I come from a long line of ToTos, we KNOW about *chisme*.

"She's a snake and I can handle it better than you. Period!"

"She is not a snake! She is a wounded child," his fist slammed his chest, "Like me!"

Tessa started at his sharpness but her words came with the same authority as ToTo Cuarto's words when Guito confronted him about the rumor of Rajiv's and Guito's sexual affair. *"We'll fix this with people,"* Toto had said.

Aurelez raised her hand to break the mounting tension but Tessa kept going.

"She's denying now. She starts the rumor then says she's just repeating 'what she's heard.' She's an expert at this Guito. We've seen it before. She does not want to be seen as a malicious gossip. That will hurt her as much as you in this town. It's how you know you are dealing with an expert."

Aurelez' hand chopped the air between them. Tessa stopped her next words and stared at her. Aurelez hesitated long enough to get Guito's full attention. "Some wounds are just too painful, Guito. People lose their civility. All they think about is striking out at another version of a person who shamed them." Aurelez breathed a deep one, "And Tessa's right about one thing, they do have something on you and Rajiv. They will not allow you to stop this. They'll kill your reputation just to get him. They know that you are the only one who can really defend him."

She could see Guito's rapid breathing. She moved closer now, leaning her upper arm into his, her eyes brimming. Alba had told her the story of Guito's youth during the interviews for her novel. "Guiito, even if these people were not physically harmed as children, they were seriously shamed." She looked away as though she just remembered something. Her gaze returned to Guito and held until his eyes met hers again. *I cannot be his therapist*; the thought returned but she plunged ahead. "Guito...it is the shame that lasts, that causes our reactions. Even if people are not physically abused, the shaming can be so deep—and the feeling of being so unlovable—some people take advantage of any opportunity to strike at others, to pass it on."

"Shame?" Each stared into the eyes of the other. "Shame?" he repeated.

"Yes. It gets passed from generation to generation." She took a measured breath while holding his gaze, "Shaming is what they do when ever the opportunity arises. And they are good at it. You are the exception, my brother."

"So, it is shame," he repeated quietly. His eyes had looked away, now they re-engaged hers, seeking his answer. "*My* shame?"

"Yours."

A small surge of satisfaction passed through Aurelez as she realized Guito had made the intended connection.

The three sat down. Tessa and Guito lost in their own emotions, only Aurelez seemed aware of the poignancy in the room. She allowed them to sit in it and they were quiet for minutes. Then she stood, went to a window and opened it. The cooling temperature outside and slight breeze cleared the room a little.

Guito placed both hands on his knees and leaned backwards into a deep breath, "Omelas." He said,

Tessa sat bolt upright. "Where did you hear that?"

"From ToTo Cuarto. He told me the story of changing from dairy to fresas." He glared at her, "While you were away at college."

Guito looked defiant and Tessa was open-mouthed now, but her face had softened, taking on a bemused look, Aurelez thought. She could see Tessa changing in the course of this conversation. It may have been Guito's adamantine position or his latest statement, but something was abating Tessa's merciless attack on the gossips.

"This is what I know." Guito said, "This community is not Omelas. It is a haven for those of us who need acceptance. All of us need a *querencia,* some more than others. Aguas

Calientes has to stay that way. There can't be many places in the world where people are so tolerant and so forgiving." His head gave a slow, side to side shake. "But I'm going to stand up for Rajiv." He glared at Tessa again, "Period."

He looked at Aurelez and then back to Tessa. "Tessa, that woman needs understanding too. We have to do both those things."

Aurelez saw Tessa retake Guito's eyes softly. She took her own deep breath, drawing out the moment. "Do you remember Lorenzo?" She said at last.

Guito shook his head, "No."

"He was the other intern. I remember what you said about him all those years ago. It was about trying to help him get over his racism towards Sochi. You don't remember?"

Guito tilted his head. "Kind of."

"Well I remember. You were carrying my groceries and said you wished you "could help him" on the way to my house. I didn't love you at the time but it was the first time I knew I could love you. I feel the same way right now." She paused, "I love you, Guito."

He reached for her hand and they sat quietly for a few moments. Aurelez was aware that a silent communication had also passed between them and felt the stir of longing for the tenderness playing out in front of her.

"You used to say that this place is magic." Aurelez said, "I think I may get it after all these years." Her head bobbed understanding and her eyes glistened. "By the way, Rajiv said exactly the same thing."

The magic in this moment fled.

"About Aguas Calientes?" Guito said. Aurelez' head nodded a yes. Guito turned toward her, "Doesn't Rajiv have anything from his court hearing?"

"I asked him that," Aurelez said. "He said they were in a leather satchel that disappeared off the cabin porch a few years ago. He used to carry them with him whenever he came for a visit, just in case something like this came up. It's been gone for years."

"Who would steal a bunch of papers?" Guito said as though trying to imagine his answer, "Maybe they could be recovered."

"What are you thinking?" Tessa said.

Guito took his time to answer. "I think it's time to talk to Don ToTo. You want to do it or me?"

Tessa looked at him now with a look that was part compassion, part respect and part something Aurelez had never seen in her. "I think you can do it now," Tessa said. She visibly squeezed Guito's hand.

The moment had softened, *But it feels fragile*, Aurelez thought, *too fragile for questions. What is Omelas?*

꙳

"Have you heard about Rajiv?" Guito spoke bluntly to ToTo Cuarto.

ToTo nodded.

"It isn't true. I need your help."

"I can't imagine it either."

"Several years ago, Rajiv had a satchel disappear from his porch. It had court documents relating to the charges."

ToTo shrugged, "We have our share of thieves, so what?"

"No ordinary thief would take a bundle of documents, ToTo Cuarto."

ToTo gazed at Guito until he realized his thinking. "You never cease to surprise me, Guito."

"Will you help me talk to Don Toto?"

꙳

Don ToTo recognized the possibility as soon as Guito explained the disappeared satchel. "But even so," he said, "it's been years." He took a deep breath and exhaled it slowly, "I'll try to find Fingersnapper. He owes me one from a long time ago." He looked off, "Still, no one has seen them for years."

A stack of yellowed documents with rusted clips and staples, securely topped by a large, mossy rock, straddled a banana frond on the porch when Guito awoke about a week later. Tessa had one of them copied and circulated. Most people were relieved, some were still doubtful and some clung to the rumor-cum-truth with tenacious glee. The document made no difference to the crones. *"There are elements in that village that find happiness in the pain of others."* ToTo Cuarto's twenty-five-year old words came back to him. *But we are not Omelas!* Guito insisted, repeating it to himself over and again, *We are the good people.*

Life Is

March 2008

Guito took the call from Luisa at four AM that morning. She and her daughter had been staying with her parents while she and her husband went through another round of fighting. "Ma has collapsed," Luisa said, "They just got her to the hospital about four hours ago...they are doing a hurry-up biopsy." He knew his mother was near the end of life. She'd been creeping up on it for the past two years. *This is probably it*, he thought and he left soon after the call. Guito also knew Eduardo would be there. Now, the idea of seeing him came noticeably with little tension.

Something had transpired with Aurelez' lesson on shame. He knew she'd taken a risk with him and was grateful. After she left the Aguas Calientes, Guito pondered how, after all these years of childhood then manhood, he'd not been able to work out how his father loved him. Or if he did. It was a knot so tight it had taken his entire life to untie it. With Aurelez' few and timely words he saw that it wasn't about him yet...at the same time it was all about him. The shame was *his* shame, and it may have been Eduardo's also. But it was his and he knew it, because of that, it could be gone. It was gone. *What will Ma's legacy be*, he wondered.[6]

Guito saw the man as soon as he turned onto the hall. He was sitting next to the door of his mother's room in a metal armchair put there for the purpose. He slumped into the chair, legs straight out, hands steepled at his mouth, eyes closed. Except for his posture, he could have been a guard. When Guito tapped the door the man looked up. Seeing Guito, he put his hands on the arms of the chair and pushed himself up. They looked at each other a moment, then both began at once, "*Buenos dias*, I'm...." Each smiled. The man said, "I'm called Rigo."

"Ahhhh...." Guito said, his expression more complicated than just interested. "I'm Guito, very nice to meet you, Rigo, finally."

"Yes, finally, the pleasure is mine." Both were quiet, searching the other's face.

"Have you seen her?" Guito asked.

"No, I've been waiting for family."

Guito's eyes caught Rigo's, "You surprise me Rigo."

"How is that?"

"I think you qualify." Guito smiled again.

Aurelez opened the door.

"Guito...oh Rigo?" She said noticing the chair, "Forgive me, Rigo, I didn't know you were here." She stood back to let them to enter. "It is not good, cancer...metastasized, pretty far along," she whispered. "She's comatose." Eduardo leaned against the bed near Alba's head; Luisa sat wide-eyed and reddened, at the foot. His brother had been there earlier and left, Aurelez told them. "Handling emotions has never been his strength," she said.

Alba slept. Guito gawked at her appearance and a shudder rippled through him. *She must have lost 30 pounds since my last visit.* Three callas leaned serenely in a pitcher of water on the bedside table. A pale light trapezoid through the window fell on her, brightening and dramatizing her desiccated face. The opposing points of light resided at her forehead and bosom as though indicating her future and the nature of the gathering. *Pa looks very lost* Guito thought and he felt the urge to enfold him, but a lifetime of habit kept his hands at his side. He pulled a chair next to the bed for Eduardo. He glanced at Guito with a small smile. That was their greeting. He stood next to his father, right hand on the back of the chair and Eduardo reached around with his right a patted Guito's arm.

Aurelez saw her father's shiver in the cool hospital air and handed a blanket to Rigo who stood between her and Eduardo. Guito watched as Rigo covered Eduardo and pushed the blanket in around the sides of his chair. "Don Eduardo, move a little to right," or "Don Eduardo, move this way a little," Rigo said, as though he were talking to a child-king. He tucked every loose fold so that the blanket neatly encapsulated the old man then placed both hands on the near corner as if to hold the chair steady. Eduardo accepted the help, he smiled at Rigo, a mere glance and Rigo smiled back. Guito sensed their mutual affection and his eyes glistened. A wave of longing swept through then out of him.

They stood or sat there for 30 minutes or so; there was little talk. Luisa explained how she had found her mother on the floor in the hallway. Guito told her that he was grateful for the call and she gave him another sumptuous smile. Eduardo said nothing. Rigo's hand moved to Eduardo's shoulder and he reached to pat it with a caressing motion. Aurelez' silence confirmed the medical opinion.

Then Eduardo looked at Aurelez, signaling somehow that it was time to go. She began to pick up things. Their mother marched on in her coma. "Can someone give me a ride back to Asturias?" Eduardo asked.

"I can," Rigo said.

"I can too," said Aurelez. "I've taken the day off."

Rigo deferred with a nod. Eduardo looked at him and raised his right hand as if to acknowledge Rigo's offer.

Luisa said, "I will stay here today."

"I will also," said Guito.

Aurelez looked at Luisa and nodded. "We'll take turns, I'll be back later...I can come back for you—."

"No, I'll be fine...don't," Luisa said looking at her sister; clasping hands, they touched cheeks.

"I can give her a ride." Guito said and Luisa smiled again at him.

ꙮ

Guito and Rigo, standing on either side of Eduardo's chair, each extend a hand to him to rise. Still watching Alba, Eduardo tugs at and pushes away his blanket and places his right hand on Rigo's extended arm, his quaking forearm resting on the length of Rigo's left. He arises, unsteady; Rigo turns to him and offers his far hand as Eduardo stands and he takes it. Guito sees them standing closely, almost as one, the frail older man resting against the younger, both gazing at his mother. It is as though the two of them now comprise an entity and that they could not have been known if apart from each other. He senses he knows both Rigo and his father at last and there is no surprise. *But who am I?* Guito looks downward at his mother's hand on the blue blanket, his attention deepens, pouring into it. A calm ecstasy arises in him.

He sees past the wrinkles, the veins and spots, into her translucent skin, sensing the universe within it. His sight penetrates her hand and into the blanket and the bed and on into a vastness. The vision rushes up to embrace him and with it comes a sense of aliveness and curiosity. His eyes rise to the room. Every thing in it, each person, hands, bodies, the light from the window, all of it takes on a clarity and sharpness that he remembers. There is nothing new here, yet, as for the first time, he sees the two men next to him, each depending on the other, helping and loving each other. He knows their feelings as he knows his own. Some time passes but no one moves to leave.

The rhombus of light has moved across his mother's chest to include his own hands, illuminating them as they rest on her covers. Guito's life reels through his consciousness in a moment. His body relaxes, shoulders ease, hands rest lightly on his mother's bed. He looks at those hands, open and relaxed as though all tension in his body has drained through them into the universe of his mother's bed. From a lifetime of habit he looks inward for himself, and sees no one. The feeling in him is the feeling in the room. He is not in his body. His body is in him, as is his mother and the others. He has known this sense all of his life, yet here it is. *I am here,* he thinks, *here*. A small joy opens within him, billowing like a slow filling sail, uncrimping and smoothing the folds as it swells, softly popping creases. To the joy comes a gladness for these people, for his mother, everyone, sweeping through him, taking possession of every cell. He becomes quieter still, flooding with gratitude. In place of the room, he sees himself; he sees his nature and that of all of them. He sees that life is as it is and that is all.

In those few moments, little more than it takes to read these words, all possibility of loss in this life slipped away from Guito. He looked at Aurelez, and saw her watching him, her face as soft as he could ever remember.

It was as simple as that.

Funeral

October 2008

He stood in the doorway of her apartment, wiping and stomping his feet and tapping the point of his umbrella on the stoop. The shadow of the portico offered small protection, and that only because the wind blew from behind the building.

"Hi, I know you are getting ready to leave—."

"Hi, Luís, come in out of the rain...I have some time, Eddy is still getting himself ready."

"I came by to offer to go with you...I can drive."

"You came out in this? That is so sweet, but I really need to focus on the family, my Pa. You never even met mother.... This is really so sweet of you." She kissed him. "I do want to take you to meet my father sometime, but some other time. Especially now."

"I would like that. I could ask his permission to sleep with you."

"Are all Cubans this crass?" She smiled, eyebrows arched, "I can just see it now, the two of us sitting in the parlor talking in code while my father listens. You are not thinking of marrying me are you?" The smile broadened into a grin.

"I'm crass? I thought you were way too modern for that."

"Are you okay?" Her smiled faded.

"Sort of...it's just that I've been thinking about things...you mostly.... Sorry, I should have called." He pushed his free hand into a pocket. "You know my father did that."

"What? Talked to your mother's father?"

"Yes.... Indeed. For three months they sat around the *salon*, with both her parents reading books. They were very traditional, doctors and all that."

"My father did also, it still happens out where I grew up...asking permission anyway."

"It's not such a bad idea."

"Luis, are you all right? Really?"

"I am." He sighed, "Sorry, I must be in a mood...funerals can do that. C'mon, I'll walk you to your car, I'm parked right behind you."

"Eddy, remember?" She pointed over her shoulder, "We still have some time, tell me more about your mother."

"She was a lot like you, started college and never stopped."

"Was?"

"A couple of years ago.... When your mama dies it's always a showstopper...no matter what your relationship was. I know you two were close."

He paused. She gazed at him.

"She taught English Literature at the University of Havana until Batista closed it." She nodded. "Mother had an interesting family.... Spanish-speaking Jews from Morocco.... They went back to Spain in the 1870's but things still weren't happy there, so they came to Cuba a few years before the Americans 'liberated' it from the Spanish. They welcomed the change and worked with the Americans afterwards."

"Jewish?"

"Yes, my mother...my father not. Tells you something about him, doesn't it?"

"I don't know...."

"He was...is, a tough old coot, a real individualist. He came to hate Batista after working for the government and emigrated just before the fall."

"Well, what about the Jewish part?"

"Does it matter?"

"Don't offend me honey." She said it evenly, gazing at him. "It's a surprise, that's all. I didn't know there were Spanish Jews in Morocco...Cuba for that matter."

"Yes, yes...I'm sorry." He sighed visibly. "You may not know that my mother being a Jew makes me one also...technically, culturally... I'm not religious, but I am Jewish. We Jews take that seriously. Ethnicity has caused a lot of mischief."

"Is that why you became a lawyer?"

He grinned, "I'm Jewish. It was either that or medicine. I can't stand the sight of blood."

"That—is a bad joke. Tell me it is, isn't it?"

"Awful. I'm just telling you that I've gotten past my funk, but, I must say...it feels odd talking like this."

Her smile started in the corners of her mouth, spreading broadly. "Yes," she said, "but endearing. That's the *bon mot*. It *endears* you to me even more." She reached up and kissed him on the mouth. "Thank you for thinking of me."

"Hello, Don Luis. Are you going with us."

"Not today *Mai*—Whoa! A tie, is this an all-time first?"

"No, but Mom tied it. Is it all right?"

"Per-fect-o, like everything she does."

"I donnn't thinnnk so."

"Hey, let's have a little loyalty around here, *Chi-quii-to*."

Eddy grinned.

Luis walked them to the car, all of them under the same umbrella. "Well, not a total loss...I feel better, much better. Thank you for being there for me." He held the umbrella over her as she wedged herself behind the wheel. "I was hoping to do the same for you. Take care of yourself, along with everyone else."

They kissed goodby.

He tilted the umbrella against a gust and watched them pull away.

❦

Eduardo buried Alba next to her foster mother in San Juan. They walked with other family and neighbors from the church to the cemetery in a cat's paw rain. Aurelez drove her father home from Alba's funeral. Eddy rode with Guito's family. Only Elizabeth, in the States, could not make the short notice funeral. Most of the drive was quiet; then Eduardo began to talk.

"I will miss her.... You know, I didn't deserve her...when I think of all the wrong choices I made in my life...I did everything wrong with you and Guito."

"You did fine, Pa. You don't need to apologize to me, Guito either. I got by all of that years ago. I'm sure...I know for a fact, that's true for Guito too." She hesitated, a smile worked at the corners of her mouth, "Besides—I got you back."

He looked up, head cocked, "Oh...." He smiled, "you mean Chiquito.... Don't you wish everyone took their revenge by giving each other little blessings like Eddy."

"You and Ma were a blessing to us during those years...I wasn't the best mother around." Her face darkened, "I wasn't around enough." *The two of you saved me*, she thought, *Guito and Tessa too*.

He became quiet, his mouth began to move well before the words came out, "I never thanked you for naming him Eduardo." He paused, "You hated me then...I hated myself during that time—

calling him Eduardo and 'Chiquito' saved me in those days."

Her attention wavered and a wheel dropped into a pothole. "I'm glad too, Pa." *Maybe that's what we do,* she thought, *we save each other*.

"I never asked...how is that you and ma raised me...not Adele"

"Well, Honey, Jorge, I think it was Jorge—."

"It was Jorge."

"Jorge didn't want a baby—you—in the house. It turned out to be lucky for us, Honey."

"Lucky for me. I thought that might be it. You know Adele supported me in medical school after he died."

"You told me."

"He was always nice to me when I was over at their house."

"He was a civilized-son-of-a-bitch. She worked hard for that money. She gave up a lot. I bet she knows it now." He took a deep breath, "Anyway, it all worked out fine, everything...even for her." They were quiet for a long moment. "I need to talk with Rigo and Guito like this. I hurt Rigo too—just to clean up my conscience."

"Well, don't worry about Guito, unless you just want to get it off your chest. Can I ask you one more about Adele?'

He looked at her but said nothing.

"Did you ever think about you and her, afterwards."

"Not after my sanity came back. Guito's changed, hasn't he? I've never felt so cared for by him. He has been home more since Ma got sick than the rest of the time put together. Usually he brings one of the girls."

"I'm sorry Pa." he nodded. "Guito's become one heck of a human being, practically a saint."

"What happened to him?"

"He was always a special person, in a different kind of way...but...." She stopped, expelled a sharp breath, *What do you call it?* then plunged ahead. "He has been trying to know God all his life; I think he has finally...surrendered," she said. She wondered where that came from, *maybe Guito used it.* They were quiet while Eduardo took this in.

"We hardly ever went to Church."

"I don't think Guito got 'religion.' Not the way we usually think about it. But he has a strong desire to know who he really is in relation to God."

"Well, I'm not sure what that means, but I'm very happy for me and him."

"Have you talked with Rigo?"

"I asked him to give me the name of a lawyer. Mine died 15 years ago and I haven't needed one since."

"Did he?"

"He got a name from that Gringo he used to work for, she's—the lawyer, she's good, a retired judge."

"She honest?"

"Everybody says so, and nice too...they are not *all* bad you know."

She glanced sideways to see if he was serious. "Who? Gringos or lawyers?" She remembered he didn't have much use for either and chuckled.

"Both."

She chuckled more. "What's it for anyway?"

"I need a will, *cariña*. Now that Ma is gone I need to start taking care of these things...should have before."

"If you want any help, I have a good friend at the law —."

"I want to do this myself, *mi amor*."

"Well, you know I need the least."

"I know that, but you know that that is not how I am."

"Yes, I do... I hope you will include all five of us."

He looked at her, "Rigo?—I haven't figured that part out yet." He paused, "You know he is a good man. I think he has always carried the torch for you."

"We are just going to have to let that be his problem, aren't we?" He glanced up at the edge in her voice. "Rigo has carried a torch or two in his life," she said. Both went silent for a long moment.

"That's been over a long time, Aurelez. He is a good husband and a good father." They approached the house.

She stopped the car in his driveway, "That was harsh, Pa. I know Rigo has always been a good man; he's made his share of mistakes...like each of us." Neither moved. She rested both arms on the wheel, "I was just a girl when all that happened, but I swear to God I loved him, and I know he loved me. Now he is like a brother," she added as she opened the door. She stepped out, then turned to get her purse from the console; Eduardo sat there, hands folded, staring straight ahead. She closed the door and went in the house.

�

The early part of the return trip to Aguas Calientes was a slow one. The funeral had been marked with rain, light then heavy then light again. But first days of summer could be gorgeous on the day after the sky drained itself and this one was like that. The sky held nothing but air, no vapor, no smoke from the fields. The blue of it was celeste, brilliant and brittle. Only the natural horizon remained to obscure one's vision. It was a trip Guito had made a hundred times while in high school, at times walking the 10 kilometers from Paso Llano to his home. He stopped twice in the drive down the mountain. At Pueblo Nuevo they could see the confluence of the Rio Fresa and the big river from the lake, the exact point that formed the Rio Vallejo, which drained the Lake and the Great Valley.

When he turned into the dirt entrance to Yamiya he paused just over the crest of the little rise where the road began its plunge, 200 feet, to the knoll on which the village sat. The panorama commenced at far right with the volcano at the head of the great valley, and its white skyward plume. The horizon persisted northwesterly, making a crenelated hem for the sky with the two volcanoes that bookended the great saddle of Aguas Calientes. In a narrow gap in the north range one could glimpse the southern end of another Cordillera as it carried the continental divide northward on its back. One could see the western end of the northern range again and the notch at the western port. The gray green ribbon of the gorge inclosing the Rio Vallejo coiled for the most of that sweep until it disappeared behind the village itself. Further out, the white tower of a cumulus, spread its anvil head out over the Western Ocean.

The normal ten-minute trip from Eduardo's farm to the turn off to Yamiya had taken a half an hour and it seemed he had scarcely started the story of his mother's childhood. He said nothing of "El Indio," and neither did Tessa. At the bottom of the hill there was the small school on the right but he turned left immediately in the direction of the *ceiba* tree where his grandmother's house had been. The road terminated in overgrowth at about 200 meters. No *ceiba* was in sight and he turned the car around, "There was an old tree," he said, "but the house was gone even when I was a kid."

At the intersection, there was a public phone and little church on his left and the blue school building directly in front. He stopped the car and turned off the engine. A small juddering breath escaped; Tessa placed her hand on his arm. Painted on the wall of the school was a mural of a feathered Indio, "Yamí," scrawled in paint above it. They sat in the car for several minutes; Salome and Anaïs looked at the painting, then their father, then the painting, and back again. They said nothing.

"I can drive," Tessa said.

"No, no...I'm Okay."

The moment opened to a discussion about their great grandmother and her brother and the Indios and the story of their father's childhood and El Indio and Aunt Aurelez spilled out, filling the car until well through the great valley, around the big lake and into the long climb to Aguas Caliente.

Afterward

2016

Late-to-diagnosis diabetes finally caught up with Eduardo. One stroke put him in a nursing home for two months and then a second got him a year later in his sleep. I should be so lucky. Guito, his daughter Salomé and Eduardo's first great grandson, also Eduardo, found him the next day.

Until their mother's passing, I had only met Guito and Aurelez a few times at some birthday parties and at Luisa's second wedding. They held the reception at the "old home place," Guito called it. I love the expression; it could have come straight from my own family. The name, Guito, I could remember, but early on, Aurelez, was near to impossible. I told her it was because I'm an *anciano* and my brain was gone when I ran into her at a restaurant. She must have seen my blush when she said that she thought it was because, "We all look alike." She quickly apologized, "It was a joke," she said, thinking that it was an American expression. Of course it *is*, but people of my age and origin can feel awkward with talk like that. The man she was with, Luís, was extra generous in shaking hands as we parted.

Aurelez wrote me a letter, on paper mind you, after my last draft of this story. Here is what she said, thinking about her father: "Our lives are like letters and other people are the punctuation. Some are commas and semicolons; our children each get a paragraph. When the letter gets too long, part of it breaks off and addresses another life, or at least it should. Run-on lives are just as confusing as run-on sentences."

No wonder her books sell.

❧

Eduardo's will left each of his children fifty or more acres of prime development land along the highway to Asturias, the "steak," as the saying goes. Guito got the parcel with the house. It came with twenty hectares of coffee and the old *almácigo*. With Rigo's help, he became a coffee farmer and the property offered enough income, combined with their savings and the social security, to retire there. They did so just this year, after the girls were settled. Salomé went to the national university, married and taught school in Aguas Caliente. She gave Guito his first grandson. Elizabeth went to college in the Seattle, married and stayed there as a physical therapist. The marriage didn't last but she remained. Anaís, followed Aurelez to medical school, "to be a real doctor though," she liked to say whenever her aunt was around. It's the kind of thing that could get old but it never did. Aurelez seemed unoffendable with the ways things worked out. She left her parcel in coffee and leased it to Guito.

Her new book drew an eager publisher but she did some research and decided to self-publish, refusing the advance. She is definitely a risk taker. She and Luis married two years ago in a very private wedding, and he attempted to adopt Eddy but his natural father objected. The father's decision seemed to be negotiable but Luis and Aurelez disdained to engage in it. And Eddy is in his first year at CalPoly, studying engineering. With his fearless gift of gab, everyone thinks he will end up in sales.

Luisa built a house on her parcel and moved there with her new husband. Their middle brother sold his parcel for enough money to enter a partnership for an auto service center in the capital. A small, one hectare piece between the Aurelez and Guito parcels went to the *peón* who had been with Eduardo since before Rigo.

That leaves Rigo. Eduardo left him the remainder of the coffee *finca*, over 500 acres. He worked as a guard for another six months until the current harvest was in and while he and Carmen built a smallish house, "to start with," he said. They had a party at the house right after becoming full-time *finqueros*.

The place was already crowded when I got there. Cars were parked all over the yard. Rigo and Carmen were welcoming people on the porch. We walked up the long straight path bordered with flowers. The porch was almost as deep as the house itself and held several leather rocking chairs.

"*Buenas tardes*, Don Rigo." He looked at me, his eyes glistened, just before that big Rigo smile split his face and he pulled me into a hug.

The River[7]

"I do not know much about gods;

But I think that the river is a strong brown god-sullen,

Untamed and intractable . . . ." [8]

Dark clouds, dark sky. I have avoided thoughts about the clouds since coming back, but today, watching the black cumulus gather above the mountain; it presses on me. That is the feeling, pressure, as though the weight of the cloud is forcing recall from the ten thousand tributaries of the unconscious, pushing it upward, giving it a form and making it into a memory.

❧

A young boy or man, one cannot say from this distance, makes his way downriver, across the broad expanse of shallows known as the three *lagunas*, in a dugout canoe. He sits just behind center, legs loosely crossed so he can unfold them quickly should the river try to wet him. He sees the sky blackening over Mt. Turu-ba-ri. It is early for rain although a storm from the Atlantic has settled itself over the eastern shore and is pumping water into the Central Valley and the next canton east. Today, the water was high enough to make for easy transit across the *lagunas* and he wants to enjoy it before the dry season reasserts itself. The river's home is the eastern canton. From there it surges from the ground as the Quebrada Maquina, twenty kilometers northeast and is joined by hundreds of smaller creeks and springs as it follows the valley slope to the Tárcoles River and on to the Pacific.

He found the log boat years before at age ten. It stood against a tree, prow wedged securely into the fork, the lower end resting on a flat rock but still pocked with rot from the surrounding mulchy soil of leaves and worms. It had been burned and hollowed from the trunk of a bitter cedar, that wasn't a cedar at all. But the bugs did not like it so there it stood for who knows how many years. The boy had dragged it, a little each day, hoping to surprise his father, but his father had found him out and the two of them lifted it to their shoulders. The *Indigenas* made it, his father said, but they had not been around here since he had married the boy's mother. The boy used it with a single bamboo pole, hollow ends stuffed with rocks for a little weight and tied off with a flap of raw cowhide. One pole for each dry season and he had been through four

He knew the rocks in this river. The stream comprised the better part of his mental map of the world. It extended from the south, from the rock escarpments of the Potencianas to a few hundred meters north of the river. By the time his children were his age, they would surrender the outside, all of nature except their pets, in favor of an electronic world of relentless non-communication. But this was his youth and the river was the part he chose when those things that had to be done were. That was how he was on it today, on the wide and slow moving *lagunas* with their wide bars of river rock and sand. His parents had taken the younger ones to the dentist in the nearest city, and to visit with a colleague in that town.

The boy and his older sister remained on the farm. He had secured the canoe with a long rope from a tree on the shore, and it beckoned to him from the wide sand and rock bar that formed the beach of the river. He hung the coiled rope from the stunted branch of the tree that served as his bollard. The shallow little craft would surf the thin water rapids that connected the three flat sections in the dry season, but his one attempt in the rainy season had resulted in near disaster and he had found the canoe near the confluence with the Tárcoles after a week of searching.

This boy-man had been born at home a month early, in 1956, delivered on a weekend by his father who, out of fear for his wife's life, had done so by an emergency caesarian. He was a veterinarian so his surgery was sterile, and considering his lack of training, one could say skillful. It appeared to be the safest option given what he had been told by a physician after his second child was stillborn and his wife endangered. The trauma of the second and third births ended any further efforts to extend the family and the boy had only his sister, older by four years, for a true sibling. But like the stray and wounded animals that found their way to the veterinarian's farm, stray and wounded children washed up at their door so that the boy now had three younger siblings, all of whom were cousins of some distant degree. His parents loved these children like their own but it was his older sister who assumed, of her own volition, the responsibility for training the younger ones to be members of the family.

Her name was Gabriela and she would leave in three months for Heredia to the university followed by veterinary school. The boy had already inherited the big black mare that she rode to high school in San Juan. The years between them were enough that she was not a reliable playmate except when her own unfinished childhood bubbled through her sense of responsibility. The happiest moments of his youth were when her loving authority dissolved into a playful equality. She watched out for him, treated his hurts as though she were already a doctor, and comforted him in the times that his little boy behavior required timeout from his parents. When he was 11 he was careless with the latch on the bathroom door and she walked in while he was massaging his new adolescent toy. In an almost incomprehensible measure of sisterly compassion and wisdom, she chose not to see. Weeks later, when she began to tease him with, *"chico malo,"* (bad boy), it felt less of a reminder of the incident than it did of his emerging masculinity and his now proper sense of who he was. She loved him and he knew it.

It was that same year that Marco came to speak to their father. Marco was older than Gabriela by two years and had helped his father with the farm from time to time. Marco played the guitar, like a real musician, the boy thought, and could sing *"ranchera,"* like the Mexican singers his parents listened too. After the talk, Marco began to come several times a week and the boy realized that his sister had a boyfriend. If it had been anyone other than Marco the boy might have been jealous but Marco was fun, for all of them, and he often brought the boy a sweet orange or mango. When he was 13, a few days before his birth day, Gabriela told him to go down to the river and remind her parents she had a test the next day and needed relief from their brothers and sister in order to study.

He could see them sitting on the old *almendro* log beneath the riverside *higuerón*. At least once a year his father would say that he was going to "cut that magnificent log into boards and make a chest one day," but it had sat there for as long as the boy could remember. The big tree cast a wide shadow and the couple shared the shade with his father's cows and the mare. The heat sucked energy from the boy and his progress was diffident, listless, down the shallow slope. He stopped a few meters away when he saw his mother's arm flail the air. "Him," she said loud enough for the boy to hear and he stopped. At the end of her arm was the paper fan with the picture of Jesus on one side and the beatitudes in calligraphy on the other. It returned to its choppy waving, low on her bosom. He could not hear his father at all but, "her," rang out from his mother and for some reason, he knew they were talking about Marco and his sister. The thought brought him alert, and then just as quickly filled him with a sadness that would require many years to understand. His mother's hands were animated the way they got when she was worried. He called out a warning and they both turned abruptly to face him over their shoulders. His father held up a hand as though to say, "wait there," and they finished whatever they were saying. His father waved the boy closer and he delivered his message. His mother had been crying.

The family lived near the village of Lagunas on a farm that sloped down to the Turubares River.

Across from the farm, lay the bleached trunk of an *higuerón* tree its trunk wedged under a boulder and its roots exposed upstream to the river. It was just last year that the boy had scrawled a girl's name on that rock on the side away from his house with a thick chalk, thinking perhaps that it might last forever, or at least a long time.

Lagunas was his mother's home. She had met his father at the university while studying to be the teacher she now was. His father, from the high elevations at the far end of the Central Valley, loved the hotness of Lagunas. He thought that being the only veterinarian in the area was propitious, even though his practice was limited to large animals and the occasional snake-bit hunting dog, and his professional fees were as often as not, paid in kind. But as families go, in any part of the world, this one wanted for little.

৪০

The sun broadcasts from the west with an unrelenting brilliance. It provides a shocking contrast when the boy checks behind; a black and towering cloud sitting over the east end of the valley. It is raining hard in the East. The boy hesitates, allowing the canoe to drift, then reluctantly begins poling to turn the craft and make his way upstream to the first *laguna*. When the canoe reenters the upstream lagoon, he can just make out the large tree trunk across from the beach where he ties off the canoe. The boy had climbed on that trunk since the first time he had crossed the river with his parents. He frequently climbed the matrix of bleached roots, which reminded him of fishing nets, although he noticed that there were fewer of them with each of his passing birthdays. The river has risen more and he keeps the craft to the sides where the current is slower. His sister waves to him from near the tree where he ties the canoe. She holds the line and runs it through her hands as she coils it into a throwable loop. Ten meters more and he would move back and rise to his knees to bring the prow up and drive the pole hard to beach the canoe. He looks at his sister and she waves again. She looks upstream, then back at him. Her right arm shoots straight out, sideways, "Joaquín," she yells.

He looks to his left and sees the wave enter the *laguna* two hundred meters upstream, a low wall of water about three feet high. The boat is sitting sideways to the current and in a frightened confusion he begins to pole the canoe to align it with the approaching wave, but headed downstream, not up. He can no longer see the wave but he hears it bearing down on him. Above the low roar he hears Gabriela; "Joaquín," she screams again, and then again. His alignment is not perfect. The wave has spread out as the water expands into the *laguna* but there is enough to catch the little craft at an angle, twisting it and flipping the aft end up and the boy into the water. Joaquin cannot swim but the wave washes him into the root mass of the tree as it floods the rock bar. He catches the roots and then works his way to the side, and climbs up, straddling the trunk as though it were the mare. He clutches the roots with both hands, gasping until he hears his sister's yell, "Joaquin—are you Okay?" He looks up and waves one arm heartily. It morphs into a clenched fist and his face into an exuberant grin. She waves back and then laughs, head back and hands on hips.

Gabriela's solution is to use the rope, already secured at the other end, as a support to wade the now waist deep water to get to Joaquín. Then together they would make their way back to beachside. It took him a moment to realize what she is doing. "Wait there," he yells, "I'll come to you." But she has already decided. She works her way across, paying out the rope as she goes. It will clearly not reach the opposite side but it will get her to the point where her paddling hands would help get to the tree. How they will get back without it was a question she has not yet considered.

The boy hears it first. He stares, eyes bound to the upstream bend as the choking sound of the twenty foot wall of water hunts the wide open *laguna*. With it comes the straight-on sound of the wave, carrying whole trees and hundreds of boulders gouged from the sides of the river, out of sight and grinding the river bottom into fine paste. The river disgorges its entire meal of thunderstorm into the flat. Time comes close to stopping as people have reported in such circumstances. The boy turns to his sister, five meters to go; she hears but she does not look. Her eyes lock his and hold him like a beam, guiding her, pulling her the last few meters. "Joaquin, stay there," he hears it as though from the end of a very long tunnel. Their eyes hold as the wave hits. He thinks she may have called his name once more before the water and sand fill her mouth and drag her under.

The boy has pushed his arms through the mesh of roots, his elbows twisted into the tough matrix of dried sticks. The initial shock twists the tree trunk and moves it sideways but it holds. Sometime during the minute or so that he is submerged, a large rock, suspended in the wave, smashes his left hand breaking the fourth and fifth fingers. Rock and debris pummel his head and face. As the tree quakes under the assault, he stops struggling and whoever, or whatever handles these matters, assumes control. They find him two hours later, pasted to the tree trunk and partly conscious. The boulder is gone.

Neighbors working with his father are assembling a rope tow using oil lanterns and a single flashlight to see in the dark. The boy is naked except for his shirt, which hangs from one arm and is twisted into a thin rope. It is wedged into the mesh of roots and may have helped him to stay aboard the trunk. Someone throws an oversized shirt over him and his father's trembling arm guides him to his mother who stands with the women near his bollard-tree. His right hand holds the left arm well in front so that nothing touches his fingers. His mother, dry-eyed, watches him approach. She holds the frayed tie down rope and works it through her fingers rubbing each of the hemp braids, "Ave Maria, full of grace," her lips moving without pause. When he is in front of her, she stops her prayers and extends her arm, her fingers feather his cut and swollen face, her stare penetrates his eyes to the back of his brain, "Thanks be to God, Joaquín," she says. "Where is your sister?"

All that happened forty years ago this week. My sister's body was never found. After the flood my family mourned quietly and deeply for well over a year. My father was able to splint and save the ring finger but the little one was crushed beyond repair and taken off at the first joint. It remains the most visible of all my scars. During that year I realized that if there was going to be another veterinarian, it would have to be me. To everyone's surprise I became a serious student, eventually graduating from veterinary school in Heredia. I went to México for more training and then joined the faculty here. I stayed in the Central Valley and never went on the river again. My mother died of colon cancer 20 years later and my father just last year. He practiced until well into his nineties and left the farm in parcels to the remaining children. I got the house and retired here.

I have heard it said that one cannot step into the same river twice. The tree is gone of course, and the boulder. The river gives life and it takes life. Perhaps it is life. As I sit here today, I remember overhearing a classmate in high school tell someone that my sister was never found because she had been washed into the Tárcoles and eaten by the crocodiles. That remark might have made me angry, or at least sad, but it did not. I had already decided that she had become the water, become the sand and the silt. The river was her tomb and her spirit became part of it. I still think so.

The Last Indio[9]

Doña Isabel had seen this boy many times on her way to the village school each day. He lived with his older sister about 400 meters down the road toward San Pedro. It was a wooden house with a rusted tin roof and shutters for windows and in bad condition. The doorsill was high and appeared to have supported a small porch at one time. It stood in the shade of a large *ceiba* tree. *Probably has a dirt floor,* she thought. From time to time a horse would be hobbled in the yard, or perhaps a man sat on the rock that served as a stoop, but the boy almost always played outside, alone.

She knew that their mother had died when his sister was a new teenager. How they survived was the subject of *chisme*, the local gossip that stood in lieu of newspapers in those days. *No lack of chisme around here,* she thought. When she herself was a child there were *Indios* living on the slope of this hill that fell away, down to the Rio Grande gorge. As far as she knew, they were all gone except for this boy and his sister. Now the boy says, he wants to go to her school.

Isabel grew up two miles west of the town of San Pedro and three from the village school. She attended the one room schoolhouse about a mile from her home on the road to the town. Her father took care of the house and grounds of a large farm for its absentee owners and was entitled to harvest its mangos. For a local man, he made a good and steady wage. His still-living grandmother was *Indio-Indio* but no one in Isabel's family was allowed to mention it or to ask questions about her. Still, Isabel knew, as did everyone, and in spite of the taboo she loved the old woman as much as any.

Isabel was the good daughter. The oldest, she assumed responsibility for household chores, for collecting mango, and for the children, without complaining and even with enthusiasm. She discovered "art" in high school and developed a rather good hand at drawing faces. Charcoal images of her entire family graced the walls of the house. In the year after her *quinceanera*, the traditional 15th birthday celebration for girls, Don Juan Carlos Aguero asked her father for permission to court her.

Her father was delighted but Isabel barely knew the man. He was ten years older and had lost his wife after the birth of their third baby. Isabel had seen him apprise her on the way to and from school and they had spoken at town fiestas; she knew that he was not ugly. He now cared for the three children, two of whom were approaching adolescence. She thought of him as a pleasant man but certainly not Francisco.

Isabel was a good girl, not at all a rebel, but she imagined herself in love with Francisco an older boy in the high school of San Pedro. In truth, the boy reciprocated but this love had gone unspoken for the weeks that they had looked in each other's eyes and smiled. The very air between them rippled and sparkled when they arranged to pass each other. *Why has he not spoken to father?* With Don Juan Carlos' proposal, her emerging dream would be as dead as she now felt. Her father knew this, but he persisted. Don Juan Carlos was more than a suitable match for this family, and his daughter.

For the first time in her life, Isabel fought. She was one of a few girls in high school, education in those days being appropriate for boys. She thrived in the stimulation, *like the spores in a petrie dish*, that she learned about in science, and she acquired the ambition of becoming a *maestra*, a teacher in the *escuela* that she herself had attended. Her father knew this also and had shrewdly spoken to Don Juan Carlos about letting her finish high school and the suitor had already agreed. But her father said nothing of this to Isabel or his wife.

When Isabel's unexpected resistance devolved into a week of crying and sequestration in her room, her father bargained with her; he would speak with Juan Carlos to see if such a thing might be possible. But Isabel sensed manipulation and with a shrewdness beyond her years she agreed to see Don Juan Carlos for the year remaining in high school. If all worked out, she would marry him. Her mother stood up for her. "No, husband," she said to Isabel's father, "she has agreed and that is enough. It will be this way or not at all."

Don Juan Carlos was annoyed. His generous agreement he felt, had been broken, but her father through up his hands, "Women!" he said, "may you understand them better than I." And Isabel was both a comely and predictable commodity as a wife.

"Very well," Juan Carlos said."

❦

That was fourteen years ago. When the agreement was struck, Isabel stopped making eyes with Francisco to the boy's visible heartbreak. But a deal was a deal, and in spite of her own *corazon destrozado*, she stuck by her part of it.

Her life as a married woman was predictable except in one respect; she did not get pregnant. After five years both she and her husband resigned to that fact. It was less of an issue for him except for the currents of invisible suspicion that flowed in the local *chisme* river. That river informed life and arbitrated truth in the villages. Isabel was a good mother to Don Juan's children but it was only with the youngest that she ever came close to a feeling of motherhood. And the youngest, a girl, had the disheartening practice of wailing for her natural mother at times and pushed Isabel away.

Any sense of motherness with the girl had to be recreated every few months. In time, that too became a stunted version of what might have been possible. Still, she knew from other women that Juan Carlos was a better than average husband. Every so often a woman friend, usually older, would congratulate her on her luck. But the reality of no children left her unfinished, self-conscious, and perhaps, a little vulnerable.

Isabel became a teacher. The one teacher in the school of her dreams, the one she had attended, never left so she found employment in the big *escuela* of San Pedro. Then four years ago, this particular village built a new school, all wood and two stories high. The village of Yamíya now had nearly 200 families within its purview and a retiring director. The school *junta* selected Isabel to replace her. The four years had passed without remarkable incident. She walked to her new post, three miles in each direction and uphill in the mornings, and as a result retained her health and her figure. In time her husband would buy her a gentle mare that would graze, hobbled, near the school. But that was still a few years off.

A great war raged in the world now but in these villages a subsistence existence continued unaffected. The country declared war on its benefactor's enemies but that did not amount to much except in the ports. This same benefactor had bought thousands of acres of *ceiba* forest only to discover shortly afterwards that the type of kapok the tree produced was not suitable for its intended use. Any boom to the rural economy evaporated without effect. Life flowed on.

She knows this boy by sight. She makes his age to be about seven, maybe eight, but he is smaller than the other boys, so there was no knowing for sure. Birth certificates were a luxury found in the Central Valley and the larger cities, *for the rich* she thinks. And today he is freshly bathed and hair parted, the first time she ever noticed. The boy says he wants to go to her school.

"What is your name *chico*?"

"Yamí."

"Is that your Christian name or your *apellido*?

The boy hesitated, uncertain, "It is my name." He looked at her with a combination of confusion and melancholy that split her heart.

She smiled at him, "Well," she said softly, "Any boy named Yamí can certainly go to the school of the village of Yamíya. Do you have a uniform?

"No *Doña Maestra*."

"Well, let's see what we have." Doña Isabel kept a few odds and ends that came to the school when the youngest child in the family finished *escuela*. She found an oft-repaired white shirt that might fit and a pair of too large navy trousers that would make do if he rolled them up. She left her office for him to change.

"*Doña Maestra*."

She opened the door. He stood there, hands shyly and tensely folded in front of him. Dust motes floated around his head in a ray of sunlight. They looked at each other for a long moment and a smile opened her face. He smiled, his eyes glistened, and she walked to him, kneeling to look him in the eye, placing both hands on his shoulders, straightening his shirt and buttoning a missed one

"I think you are very handsome in this uniform, Yamí. School starts tomorrow at 8:00 AM. Would you like to walk home with me, I will talk with your sister.

Before leaving for home that afternoon, when she added the boy's name to the roster, she wrote " Yamí Purísima," then added "y Purísima," for good measure. The other teacher, who knew of the situation, chided her gently for the subterfuge.

"*Buenas tardes*, señorita, Yamí has spoken with me. I am Doña Isabel, the *directora* of the school." The girl, perhaps 16, looked at her, then past her to Yamí in his new clothes. Her face broke into a broad smile.

"Oh *muy buenas tardes* Doña Isabel, *mucho gusto*." Her hands clasped each other at her throat, "Thank you, thank you so much. We do not have the money for the uniform."

"Yes, perhaps we can find clothes as they are needed. We are looking forward to seeing Yamí in class. Can you, perhaps," hesitating, *not likely,* she thought, "can you adjust the pants a little?" The house was more wretched than she imagined and she left as soon as might be polite, resolving to bring needle and thread the next day.

The walk home found her in a mood. The girl was doing the best she could, Isabel was sure of that. *How would I handle her twist of luck? Better? Maybe, But just maybe*, and her uncertainty blossomed into a grudging admiration for the girl's grit and her will to survive;

Isabel brought the needle and thread and many other things as the school year progressed, a loaf of bread from the previous day, pieces of fruit, and at times a plate of left over salsa de carne or pinto covered by a cloth. The girl was always grateful and had the plate cleaned and ready for

Doña Isabel at the end of the day.

When the boy walked with Isabel, he always remained close and when other children appeared to grab her or talk to her, the boy would press even closer to her leg, his head barely reaching the top of her thigh. Once on the way home they passed a man trudging uphill from a day in the fields. He wore a machete and a cotton *lona* on his head. It used to be white, but was now dulled gray and brown from sweat and grime. The boy was chattering at Isabel, looking at her and did not see the man until he loomed in front of them. Yamí gave a small cry, stepping behind Isabel as he tried to push his arm between her legs holding her tight and hiding in her skirt. A wave of embarrassment flashed over her followed by recognition of the boy's fear and its object. Anger rushed to the surface and she glared at the man, refusing his "*Buenas tardes.*"

Another thing, essential to our story, came to Isabel's attention during those first years. Once in the rainy season she arrived early at school to find Yamí sleeping on the porch, its roof covered the entrance to the school. His uniform was wadded into a ball and his head slept on it.

"What happened *mi amor*?"

"They put me out last night."

"And you slept here?"

"Yes, *maestra*." He looked up to her face, "I am sorry, forgive me."

"Do not worry yourself, Yamí. It is all right *mi amor*. Tell me, is your sister okay?"

"Yes, I think so, *maestra*."

But it was not all right. *There is nothing 'all right,' about it*. And that afternoon, Friday, the last day of the school week, she asked his sister if she might take the boy home for the weekend. "Yamí needs a little additional work on his letters and I can give that to him on the weekend."

The girl looked at her, searching her face for some hint of condescension but there was none. Empathy for the girl herself and her struggle perhaps, but no pity. When Isabel said that there were many children around to play with and that she would stop by on Monday morning, the girl relented.

What Doña Isabel's husband might think of this had not occurred to her, and as the two walked downhill, she thought of Don Juan Carlos.

It doesn't matter, she thought, *maybe I am a rebel in my old age*. At thirty-two, the thought made her chuckle; her humor flowered into bravura. *Yes by God, this boy needs me as much as he does.*

When they got to her house she simply

introduced Don Juan Carlos to Yamí and announced that the boy is, "visiting us for the weekend." Juan Carlos was no fool, and after 15 years of marriage he could recognize a certain tone.

"Yes dear. Welcome Yamí, is that your first name or your last?" He chatted amiably with the tongue-tied boy as he showed him to a bedroom and the bathroom. Later he said to his wife, "My dear, I hope you will do me the favor of talking first if you are getting ideas."

A year or so into the arrangement, Yamí returned home with a charcoal image of himself, a smiling boy leaning against a picket gate. It arrived with a tack and remained on the wall until the house was abandoned many years later. In time, Don Juan Carlos warmed to the boy and began to spend time with his wife and Yamí. To a casual observer, they appeared as a family on those days.

Her husband was way ahead of her. He had learned to anticipate his wife in the manner of some older men who become more solicitous as time passes. And after two years of spending almost every weekend with the boy, Doña Isabel began to "get ideas." *The boy is thriving in this home*. This time she spoke first with her husband.

"I cannot agree or disagree at this point

querida. You must talk with his sister first. I do not know her but I would not be surprised if money must change hands.

The schedule had evolved so that Isabel had not seen Yamí's sister for some time, routine having taken the place of polite amenities, supplemented perhaps with some modesty on the part of the girl. So there was a shocking moment on the following Monday afternoon when Isabel stopped by the house. His sister was clearly pregnant. Yamí had said nothing about this. After the usual greetings, the girl spoke first,

"As you can see Doña Isabel, I am unable to earn much and it will get worse soon. I need Yamí to help with the house and perhaps to earn a little money for us."

The announcement and the girl's pride, *stubborn pride,* Isabel thought, shocked her. Her first thought was to the girl's well being, and the compassion in her face may have been misunderstood by the girl-woman. The second was to the options, *how can we do this differently?* Her husband's prescience rose to the surface, *I would not be surprised if money must change hands.* "If it is a matter of money perhaps we—."

"No, señora, Yamí must stay with me." The girl reddened; she seemed to suffer from a guilt, an inexplicable guilt to some, when it came to letting

Yamí go with Doña Isabel.

They talked further, Isabel trying to find a way for the girl to change her mind but the steadfastness of her resistance, *her stubborn pride,* the thought repeated itself, led to Isabel's capitulation and a decision that would haunt her for the rest of her life. "Yamí," she said, "you must stay with your sister. You can come visit us whenever your sister says so."

The boy said nothing, he stood there staring at Isabel and sobbed.

Then Isabel sobbed, and they held each other until well past time to leave for home. The next morning, despite her repeated entreaty, the boy would not go to school with her. That night Isabel's distress became physical, migraines and nausea. She stayed at home for over a week and when she returned the other teacher told her that Yamí had come to school for three days, but had not been back.

❧

The boy's attendance in school became episodic. Within a year, the river of *chisme* developed a new channel and rumors began to arrive to the school that Yamí was busy at night, that in fact, the boy had become a thief. The good people of the village began to take precautions. In time, Isabel heard that the boy was seen sporting a *cruzetta*, a sword like machete with an actual hilt that grown men often wore to fiestas, and with which they sometimes fought each other. *Where did he get the money for that?* Doña Isabel's dissonance became so great she went to talk to his sister, her husband having agreed to offer a substantial amount of money.

Yamí was there but he feigned politeness then slipped out the door. His sister said she would consider the offer but only to let the boy resume his earlier schedule. She had another mouth to feed now and she needed Yamí's assistance in looking after the little girl.

It was the measure of her desperation that Isabel had talked her husband into a lump sum contribution. Afterwards, Yamí did spend a few weekends but he had friends now and he spent much of the time with them. The visits were almost always disappointing in some manner for the couple. Then things began to disappear from the house and finally, after one weekend visit, Don Juan Carlos could not find the revolver that he kept in his drawer next to the bed. Yamí never returned. The couple did not report the loss but Don Juan changed the locks on the house.

❧

When Yamí was fourteen he fought an older and

larger bully for, he thought, the affection of a girl. It was an adolescent, hormonal brio but it led to his severe beating. The other boy held him down and pounded his head into the hard, cracked earth and had to be pulled off Yamí, almost too late, by the girl's older brother. Yamí spent weeks trying to recover without medical care in his sister's house. At times it seemed the boy would burn up with fever.

Finally, his sister panicked and fled to the school to find Doña Isabel. She arranged for the boy to be taken by ox cart to the railroad stop some 15 kilometers away, then by train to the capital and ambulance to the hospital, an agonizing trip of nearly two days. Isabel went with the boy and nursed him. She took a room in the capital for the two weeks of treatment and observation in which she visited him daily. The prognosis was that the he would never be quite right but that he would be able to live a normal life. *Not quite right but normal?* Isabel felt that she herself deserved that same verdict. *Not quite right but normal. My God, what have I done?*

One of the losses the boy suffered was any sense of connection to Doña Isabel and Don Juan Carlos. He returned to his sister and led an ordinary, in some ways exemplary, life as a *peón*, working day jobs. Isabel could not say that the boy-then-man was unhappy. She watched him work as the years passed. He was always friendly yet her heart never failed to produce an ache whenever she spoke to him.

A few years after his return, his niece was taken from her mother by the authorities, a forcible removal that unhinged what remained of his sister's self-respect. Or perhaps it had the opposite effect; who can really say. His niece's departure seemed to have little effect on Yamí but one morning his sister walked out of the house *pata en suelo,* barefooted, and never returned. Someone saw her in a nearby town and said that she was cleaning houses. He continued to live in the house and did work for the local farmers and occasionally for Don Juan Carlos. In time, the channel of *chisme* that had labeled him as a youth, dried up. He died, the river said, of something in the brain in the 1960's.

In 1970, for her sixtieth birthday, Doña Isabel and Don Juan Carlos were invited to the dedication ceremony of a new school. The fiesta was to be in her honor for the years she gave to village of Yamíya and she was to dedicate the new building. Her request was that she be allowed to paint a mural on the school's wall of the indigenous that gave their name to village. It was a bust with a few headdress feathers, and to some it looked familiar.

The Walk

There is a road from Quebradas to Bolson. It is an old road and buried beneath the layered sand and soil is a cobbled trail that served the ox cart caravans from the Central Valley. This road goes down the mountain to the big river and then up another mountain to Bolson. In the dry season the road is white and dusty and that is the way it is today.

The big birds, *zopilotes* and *gavilanes* patrol the road; the one looking for the dead and dying; the other for the fresh and living, caught in the road's bright nakedness. A young girl, who has perhaps 13 or 14 years, makes her way down the road barefooted. She wears a worn dress of plain white cotton and she carries a package in her right hand. It too is wrapped in white cotton. One's sensibility is that of a youth, young in all the ways one thinks of young people.

Perhaps it is the whiteness that offers this sense, or perhaps it is the manner in which she progresses. She stares at the road. She has no staff but her right arm thrashes outward with each step offering a tare to remain upright. The toes of her right foot grasp the road as though they were fingers; the heel and side of that foot press into the road with the tenacity of a fence post. Her progress is a rocking motion as her left foot is turned inward like angle iron, so that she must offer the calloused side and top of it to the road. Movement is hard work and she walks in this manner without rest for the better part of an hour.

The old man studies her approach as though he has never before seen the lame. His right hand plays with the tips of his untrimmed beard. It is as white as his hair, which curls from underneath his *lona*, framing his ears and covering his neck. He also is dressed in white cotton and his shirt has a button only at the top to allow his head to enter and it hangs out and over white cotton pants. He wears homemade sandals made from rubber tire tread. He is resting against a large rock in the sparse shade; his staff leans against him, his left arm loosely wrapping it.

"A very good morning to you, *abuelo*," the girl says.

The man hesitates as though assessing her greeting, "Good morning girl. From where do you come, and where might you be going?" he says this in the manner that old people speak to those who know less of the world.

"I used to live in Quebradas but I am going to my aunt in San Pablo. I am going to live with her."

"San Pablo is very far and the day is hot."

"Yes. It is. But I have the day, and food for tomorrow if I need it."

"Why do you not stay with your mother?"

The girl studies his face, "She has a new husband and a baby and she cannot take care of me." She says this with neither dare nor poverty of spirit.

The man thinks on this news for a moment. "People do the best they can."

"Yes, she does."

"Near the bridge it is very steep and uneven."

"Is it?" she says as though this might be her first warning.

"Perhaps it is risky, can you make this passage?

"Thank you for your concern, *abuelo*, but I do not know yet. I have never been to San Pablo. May I share your rock with you?"

"Of course, señorita." and he moved to his right to make room for her. He speaks now as a man who has detected something other than youth in this girl. His speech is thoughtful in the manner of the educated, education or no.

"I have learned the hard lessons of risk. I wish I had learned them at your age," he said.

"Yes, *abuelo*. You seem very wise."

"Yes, I think so. I am going to Bolson, perhaps we could travel together. I may be of help to you."

"I would be very grateful, *abuelo*."

"You must take the left fork at Bolson."

"Thank you, *abuelo*, you are already a big help to me. Were you a strong boy when you were my age?"

"Yes," he answered promptly then paused, "I was the strongest boy in Escobal." His free hand wiped across his mouth as though there were crumbs there. The little smile that emerged was gone. "I had a girlfriend in those days, the prettiest one, she looked a lot like you. In time we married and had a baby and were happy. Then she became pregnant again and we were so happy. But she and this baby died of the bleeding." He paused and looked at the girl as if trying to decide if she might understand his story. "After a few weeks I gave over my hopes and became a risky person and joined the coffee caravans from the Valley and left my little boy with my younger sister who had no children of her own."

"Oh *abuelo*, that was a mistake, wasn't it?"

"Yes, ...you see my story already. I was risky, as I said. " He paused, "We were away over two weeks. Some of us stayed in the port for a few extra days and drank whiskey with the women there." He looked at her, "Forgive me for saying so señorita, but it is the truth." He paused, "I was gone for nearly three weeks. When I returned, the baby, his name was Pablo, Pablo was burning up, he could hardly breathe and when he would cough a bloody mess would come out." He paused, staring at the road as though the story were written there. A squirrel began to chitter at the pair of them. A swirl of dust levitated in the breeze.

He shifted his position a little, "In those days there was a doctor in up in the town, he pointed in the direction from which the girl came. I and my father took the baby with my sister in a cart. But we had waited too long and he died during the night as I held him." He paused for a long moment. "That was how I learned that riskiness leads to bitterness. And now, I see that bitterness is just part of life. Closer to the end one can see what needs mending but then...." His free hand resigned open for a moment then dropped to his side. "That is the most bitter part."

Neither spoke for awhile, then she said, "I am very sorry, *abuelo*. What happened after Pablo died?"

"In truth, that is the end of the story. That is all there is to say."

"There must be more, *abuelo*, tell it to me, please."

"Later, perhaps. We should start walking; are you rested?"

They began to walk, the old man slowing to stay even with the girl. He put his hand to her elbow but she said, "Thank you, *abuelo*, it is easier to do it the way I do it."

"You may have known some bitterness yourself."

"Yes, for many years...many to me," she glanced a smile at him. "It is hard to want to play and not be able to keep up. I am so different." She glanced again, still smiling, then she looked at the road to mind her step. "I have to be careful of the rocks with my little foot." He said nothing but began to move a rock here and there with the end of his staff. They walked on in the dust. The sun now shown down directly through the thin tops of the trees,

"The sun is heavy today," he said.

"Yes." She said it as though first giving it thought. "On the day of my first reconciliation I confessed that my foot was penance for something I did as a baby and I wept. But the priest told me that God loved me always and he whispered to me that Our Holy Father had said in a scripture that 'Heaven was all around us but we do not see it.' And for the rest of that day I thought about that. How could that be so? I thought."

"Yes, I have had such thoughts myself."

"But our Lord said it, it must be so."

"Yes, without doubt *señorita*, but I have never heard that said before."

"At first I thought it meant that heaven was all around like all the other kids playing and liking each other. That must be Heaven I thought. But then, I could see that sometimes they did not.... For no good reason they put themselves in my Hell. When they did that, the one they kicked out or the one that left for his own reasons, that one would come and play with me. We are both in Hell I thought but I did not say so, I was too grateful."

"Of course, *señorita*, that is very sensible."

"And then, one day, I thought, maybe I put myself in Hell like the kids do to each other. Why I thought that, I cannot say. It just came to me. But from that moment, when I was upset or feeling poorly, I would think, 'My Lord Jesus is not doing this to me, who is this person who puts me in Hell?'

"Perhaps the Virgin was talking to you through your thoughts."

"Do you think so? It makes me happy to think that."

"*Quien sabe?* I would not be the one."

"I began to look for that person." She paused for a long moment. They moved to the outside of the road to avoid a deep rut in the curve, the cobblestones clearly exposed. "I looked and looked and looked... for many years," they glanced and shared a smile. "But guess what, *abuelo*, there was no one there. There is no one there to put me in Hell."

"This talk is very strange to me *señorita*, it is very strange. I must think about this." They walked in silence until the sound of the river roiling in the narrow channel below, began to reach them. He stopped and turned to look at her, waiting until she caught his eye, "*señorita*," he began but hesitated as though searching for the words. "*Señorita*, thank you for calling me *abuelo*. The young people these days do not show so much respect."

"You are someone's grandfather, *Abuelito*," she grinned at him and began to move ahead, but he remained still, searching her face, she paused,

"Are you in Heaven *señorita*?"

"*Abuelito!*, who can say such a thing? Only our savior could say such a thing. I am here, with you, am I not?"

He nodded, "Certainly."

But *Abuelito*, I am not in Hell."

"*Gracias a Dios.* I can see that you are not. But how is one to know these things *señorita*, if one does not ask?"

They rested on the steep slope above the bridge. The gorge was illumined by the slanting rays forming shadows on its high rock walls, drawing them into high relief. The time of day and the breeze of the gorge robbed the sun of its brutishness. After a while the old man spat in the sand and wiped his mouth with the heel of his hand. He looked through the trees at a small waterfall on the other side of the river. "That is the water for the people in San Pablo. We should drink, it will be all there is until the top of the mountain." On the bridge he paused for another long moment; he leaned to the railing and stared into the white water below. "I remained a risky person after my son died, and for about two years, I drank *guaro* every night. Then I met another woman," he paused and turned his head to her, she was watching him, and he lowered his gaze to the torrent, "she wanted me to stop and I did for awhile. We did not marry in the church but we lived as man and wife for the span of seven children. I was good to them sometimes, but I made mistakes with each of them. In the end, they stopped loving me and I went to another town."

"How did you know that they stopped loving you *Abuelito*?"

"They were angry with me...I could feel that they did not love me anymore.... My oldest son hit me...he cursed me."

"That is hard indeed." She placed her hand on his arm but he jerked it, turned and strode across the bridge. He waited for her at the other side. After a moment she joined him.

"Where are they now *Abuelito*, could you see them if you wanted?"

"I do not know. They live in different places. Some of them on this side of the river others on the other. I think some of them turned out well, others not.... It is a sorrowful thing in truth, but it is the way things are."

"Are you in Hell *Abuelito*?"

"I thought not. But now, I do not know.... I think, it is like I said *señorita*. It is best to accept life as it is."

"Perhaps so *Abuelito*, perhaps so. But can you tell me, how is it? This...life?"

"How is life? Life is how I feel, how we all feel. Is that not obvious, even to a child!"

She started. His head dropped forward. "Forgive me *señorita*. I do not understand your words. Perhaps I am too old to learn now."

She took his hand in a manner that he could not easily withdraw it; her eyes locked his. "It is not important *Abuelito*. Understanding is not important. But, perhaps, perhaps some morning you may wake up and ask yourself, 'who is it that feels such shame, who is there to put one in it?' That is all one needs."

৪৩

It took over an hour to reach the crossroad where one goes left to San Pablo and right to Bolson. A small school squatted off to the left and two small boys gaped at the girl.

"Is this Bolson?"

"Very close, the village is off to the right. You must take the other fork."

The old man studied the reddening clouds over the Nicoya, "There will not be another whole hour. You can make it to San Pablo I think…if you hasten." He paused and took a deep breath. "*Señorita*, before we say goodbye…thank you again for calling me *abuelo…gracias,* and may God bless your path."

"Thank you for helping me *Abuelito*. I have learned so much from you. And I will be safe, my aunt wrote that the people here are good people."

"I would walk with you if you thought your aunt would let me sleep on the porch or in the shed...perhaps a little dinner."

"You are so good to me *Abuelito*, I would love to stay with you a little longer and I'm sure she would permit it. She sent a letter saying she has lots of room, and dinner, of course."

The sun is buried in the pink and purple heavens over Cerro San Pablo, too weak now to cast shadows. The old man and the girl hesitate in front of the large house as though just arrived on a foreign shore. The house sits in the curve of the road as it turns right into the plaza. Wrapped around the beam that heads the roof is a thick dried vine, snaked as an ornament. The angst of the singer's broken heart reaches the travelers from a nearby radio. A coconut chooses that moment to drop, bounces into the drainage ditch and comes to rest there. As though emerging from a spell, the girl holds up a scrap of paper and reads it again. "This must be it, that is the vine," she says, then she looks at him and takes a deep breath and calls out, "*Upe! Upe!,*" as loud as she can.

"Isabel?" A woman's voice calls from inside the house, "Isabel!" and in a moment she appears on the terrace, her eyes already moist, "*Oh Isabel mi amor*." She plunges from the porch taking the four steps in two, pulling off her apron as she and Isabel meet in the walkway. They hug, rocking together for many breaths and kisses. The woman strokes Isabel's hair until her eyes meet those of the old man, leaning on his staff. The stroking and the rocking pause for a long moment, then she begins again, more slowly this time, still holding the girl, her shoulders shaking. "Oh Papi," she says, "Do you remember me?"

La Novena

My father died. It was it late August, just before I left for my first year of college. I am the first person in my family to finish high school and the first to go to college. It created an odd situation with everyone except my father who told me how proud he was of me many times including the very night he died in his sleep. My mother brags to everyone about my going to college, but to me, it seems like my studies are more of a nuisance to her. I know she worries a lot about money. I have a scholarship for books and other expenses, and it is based solely on my high school performance and some test scores. (The Director told me that I am the best student to ever graduate from my high school.) There is also some local assistance for as long as I can keep my scholarship, but that looks certain now as I am in my last year.

My father was a *sabanero*, a "rancher." I put it in quotes because I don't think we ever had more than a dozen cows and often much less; it was never enough to make ends meet. We had to rent land to graze them and 10 or 12 are just not enough to live on. I suppose that if we lived near the Central Valley where land is expensive we could not have made it at all. My younger brother always said he wanted to be a teacher, but he would not study enough to finish school. He contributed some to the family but not much, so my father worked part-time for several years for another rancher, a Don Beto, who was a very nice man. He was rugged yet handsome like a "Marlboro Man," except for the beginning of a little pot belly, and he was a widower or divorcee, we could never be sure which.

My outrageous girlfriends could be quite explicit about their plans for Don Beto. We had fun talking about him and it always seemed to come up when we tired of talking about "boys." My girlfriends often laughed about how men look at us. They all agreed that often you could feel it as much as see it. One claimed that she looked "right back," and I do not doubt her at all. (I have always wondered, *can boys feel the looks that girls give them?*) We talked about how to stand and move when boys were around to get them to look, and one of my friends said she practiced whenever she saw Don Beto. "So far," she said, "no luck, but I have some new heels and I am not through with him yet." We laughed because we knew she might be serious. Our talks were the usual thing at that age, kind of giggly, but our friend seemed quite serious about how she intended to move her plan along. I laughed with them, as much as anyone, but I still felt shy about such talk. I did not to say anything about this to my mother.

I was seventeen at the time my father passed and I think I had already begun to look like my mother. My face is clearly that of my father but I have my mother's mouth. I am much more intellectual and quieter than she. I have never known her to actually read the front page of a newspaper and it is something of a miracle that I study literature in university. Perhaps my father was very smart and we never knew it because he was so nice, such a really good man actually. I was always his favorite. The funeral was the day after he died. Afterwards, I followed my mother as she walked up the road with a neighbor. I remember that she walked with her head held high. I knew, as well as anyone, that the last five years of my father's life, when he couldn't work, were drudgery for my mother. It was hard on all of us, beginning from the time of his diagnosis a year before he stopped working. And I sympathized with her even then, as I do now, when I remember what she had to do and to put up with. His kidneys slowly gave way and he should have been on one of those machines but he insisted on leaving the hospital. I guess my brother and I could have been more helpful during those years, but what is done is done.

Don Beto visited more than a few times while my father was sick, especially for the last year and a half when he could barely sit upright in a chair. He would always bring a small gift and very soon he and my mother dropped the "Don" and "Doña," when he would stay for dinner and talk with my father. He calls her "Yola," her nickname, and over time he changed from "muchacha" to "señorita," for me. At the *novena* he called me "Patricia," and I finally felt grown up in his eyes. Don Beto's visits were the few opportunities that my mother had to dress up a little and to have something interesting to do, perhaps even fun.

We hosted the *rosario* at our house for nine days in the evenings. The religion teacher in our high school volunteered to recite the rosary for us for the entire *novenario* without a fee. We could not afford music, but our neighbors and family were generous with food at the end of each evening. I have always wondered if Don Beto had something to do with the teacher's volunteering.

At the graveside, Don Beto was solicitous and he took my elbow and my mother's to help us across the drainage ditch that bordered the cemetery. For the *rosario* that night he brought a large pot of chicken and rice, enough to feed everyone. *Who prepared that?* I thought. When she had time to sit, my mother would sit next to him during the service. The chair next to him always remained empty and I wondered if he saved it for her. By this time I was over being jarred by father's death. *She's done her duty,* I thought, *maybe she can be happy again.* Except for my uncles, and a poor relative who had little food in his own house, Don Beto was the only man who came every night.

The third night, after the *rosario* while my mother was busy talking to another guest, he brought his plate and sat in the chair next to me.

"Are you excited about your new life?" he asked.

"Not yet," I said, "I'm more worried about keeping my scholarship and about criminals in the capital." I wanted to sound like the serious person that I really am. In truth, at that time I really was unsure how to talk about myself with a man.

"Well, I have heard that it is not good to go into the parks at night. But if you are ever afraid, just call me. At the least, I have friends in the city who can help you."

I started to thank him, but my mother came up, "Beto, I see you have found someone to talk to," she placed a hand on his arm. "If you get tired of schoolgirl talk, I am sitting right over there." I blushed, it took a moment but humiliation just rolled over me. *I am NOT a schoolgirl!* I thought. I am sure my mouth dropped open but I could think of nothing to say.

She literally swished away. My embarrassment morphed into anger and I could not respond when he tried to recover our talk, "This does not feel like schoolgirl talk to me." He said it kindly and I mumbled something, but our conversation dribbled off into eating. Finally I got up and excused myself and went to my room. *How does Ma manage to do it,* I thought, *why did she say that?* I could hardly sleep, and I got up the next day still angry with her. I wondered if Don Beto would ever speak to me again except as a little girl.

I did my chores the next day without talking to her but I thought about him. *I wonder if he looks at her? I doubt it, she is getting piggy.* I began to concoct a whole series of clever conversations that I would have with him, none of which would be remotely "schoolgirlish." I remembered my girlfriends talking about standing and walking around boys and I even thought about how I might comport myself. These thoughts had almost lost their steam when mother told me to go to the little grocery store to get juice for the evening *rosario*. It was a two-kilometer walk and only an hour remained until people were to arrive. I began to fret about having time to wash up and put on something clean to wear. On his way home from the auction, Don Beto stopped in his big blue cattle truck with the four doors and high wooden sides.

"Buenas tardes, Patricia, may I offer you a ride."

I had at that moment been thinking about him and I am afraid that my practiced aplomb was not readily available. But I was happy for the ride and climbed in. "Muchisimas gracias, Don Beto. I scarcely have time to get home and clean up."

"You look just fine to me," he said, "and don't call me Don Beto. My name is Alberto—Beto. We are friends and you are no longer a schoolgirl."

The reference made me blush deeply and he saw it. He looked pleased. "I think your mother was distracted last night and perhaps a little thoughtless, just a mistake perhaps."

A little thoughtless!.... I could have gone further down that road of thought but I was so pleased to be talking with him again. It was a short ride and he said goodbye and that he would be back in 30 minutes. It was that moment, on the night of the fourth rosary, that I felt him watch me as I walked away from the truck. And I was very conscious of my walk.

When he returned, most of the people were already here. My mother had held up the beginning of the recitation and she signaled the reciter as soon as Beto said his hellos. I held back, not wanting to appear too glad to see him. When he did come over the faint odor of cologne wafted from him. " Beto, it is a pleasure, again." And I put out my hand a leaned into him for a buss on the cheek. I thought I sounded sophisticated, especially with the " Beto." My mother, who came over to take his arm, looked horrified.

A few minutes later, just as everyone turned to face the reciter, she came up behind me, "It is," she hissed, "*Don* Beto."

"It is *Beto*," I smiled straight ahead. "Ask *him* if you don't believe it," and I kept my attention on the reciter. She pinched the skin above my elbow but I clamped my lips tight and refused to acknowledge it.

The meals of the fifth, sixth and seventh *rosario's* were like the fourth night, only more so. The chair next to Don Beto was used by others more often. I kept myself available if Beto wanted to talk and as the *novenario* progressed, I also began to sit in the chair. Gradually he spent less time with my mother and the other guests and more with me. My mother seemed confused at first and her vulnerability increased my boldness. She slowly pulled away from both of us. By the eighth and ninth nights she hardened herself and kept busy with other people, ignoring Beto and me. It was as though she had been defeated in battle and she left the field to me. Or maybe she was plotting her comeback, *or whatever*, I thought, *it hardly matters*. She was very distant with me at other times, barely speaking, but I felt exultant. Sometimes I pitied her. My brother looked at me knowingly or, perhaps appraisingly, I am not sure really, what it was. *Has Beto said something to my brother?* Beto and I exchanged cell phone numbers and he called me, "just to test the number," he said, but by now I knew that he wanted to know me better and I was feeling the same way. "Boys" disappeared from my catalogue of interests and discussion. My girlfriends had heard something, even before I regaled them with the news. They were mostly on my side but one of them was a little horrified. All of them treated me with obvious respect, and I left for college feeling more independent than I had ever felt in my life. We lived in a small village west of Santa Cruz in the Guanacaste. It was too far to commute and I had to rent a room near the university.

Beto called to ask if I wanted a ride, to take my things to the university but it was strange, I was feeling independent of him also and told him I had already made plans. "You could change them," he said, but I declined. "Well," he said, "I come to the capital a lot on business, perhaps we could have lunch, or dinner."

"For sure," I said." Be sure to call when you are coming."

≔

College was incredibly busy. And I am a conscientious student and do my work everyday. I had a roommate then, and we became good friends. It was the first time she had ever lived away from home also, but it was obvious that her family had money and she seemed to handle the changes better than I did. A trip to her home convinced me that her family was richer even than Beto. I thought she would appreciate, perhaps admire, the fact that an older man was interested in me, but she acted like it was ridiculous. "Oh sure," she said, "all those old guys want to get in your pants. Especially the first time." It added a new meaning to "outrageous" for me, and I began to suspect that my other girlfriends were not so sophisticated. I guess that I cannot say I was shocked, but it was clear she came from a much different world than I did. She studied as hard as I and with all the changes, we had so much to do both of us lost touch with our friends at home. After the first month, I never went home on weekends. There were lots of men in college, and I fell in love with my history professor (from a distance of course). It was all just so "eye-opening," I guess.

Beto did call several times. And about three months into the semester I met him for lunch. I asked my roommate to go with us but she just turned her mouth down with her, *you must be kidding* look and said, "I don't think so girlfriend." I was on my own. How should I say this? I was not happy nor unhappy to see Beto. Bemused might be the better word from the distance of four years. He was all dressed up wearing his best Mexican boots, a large shiny buckle with silver cow horns and a string tie. He wore a new, wide brim cowboy hat of white felt and seemed very much a part of the *sabanero* world from which I came. In the restaurant, he looked like an old fashioned movie star and he did his very best movie star elegance. A waiter came over to remind him of the no-smoking rule. I felt like other people were watching us and I became uncomfortable. He was, no doubt, out of his own comfort zone, but he acted encouraged and intensified, if possible, his performance of the "dashing caballero." Honestly, I felt ridiculous. *He is perfect for mother,* I thought.

After that, with a little coaching from my roommate, I discouraged him.

When I went home for the December vacation my mother had changed; she seemed quite happy to see me. She kissed me and held me for an extra long time. My brother also. I loved the new spread for my bed with matching curtains, and it felt good to do my old chores. But now, my mother would ask me to comment on things that, in the past, she assumed to know more than me, about the news or even on something political (as though I keep up with such things), and it felt like being appreciated in a different way. I found myself silently disagreeing with her opinions, *not very educated,* I thought. Still, I began to relax into what felt like a different family and I admit it, I liked being there. On the first Saturday my mother prepared a large lunch and invited some family to join us. They brought food and there was a little beer and *chicha* so it became a kind of a welcome home party. People were full of questions about college life; the conversation was loud with laughter and everyone joined in. I was having fun and feeling special. Mother was a wonderful hostess, *How is it that I never knew this?* I sat next to her and about halfway through lunch,

"Have you seen Beto?" I asked.

She turned to me and hesitated. Her face locked up, stone like, her mouth twisted into a tight smile, "No...I hope you are happy." She said it so only I could hear.

"What do you mean?" The stone cracked. I thought she might laugh.

"Excuse me," speaking to the table, and she walked into her bedroom. I must have looked confused; the conversation at the table stopped, then resumed slowly. I knew something terrible had happened.

Those of our family who accept the responsibility for keeping things easy doubled their efforts at conversation, but I did not participate. I sat staring at, then dawdling with my food. It must have taken 10 or 15 minutes, while the whole Beto thing replayed in my mind. This time the view through Ma's eyes sat side by side with the way I remembered it. In that small space of time I came to understand one thing; I excused myself and walked to her bedroom door.

"Come in," she said.

I closed the door behind me and stood there; she sat on the end of the bed. "Ma, I am sorry. Please forgive me."

Her face was haggard and streaked. She looked as though all the fight, hope, and life were draining from her, right in front of me. She wasn't crying but tears seeped from my eyes. From this distance, I imagine that it was from some deep pool, a deep reservoir of motherness that allowed her to look up and reach out for my hand. We sat there alone until people went home.

La Llorona

"I want to tell you a story," my grandmother said. Even at that moment I knew it was odd; I was always the one to beg her for a story because she never imposed herself. I guess it was the bluntness of her announcement that got my attention. I had been in my bedroom all morning and would not allow my younger brother, whose room it was also, to come in. As my family told the story over the years, I wailed all morning and would not be consoled. My father said I cried and yelled and threw things so that he could not even think. Grandmother finally took charge.

The reason for my upset was that my father had announced at breakfast that we would make our yearly trek up the mountain to spend the month with family in Santiago. We were going to leave in two days from Colon where we lived in those days. We would walk up the mountain for three nights, camping by the streams. Even at that age I new our camping spots by heart. The problem was simple to a second grader; I did not want to leave my best friend Yamileth. We just finished first grade and decided that we would go to school together while we were kids and would be best friends for life, having no other friends, ever. It was a very serious pact and had we known about such things I'm sure we would have sealed it by mixing our blood in a solemn ceremony. Then Yami's father decided to move away for a better job. You cannot imagine the cruelty of that decision. We had only two weeks to spend together and now, my father said, I had only two days. I'm sure you can understand the problem for me; my behavior was absolutely and totally appropriate. But I've lost track, as usual. This is about my grandmother's story and I will tell it as I remember it. But I must warn you; it is a difficult tale.

Once upon a time, there was a beautiful young woman in a village near the *lagunas* of the river. She heard all of her life that her beauty was so stunning that none of the men in her town were handsome enough to deserve her. For that matter, neither were any of the men in the nearby towns. Although, all of them, even the grandfathers were so touched by her radiance that they could not help themselves but to fall in love with her. All day long the men would troop past her father's home hoping for a glimpse of her and sighing as they had to move on to make way for another lovestruck. The young woman, as you might imagine, became quite haughty and disdainful of "mere mortals," she said.

One day the village was visited by a Federal policeman, Rurales, they were called in those days. He was new to the canton and was visiting each town introduce himself and to get to know the *pueblo* and to find out if he could be helpful in anyway. On this day he was tracking a very mean *hombre* and wore his pistola in his belt and carried a rifle on the saddle of his fine-looking palomino. He had a full and beautiful beard and sat quite tall in the saddle. All the young women of the town, except for the beauty of our story, followed him as he walked his horse to the cantina. He spoke to each one of the men in a polite and humble manner and they immediately respected him. When he looked at the young women, some of them fainted at the sight of his beauty. One of them ran to get the young woman of our story. She was busy cleaning rice at the *pilon* and the prospect of looking at another man did not interest her. "You may be surprised this time," her friend said, so the young woman went with her friend to stand at a distance from the porch of the cantina.

Well, how can I say it? When the Federal came out of the cantina, he was smiling from the effect of the *guaro* and his teeth were brilliant. He carried himself with a confidence the young woman had never seen before, and she felt her knees go weak. She leaned against a nearby tree lest she faint herself. "Oh my God," was all she said. Her friend ran to get the young woman's father, but he was unimpressed, or at least, he acted that way. "Impossible," he sputtered, "Impos-si-ble. He is a policeman, he has no money."

But there was nothing the father could do. The beauty of the young woman drew the Rurale's eye and he stopped, cold in his tracks for several moments. Then he walked toward her and her father knew that all was lost.

The policeman was from the capital and he spoke of things that the young woman had never heard before. She could scarcely believe her ears when he told her of the wonders of automobiles and pipes with water in the house. But the policeman was very traditional and he spoke to her father who grudgingly said "okay," to the request to court his daughter. For a few years their love was "vital" as people sometimes say. They lived in a small house in the village and even though the policeman was gone a lot in his duties throughout the canton, when he was home the couple were rarely seen, preferring to share their love in private. Soon, a baby boy arrived on the scene and the young woman was even more happy and she thought her life was "so perfect," she told her mother and all who would listen. Then a little girl arrived and the young woman thought she might actually be in heaven. She told everyone, but some people had stopped listening.

One day, her husband came home with news. He had to return to the capital to a new assignment. He would go ahead, he said, and find a place to live. At first the beautiful young woman expected him any day. But after a few months of no word from the capital, a small current of *chisme* developed; "The handsome policeman had abandoned his beautiful wife and family," it said. The current grew into a river of rumor and the young woman thought she might go insane with worry and fear. She no longer looked as beautiful as people remembered.

One day she brought her children to her mother and said she was going to the city. Her parents tried, but the young woman was desperate and would not be dissuaded. "Give me some money," she demanded, and with great fear, her parents did as she asked. That very day the young woman paid a local man to take her by horseback to the city. He left her at the steps of the Government, and she went in to inquire about the policeman. *They should know where he is*, she thought, but no one could, or would, tell her where he could be found. As she walked away, a smitten young man from the office followed her and told her where the policeman was living. She found the rascal with another younger and more beautiful woman. The policeman would not look at her and refused to talk. *But I am the most beautiful woman in the world,* she thought, *how dare he!*

Well, to make a long story short, the now not-so-young-woman, wandered for days around the

Capital gradually spending all of her money. Men came up to her wanting to pay her for love. *Why not?* she thought. *I have nothing left to live for.* And soon she lost her mind completely and it filled with a terrible rage.

After a few weeks she found her way back to the village and took her children from her parents. She went straight down to the lagoon, and holding the children in her arms, she drifted out into the current until she could no longer stand. She released her two children to the water. The three of them drowned in the river that day. Her body was found but not the babies.

My grandmother swore on the Bible that what happened next is true. When the woman's soul appeared at the gates of heaven, the Lord God asked her, "Where are your children?" The shame of her act overwhelmed her and she confessed that she did not know. The Lord ordered her to find them and bring them to Him. "You may not rest until they are with Me," He said.

One night about a week after the woman was buried, a villager saw a strange and luminescent figure wearing a white burial dress floating over the river. "Ooooh, ayyyyeee," it cried out. "Where are my children?" Then other people saw the figure, and heard it call out, "Ooooh, ayyyyeee." The villagers said she wanders the streams and canals looking for her children. Children began to disappear. When my grandmother was a small girl, she saw the figure and it tried to grab her, but she ran, quick as a rabbit, back to her house. Soon it became clear that the deseparecidos were children who were naughty or who cried a lot, and the villagers began to warn their children about the consequences. They gave her a name, "La Llorona," the wailing woman, they called her, and people still see her to this very day.

So mi Amor, that river is not far from here. Your mother and your father love you so much, as do I and your grandfather. I think you must stop this crying lest La Llorona comes to take you away from us.

The Good Policeman

If you were to ask, why are you writing this now, after so many years? My answer to you would be, sincerely, I do not know. I have never been one to keep a diary or a notebook. Perhaps I want my father to live forever in the minds of his countrymen, perhaps I would like to do so as well, or to explain how I feel about being a policeman in the service of my country. Perhaps, this is what old men do when they stop working on their careers and begin to think on the old conundrums. But sincerely, I do not know.

My name is Juan Pablo Alfaro Mereía. I was born on September 15, 1948, a propitious date in this country. The day is the day of independence from España, and 1948 is the year my father, Juan Pablo Alfaro Salazar died; in Cartago, to birth the Second Republic. He was a policeman in the first republic; I normally do not capitalize it as it would have been the last but for misguided ambition. My father was of the family of the would be dictator, which is no doubt how he came to be a *capitán* while so young, but that did not stop him from following don Pepe when the time came to act. With his rank and training, and family, he became the commander of a company of volunteers, mostly men without any of those qualifications. He had one sergeant who defected from the old Army to help with discipline and training, a Sergeant Mereía. We have an old photo of the two of them.

On the back was the note, "To my darling Miriam, I will love you forever." It is dog-eared from the years of my holding it as a child. When my mother would tell me stories about my father's service, she usually mentioned Sergeant Mereía's name, "But he is not family," she would say. That meant something to her. Of course, at this age I cannot pretend not to know about such things, but I think, or at least I feel, that she held Sergeant Mereía in genuine affection in spite of the differences. I know she had hoped he would keep my father safe in the war. In the photo, my father is taller and lighter than the sergeant, *as it should be*, I thought. And he looked to be older. It was a grave disappointment to me to discover in adolescence that I would not be as tall as my father.

When I was four years old, my father's father died and we went to his family home in Santa Maria de Dota and for the first time that I remember, I met my uncles, aunts and cousins. My father's family are coffee farmers and most of my uncles still worked the large farm. "This is where your father became acquainted with don Pepe," my mother told me. "Don Pepe is now our *presidente*." A few days after we came home, my mother read to me my grandfather's obituary from the San Jose newspaper. They called him a "well known planter and patriot," and I felt almost as proud of him as I did of my father. I was to learn that my mother's family had pineapple farms near La Gloria in Puriscal. They were big farms, which allowed us to continue living in San Jose after my father died. I cannot say why, but I felt more proud about the coffee side of my family.

I would ask my mother when Sergeant Mereía was coming to visit. After the Army was abolished and the Guardia Civil was formed, he was made a *teniente*, a lieutenant in the new service with big responsibilities in San Jose. Nonetheless, he came often. When he was coming my mother would tweak my nose, my *narizon*, she called it because of its large size, and say, "Oh *mi amor*, guess who is coming to visit you?" When I was five I would ask him to tell me stories about my father. He did so on most visits until those visits stopped when I was twelve.

"Sergeant, tell me what happened the day my father died?"

He stretched out in the big chair on our terrace and folded his hands over his leather belt. "Well," he would say, "that is quite a story." Then he would say, "Go over and turn that fan up a bit." And I would do it. "That is better. This day is a lot like that day, a very hot day in March. We were camped temporarily in the hills south of Cartago to be available should the need arise for a stout group of *muchachos* such as ourselves. The Legionnaires were the best trained but of the Tico volunteers, we were the best. Most of the men had little or no training but your father insisted that we train whenever we were not doing something more important. He insisted and that was the reason we were considered the stoutest and most able of all the volunteer companies. On that day we were training in fire and maneuver. We were too close to a village to fire our weapons; we had no ammunition to waste anyway. We would simulate attacking a position with one squad covering while the other charged for a short distance, then dropped to the ground and covered for the first squad. It was tiring work, all that running and falling down and getting up and running again, but your father knew that the men had to learn to be good soldiers in the fight."

"What did you do, Sergeant?" When we talked liked this I called him "Sergeant Mereía," but otherwise my mother insisted that I call him *Teniente* or *Tío,* Uncle Mereía. He would always smile when I called him "Sergeant."

"You even sound like your father," he would say. "My job was to follow the orders of your father and to see that the men worked hard. And sometimes I would give advice on how things were done in the Army. Anyway, we were tired from all that hopping around when a courier arrived with the order to proceed immediately to Cartago, 'On the double,' the order read. We broke camp immediately taking only what we would need for the fight. Many things that the volunteers had brought with them had to be left behind. After we formed up, your father gave a very brave speech and said that we would force march to Cartago. He said that he knew we were tired, but he knew that we would not miss this fight for anything. The men cheered him, I did also. He was a very fine leader your father. Then he went to the front of the column, gave the order, 'Forwaaard, MARCH!'" I jumped as the Sergeant's voice boomed. "Your father said this in a fine voice and set the pace, staying in front for the entire march without rest."

"What did you do then Sergeant?"

"I stayed at the rear to keep the ranks closed up and to deal with stragglers. But, I must say, that when we reached the first houses of Cartago, the most of the men were still in formation and *that* was due to the training that your father gave the men. Just think Chico, eight miles in two hours, now that is a march."

"Wow," I said, near speechless; my mind was bursting with images of the company and my father.

"We were met on the outskirts by a runner from the local commander's headquarters. He told us the opposing force was comprised of some regular Army with some of the Communist militia, all stout *muchachos* who were willing to fight as well. He suggested to your father to remove his insignia as there was a sniper in the neighborhood. Your father looked at me and I nodded, 'It is a good idea I said.'"

"What is a sniper?"

"That is a soldier who is a very good shot with a rifle. He will hide by himself and look for important people in the enemy and shoot them."

I shuddered. "Were any of the enemy friends of yours Sergeant?"

"Oh, I suppose I might have known some of them. But life has a way of changing things, even friendships.

His mouth twitched and I thought he might smile but he did not. "Anyway, back to my story. The men were resting, sitting or lying on the ground and waiting for the stragglers to come up. There was black smoke from a burning truck over near the Plaza and a lot of gunfire. After about 15 minutes we were almost full strength and your father gave the order to spread out and take our assigned position. We were to occupy the area around a small church and use its steeple for a lookout and to stay out of the fire of the enemy until more orders arrived. We were about two blocks away from the center and about six blocks from the Basilica of LaNegrita. The courier said he thought that we would be part of the force to attack the plaza and city hall where most of the Army and Vanguardia militia were located."

He paused and looked away as if in thought. His hand went to his mouth as though wiping it down to his chin. When he began again his voice was hoarse, "After the men were in proper positions, your father and I went to the bell tower to look for the sniper. After a while he handed me the glasses and said, 'Look in the window of that gable, the one with the *arcilla* roof.' I looked and sure enough there seemed to be someone in there. At that moment," he hesitated again, "at that very moment, I saw the puff of smoke and then heard the report of the rifle. 'That's him, I yelled,' and I turned. Your father was lying on the floor." Sergeant Mereía hesitated again, his hand went to his mouth and chin like before. "I yelled for help and tried to stop the bleeding but the bullet had severed the big vein in his neck. Your father's heart was strong until the end; it pumped enough blood to kill him in only a minute or so." The Sergeant looked at me and pulled me close. I sat in his lap and wept for several minutes. My mother must have heard the silence and came out to check. We both looked at her and the Sergeant waved his finger saying, "Not now, *Querida*," and she backed inside the room still watching us. "Later that evening after the fight, that old bell from La Basilica rang out, signifying our victory, but with a peculiar tone this time. I have never heard it sound that way since." His look was off, somewhere in the distance and I waited for him.

After a while I began to stir and the Sergeant said, "Just one thing more, Chico." Again he hesitated, "As I bent down to help your father, he said, 'take care of them,' meaning, I have always thought, you and your mother." I looked at the sergeant's face then lay back against his chest.

Finally I asked him, 'What did you do then, *Tio*?'

"After a few moments, I went below. I took a couple of squads and attacked the house with the sniper. The fool had remained at his station and did not try to flee until he saw us coming. He was a brave Tico, I must say. He fired at us from the door and wounded another man in our attack but the squad did not falter, we wounded the sniper and he surrendered. Your father would have been proud of us. Even of the sniper, I think."

I heard that story several times more between those days and up until I became a teenager. On at least a couple of occasions my mother sat with us and she always had little tears on her cheeks. Once I asked him, "Were you mad at the sniper,

Sergeant? Were the *muchachos* mad at him?"

"Some of them, yes. I was not. Men do their duty in these matters, Chico. It is best not to take it personally." I remembered this instruction all my life and it has served me well on more than one occasion.

The Sergeant would always repeat my father's last words and look at my mother if she was there and she would get up and leave the room.

One time after the Sergeant's visit, I must have been 11 or 12 at the time, I asked my mother, "How did the Sergeant and my father get to know each other?" I fully expected that the Sergeant was assigned to my father's unit by the commander of the rebels, maybe don Pepe himself. But she looked at me and said, "Well, there is a little more to that story. The Sergeant was stationed at the barracks in San Jose, not far from here really." (We lived in Barrio Los Yoses). "In November or December of 1947, he came to the house to tell me that he was going to leave the Army if the fighting started and asked me to tell his parents if anything happened."

I was stunned. *She knew the Sergeant from before.* I could not speak. She watched me, closely I think.

"Your father had already gone to San Isidro in

the Valle General to wait for the Legion from Mexico. We had been married over five years by that time and we had never been apart. He came home once but it was dangerous because there were policemen watching the house in those days. It went on for several weeks."

"You *knew* him! You knew the Sergeant from before!"

She sighed deeply and smoothed the lap of her skirt, looking down. She sighed again, another long one. I got up and adjusted the fan and sat back down; her eyes followed me. "Yes, Sergeant Mereía is from La Gloria, his father worked for my father."

My voice squeaked in those days and I barely got out, "No!.... Why didn't you tell me this?" My anger boiled to the surface; I felt betrayed in some way.

"Well, Juan Pablo, I guess, well, I guess I thought you needed to be older."

She did not look away and something about the way she acknowledged my being old enough to understand things smoothed the anger; it flattened like dough under a rolling pin. It was replaced with a manly feeling, a little jangled but manly nonetheless, for the first time in my life. "Tell me about La Gloria, Ma."

She took her time, looking at me as though to

make sure I really was old enough. "Hernán, that is the Sergeant's name, and I grew up in the same village. His father worked for my father, the name Mereía is a mere coincidence." She looked up at the ceiling, then "I think it was, yes." Her gaze returned to me, "He was more than a year older than me and the smartest boy in town, but he would have gone to work in the fields after elementary school except that my father had great regard for his father, and for Hernán also, I think. When it came time for high school, my father made it possible for Hernán to attend. So, we attended high school for three years before I was sent to boarding school in San Jose. We were good friends." She waited as though to see if that was enough.

It wasn't. "Then what happened?" I wasn't letting go until I got the whole story this time. I can still remember my determination, *I deserve to know,* I thought. It must have felt like an interrogation, but my mother was prepared.

"After my 16th birthday party, I visited the home of a friend from the academy. I met her older brother. He was a police lieutenant at the time, twenty-five, and very handsome, his name was Juan Pablo Alfaro Salazar. And two years later we married in the big church in Puriscal. My father was very happy that day."

All of this was so new to me. I didn't know what to ask next. Finally I said, "What happened to Tío?"

"In the year after I left La Gloria, he had almost finished high school but left for some reason and came to San Jose. After that, he joined the Army. It must have been 1938."

I thought about this for a long time. My mother said nothing more, waiting for me. Today, as I think about this, I imagine that she was watching my 'wheels turning' as people say. I looked at her and she was smiling at me.

"Well," I said from my new manliness, "I would love to hear the Sergeant's version of all this."

She looked at me, sad it seemed, certainly not smiling anymore, "The Teniente Mereía cannot come by as much as he used to. He has been transferred to the *delegación* at Alejuela. And, he has been promoted, and..." I thought it was difficult to for her to say it, "he has a new wife. I'm sorry, *mi amor*, it was so sudden, he did not have time to come by." Then she added, "I'm sure he will, when he is back in San Jose."

For the second time in the conversation I was lost. From the vantage point of all these years, I can still feel the shocks of her announcements that day. I imagine myself staring at her, mouth open.

He did come by, once or twice a year over the next six years. He was always pleasant and very warm to me. He kept hugging me until I got older and became obviously exasperated. After that he observed my preferred decorum. He wrote me letters to tell me how proud he knew my father would be of my various accomplishments, regardless of how undistinguished they might have been. But the old Sergeant was gone, vanished into the ether of career and of a life having moved on.

Things changed after the Sergeant moved away. I thought that my love for my father was changing and I felt guilty. I could not put words to it early on but it felt like, without the Sergeant's presence to remind us, we did not talk about him so much. I did not think about him so much. It was though he became just a photograph of someone I never knew. And I felt guilty and the guilt became a conundrum; I knew that I should not feel that way and I would try to visualize him and remember him and to make him a polestar for direction in my life. But try, as most surely I did try, it did not work and the guilt would not leave me. At times I would sit on my bed and say, "he loves me," over and over, trying to feel it. Once my mother put her head in the door and said, "What did you say *mi amor?*" but her voice broke and her eyes were moist and I knew she had been listening.

"Nothing," I told her. But she pressed me and it made me angry.

The Sergeant's yearly visits did not serve. He tried to keep me connected to my father. I could sense his efforts, but his life had changed also and talking about my father did not make him live for me anymore. I came to think that I wanted the real flesh and blood presence of my father and I knew, in a flash one day, that the Sergeant had served that purpose until he stopped coming. I tried once to talk to my mother about this after one of his visits but it only made her sad and I found her crying later so I never spoke to her about it again. I dealt with the guilt by putting my father into a category. I don't know an exact word for it, perhaps, "someone to aspire to be like." Pride for him replaced longing and served in the place of his affection.

❦

I graduated from university and earned a commission in the Guardia Civil in 1973. My mother was too sick with her final illness to come to my graduation from the academy, but Comandante Mereía gave the commencement address, reminding us of the sacrifices of an earlier generation and exhorting us to loyalty to a democratic government. He came up to me at the graduation party and asked me to have dinner with him afterwards. It was a polite request, but now that I was in the service, there was no refusing. (That sounds ungrateful of me, shameful for me to think that, now that I re-read it. I gladly went to dinner with him.) We went to a modest restaurant in San Jose that had been a favorite of his from the Army days. It was located in what would become the San Jose Chinatown in later years, lots of smoke and loud talk.

"How is your mother?"

"I am afraid this may be it, a few more months perhaps." His head started a little bob, shaking in agreement or understanding as he watched me. He looked away for a moment or two, then back at me, his head still slowly bobbing. We had been drinking some and that may have accounted for the watery eyes, but maybe not.

"Mother would love to see you."

"Yes," he said looking away, "yes, I will do that right away."

"Mother told me a long time ago that you and she knew each other in La Gloria."

"Yes, is that all she said?"

"Except that she came to boarding school in San Jose and that you joined the Army."

"Yes." He picked up the shot glass of *guaro* then thumped it back down. He half-turned in his chair and slung one arm over the back. "Did she tell you that my father worked for hers?" I nodded. "And that her father paid for me to go to the high school?"

"Yes."

"Well, I'm sure she did not tell you that when we were in high school we were sweet on each other."

By 1973 I was, of course, more worldly than in 1959, but I riveted to his words.

"I loved your mother more than I can say, and I think, I'm sure, that she loved me. It certainly felt that way to a teenager. But I was naïve. I was 16 and she was 14 at the time. In defiance of the warnings of my father, he 'prohibited' me, I asked your grandfather if I could court his daughter. It is pathetic, laughable to think about it now. But your grandfather did not think it was funny. He sent her away to boarding school in San Jose within the week, took her himself. He forbade me to see her, 'Ever' he said. But for some reason, he did not keep me from finishing high school. I did that myself.

I was frantic. I took, 'stole' is more honest, some money from my father, hitchhiked to Santiago and took a bus to San Jose, but she could not see me. The administration of the school would not let me enter. It had taken two days to find the school; I walked all over this damned city." His lips pursed into a gritty smile. "That school is only three blocks from where we sit." He pointed east, then swung his arm north, "and the barracks are right over there. I had had it with walking. I had my first beer, spent my last centavo and joined the Army, one-two-three, a pretty sad story don't you think?

I did not know what to think. It was definitely sad but agreeing with him did not feel right. "I am sorry for bringing this up Tío, I wouldn't have—."

"Oh, it's okay among brothers in arms. You are old enough to know, Chico." He had not called me that since 1960. And there it was again, *when is one old enough to know everything*, I thought.

"Anyway, I did not see your mother again until just before the revolution of '48. It had been ten years or so and for some reason I took a chance on calling to ask if I could come by; to tell her something important of course."

I nodded, "Of course."

"It was a few weeks before Christmas of 1947; she was then a married woman for several years. I came to tell her that I was going to leave the Army if don Pepe started the fight. I thought it would be soon and I hadn't spoken to my father since I left home and I asked her to let my parents know if all that came to pass."

"'You should do that, now,'" she said, but I told her that I could not face him yet and we started to talk about the old times."

"Did she say yes?"

He looked at me disoriented, reeling perhaps, as if not understanding my question, then looked away. "Yes she did. There had been so much time, so much water over the dam, that we could be friends again. It was a little like old times, as much as those can be. We laughed at the memories, even my audacity to talk to her father. It was funny, almost, by that time. I remember feeling like I had missed my life somehow, ten years of it. But it was worth it, just to laugh with her again."

"Is that when you met my father?"

"No," he harrumphed, "your father was the real patriot. No waiting for him, he was already in San Isidro, spoiling to get on with it. But your mother asked me to find him and look out for him and that is what I did, in February, when I abandoned the Army."

He told me he saw my mother a few times before leaving the Army, but that the police made it dangerous to be seen doing so. We became quiet, he studying the shot glass, me struggling with the question that had to be asked. "Did you ever speak to her of love after he died?" I felt my heart pounding in my temples, in my ears. I was frightened, and to this day I cannot say why.

He looked at me squarely and every sense told me that again, he was sizing up my maturity. Finally he said, "Yes. More than once...but she would not have me and I married another."

We talked awhile longer. I filled him in on the things he did not know about my life; I had a girlfriend by then for example, and it made him smile. I told him that I was thinking about buying an automobile with my new wealth and he just shook his head, but he said nothing.

When it was time to go we stood and embraced. He kissed me on both cheeks and told me that both he, and my father, were proud of me. It was awkward as our big noses got in the way of each other when we switched cheeks and we both laughed. By the time that the *Fuerza Publica* was formed in 1996, and we all transferred over, he was gone.

കൈ

My final assignment was, at my request, to command the *delegación* of Puriscal in Santiago. These days it is just over an hour or so from La Gloria and I found a farm here to retire to. I have cousins and their families still living here and the Sergeant has family left also. They are all like family now. As I finish this I am staring at that picture of my father and the Sergeant for the thousandth time, *which one of you wrote that? 'To my darling Miriam.'*

GLOSSARY with Characters

Note: Spanish words are defined in the story text. The glossary is for backup and further explanation.

Abuelo (a)- Grandfather (or grandmother). Also a term of respect or affection for older people. In this story.

Aguas Calientes or "AC"- Literally, hot water; came to be the name of the rain forest and surrounding area.

Adele- Aurelez natural mother.

Alba- Guito's mother and Eduardo's Wife.

Amigo- Friend.

Añoranza –(An-yo-RAN-za)- A particularly beautiful Spanish word translated as homesickness.

Archivo- The military commitee that made decisions to disappear people in the '70's, '80's and '90's. It was a later manifestation of the National Committee for the Defense Against Communism in Guatemala.

Aurelez- Guito's younger sister, daughter of Alba and Eduardo.

Cabina- Cabin.

Caldo- Soup or stew.

Sochi/ Sochi/ Cólera de Dios- Guito's best friend in the AC.

Capitán- (Ca-pi-TAN)- Captain

Chapin- Slang term for a person from Guatemala.

Chirimia- A primitive oboe called a shawm by European conquistadors. Assimilated into indigenous culture.

Comarada- Comrade.

Commandante- Commandant in English. It is used generically for a rebel leader but also as the denoted term for "major," in the military.

Compañero (a)- Companion. Used to refer to associates in a work, university or school setting. Also used for co-guerrillas.

Compa- Short form for either compañero or compañera. Used specifically among the guerrilla forces.

Con permiso- With permission or excuse me.

Cooperativa- A coop or cooperative.

Departamento- Department, the Guatemalan designation for province.

Derrumbes- An area demolished by a landslide or falling boulders from a volcano.

Desaparecido- Literally "disappeared" or "missing." It has come to define all persons who were kidnapped and killed in the repressive Latin American regimes of the Cold War.

Doña- (Don-ya) A term of respect for a married woman.

Don- A term of respect for a man.

Edurdo-Guito's father.

EGP-Ejercito Guerrillado de Los Pobres- Guerrilla Army of the Poor, formed in 1972. One of four armed groups, it operated mostly in the north (Ixil) territory, and Ixcan. There were also units in the east, south and in Guatemala City.

Elena- William's love and Dr. Rodrigo's daughter. A nurse at the State Hospital.

EM- An English designation for "Emergency medicine."

Entrada- Entrance.

FAR- Fuerza Armada Rebelde- Armed Rebel Force, the first of the insurrection armed forces led by former army officers. One of an eventual four armed groups, it started in 1960 in reaction to CIA coup of 1954 and the reversal of democratic policies and land reform legislation. In theory, the FAR operated under the political leadership of the PGT. The relationship was historically tenuous and eventually the FAR separated from the PGT in order to pursue a more aggressive military posture.

Finca- A farm or ranch.

Flor- literally, flower; the name of Guito's friend.

Grácias- (Grá-see-as; or Grá-thee-as, in Castillian Spanish)- Thank you.

Guerra Sucia-Dirty war; used in reference to the manner governments conducted the wars in Guatemala and El Salvador.

Higueron- A ficus tree native to Central and South America. Many varieties.

Hola- Hello.

Huípil- (HWEE-pil) Traditional Mayan pullover top for women. These were decorated with designs specific to a language group and sometimes to specific villages.

Igualmente- Equally. Used informally as in "the same to you," or "ditto."

Indigena- Indigenous.

Indio- Indian, in Guatemala a derogatory term.

Indita- Literally, "little indian," woman or girl.

Itz- Mayan, the basic stuff of the universe. Comes to man from the Other World.

Itzmam- Another word for shaman, leader of the Mayan familial lineages that comprise the village groupings.

Ixil- A language group of Mayans occupying north central Guatemala.

Jefe- (Hef-a) Spanish for "Chief" or "head of." Can be applied to any level of organization.

Judicials- A quasi-official group of thugs that functioned as "death squads."

Lorenzo- An intern during the first year that Guito was in the AC; held racist attitudes towards Indios.

Lucha- Struggle or fight.

Mucho gusto- A polite phrase meaning "with much pleasure" used when one has been thanked or upon meeting someone.

No- No or not.

Novio (a)- Boyfriend or girlfriend. In some cases a fiancé.

Oreja (O-reh-ha)- the outer ear, slang for an informer.

Padrón- Literally, one's patron, usually meaning employer.

Pase adelante- Come in or go ahead.

Por lo menos- At least.

Problema- Problem, as in, "No problema."

Puta- Bitch (derogatory) or whore. Used as in, "puta communista."

Puesto Policial- Police post or station.

Quarteto- Quartet.

Quebrada- (Kā-bra-da)- Spanish for broken. It is used to apply to mountain stream beds (broken rocks).

Querencia-(Kā-rān-cia)A Spanish bull fight term indicating a place in the bullring deemed a place of safety by the bull. Not directly translatable, it is used metaphorically.

Que vaya con dios- Go with God. A common form of goodbye.

Q'eqchi- An indigenous language group occupying the north, central and southeast parts of the country.

Rajiv- Bird researcher in the AC and Guito's spiritual teacher.

Rurales- A common designation of national police that serve non-urban areas.

Salchicha- Sausage.

Sem Problema- No problem in Portugese.

Sor- Sister, especially a member of a religious order.

Temblor- Earthquake, a shaking.

Ten Cuidado- Be careful or have care**.**

Tessa- Guito's girlfriend and later, wife.

Tia- Aunt.

ToTo- The nickname of each of the Juan Carloses Torquemada y Torremolino whose grandmother came to th AC after the First World War. Each is numbered sequentially, (ToTo, ToTo II (Segundo), III (Tercero), IV (Cuarto).

Volcán- Spanish for volcano.

Wym- Botanist and Rajiv's one-time lover.

Yucca- Manioc. A tuber cooked and served like potatoes in Central America.

Notes

1. The imagery in this chapter comes from a Chapter of the same name in Allan Wheelis,' book, *How People Change*. I read it in graduate school and it resonated with the punishments my sister and I knew as children. *How People Change* has been in my possession for over 35 years and still serves as a guide to understanding behavior.

2. The name "Omelas" comes from the short story by Ursula K. Le Guin, The Ones Who Walk Away from Omelas.

3. Apologies to Willow Zuchowski and Bruce Young who described the nest in 2003 in a refereed journal.

4. Thomas Szasz, *The Myth of Mental Illness*.

5. The concepts presented in this chapter are found in *Polarity Management: Identifying and Managing Unsolvable Problems*, HRD Press, by Barry Johnson, Ph.D.

6. The imagery from this paragraph is taken from the poem, *Knots*, by Joseph Stroud.

7. The imagery for this story has been taken from the poems, *River I-VII*, by Jim Harrison, Songs of Unreason.

8. T.S. Eliot, *Four Quartets*

9. This is a work of fiction. The village and the school exist, under another name. Other than the near mythical character of Yamí, (Purí all the characters and the storyline are from the imagination of the author.